Kat Richardson is a former magazine editor who escaped Los Angeles in the 90s. She currently lives on a sailboat in Seattle with her husband. She rides a motorcycle, shoots target pistol and does not own a TV.

Visit her website at www.katrichardson.com

VANISHED

A GREYWALKER NOVEL

KAT RICHARDSON

piatkus

PIATKUS

First published in the US in 2009 by ROC,
A division of Penguin Group (USA) Inc., New York, USA
First published in Great Britain as a paperback original in 2009 by Piatkus

A CIP catalogue record for this book
is available from the British Library

ISBN 978-0-7499-4076-8

Printed and bound by CPI Mackays, Chatham ME5 8TD

Papers used by Piatkus are natural, renewable and recyclable
products sourced from well-managed forests and certified
in accordance with the rules of the Forest Stewardship Council.

Mixed Sources
Product group from well-managed
forests and other controlled sources
www.fsc.org Cert no. SGS-COC-004081
FSC © 1996 Forest Stewardship Council

Piatkus
An imprint of
Little, Brown Book Group
100 Victoria Embankment
London EC4Y 0DY

An Hachette UK Company
www.hachette.co.uk

www.piatkus.co.uk

THIS ONE IS FOR "THE MUMS," JOY AND SANDRA, WHO
ARE NOTHING LIKE HARPER'S MOTHER. THANK GOD.

ACKNOWLEDGMENTS

This book was a big group effort, as they all are, but it had some unusual challenges, like . . . oh . . . England. . . .

So special thanks go to the family and friends in England who supplied information, entertainment, books, lodging, food, friendship, and much love: the Scotts, who proved you can be married for forty years and still be very much in love—and who also had lovely asparagus that I ate more than my share of; the Harrises and the hospitality of their charming old house at the edge of the fields; the Carpenters and kin; Rik and Carol and Mr. Monkey for the *Lost Rivers of London*, the Canal Museum, and so much more; Liz de Jager and Milady Insanity—sorry we didn't get more time; and Maxim and his minions at the late, great Murder One bookstore. And thanks to my father-in-law, Arthur "Bogus" Carpenter, whose Norfolk accent was the starting point for Marsden's curious way of speaking.

I owe a great deal of creative thanks to my British agent, John Parker of the Zeno Agency, for suggesting Clerkenwell as the haunt of vampires. And to my UK editor, Donna Condon, for checking my London facts and helping this book be more "English." I'm overwhelmed by the work and support the Piatkus team has put out on this book; from marketing and publicity through editorial, and the beautiful art and cover design for the UK editions, they've all been terrific.

My US publication team is also no collection of slouches. Many thanks for the patience of my US editor, Anne Sowards, and the fantastic work of my copy editor—who makes me look like I know what I'm doing. I'd also like to thank the anonymous proofreader who saved my butt on the last book with a timely continuity catch. I've been blessed with lovely art and design on all the books and I can't say "thank you" enough to everyone involved in that. And of course, my agent, Joshua Bilmes, without whom nothing could happen.

Huge thanks to my former publicist Valerie Cortes for keeping me sane during the 2008 tour, and to my former agent, Steve Mancino, who was fantastic—con bars will never be the same.

Of course there are the friends at home who are too numerous to name, but a few who deserve drinks and hugs include (but aren't limited to): Cherie Priest; Richelle Mead; Mark Henry, who kicked my ass in just the right direction and time; Caitlin Kittredge, who read and critiqued "Brit speak"; Mario Acevedo, who kept my spirits up con and con again; Charlaine Harris; clan Jordan of Crimespree fame and all the crazy folks who toil in those fabulous fields; Penny Hale, librarian extraordinary; Paul Goat Allen; my Seattle book pushers at University Bookstore, Seattle Mystery Bookshop, Third Place Books, and the downtown B&N; Andrew "Blue Ninja" for setting up my Web forum; the real John Purcell, who doesn't mind being a vampire; the real Christelle LaJeunesse, whom I agreed to kill off in this book; Alan Beatts, who surely knows why; Tobias Buckell; John Scalzi; Richard Foss and Marc "Animal" MacYoung for remaining true friends and lunatics through . . . a lot of years; Toni L. P. Kelner; John Hemry, Elizabeth Moon, and Lee Martindale for the best Dead Dog dinner ever; and Charles Stross for being funny and gracious when I was scared to death of him.

A quiet and heartfelt "good night" to Dexter the ferret, who made life much sweeter and funnier by his presence, and who taught Taz that toes are not for biting—unless they are your own toes.

Finally, thanks to my family who put up with so much, especially "the mums," who must have wondered when I'd finally get around to dedicating a book to them.

VANISHED

PROLOGUE

When I was a kid, my life seemed to be run by other people's designs and not by mine. Once the time was ripe, I escaped from the life other people pushed me into and made my own. Or so I thought. Now it appears I was wrong about . . . well, everything. But I'll get to that later.

Two years ago, I died for a couple of minutes. When I woke up, things had changed: I could see ghosts and magic and things that go bump in the night. You see, there is a thin space between the normal and the paranormal—the Grey—where things that aren't quite one or the other roam. It's not a place most people can visit; even witches and psychics only reach into the surging tide of power and the uncanny and haul out what they need. But once in a while there's someone like me: a Greywalker, with a foot on each side of the line and fully immersed in the weird.

Sounds cool? Not so much. Some of my friends in the know are fascinated by it, but to me it's more frequently a royal pain in the ass. Because when I can see the monsters, they can see me, and if they have problems, I'm the go-to girl. I've been a professional private investigator for ten years, and it's a job I've come to practice on both sides of the vale because ghosts, vampires, and witches just don't take no for an answer.

Since I'd died, I'd made my accommodation with the Grey and I thought I had it pretty well figured, even if some things were still a mystery to me, like, "why me" and "how does this stuff work?" It just did, and I did my best to get along. Until May of this year, when things got rather personal, starting with strange dreams and a phone call from the dead.

ONE

I t started just like it had in real life: The man belts me in the temple and it feels like my head is caving in. I tumble out of the chair, onto the hardwood floor. In the dream I can see its pattern of dark and light wood making a ribbon around the edge of the room, like a magic circle to contain the terror.

I grope for my purse, for the gun, for anything that will stop him from beating me to death this time. I am still too slow. He rounds the edge of the desk and comes after me. I roll up onto my knees and try to hit him below the belt.

He dodges, swings, and connects with the back of my head. Then he kicks me in the ribs as I collapse again. This time I don't shriek—I don't have the air—and that's how I know something's changed. It's not just a memory; it's a nightmare.

The man's foot swings for my face and I push it up, over my head, tipping him backward. As he falls, I scramble for the door into the hall. This time I'll get out. This time I won't die. . . .

But he catches up and grabs on to my ponytail—an impossible rope of hair a yard, a mile long and easy to grip. Was it really so long? I can't even remember it down to my hips like that. But in the dream it's a lariat that loops around my neck and hauls my head back until I'm looking into the man's face.

But it's my father, not the man who beat my head in. Not the square-jawed, furious face of a killer, but the bland, doe-eyed face that winked like the moon when I was tucked into my childhood bed. He read me Babar books and kissed my cheek when I was young. Now he calls me "little girl," and slams my skull into the doorpost.

I don't fight back this time. I just wrench loose, leaving my long hair in his hand. He lets me go and I stumble toward the ancient brass elevator, my legs wobbling and my pace ragged. I feel tears flooding down my cheeks, and the world spins into a narrowing tunnel.

I see the elegant old elevator at the end of the tunnel, the gleaming metal grillwork shuffling itself into shape, as if it is formed from the magical grid of the Grey. There's a vague human figure inside, beyond the half-formed doors. There never was anyone there before. . . .

I stagger and fall to my knees at the elevator door. The ornate brass gates slide open and I tumble into the lift, sprawling like a broken toy at someone's feet.

He's much too tall from my position down on the floor: a giant blue denim tree crowned with silvery hair. My dream vision zooms up and in, and something tightens in my chest until I can feel it strain to the breaking point.

Will Novak, my ex-boyfriend, looks down at me with a cool glance. "Oh. It's you," he says.

The too-tight thing in my chest pings and breaks. Pain lashes through me like the unwinding mainspring of a broken clock.

I woke up with a scream in my mouth that twisted into shuddering tears. I huddled into my bed and cried, feeling that something had been wrecked or wrenched apart in a way I didn't understand. I wished I was cuddled up with Quinton in his safe little hole under the streets and not alone with the lingering desolation of my nightmare.

I'm not much for emotional outbursts. They're counterproductive and ugly and they tend to put someone at a disadvantage. Even alone in my condo I felt a little ashamed of weeping like a brat, and I was glad the ferret wasn't going to tell anyone. But I still felt bad about it.

The dream was a bad start to a bad day filled with unpaid bills, lying clients, dead-end investigations, and ghosts behaving badly. So with the past and my death on my mind, I guess it wasn't such a surprise that I got a phone call from a dead boyfriend. The dead seem to have a thing about phones.

I didn't recognize the number, but that never stops me. I answered the phone, "Harper Blaine," like usual.

"Hiya, Slim."

"I think you have the wrong number."

"Ahhh . . . no. I had to whistle pretty hard, but I think I got it right."

Whistle? What the—?

"Hey," the voice continued, "you know how to whistle, don't ya?"

I couldn't stop myself from finishing the quote. "You just put your lips together . . . and blow." That was Slim Browning's line from *To Have and Have Not*. Lauren Bacall to Humphrey Bogart. My favorite film. It was someone else's favorite film, too. . . .

He laughed. "I knew you wouldn't forget."

A chill ran over me. "Who is this?"

"You're disappointing me, Slim. It's Cary."

"Cary . . . ?" I echoed, feeling queasy.

"Malloy. From LA."

Cary Malloy had mentored me through my first two years as a professional investigator. We'd broken the rules about interoffice romances. Then he'd died in a car accident on Mulholland Drive. Two fast cars racing on the twisty road with a distracting view across the nighttime basin of lights; a bad curve; Cary's car parked on the shoulder as he observed a subject's house, pretending to admire the view; one car swinging a little too wide, sliding out the side of the curve . . .

I hadn't been there, but I always felt as if I had, as if I'd heard the sound of the cars colliding, scraping across the road in showers of sparks and the screech of metal. The two cars had tumbled over the cliff, milling down the canyon side as the third rushed away into the darkness.

The subject had called it in. After all, it had happened right across the street, and the small fire started in the dry chaparral by hot metal and spilling gas was a menace. The entangled state of the burning cars made it plain both drivers were long dead by the time LA County Fire arrived. The residents of the canyon had simply stood at the edge of the road and watched. There was nothing else they could do.

My silence gave my thoughts away, I suppose. Cary's voice said, "Yeah . . . dying really bit."

My own voice shook a little when I replied, "That's what I hear. Umm . . . why did you call?"

"It's complicated." I could almost hear him shrug. "But, look, I have to tell you—" He choked and coughed, his voice straining now. "Have to say, it's not what you think."

I could hear a noise, a crackling sound.

"You don't know what you really are, Slim. You need to come here and look into the past," he muttered, his voice fading as if he was moving away from the phone. "There're things . . . waiting for you. . . ."

"Cary? What things? Cary!" I shouted at the phone, feeling tears building and trembling over my eyelids.

But he'd already faded away, and the flat, dull hum of the dial tone was the only sound from the phone. I put the receiver down and pressed my hand over my mouth, squeezing my eyes shut against the burning of saltwater tears. Coming on the heels of the nightmare, this was too much. But I wasn't going to cry. Not over Cary Malloy. Not again and after so much time. I wasn't twelve anymore, and blubbering wasn't going to help anything.

I wasn't crying when Quinton came tapping at my office door a few minutes later, but I must have looked pretty horrible. He glanced at me and slid in, locking the door behind himself as he dropped his backpack on the floor. He crouched down beside my chair and tried to catch my eye.

"Is the ferret OK?"

I frowned in confusion. "What? Why are you asking *that*?"

"Because you look like your best friend just died. What's wrong?"

"I just got a phone call from a guy who's been dead for eight years."

"That's never bothered you before."

"I used to date him. He died in a car wreck."

Quinton straightened and leaned on the edge of my desk. "That is a little weirder than normal. What did he want?"

"I'm not sure. He wasn't very clear. He wanted me to come . . . someplace and look into the past. He said things aren't what I think— he said I'm not what I think. And then he faded out."

"Was he always a cryptic pain in the ass, or is that new since his death?"

I had to snort a laugh—it was kind of funny imagining clean-cut, preppy Cary in the role of oracular spirit. "No! He loved spy novels, but he himself was about as cryptic as a bowl of cereal. He didn't hide information; he just kept his mouth shut if he didn't want things to get out."

"But he called you. After eight years. Maybe I have some competition here. . . ."

I made a face. "I don't think so. But that's not the only weird thing. I dreamed about my death last night."

Quinton looked uncomfortable and sat down on the edge of my desk so he could avoid looking me straight in the eye. "You mean . . . in the future?" Some things still freak out even Quinton, I guess.

"No, I mean when this all started two years ago; when I died in that elevator," I explained. "I don't see the future."

He gnawed on his lower lip and thought a bit, holding my hands in both of his. His grip was warm and comforting, loosening a tension in my shoulders I hadn't noticed until it slid away. "It's an interesting coincidence. Do you think it's more than that?"

I made a face and shook my head, slightly disgusted with the direction my thoughts were turning. "I have decreasing confidence in coincidence. Freaky Grey events almost never 'just happen' together. It's like a pond where the ripples of one event can set off a whole series of others."

Quinton raised his eyebrows expectantly but said nothing.

I sighed. "All right. I have the feeling that something's building up. There's a lot happening around here lately with the ghosts and vampires and magical things. I have three open cases right now involving ghosts, and Edward's been sending more invitations—of various kinds—for me to come to work for him. You know how much he wants to control me."

"Yeah. The vampires have been kind of restless lately here in Pioneer Square," Quinton added. "Do you think that's something Edward's doing to get to you?"

Edward Kammerling was the leader of Seattle's vampire pack; he was also the founder of TPM, one of Seattle's biggest development groups in a city historically run by developers of various stripes.

"I don't know," I said. "I can't see how he'd benefit from drawing attention, do you?"

"No," Quinton confirmed, shaking his head with a grim set to his mouth. "But even with the stunners I gave to some of the homeless to drive the bloodsuckers away, there's definitely more biting going on. But it's kind of hit and run—I'm not seeing a pattern, just an increasing frequency of attacks."

Quinton had developed cheap, battery-operated shock prods that he called "stunners" that incapacitated vampires for a few minutes. The jolt was not strong enough to kill them but enough to give the near-victim a head start on running away. He'd distributed them to some of the more stable of Pioneer Square's indigent population to reduce their chance of being an unwilling vampire lunch. Most of the "undergrounders," as we called them—the homeless who lived in the hidden spaces under the city or simply preferred life below the rest of the world's radar—didn't always know their assailants were undead and they didn't care. They just wanted to be left alone, like Quinton himself. He was their personal mad scientist.

"It could be another faction war . . ." I suggested. When I'd first fallen into the Grey, I'd discovered that vampires jockey for position constantly. At the time there'd been at least three individuals who wanted Edward's head on a plate and were looking for ways to get it. One was now dead—or re-dead if you prefer—one was apparently biding his time, and the other was currently holding to an uneasy agreement I'd helped to hammer out.

"Could be," Quinton admitted. "But who knows?" Still knitting his brows, he muttered to himself, "I wish I knew when ghosts were more active. If there's a rise in paranormal activity . . ."

"Then what?" I asked.

"Huh?" he grunted, jerking out of his thoughts. "I'm not sure, but I'd like to know. Maybe there's a correlation between ghost activity and vampire activity, or maybe there's something more personal here. I mean, if your dead boyfriend thinks there are things you should know and if there's a rise in paranormal activity at the same time, I'd think that's significant. But we don't know what it's indicative *of*. I wish I had some more equipment. . . ."

Quinton was having a geek moment—that sort of glazed-eyed mental gymnastics session that ends in the discovery of penicillin or the invention of the Super Soaker and the resulting battalion of wet cats. I left him to it while I pondered what he'd just said.

There was a lot more going on in the paranormal than usual. Cary's strange call only highlighted the fact that the activity seemed higher around me, something I'd been either missing or ignoring. It was unwise for me to turn a cold shoulder or blind eye to that sort of thing. Usually I don't put a lot of trust in the words of ghosts—they tend to lie or know only a fractured, incomplete version of the truth, just like live people. But Cary had more weight with me when alive than most people, and his sudden call had come with the freight train impact of the dream that preceded it. If that was a coincidence I'd eat the proverbial hat.

"I'm going to Los Angeles," I announced.

Quinton twitched from his reverie and raised his eyebrows at me. "Why?"

"Because I can't think of any place else Cary could mean by 'here' when he said I needed to 'come here and look into the past.' There's too much of my past coming up all at once, too much strangeness, for his call to be meaningless. I know this isn't the best time to go," I added, stopping Quinton before whatever words forming on his lips dropped into the air, "but if there's really something going on that will affect me, maybe I should get a jump on it first."

"You sound like you think I'm going to argue with you."

"Well . . ."

He shook his head. "Oh no, Harper. I'm not getting between you and a case. I know better."

"A case? This isn't a case. It's me."

"Even worse. If you think there really is an answer in your past to what's going on now, or to why you are what you are or how you got that way, I know nothing will stop you from pursuing it. I'm not going to throw myself in front of a runaway train. I'll hold the fort here and I'll look after the ferret, and we'll take on whatever's going on in Seattle when you get back. I think Chaos and I can manage that."

Chaos, my pet ferret, adored Quinton and his many pockets. Quinton was more than capable of keeping tabs on the strange and otherworldly while I was away. He couldn't do much more, but unless hell literally broke loose and rose to the surface of Seattle's streets, I didn't think he'd have to.

I bit my lip, uncomfortable about heading back to the place I'd escaped from and not sure I liked the idea of being a "case," or having to look at my past, or tracking down an old, dead boyfriend to find out what he was talking about, or dealing—as I would have to—with my mother, either.

Maybe all that showed on my face. Quinton gave me a crooked smile and leaned forward to kiss my cheek, murmuring, "The sooner you're started, the sooner you're done, right? And then you're back with me, and whatever's wrong, we'll fix it."

That did put me over the edge, and I clutched him close and kissed him back very hard. I could feel the pent-up tears flow down my cheeks and a juddering sensation shook my chest. Why does love feel like hiccups? I snuggled into the warm sensation for a moment before I got back to the drudgery.

I'd have to rearrange my schedule, but no matter how much I didn't like the idea, it appeared Los Angeles and my mother were inevitable.

Two days later I was on a plane to Los Angeles and sharing my row with a dripping-wet dead teenager. She was pissed. I almost wished I'd driven down from Seattle, but the temptation to dawdle might have been overwhelming. So instead my sleep-deprived self was wedged up against the window seat to avoid the creep on the aisle and the glowering ghost in the middle.

She was about thirteen years old, I'd guess, and soaking wet. Her very long blond hair was pulled back into a ponytail so her angry face was unobscured. She'd appeared somewhere over Oregon and didn't say anything for a while; she just scowled. I wanted to talk to her and get her story, but the man on the aisle was already giving me more attention than I wanted and might take it as an invitation. Instead, I got up and went back to the lavatories. The dripping specter followed me.

"What do you want?" I asked when we got to the back of the plane.

"It's all your fault," she hissed back.

"What's my fault?"

"It's your fault, Harper."

She didn't tell me what was my fault. She only repeated her ac-
cusation over and over for the rest of the flight. Even retreating to the
mindless noise of in-flight music couldn't block her out of my head,
since ghosts seem to have an affinity for electronic equipment and her
uncanny voice seeped into the headphones to harry me.

There are a lot of types of ghosts, from the nearly alive to the merely
present. Repeaters—ghosts that are essentially memory loops on endless play—are among the least annoying most of the time. They don't
interact with anyone. This dreadful drowned child was something a
bit more than that, but not a lot. She annoyed the hell out of me
while instilling the discomforting sensation that I'd done something
wrong. But I couldn't recall having anything to do with any drowning
victims, so I didn't know why I should feel guilty, though for some
reason I did. The ghost disappeared somewhere over Santa Barbara,
but by then it was too late to rest.

After my unpleasant flight, I was not in a good mood when I arrived at LA International. The baggage people at LAX added to my
irritation by refusing to hand back my bag. It seemed that the X-ray
tag that let them know there was a properly inspected and secured
firearm in the case had gotten buried, and someone had freaked out
when they saw the shadow of my pistol in the scanner. I had a long,
boring, and circular discussion with everyone at the baggage office
about handing it back. When they wanted to read me the riot act
because they'd bungled the tagging and given some poor monkey on
the X-ray machine a fit, I got a little testy, and that's not a good idea
with security people. By the time the luggage supervisor was involved,
everyone was beyond pissy and I'd spent an extra forty minutes just
trying to get my property back.

Therefore I was a bit short with the car rental clerk. It was nearly
nine o'clock in the evening and I had very little tolerance left, so
when he smirked at my chest, I snapped at him.

"What?" I demanded.

"Umm . . . your shirt's funny. . . ."

I looked down, having forgotten what I'd thrown on under my Seattle-necessary leather jacket for the flight to the warmer climes of Los Angeles in mid-May. It was a dark blue T-shirt with van Gogh's famous evening sky above a picture of a giant, gore-fanged bunny menacing a tiny human figure. "Starry Starry Night . . . of the Lepus!" it read. My bookstore-owning friend Phoebe had given it to me for my birthday on the principle that if you won't shop for yourself, your friends have carte blanche to give you things they think you should wear.

"Oh, gods," I groaned. The shirt was too conspicuous. I'd have to dump it at my first opportunity and hope Phoebe would forgive me.

"I wasn't checking you out, I swear!" the young man objected. "I'm just kind of into schlock film," he added, pink-faced and defending his casual glance at my chest.

"Right."

"Hey, it's *Night of the Lepus*! One of the worst films ever made— mutant rabbits attack Arizona. It's—umm . . ." He could see me losing interest and patience. He shifted back to business, and I wouldn't have thought anyone's face could have gone that shade of red without makeup. "So . . . would you like to upgrade to a midsize car for only six dollars more per day?"

"No. Thank you." We wrangled for a while longer before he let me have the compact car I'd reserved and I set out into the spring twilight looking for my hotel.

THREE

Most people visiting out-of-town relatives will stay with said relatives—especially if they live in a house like my mother's four-bedroom cliff residence. But my mother's ideas about my life and my own aren't exactly in sync, and it's better that we not occupy the same house—or the same state—for long. The prospect of interrogating Mother about my past was already about as attractive as swimming in razor blades; I didn't need to live with her while I did it. By the time I'd checked into my hotel, it was after eleven and late enough to ignore any urge to call and let my mother know I had arrived.

But morning was inevitable and I made the call as soon as I was up and dressed—which wasn't that early.

A sultry female voice answered the phone. "Hello?" Mother was feeling femme fatale–ish.

"Hi, Mother," I said. "I got in late last night, and this was my first chance to call you."

Her voice swooped up in theatrical delight. "Snippet!" In spite of the fact that I tower over her by five inches, that's been my mother's nickname for me since I was five and suddenly a real human in her eyes, instead of a parasite. "I'm just having breakfast. You have to come up and join us."

"Us?"

She ignored that. "Come up, sweetie! See you in a few!"

And, having issued her orders, she hung up. As much as I hated feeling summoned, I wanted to get it over with, so I headed down to the ghost-stuffed lobby of my once-grand Hollywood hotel.

The building was like something out of a Stephen King novel to me—ghosts, murders, crimes, and monstrosities lurked in every shadow—but at least I could see them first. I considered that I should have booked a more boring venue, but the haunting ratio isn't a lot lower in most newer buildings—people just want to think it is—and I'd loved looking at the crazy California rococo facade back when I'd never seen a ghost. It tickled me a bit to finally be a guest. A dead flapper scurried, blood-spattered, down the hall, things watched me as I passed down the staircase of painted tile, and a tragically beautiful face gazed at me from a mirror. I didn't stop to find out what any of them wanted. I didn't need another mystery right now. I just retrieved the rental car and drove.

My mother's house clung to a hillside far from the site of Cary Malloy's death—I wasn't ready to face that twisting bit of road yet. I stopped the car for a moment at the bottom of the street, peering out the side window at the curvaceous white plaster building hanging from the steep canyon walls like a hornets' nest buzzing with orange and yellow energy clouds. She had one part of her dream, at least—she'd always wanted a house in the canyons. Judging by the colors around the place, I figured it hadn't mellowed her out much, but I guessed I'd find out for sure in a few minutes. I hadn't seen my mother since acquiring my Grey sight and I wasn't sure if the manic flares of energy around her home were better than what she'd have shown me a few years ago. I shoved the car back into gear and growled up the twisty, eucalyptus-lined road.

The smell of the dusty trees, cholla, and canyon weeds reminded me of long treks up the ridges as a kid and of baking-hot days on "ego duty" with Cary—watching the houses of minor celebrities for suspected stalkers and known exes with grudges. It was the scent of the seemingly endless summer of southern California childhood. It should have made me smile, but I felt my brow creasing into a frown. Something nagged in the back of my head, making the memory bitter beyond the remembered misery of sweltering hours of dance rehearsals and auditions wearing fake smiles and unbroken shoes that raised bleeding blisters for the sake of five minutes' beauty. That particular sunshine made me morose.

The house didn't seem any more restful when I got closer to it, in spite of the architect's best efforts. It was still too active in the Grey for my comfort. I pulled past a gate that shut behind me and into the narrow, trellis-covered shelf that served as a carport, between an older, forest green Jaguar convertible and a spanking-new Mercedes coupe. That brought my eyebrows up, but the thought that prompted it got no further as I was hailed by my mother's voice from a speaker set in the creamy white wall.

"Sweetie, come through the gate to the terrace. It's on the left."

I left my bag in the car—who was going to steal it?—but I kept my jacket on. I walked through the rustic gate in the plastered wall, which was as white and perfect as wedding cake frosting. My boots clacked onto a bed of smooth indigo stones pretending to be an oxbow surrounding the white marble island of the terrace. The view spread beyond the wall in the perpetual canyon haze of blue eucalyptus dust as if the pebble watercourse had widened into a river of sky. It would have been a restful haven if only my mother hadn't lived in it.

My mother and a man who looked like an accessory to the fake-Mediterranean decor sat at a round redwood table facing the view over the scattered remains of the morning meal. So much for "join us for breakfast."

Mother smiled and waved like Princess Grace. I admit she looked great, if too thin. She'd given up the battle against gray hair and embraced a dramatic sweep of silver through her chestnut mane. Makeup and artfully casual clothes added to her morning polish. It would have looked better without her apple green aura— possessiveness? Jealousy? I wasn't sure.

The man stood up, bending to give her a quick kiss on the lips before walking toward me. He put out his hand as he got close. He was Hollywood's idea of sixty-five and dressed like a 1940s gangster on vacation. I smothered a snicker.

"So, you're Ronnie's Snippet. I've heard all about you. I'm Damon."

I took his hand, but I didn't shake. His palm was warm and dry, but the gleam of energy around his body in the Grey was sickly olive green. Mother's complementary green energy trailed after him like a thread raveling from his sleeve. I guessed he was the owner of the quarter million dollars' worth of Mercedes in the carport.

My mother's name was currently Veronica Geary, and she'd always hated the nickname Ronnie, so I had to assume that she was angling to make Damon into husband number five, or she would have chilled him to the bone for calling her by the despised moniker. I wondered if she knew there was something wrong with him, though whether it was physical or mental, inward or outward directed, I didn't know. I only knew the size and color of his aura weren't good. I didn't like seeing my mother's energy tied up to his that way; there was something squick-worthy about it.

"I'm sure you haven't heard it all just yet. And I'd prefer 'Harper,'" I replied. "I think I'm a bit tall to be a snippet." And "Snippet" hadn't always been an endearment, either.

His hand fell away from mine. "Ah. Well. I was on my way out, so I'll let you two have some privacy, then," Damon said, not quite frowning.

"Thanks."

My mother waved and blew him a kiss. "Be good, Damon! Dinner at Marmont—don't forget!"

"Of course not, bunny," he answered, waving as he passed through the gate.

I just stood still until I heard the Mercedes purr to life and crunch away across the eucalyptus pods scattered on the pavement. I walked over to the table and stood beside Damon's vacated chair—all the others were up against the cool white wall.

My mother looked me over, scowling. It didn't become her. "Good God, baby, aren't you sweltering in that jacket? Take it off; you're making me sweat just looking at you," she added, flicking her hand airily at me. Queen Veronica.

"I don't think that would be a good idea."

She glared and leaned forward, all trace of the royal charm wiped away. "I said take it off, Harper."

I shrugged and slipped out of the jacket, dropping it onto the back of Damon's chair before I sat down on the seat.

My mother stared, aghast, at the holster tucked into my jeans. "Jesus, Harper! You bring a gun into my home? Into *my* home," she repeated. She clasped a hand to her chest like someone from a silent film. I didn't think it was the gun that offended her so much as my having it on my person.

"I bring a gun everywhere, Mother. I have a license for it."

"But this is my *home*! How could you possibly think you'd need a gun in my house? This is a safe place! Not a . . . a barrio pool hall."

"I was killed in a 'safe place' two years ago."

"Don't be so dramatic, Harper. You're not dead."

"How would you know? You're listed as my next of kin, but I never saw you at the hospital, Mother. If you'd bothered to show up, they'd have told you I died for two minutes."

"You were fine! I called."

"Not while I was conscious."

She waved my words away. "How did I raise such a drama queen?"

"Because that's what you wanted. Twelve years of professional dance and every audition and road show you could get me into was kind of a hint. I'm sure you remember it as well as I do. Like, when I was ten and instead of summer vacation, I did fifty-four performances of *Annie*."

"In the chorus! And if you'd only lost a little weight, you'd have been first understudy!"

"I am not fat and I never have been. But I was much too tall to play a ten-year-old orphan. I'm five ten, for heaven's sake!"

"Well, you weren't then." She looked me over and snorted. "And you could stand to lose five pounds. . . ."

Since I'd worked hard to put on that five pounds of muscle, I disagreed, but I didn't say so. Instead I answered quietly, "And, if we're slinging personal criticisms, you could stand to gain a few." A woman in her late fifties shouldn't have the body of a heroin-addicted teenager. I didn't like my mother, but that didn't mean I wished her ill.

She glared at me and kept her mouth shut—score one for me. She picked at the pineapple rind that sat on her plate and sighed, exasperated. "You don't know how hard it is to compete in this town, sweetie. . . ."

I shook my head and rolled my eyes.

"You don't," she insisted.

"Do we have to have this conversation?"

"It's entirely your choice."

I'd heard that before—usually before emotional blackmail. "Then my choice is that we don't."

"Fine."

We sat there in silence for a minute as birds called and traffic grumbled in the canyon below. Finally, I leaned forward and said, "Look, Mother, I need to know some things about the past—things about me. And maybe you and Dad, too."

"What? You have a medical condition or something? I assure you, sweetie, no one in our family—"

"That's not it. I'm not dying of cancer or anything screenplay-worthy. There have just been a few . . . things lately that indicate something creepy or bad happened sometime in the past. Do you have any idea what that could be?"

She looked surprised. "Well, dear, of course! Your father killed himself."

FOUR

Sitting in the sunny perfection of her tiny mock-Mediterranean villa, I stared at my mother. "What?" I felt like someone had punched me in the chest and pushed me off a cliff and I was hanging in the air like Wile E. Coyote, waiting to fall. I stammered, shook my head, and kept repeating myself. "What, what, what?" It just didn't make sense. My mind rejected it and everything sensible screamed in my head that it wasn't—couldn't be—true.

My mother grabbed my nearest arm and shook me. "Baby, stop that! You're a trouper—we just go on; we don't go to pieces over this sort of . . . thing."

"'This sort of thing'?" I shouted, yanking my arm out of her grip. "What sort of thing? Suicide? Holy shit, Mother!"

She slapped me. "Don't you talk like that, Snippet! I won't have it! You're not a filthy little street urchin to be using words like that. Buck up!"

I knew that phrase, that tone. What she meant was "Shut up and don't embarrass me," but I didn't see anyone around who needed to be impressed by my restraint. I articulated with venom and care through my confusion and a sudden flare of rage. "I will not buck the fuck up, Mother. This is not an audition. I don't need to be a little lady. You just said my father killed himself! Don't you think that deserves a bit more explanation than 'buck up'? You always told me Dad's death was an accident!"

She rolled her eyes and waved my upset away. "Drama, drama, drama . . . He was a dentist. Dentists don't have accidents. What would they do? Slip with a drill? Die from a leak in the laughing gas? He blew his brains out. It was just so . . . nasty, I never wanted to tell you. There. Is that awful enough for you?"

I just kept gaping at her. "What the hell . . . ? My God, Mother. Do you know why? Did he say? Did he leave a note? Something?"

"He left a note, but it didn't make any sense, and I don't know why he did it. He was depressed. All dentists are depressed. If I'd known, I'd have married a plastic surgeon."

I was flabbergasted. What could I say? I didn't remind her that husband number three *had* been a plastic surgeon. No doubt a contributor to the fact she looked closer to forty-nine than fifty-nine. I didn't scream or throw things, even though they both sounded like more reasonable reactions than her unreal calm.

"He had nightmares," she went on. "Your father was losing his mind. I should have seen it coming. . . ."

I was still staring, shaking my head, and not sure what to think, but my investigator instincts started kicking in. "How?" I asked in a quivering voice. "What did he do?"

"He stopped talking to me."

I couldn't fault him for that. I'd stopped talking to her for years.

"He got quieter and quieter and sometimes he'd just . . . leave."

"Go out of town without telling you, go on benders . . . what?"

"No, I mean he'd sneak away. He'd just leave the house and I didn't know he'd gone. Then he'd come back and sometimes I didn't know he'd come home. He was so odd . . . spooky even, by then."

"He wasn't always odd?"

"Oh, yes, but I thought it was kind of charming at first. Like the way Lyle was charming—you remember Lyle?"

"The guy with the dogs? The TV writer?"

"Yes. That Lyle." At least she hadn't married him.

He had been a very funny guy—he'd made me laugh even when I was still crying over my dad and on the days my whole body ached from dance classes and dieting—and he'd had two ridiculous retrievers he'd called "the labradork twins." We'd moved in with Lyle and the labradorks about six months after my father died. Normally the dogs had the run of the house, but Mother had put the dogs in the yard when one of them started using the carpet as a toilet, and that, for some reason, had been inexcusable to Lyle—the expulsion, not the piddling. When he'd come home from work and seen the dogs in the yard, he'd hauled back and smacked her hard enough to knock out one of her front teeth. She'd packed both our bags and we were gone within fifteen minutes, me carrying her knocked-out tooth in a glass of water while Lyle ran after us, babbling, "I didn't mean it, Verry! I'm sorry, Verry!" She'd mailed the glass back in one of my tap shoe boxes two days later. The Lyle incident had cemented her aversion to pets; we never had another dog, cat, bird, or even a fish after that.

It had been the first time we'd lived with a man who wasn't my father, but it wasn't the last, though she'd held off on marrying any of them until I was in high school. I'd always been a better judge of their characters than my mother had, which hadn't made our relationship any easier. But no matter how rough it had gotten or how horrible the man-of-the-moment had been, I'd stuck it out. And to give her credit, she never let any of them physically abuse her or me again.

Then it hit me like a brick that I'd fallen into a similar pattern with boyfriends for a while myself, not drawing the line until one finally belted me. At least I'd stopped putting up with that. Mother didn't seem to have learned to stand on her own feet and refuse to take that treatment just so she could have someone around. Even as I steamed at her, I felt terrible and even more confused and upset. Was I sup- posed to feel better or worse at discovering our mutual flaw? Enlight- ened? I didn't feel better, that was for sure. I was still angry and I still didn't like her.

While we'd been staring at each other and remembering the past, the sun had moved higher into the sky. Now its rays hit the glittering white stone of the terrace from a harsher angle, reflecting glare into our eyes and doing unkind things to my mother's face. She cupped her hands over her brow and glanced around as if searching for shade, pursing her lips in disapproval at the sun's temerity.

"Let's go inside," she said. "I think I have some of your father's things still, down in the junk room. We can talk while you go through them."

I glared at her. She ignored me as she flitted out of her chair. I hadn't come to help her clear out her collection of boxes. I hadn't come to help her at all, and I wasn't feeling any more generous now than when I'd arrived—maybe less. I wasn't just bewildered by this revelation; I was pissed off at being lied to for years. I longed to tell her off, but I was piqued by the thought that there might be clues inside the dusty cartons in the basement—such as it was. Dad com- mitting suicide, while it was shocking and upsetting, didn't seem like much of a triggering event for what had happened to me. How were they connected, if at all? And what had he been doing in my dream? Suicide couldn't be the deciding factor—could it?—but what about the motive? Or perhaps some other event associated with it was the key . . . ? Those might be worth discovering, even if it meant a day or two sifting through the accumulation of castoffs. It couldn't be any worse than the days I spent in the County Recorder's Office, troll- ing for information on witnesses or other people's prospective spouses and employees. Except that I would have to deal with my mother while I did it.

I trailed her inside and down a switchback staircase to a small room at the bottom of the house. It was almost isolated from the rest of the structure, stuck on like an afterthought that had been cobbled up and jammed on at the last minute when someone realized they desperately needed a place to put the construction supplies. It was such an oddly shaped space that I couldn't imagine it had ever had any other purpose than being a place to stash unused items. Or over-worked maids. Mother unlocked the door and groped for the light switch, leaning in through the doorway as if something inside would leap at her if she stepped over the threshold.

The light snapped on with a pop, revealing several dozen heavy-duty cardboard boxes. They were stacked a bit haphazardly from wall to wall, two or three high, taking up most of the room except for a ragged triangle starting at the door.

My mother made a vague wave of her hand at the room. "Your father's things are in here someplace."

I sighed with irritation. She acted like he wasn't a person, like he was nothing but this collection of junk that she'd shoved down here and forgotten. I was being irrational, I knew. Dad had been gone for twenty-two years and this really was just a load of things, not a human being. I told myself to let go and start digging.

I hung my jacket on a hook beside the door and walked deeper into the room, taking mental stock of the piles and labels on the boxes while I scanned for any sign of something Grey and gleaming among the heaps. Mother walked out and returned with a handful of white cloth towels. She used one to dust off a small stepladder, which she then unfolded and perched on, setting the rest of the towels on the top platform beside her. She put her elbows on her knees and rested her chin on her hands like Audrey Hepburn in *Breakfast at Tiffany's*. All she needed was a long cigarette holder and a little black dress.

I kept turning my head side to side, looking for the telltale gleam from the corner of my eye that would indicate something Grey in one of the boxes. I saw something blink and die out and then blink again. I pushed deeper into the maze until I found a stash of three old boxes shimmering with an edge of Grey. Two of them were marked

PHOTOS. The other was marked ROB'S OFFICE. That was my father's stuff, I thought, and felt a quiver of indecision. There was no guarantee that whatever had winked at me was important—lots of things have a trace of Grey—but I had to start somewhere, and this looked more likely than most of the boxes, if I really wanted to know. And I did, didn't I? Cary had said I should look. . . .

"You know," my mother suddenly declared, "your father was an odd duck."

"Yeah, you said," I replied, flipping open my pocketknife to cut the tape on the box of office paraphernalia. "If he was so weird, why did you marry him?"

I could almost feel her frown before she dismissed my hostile tone as flippancy.

"Why? Sweetie, I lived in Montana! I wanted out of that place so badly I'd have married a serial killer to get away. Your father—who adored me—had a professional degree and was heading somewhere far away from three hundred acres of cow flop. I have never been one to look gift horses in the mouth."

"Until they clock you one," I muttered.

"What was that?" she snapped, narrowing her eyes to glare at me from her perch.

"Seems kind of mercenary. If you thought he was a freak and only saw him as a meal ticket, why'd you stick around?"

"That's not what I meant. I liked your father. But he had strange ideas sometimes and they got stranger after you were born. That's when he started being mysterious and sneaking off. And what was I supposed to do with a baby to care for? I had to quit dancing when I got pregnant and I didn't have a fancy education like he did. I had nothing!"

"Cry me a river."

"Don't smart mouth me, Snippet."

"Then don't play the martyr," I replied, looking up. "You seem to be doing pretty well for a woman who claims she had nothing and was practically a prisoner at home with a baby. You did everything you could to have the career you wanted through me, and I don't recall you being so broken up over my dad's death that you didn't find someone else to promote your dreams as soon as he was gone."

She looked shocked. "Baby, how can you say that? Everything I did was for you! You needed help, direction, discipline. I got that for you. I got you a career. I got you a *place*!"

"You got me *your* place! You got me what you wanted, not what I wanted. I was a doormat. A doll for you to wind up and set onstage."

"You were happy—!"

I barked over her, drowning her voice under mine. "About ten percent of the time. The rest was hell. Why do you think I ditched the dance gig at my first opportunity?"

"Because you're an ungrateful brat!"

That was enough. I picked up the box and started toward the door. "Then I'll take this and get my ungrateful self out of your house."

She jumped down from the ladder and blocked the door, spreading out her arms in a rage of red fury. "Don't you dare! Don't you dare talk to me like that. And don't you dare take my things!"

I fought to make my voice calm and reasonable. "Mother, it's not yours. It's Dad's. And you clearly don't want it. Nor do you seem to want me—at least not as I really am. You want a Shirley Temple doll."

"I—I want a daughter . . . who won't get herself killed by some idiot. I just want . . ." She trailed off, shrugging helplessly.

"Hollywood. You want glamour and movie magic. I just want to go back to my job."

"Oh! I just don't understand you." She stomped her designer-clad foot. "How can you do that? It's such an awful job."

"Not to me," I replied. As I said it, I felt better, because it was true and I wasn't unsure or bewildered for the first time since I'd entered her house. "I love doing what I do and I love being the person in charge of my life." The box was poking into my hip, but I'd be damned if I'd put it down. "When I was a kid, I wasn't in charge of anything. Even when I went to college, I was someone's student or someone's girlfriend or some director's chorus girl. Someone's whipping girl. Someone's doll. I was Veronica's daughter. I wasn't Harper Blaine."

My mother let out a scream and lashed her fists at the box, knocking it out of my hands. "How can you say that?"

The box went down like a sack of flour, sending up a cloud of paper and small objects and the smell of dust. Grey whorls spun from it as it struck the floor, gushing its contents from split sides.

"Look what you've done!" Mother shouted, sweeping her arms around.

I sighed and crouched down to pick up the pieces. A piece of paper glimmered like silver and floated in the air, drifting with unearthly languor toward the ground. I reached for it, feeling the buzz of Grey before I even closed my fingers on its yellowed surface.

It was old. Twenty-two years old, in fact. The cream-colored paper was stained with splatters of brown and the writing had faded to a dirty spiderweb scrawl. "There must be no more," it read. "I'm sorry, Harper." It was signed "Robert." Not "Dad," though it was clearly him.

I felt sucker punched once again—he wrote it to me? Signed his name as if I were an adult? Why? I'd been twelve! I gaped up at my mother. Unable to say anything else, I blurted, "You kept the suicide note?"

She glanced aside and shrugged. "Everything was just shoved in a box when we moved."

"Bullshit. The cops would have kept it with the file unless you requested it. Why did you ask for it back?" And why didn't I remember any of it? There must have been cops around, asking questions. They must have asked why he'd apologized to me, but I had no memory of any of that. It was as if there were a yawning hole around everything connected to my father's death, and I could not recall anything of the time or the circumstances.

My mother flapped her hands in the air, as if distancing herself physically from the sheet of paper. "I didn't ask for that. I just wanted the property they took. When I asked, they just gave me everything."

"The gun, too?"

She didn't reply; she just looked away, wan faced.

I pawed through the heap the box had spilled forth, stirring and sorting until I found it: an old-school Smith & Wesson revolver. It was still in an evidence bag, gritty and smeared. No one had cleaned it off. I felt sick and swallowed bile. But the gun had no glimmer of Grey to it. It was just a dead object, less active than most. The note was Grey, but not the instrument my father had used to end his life. That was strange.

"Was this his?" I asked.

My mother shook her head and didn't look in my eyes. "No. Rob never owned a gun that I knew of."

So where had it come from? I had a lunatic thought and asked, "Was it yours?" My mother had grown up on a cattle ranch, after all. She'd been around guns and horses and hard men from the cradle. She'd flipped out because I had a pistol on me, but she'd been more upset that I'd brought a gun into her house than that it was a firearm per se. Was she just being a dramatic hypocrite or did she have some particular problem with the idea of guns now? Or was it me and guns?

She sighed. "Yes. It's mine." Her shoulders slumped as if the admission had taken something from her.

"Ah." Once the case was determined to be a clear suicide, and not a homicide, the cops had given her the note as part of his belongings. But they'd given her the gun because it was hers.

My mother's gun. My father's death. And a dead boyfriend telling me it was time to figure out how it all made me what I was. Cold tripped down my spine. This just kept getting freakier.

I stared into the mess around my feet, searching for other glimmers of Grey. A general haze of silver mist lay over the pile like dry-ice fog. There was a lot of stuff to sort through, but whether any of it would present a clue or not, as a body, it already told me Dad had had something Grey going on. I'd have to find him, too, if I could. I didn't relish the idea of hunting through the Grey, through layers of time and memory and horrors, until I found his ghost—if he had one. I shuddered.

"This room is always so chilly," my mother said.

"What?"

"You shivered, sweetie. It's because the room is cold."

I let that pass. If my mother believed that, she was less canny than I'd given her credit for.

"Do you have another box I could put this stuff in? I want to sort through it at the hotel."

"But you can do that here!"

"I'd rather take it somewhere else, out of your way," I replied. I knew my tone was cold, but I didn't care. Fear was creeping in and I wasn't going to give in to it, not in front of her.

My mother frowned but surprised me by just going away to fetch another box and not arguing. Maybe she realized that it wasn't an activity she was going to enjoy. She handed the flat-folded box to me along with a roll of tape and climbed back up on her ladder to watch while I repacked the contents of the split carton.

"You'll bring the rest back when you're done, won't you?" she asked as I hefted the box up into my arms.

"Yeah. Tomorrow probably. There are a few other boxes I'd like to take a look at, if you don't mind."

"No, I don't mind." She sounded eager in spite of my frosty manner, and I supposed she was a little lonely—or just bored—during the day, while Damon was off doing whatever he did until dinnertime. I couldn't imagine what she did all day. I knew she didn't have a job; she lived on the proceeds of divorce and widowhood and whatever man she was clinging to at the time. Judging by her earlier comments, she saw other women as "the competition," so I didn't imagine she spent her days hanging out with them, lest she come off the worse by comparison.

I forced myself to unbend a bit. "Mother, what do you do all day?" I asked as she followed me back up the stairs.

"What do you mean, sweetie?"

"What I said. What do you do all day? You don't work; you don't cook and clean—or you never did after Dad died. How do you kill the time all day?"

"I play golf. I go to my yoga class. I shop. That sort of thing."

I don't know why her reply surprised me, but it did. "You don't dance anymore? At all?"

"Oh, no, not other than socially. It's just too painful to see all those skinny little girls prancing around the studio like dogs in heat."

Another exasperated sigh escaped me. You just couldn't win with my mother: you were either too fat to be pretty or too pretty to be borne. The philosophical aspects of yoga seemed not to have taken root in her angry little soul. Had she always been like that? I thought so, but I was not objective.

We walked up to the carport, and I put the box into the backseat of my rental car. I turned back to look at my mother, feeling strange at how much larger I was than this diminutive tyrant of my childhood.

"I'll bring these back tomorrow, if you want them."

"Of course, sweetie!"

"I may have questions. . . ."

"That'll be fine. I'm just . . . so happy to see you!" she added, forcing a hug around my chest.

I didn't know how to respond to this mercurial monster. Was she crazy or just controlling? I didn't know. I squirmed away. "I may want to look in other boxes," I reminded her.

"I don't mind," she said. "Call before you come, though—I might be out."

I didn't ask what she'd be doing. I didn't care except that it might slow me from getting what I wanted and getting out of that smog-bound lotus land and specifically away from her.

FIVE

I thought I might regret it, but I drove away from my mother's house and around the backs of the Hollywood hills toward Mulholland Drive. I wasn't looking forward to this meeting, either, but I had to try to talk to Cary one more time before I got any deeper into the mystery of my own past. I wanted to know why he'd popped up now and what he'd meant by "things waiting" for me.

No matter what a ghost tells you, there's always the possibility that it's a lie or just plain wrong. They aren't omniscient or instantly truthful just because they're dead. They're as stupid and opinionated as they were in life, and even more limited in knowledge most of the time. Once in a while, they get hold of information that exists only in the Grey, and then things get a lot more complicated. I was betting that Cary had remained, in death, a lot like he'd been in life: curious, stubborn, cautious, and foolishly romantic.

I took the grumbling little car up the twisty roads of the hills until I reached the saddle where Mulholland crests the ridge from the southeast and starts down into the valley on the northwest, crossing Coldwater Canyon Road above the reservoir. I parked the car in the overlook—no more than a dusty, extra wide bit of shoulder to accommodate the desire of drivers to stop and stare at the view spreading on both sides of the road.

Just behind my car was an odd little hump where the roads met and a lone house perched at the top of the rise, glimmering through the brushy chaparral at the top of a gated road. On the other side of the turnout was the place Cary had parked the night he died so he could watch that house. I didn't want to put my car there, so I left it where it was and stepped out, being careful of the blind traffic coming across the ridge. I walked along the crumbling edge of the packed dirt. The scent of the dust and the plants swelled in the warming afternoon air, poisoned with the acid of exhaust.

To the south I could look down into the steep, storm-forged canyons of Los Angeles and its colony of rich and famous recluses and Spanish revival houses set in the twists of the arroyo walls. To the north the broader, rolling floodplain of the San Fernando Valley offered its more sanitized and spreading estates in the descending hills of Sherman Oaks and Studio City before the valley turned into an endless bowl of suburbia smothered in smog.

I came to a boulder that had been shoved and wedged at the edge of the turnout by the last big landslide, and I sat on it, waiting. If Cary was going to show up, I figured this was the place: about a hundred feet straight up from where he'd died.

After a while of sitting in the sun and staring into the Grey, I saw him, trudging up the canyon side, trailing uncanny flame and smoke. Cary didn't quite levitate, though his feet made no impression on the ground or plants he passed over. He reached me and stopped, swirled in fire that crackled and stunk of burning creosote and charring flesh.

I gagged, but held it down with difficulty. A desire to shake and scream and cry and hide my face crawled beneath my skin. It wasn't just the smell but the presence of the man I used to love amid the flame and the sunshine and the odor of past and present warring in my senses. I'd never seen a ghost so horrible.

"Hiya, Slim," he said, staying a few feet away from me as if he thought he might set me alight if he drew closer. I wasn't sure he wouldn't.

"Hi," I faltered back.

"You look sad. What's wrong?" he asked.

"I don't know. You called me and now . . . things are crazy. My dad killed himself. Did you know that? Is that what you wanted me to discover about my past?" It sounded angry and accusatory, and I don't know why I said it that way—it just came out.

"No. I don't know what you need to find out. I just know . . . We're not like you. Dead is like being locked in a room in the loony bin with only a cruddy little window some tree's grown in front of. Sometimes you get out on the ward floor, but usually you're just in your room. You can't see much and you can't go out unless someone opens the door."

"Who opened it? Who let you out?" I thought if I knew who, I might be able to figure out what I was supposed to know.

Cary shook his burning head. The long-gone flesh was blackened and crisp, but the face was still his, though his eyes were only coals and his smile showed tombstone teeth against the inferno that engulfed him.

"I don't know," he replied. "I had the chance and I took it, but that window's starting to close. I'll have to leave soon."

"Then you'll have to talk fast." My voice caught in the back of my throat like smoke and stones.

"I don't have a complete picture," Cary said. "Just the outline. What I can see or hear from my tiny window. I heard about you when you first came here. I couldn't believe you were dead. I tried to get to you then, but by the time I got close, you weren't with us anymore. And then it got so much harder to get near you. There are things after you. Things near you all the time. I don't know what to call them. They aren't the dead and they aren't the living. They watch you and they have been for a long time. They were watching you even when I died and since before then—a long time. Now something's happening. Something's . . . breaking. Suddenly it's like everything is unlocked around you and the things from your past are flooding out. I snuck out with them, but I can't stay. I don't think they mean you any good. They're . . . evil things. That sounds so crazy. . . ."

He was fading. I tried to reach for him, but my arms felt scorched and I jerked them back. "It's not crazy. Cary! Don't go!"

He put out his incorporeal hand, wreathed in fading fire, and stroked my cheek, sending a whisper of burning and chill over my face. "I'm sorry, Slim. If I told you I loved you, I lied. I miss you, but I don't want you here. I'm . . . so sorry. Be careful. They come out of the past. They come . . . from . . . evil."

"No!" I shouted as he snuffed out and disappeared into the smoggy canyon air in a dwindling stream of smoke. I snatched at the dark plume as it dissipated and got nothing but a handful of eucalyptus leaves and the odor of doused campfires.

"Cary!" I screamed, willing him to come back, knowing he was gone and I couldn't bring him back. I was outraged and hurt and torn into pieces. I thought of Quinton's uncomplicated affection and I hated Cary, but I kept yelling his name until I had to lay my head on my drawn-up knees and gulp my breath.

I sat huddled in the umber-tinged sunlight until the dreadful sensation of loss was bearable. Not just Cary Malloy and whatever I'd thought we'd had, but my father and my belief in my past had all been swept away at a stroke, and I howled at the gashed hurt of fresh loss. Not even thoughts of Quinton and my home and my life could stop the ache of betrayal. The sound that tore itself out of me was not just of grief, but of fury. I wanted to find the truth—whatever it was—and devour it so I could never be lied to again. No matter how it hurt I was going to hunt it down.

SIX

I returned to my hotel with that resolve to hunt the truth still as hard and shining as steel, and the box of my father's things was the first hunting ground on my list. Resolve took a bit of a hammering as I dug into that messy cardboard repository of the past.

I started out trying to sort the items as I pulled them from the box, but in the end it was easier to just dump it all on my bed and sort by eye. A lot of the things in my father's box were obvious on sight: his appointments book, his desk diary, some kind of medical notebooks, catalogs for dental equipment that was twenty years out-of-date, checkbooks, ledgers, patient files, X-ray envelopes. . . . They all went into piles along with useless objects like a dozen yellowed, packaged toothbrushes and samples of dental floss. It took a couple of hours to get the piles sorted enough that the eerie glow of the Grey became easier to isolate.

I removed all the Grey items from the piles until I had one gleaming pile and a lot of dull ones. I shoveled the dreck back into the box for another time and only considered the things that throbbed with the traces of ghosts and magic. What I had—aside from a headache—was a small pile of notebooks, my father's appointment calendar, the suicide note, and a small metal puzzle that looked like a flat bunch of fancy, interlocked paper clips.

I recalled him carrying the puzzle in his pocket, and seeing it again brought on a rush of tearstained nostalgia. He'd always had a box full of small, cheap toys for his younger patients to take a "prize" from after they'd endured their cleanings and fillings, but this toy had always been much more interesting to me. He'd let me play with it once in a while, though I didn't remember ever solving it. Dad had always solved it with ease. Maybe that had been the beginning of my obsession with puzzles and mysteries. I dimly remembered his dismantling and solving it over and over on some occasions, the way some people use a stress ball or prayer beads.

I picked up the toy and slid a few of the metal parts back and forth, melancholy in my contemplation of it. It tingled slightly from the Grey energy that clung to it, but I got no particular feeling off it aside from that. I still wasn't sure I could put it back together once I'd taken it apart, and the preternatural gleam of it gave me pause, too. It might have been Grey just because it was associated with my father— some of the things I handled every day had similar Grey traces—but the thought that there could be a more sinister reason turned my reverie cold and I laid it aside.

Next, I picked up the appointment calendar and leafed through it, seeing mundane bookings for the usual dental business up to and past the day he'd died. He hadn't made many notes other than the usual run of business, such as "needs flossing instructions," and so on. I put that aside as well and turned to the notebooks.

These were less business and more personal, and the books were chronological. I put them in order and saw that they started four years before his death, about the time my mother had pushed me into dance classes. That was an interesting coincidence. I started the first entry and was soon sucked into my father's strange narrative.

One entry began:

Veronica has given up on me and turned her attention to Harper. I feel sorry for the kid, but I don't suppose it'll do her any harm. I'm sure no good for them, but the watchers won't bother them if they aren't near me. They're watching all the time, but I don't know what I've done to get their attention. They even come to the office now. They just won't leave me alone.

It sounded like my dad was paranoid and I supposed that was what my mother had been hinting at when she said he was odd. I was startled at the mention of "watchers," echoing what Cary had told me about things that kept an eye on me, but I wasn't sure how they connected to my father. Still, the parallel sent a chill over my skin.

The entries went on for a while about his frustrations with my mother and increasing references to "they" and "the watchers." A little over a year later, the tone changed and the entries rarely spoke of business or even my mother and me.

It's the nightmares. They've crept out into the daylight. How could I have missed that for so long? Maybe because they changed shape? They invade everything, infest everything. They're like weevils, burrowing into the heart of everything and chewing it up from the inside out. They don't even leave my wife and kid alone now. I see them trailing after Veronica and Harper when they leave for class. I have to make them stop.

He rambled on for a couple more years, trying to put his mysterious watchers off the scent, having nightmares both sleeping and awake. Then someone had come to see him—or that's what he said, but I wasn't sure if it had been a real person, a ghost, or some figment of his increasingly fractured imagination.

He's not like the rest. He bends them and they sway to his will. White, white, white, pale and ghastly. God help me, I can't think of anything but that horrible film about the worm-man. Or did I dream that? I don't know. I just don't. I can barely work some days, they're so close. But I have to work. I have to! The patients, the singing of the drill, the routine suck them in and push them away at the same time. And this man—but he can't possibly be a man—he knows everything they see. They're his rotten little spies.

He drifts in on a red tide, saying he owns me and taking what he wants. He took Christelle. He lured her away somehow, and she came back changed into one of them and now she's watching all the time, too. I tried to make her leave. I tried to fire her but she came back and I can't make her go. Veronica's furious. She thinks I'm screwing Christelle, but I could never touch that thing that's hiding in there. I know she's one, too. . . .

What had my father thought was hiding in his receptionist? An alien? A demon? Had there been anything at all or was he really, as my mother claimed, losing his mind? I'd thought I was losing mine when I first became a Greywalker. If Dad had also been in touch with the Grey in some fashion, but without the help I'd gotten from the Danzigers and others, maybe he had been going crazy. Or maybe not. Maybe he *had* seen things that watched him.

He might have been some kind of psychic or medium; he didn't seem to be a Greywalker. He wasn't describing the same kind of experiences I'd gone through: He didn't speak of another world or the mist or the power grid; he never mentioned ghosts or vampires or any other monster I knew; he only wrote of the watchers and the white man-worm thing that threatened and cajoled him by turns, and some creature he called "the Thousand Eyes."

Whatever was going on with him, he'd been alone with it and it had been driving him insane, whether it was real or all in his head. The thought brought a fresh wave of grief for my crazy father in his solitary battle. Picking up this diary again was difficult. I saw the dates, and the horror of what I now knew and what I was seeing in his writing only grew with each word.

He'd finally lost his grip completely about three months before he killed himself.

> Christelle won't come back this time. I killed the thing in her, but there wasn't any Christelle left once it was gone. There was just black stuff, like cremated remains. Poor Christelle. How long had she been gone? I thought I'd see her for a moment or two sometimes, but I was wrong. There was no Christelle in that thing I killed no matter what the worm-man said. But if Christelle was gone, when did she go? Did he kill her back at the beginning? Or did I? And he's so happy about it! He's happy, the monster!
>
> I can't believe what I did. Or how. I just reached, somehow, with my mind, not with my hands, and something came out of me and ripped her into bits. Oh, God, I'm sick. I can't stop throwing up. It's just blood and bile now and I feel like I'm going to die from the rot in me.
>
> He's pleased. But not all the watchers are. The Thousand Eyes doesn't like it. It hates me now as much as it hates him. I can feel its loathing like radiation from a nuclear bomb that strips my skin and burns me alive. I won't do whatever it is the worm-man wants. I'd rather be eaten by the Thousand Eyes and burn in its gullet forever than let the other one win. He's evil. And I'm evil just by being near him.

He didn't write much after that, except taunting notes to the watchers he now assumed read his journal and reported all to the worm-man: "I have a way to stop you" and "I know how to get help you can't kill, even if I told you who."

The last entry was the worst.

> There were more. Like me. Before. But not like me. No, he says I'm special and he won't let me slip away from him, not even if I die. But I think he can't stop me. Veronica won't care—she's got everything

she wanted. But Harper I feel bad about. She's so sweet, my little girl. I don't want her to have a monster for a father. I will stop it. There must be no more of this. No more of me, of things like me. I hope she'll understand it's not her dad who's done bad things, but a grown-up man who has to do something awful to keep what he loves safe.

The bottom of the page was torn out raggedly, and I didn't have to fetch the thing to know the texture and shape of the missing page would match that of his final note. A note meant for me.

I felt sick and I covered my face, but tears didn't come this time, only the black sensation of horror and pity.

SEVEN

I needed to talk to my dad, however dead he was. Whether he'd been crazy, or paranoid, or dead-on truthful, he'd been connected to Grey things. I'd have to go for a walk in the Grey and see if I could find him. The problem was I'd never done that, and though I thought I could, I wasn't sure how to find a specific ghost in the roiling, uncertain mist-world between the normal and the paranormal. I wasn't a medium or a necromancer; I couldn't just call to the spirit I wanted and expect it to show up. At least I didn't think I could, since that wasn't how my abilities worked for anything else—I'd gotten lucky with Cary showing up since he'd been trying to reach me as much as I'd been trying to find him.

There was also a practical limit to how long I could spend wandering around in the Grey. It was exhausting to move through fully immersed, and it was just as big—in some places bigger—than the normal world. The Grey was filled with the sinkholes and rifts of time layers I called temporaclines, which stopped and started and broke or rose as they pleased. There were lots of places in the Grey where something in the normal or paranormal created a barrier that could only be negotiated by emerging back into the normal and going around the ordinary way.

It was almost dinnertime—I'd missed both breakfast and lunch—but I put off eating a little longer to pick up the phone and call the Danzigers. Sometimes they don't know the answer to my questions, and sometimes they had an answer that was wrong, but they at least had more experience with the bizarre than I did, even after two years more than knee-deep in it.

The phone rang longer than usual before Ben answered.

"Hello?"

"Hey, Ben. It's Harper." Background noise at the other end washed the emotions out of my voice.

"Oh, hi, Harper! How's Los Angeles?"

"Like the antechamber to hell. I have a question."

"All right."

"Any ideas on how I can find a specific ghost? I need to talk to a particular individual who's been dead for about twenty-two years."

"Well, you could— Oh, no . . . you can't call them. Hrm . . . Hang on. . . ." I could hear him cover the mouthpiece with his hand as he turned to call for Mara.

I could barely hear some mumbling on the other side. Then a thump as the phone fell out of Ben's hand and dropped onto the floor.

A very young voice cackled into the phone. "Harper! Hahahaha! Come play with me!"

"I can't today, Brian. I'm way far away."

"Are not! You're in the phone!"

A few more noises preceded the return of Ben's voice, although his son's carried on in the background. I figured he was probably holding on to the kid while he talked. "I'm sorry. . . ."

"That's OK. So what do you two think?"

"Well . . . we're agreed that you'll have the best luck looking in the places strongly associated with the person who died. Like their home or office or the place they died. You know a ghost can haunt several places simultaneously, but they manifest intelligence in only one at a time."

"Yeah, that's kind of what I thought. I know I can't always get the attention of a repeater."

"And if that's the only manifestation they have, it's going to be hard to get any information out of them."

"Nearly impossible, actually."

"Really? I should write that down. . . ."

Ever since he'd been mauled by a legendary monster on Marsh Island, Ben had been on disability, staying home with their precocious son while Mara taught full-time. Bored, Ben had started working on a field guide to ghosts, mixing the research he'd been doing for years with the proofs-through-misadventure that I'd made Greywalking for the past two years.

I thought over his suggestion and decided it seemed plausible. I'd have to give it a try. Of course, I couldn't remember the addresses of our home or Dad's office. I thanked Ben for the idea and hung up, staring at the box of junk. I stiffened my spine and wondered if I could find the addresses in there and not have to go back to my mother right away. I'd have to show up again eventually; I wanted those shining boxes of photographs and I wanted to know what had actually happened to Christelle. Maybe my father had just gone crackers and only imagined the destruction of his receptionist. . . . I wanted to believe it, but I doubted it.

I scrabbled through the shining pile for the appointment book, hoping someone had thought to put the office information in it. It had Dad's name and office address on the cover; it was in Glendale, a middle-class suburb just northeast of Hollywood. Since he'd died there, the office seemed like the best place to start looking for him.

EIGHT

Before I went anywhere, I called Quinton just to hear his voice, though all I actually got was his pager and he didn't call back, so I knew he was busy and I hoped it wasn't because of anything too creepy. Creepy was becoming the order of the day. Then I had dinner downstairs, thinking rush hour would have dissipated by the time I was done. I stopped at the concierge desk on my way back up to my room to fetch the documents from Dad's box and asked about the best route to Glendale. The concierge printed a map for me from the computer built discreetly into his Spanish revival desk and told me traffic might still be a bit thick on the freeway until after seven p.m., but it wasn't very far away and I could take Los Feliz Boulevard instead and make about the same time if I was leaving right away.

Los Feliz was a strange street, starting out wide and smooth as it ran diagonally into the hills below Griffith Park. I glanced up at just the right time to see a few letters of the Hollywood sign with the copper dome of the observatory rising over the hilltop above. If not for the haze, the glimpse could have been mistaken for a postcard. As the street ran on, past the zoo's massive parking lot and over the cement -bound Los Angeles River, it narrowed and grew more potholed, passing through an industrial slum thick with old warehouses and light manufacturing that left the roads and sidewalks dusky with grime.

After a sudden turn and a cluster of dark-shadowed thugs on a street corner smoking cigarettes and eyeing passing cars, the neighborhood changed. It got clean and slick, with mid-rise office clusters and condominiums lining the street in profusion.

I turned onto Brand, looking for the office address, shadowed by recent developments of white steel-and-glass towers. I passed a shining new shopping center with a massive open plaza and spools of neon lighting that cast color onto the street. The effect was like the change of *The Wizard of Oz* from black and white to Technicolor. I expected Munchkins and wondered if I'd really lived here.

Passing the Alex Theatre with its old movie palace marquee under the lighted, flowerlike spire that pointed to the sky, I felt the déjà vu like a blow. The farther north I went, the more familiar the scenery grew. I passed under the Ventura Freeway and into the smaller, older neighborhood that urban sprawl hadn't overrun yet. My eyes watered, and not just from the yellow haze in the evening air. I knew I had walked along this street with my dad, hand in hand. Stopped in at that building for milkshakes (forbidden treats!) when it was a retro-fifties diner. Bought makeup and school supplies in the drugstore right there. . . . The feelings that poured over me weren't just nostalgic, though; an emotional darkness now tainted every memory and put a stone into my chest. I pulled the car into a parking space at the curb and got out to walk before I hit something from my inattention.

The sidewalks were so clean they sparkled in the late sun, even through layers of ghostly pedestrians and older shadows of orange groves and rolling, empty scrub. I noticed that many of the names on the businesses ended in -ian or -ianian; what had once been a solidly WASP neighborhood was now just as solidly Armenian, and cleaner than ever. The current residents clearly didn't tolerate sloth or dirt. The shops were mostly closed—only a few restaurants were open at this time of evening—and no one, corporeal or ghostly, paid much attention to me as I went up the street, looking for the building that had once housed my father's dental office.

It was a three-story brick-and-glass building that had been brand-new when we moved into the area. It looked a little less polished and swanky than its newer neighbors to the south, but it was still a very respectable address for small offices. Dad's was on the second floor and the main door was locked for the day, but I walked around for a few minutes and found a smaller door at the side that was still open and sporting a sign that pointed up to BELLES SAUVAGES DANCE AND EXERCISE STUDIO.

More déjà vu. I'd never danced there, but as I went up the stairs, the familiar odors of sweat, old shoes, floor varnish, and rosin curdled the air. I could hear the thump of music and feet in rhythm on the wooden floor. As always, that combination of sound and smell roused mixed feelings in me: remembered anxiety and learned—or faked—happiness. I hadn't hated to dance; I'd hated the emotional freight and unending demands that went with it.

I took the second-floor exit, which should have been locked but wasn't, and went down the hallway looking for number 204. The suites had been cut up since my father's time and I discovered that his office was now split between a chiropractor and an accountant. I wasn't sure which of the new tenants occupied the room where he'd died, but I didn't think I needed to be right in the room, just near enough. I looked up and down the corridor for cameras, though I didn't think anyone observing would believe what they might see, and let go of normal.

The Grey in full flush rushed upon me, making the normal world into a dim watercolor beneath the realm of silver mist and lines of hot energy that throbbed as if alive. The layers of time were broken chunks, tumbled at all angles like striated rocks in a flood-plain. The displacement of the disjointed temporaclines was much worse than I'd ever seen it in Seattle, and I wondered if it was related to Los Angeles's famous earthquakes or the near-constant state of construction and reconstruction that went on in the area. I hoped I could do this without recourse to climbing and sliding through those ragged bits of time.

I glanced around and spotted the Grey outline of my father's office door, still lingering where it had stood for so long. It would be a pain to get through it; it might have been a door once, but it was a wall now. It was much harder for me to move something that had no current existence in the normal world than to utilize the momentary memories of passages opened by ghosts. I could try to find the right stretch of time and get through the door there, but that didn't look like the safest option. Relegating the temporaclines to last resort, I paced outside the phantom door and waited for a ghost.

After ten minutes that felt like an hour, the ghost of a young woman strode down the hall and unlocked the door. She was average-pretty behind purple eyeglasses and wore her long light brown hair pulled back with a clip. I wasn't sure I recognized her, but I thought she might be Christelle LaJeunesse—Dad's receptionist. I pushed through the doorway in her wake, and she stopped to stare at me.

"Do you have an appointment?" she asked as we went into the ghost of the waiting room.

I was a little surprised at her attempt to interact with me. I couldn't recall a ghost simply talking to me as if I were part of their context before. Usually I had to force myself upon them if they hadn't come to me first.

"Uh, no," I replied.

She went around behind the reception desk and looked back at me from her position of authority as the office gatekeeper. "Do you want to make an appointment?"

"I just want to talk to Dr. Blaine for a moment," I said, on the off chance she could summon him.

"I'm sorry. Dr. Blaine's not available right now. You'll have to make an appointment."

"When will he be available?"

"I don't know. He isn't in yet." She looked around the shadow form of the empty waiting room. "Actually," she added, "he hasn't been in for a while. I think there's something wrong." As she said it, her demeanor changed and she became frightened and sad, aware, perhaps, of her own disjointure from life, of something precious lost or broken.

Ghosts have a strange relationship to time, and this one was odd but not unheard-of: She was aware my father's absence, but she didn't know he was dead. She wasn't quite in sync with either her own time or mine. She seemed to think this was a day when Dr. Robert Blaine simply hadn't come to work, but it disturbed her, and she wasn't sure why.

"What do you think's happened to him?" I asked.

She made a sour face. "Maybe his crazy wife shot him. She thinks he's humping me. Silly woman. He's been all paranoid lately. He thinks people follow him around. I think it's her. Or maybe that creepy albino guy."

That was interesting. "Albino guy?" I asked. "Who's he?"

"He won't give a name and I don't know what he wants," the ghost of Christelle replied. "He comes by once in a while, says, 'Tell him I'm here,' and Rob gets kind of freaked out. It's like he knows when the guy's here before I say anything. And he always tries to ditch him and slip out somehow or not go home until he's sure the guy's gone."

"Tell me about this guy," I said. "Do you still see him around?" I needed to look for Dad and I was possibly wasting time, but I'd be willing to bet this "creepy guy" was the same one my dad had called the "white worm-man." So he wasn't a figment of Dad's imagination, but what had he been? He wasn't a ghost if Christelle had seen him. A vampire? Just a disturbing man who happened to be albino? What had he wanted with my father?

Christelle shook her head as if she were trying to shake her thoughts into place. "Well . . . I haven't seen him in a while. Like . . . about as long as I haven't seen Rob. As to his appearance . . . he's really pale and he gives me the willies but it's not just the way he looks. He's got those scary kind of washed-out eyes that kind of stare through you. And . . . he wears eyeliner. Somehow it just makes him creepier." She shuddered and then her face went blank and she returned to the repetitive track of her remnant existence.

"Did you want to make an appointment?" she asked again, forgetting our prior conversation. "I'm afraid Dr. Blaine isn't in today. . . ."

I tried to get her back, but her attention faded from me and she started going through her daily routine, oblivious of my presence now. I wanted to ask her if she knew what had happened to her, even if she didn't know what had happened to my dad, but I couldn't get her off her loop again.

Disappointed, I set myself back to my original task. I had no idea which part of the suite Dad's body had been found in, but I guessed that his personal office was most likely to hold some shade of him, even if it was just a loop of time playing over and over.

As I made my way through the glimmering fog-forms of corridors and treatment rooms, bright shapes darted past me, trailing blazing threads in every color. They weren't ghosts as I knew them, just bits of energy and not quite like anything I'd seen before. They moved erratically and one or two hit me, zipping through my body with a sizzling, burning sensation and leaving a short-lived tremor in my limbs and a touch of nausea in my belly, as if I'd been mildly shocked. I couldn't find a source for them. And I couldn't find my dad.

I searched the office, increasingly tired and frustrated and dragging myself through the thickening Grey. The harsh little energy bolts took a greater toll on me with each strike until I was shaking constantly. I sat down on the shimmering floor, panting.

"Dad," I called out. "Dad . . . are you here?" I wasn't sure it would have any effect, but I was getting desperate. There was no trace at all, not a shadow, not a loop, not a glimmer that was Robert J. Blaine shaped, not a voice or a reflection. I even tried stepping out of the Grey and back in with a piece of mirror in my hand to try to catch any image of him that might be lingering around. I almost didn't make it out, much less back in to look for him.

The ghost of Christelle drifted into his office, unaware of me, and bent over the desk, talking as if he was there, but he wasn't. He should have been, since her lack of reaction to me this time indicated I was seeing a memory loop, and there was no reason he shouldn't have shown up in it. I was feeling sick, and my whole body was quivering with fatigue and the effects of the energy blobs that zipped about like drunken insects.

I struggled out to the hall and collapsed onto the floor, gathering the normal back and rolling onto the ordinary wood of the corridor. The thumping from Belles Sauvages was still going on. What had felt like hours wandering in the memory of my father's office had been about forty minutes of normal time, and I felt starved and sick, as if I hadn't eaten in days. I levered myself up enough to prop my back against the nearest wall, panting and shaking.

"Hey," came a voice from the stairwell end of the corridor. "Hey, you're not supposed to be down here."

I could see a dark-skinned man in a uniform coming toward me with care. He held a flashlight in his hand, not a gun, so I guessed he was a security guard.

"Sorry," I croaked back. "I wasn't feeling well, and I took the wrong door. Is there a restroom . . . ?"

"There's one upstairs in the studio," he said, drawing near. He stopped and peered at me. "You don't look good."

"I feel awful." I could tell he was debating whether I was danger-ous, drunk, or just ill. I tried to smile and I knew it was pathetic. "I just want to get some fresh air," I added.

He grunted and made up his mind, putting out his free hand. "C'mon, I'll get you out of here."

I accepted his help getting to my feet and made my way out of the building under his aegis. It was frustrating to have nothing after look-ing so hard but I wasn't sure there was anything to find. I might come back in the daylight and see if I could get at Christelle or the temporaclines, but I wasn't convinced the result would be any better. There was something wrong with the space my father had once occupied, and the hole frightened me and left me with more questions than ever and a feeling of loss more profound than any I could remember.

I didn't know what the energetic balls of light were, but I was pretty sure they were connected to whatever strangeness was going on in the office. As disturbing as it was, I thought I'd like to see if they appeared again in the temporaclines. Not that I'd know what that meant if they did, but it was information, and with so little else to go on, I'd grab for whatever data I could get. I walked slowly down the spanking clean street to a small coffee shop, sad and exhausted.

I bought hot chocolate and a sandwich, feeling the need to raise my blood sugar fast and bask in the warmth and life of the busy little restaurant. The shaking in my limbs was visible to anyone who cared to look and my hands trembled so hard I had difficulty holding the cup at first.

The waitress, a large woman in a bright blue dress and frilly apron with the name LILA embroidered on it, paused to watch me. "You all right, miss?"

"Very hungry," I mumbled.

"Eat slower, or you'll make yourself sick. That's too good a sandwich to waste. I'll get you some more chocolate."

Lila whisked my cup away and brought it back refilled and overflowing with whipped cream. I'm not usually fond of sweets or chocolate specifically, but this was hot and stopped the quivering. I thanked her and asked for some water.

"You sure you want water now? It gives you cramps if you drink too fast."

"This is good, but sweet."

"Oh, yeah," she agreed. "I'll get your water. You eat that sandwich while I'm gone."

I'd forgotten that you have to ask for a glass of water in California.

The state's so frequently in a drought that even in good years, a glass of water is treated like a luxury to be doled out one at a time. Some places even charge for the glass to offset the cost of washing it.

Lila returned and put a red plastic tumbler filled with water near my hand. "You came down from the dance studio?" she asked.

"Umm . . . yeah." I'd have sworn no one saw me or that it was not even possible to see from the diner to Dad's building. "How did you know?"

"Oh, lots of folks come in after class. Replace those calories they sweated off. But you . . . look a little more serious. . . ." she added, giving me a speculative look.

I'm not one to ignore an opening. "Well, really," I started, "I'm scouting stories. I heard the place was haunted. . . ."

She gaped and made a squeaking sound. "You mean like on *Ghost Hunters*?"

I only shrugged. People will fill in their own blanks if I keep my mouth shut and it wouldn't hurt to let her think I might work for a spooky TV show if that got information flowing, though I felt a bit grimy for the ruse.

She nodded to herself before speaking again. "I guess that's not so strange. I mean . . . after what happened there, you'd think it would be haunted, right? Not that I've ever seen a ghost over there and my chiropractor is right in the office it happened in, you know."

"Really? So what did you hear about it?" I asked.

Lila glanced around to be sure no one wanted her attention and then turned back to me and lowered her voice. "Well, back a while ago there was a doctor up on the second floor. Must be . . . twenty years ago—before I moved up from Long Beach, anyway. So, anyhow. He was having an affair with his nurse and then one day she just up and disappeared. No one knows what happened to her, but they say he killed her and hid the body somewhere. But whatever happened, she was never found, and one day he just shot himself. Dead."

NINE

I t hurt to hear my dad described as a womanizing murderer. Even if I suspected he might be responsible for Christelle's death—and with her ghost wandering the remnants of the office, there was no doubt in my mind that she was dead—it didn't feel good to hear someone else say it. I decided to pretend that it really was not my father and Christelle she was talking about, but some nameless doctor and his nameless nurse. That I could talk about without feeling queasy.

I swallowed some water before speaking. "So he killed himself?" I asked. "It wasn't his wife, or the girl, or her boyfriend who shot him?"

Lila shook her head. "Not the way I heard it."

"Interesting. Do people see his ghost there? Or the nurse's?"

"Well, like I said, my chiropractor has that office now. I've never seen anything weird there, but . . . it's funny how the room is always too warm."

"Too warm? Most people say ghosts are cold."

"Yeah, well, you'd think so. But this one's warm. And there are noises at night."

"I couldn't hear anything over the music in the studio," I said. I hadn't heard anything at all, not even the sound of Christelle open-ing the door, now that I thought about it. Usually the Grey is full of sourceless muttering and the singing of the grid, but except for Christelle's voice, the general Grey buzz, and the zing of the flying energy balls, there'd been no sounds in the ghostly office. I'd have to take another look, but this time I'd try to get into the right layer of time and see if that made a difference.

"Do you think your chiropractor would let me look around his office? After dark, that is. When the ghosts are more active."

"Oh, I think so. He's a nice kid. Paul Arkmanian, that's him."

I raised my brows. "Kid?"

She turned her head and blushed. "Well, not really a kid you understand: He's Sandros Arkmanian's son," she said, as if that not only made sense, but made him perfectly safe. On the sense side, I wasn't so sure, but considering how tight-knit the neighborhood looked, maybe "safe" wasn't so far out. Everyone knew everyone and everyone's children, and they probably knew who was having an af-fair with whom, who was drinking too much, and who was dying of which tragic disease without their selfish kids ever coming around to visit. They'd all know who was "good folks" and who wasn't. I'd bet the neighborhood ladies brought casseroles and baked goods around for christenings and funerals, too.

Lila was glancing around the room again, her face lighting up as she waved a hand at someone, beckoning the person closer to our table. A burly, square-shouldered man got up from his own table and strolled over to us. He looked to be about six feet tall, mid-sixties, and prosperous without being full of himself over it. He gave Lila a kiss on the cheek when he reached her side.

"What can I do for you, Lila?"

"Sandy, this nice woman wants to meet Paul. She works for that ghost hunter show and they want to talk to him about the office ghost."

Sandy looked a little less excited at the prospect than Lila had.

"That's just a story, Lila. Paul's office isn't haunted." He turned his attention to me and gave me a hard, evaluating stare. "You sure it's the place you want?"

"Suite 204," I replied. "I just want to take a look."

He shrugged his eyebrows and sighed. "Well . . . I suppose that's OK. Really, I don't think it's haunted." He looked at his watch. "You want to come over, have some coffee? We can talk it over, see if Paul's all right with the idea."

"Now?" That startled me. Even Seattle's notoriously friendly residents don't issue invitations with such alacrity.

"Of course now. What's the point in waiting?" He turned toward the table he'd come from and waved. The three other men sitting there waved back. "I'm taking this pretty girl home to meet my son!" he called.

They laughed and flapped their hands at him, waving him away. "Good luck, Sandros!" one of them called back.

I finished off my sandwich in a couple of huge bites and left money on the table for Lila. I had a bad feeling about Paul Arkmanian as I followed his father down the street. Was he gay? A misogynist? What was the big deal with going out with a female? But I wanted into that office without having to do another Grey version of a B and E, so I was willing to try anything.

We went down Brand and turned onto a much smaller side street. In a few blocks, all signs of business had vanished and single-family houses in neat little yards appeared. It was like something from a fifties sitcom, and I recognized the houses as the sort I'd walked past every day as a child. The nostalgia was thick enough to choke on and my eyes watered a bit.

Arkmanian stopped and unlatched the gate of a pink house on the right. "This is it." He glanced toward a side window that flickered with television light. He sighed. "And Paul's home. Let's see what he says. . . ."

We went up the flagstone walk and into the house, which wasn't locked. The flickering blue light from a computer monitor turned the room the harsh metallic color of dance clubs. Sandros Arkmanian turned on the overhead lamp, killing the shadows that held sway in the living room and driving the rest back into the dining room.

The dining table was probably an antique, given the heavily carved legs that I spied under the mass of books and computer equipment. It was like a microcosm of Quinton's lair crushed into the ten-foot-square room. A man I guessed to be Paul Arkmanian sat behind the table. He was in his late twenties, tall like his father but rangier, judging by his arms and shoulders. He wore a pair of expensive headphones and was deeply immersed in whatever was displayed on his computer screen, twitching his mouse and keyboard and staring without blinking while he grimaced at something.

Suddenly he reared back, pounding the table and shouting, "Damn it! Damn, damn, damn! Stinking orc!"

I glanced at Sandros. "Computer games," he explained. "From the moment he gets home until he goes to bed. I tell you, I don't understand it. He'd rather play with imaginary monsters than have a date."

Better imaginary monsters than the real thing, I thought, but still, I didn't think I'd ever met an adult man who'd rather romp with pixels than with women. He wasn't bad looking, and he was plainly not stupid, judging by his reading material, so . . . where was the problem?

Sandros walked around and tapped Paul on the shoulder. The younger man jerked, blinked up at his father, and shoved the headphones down onto his neck.

"Oh. Hi, Dad. Am I making too much noise? Did you want to watch TV or something?"

"No, Paul. I brought this young lady to meet you. She's interested in your office."

Paul Arkmanian frowned at me. "My office? It's not for rent." His eyes flickered back to his screen for a moment. He wanted to get back to his game.

I'd have to be more interesting than a computer game, and I knew that wasn't as easy as it sounds. "I don't want to rent it," I said. "I want to talk to your ghost."

Paul pulled the headphones off his neck, setting them on the table. Behind him I could see Sandros raise his eyebrows at me, surprised that I'd managed to snare his son's attention from the realm of computerized mayhem.

"Who said there was a ghost in my office?"

"It's pretty common knowledge. Lila was filling me in, but I had already heard it before."

"She works for the ghost buster show—you know the one," the elder Arkmanian said.

"*Ghost Hunters*? Yeah, I've heard of that. You guys really think the place is haunted?"

"Do you?" I asked. "After all, a previous tenant did die there." My voice didn't shake, though I'd feared it would.

Paul bit his lip in thought and glanced down at his keyboard. "I don't know. . . . Oh, hang on." He made a few motions with his mouse and keyboard. Then he reached up and turned his monitor off, leaning back in his chair to get a better look at me. His father stared at the back of Paul's head with his mouth agape. "OK, now that I'm not going to get killed by the first NPC that comes by, let's talk." He stood up and went into the living room, expecting us both to follow.

I did, but Sandros paused a moment in the dining room. "I'll . . . get us some drinks, yeah?"

Paul started to wheel back around, saying, "Thanks, Dad, but I can get that—"

"No, no! You have a guest. I'll get it. Sit down with the lady and talk. What do you want?"

"Oh. Umm . . . whiskey and Coke?" the son replied as if he wasn't sure that was acceptable.

"Sure, no problem! You, young lady—what is your name, anyway?"

"It's Harper. Coke would be fine, thank you."

"All right then, Miss Harper. Coke it is." He vanished through a swinging door to the kitchen before I could correct him. But in retrospect it was probably better if he didn't notice I had the same last name as the man who'd died in Paul's office space.

Paul gestured to an armchair by the tiny fireplace in the living room's outside wall. "Please . . ."

I took the seat, although it did put my back to the door and windows.

"So . . ." Paul started.

"So, I'd like to take a look at your office during the evening hours. That's the best time for judging if ghosts are around—when there aren't so many live people around to disturb the indicators."

"Indicators? How do you tell?" Paul asked, sitting down on the sofa across from me and leaning forward. He watched me with serious, earnest eyes, and I understood why the neighborhood couldn't figure why he wasn't dating someone. He had that gaze that makes the object feel they're the most important person in the room. Cary had had that, damn him. I shoved that idea aside and carried on, my emotions about my dad stabilized by the chill of my most recent memory of Cary.

I winged it, based on past experience with poltergeists and Quinton's ghost detector ideas. "Oh, air pressure, humidity, atmospheric charge . . . that sort of thing. And noise. You can hear ghosts on recordings sometimes." I certainly wasn't going to say I could see them.

"Really? What about temperature?"

I nodded. "That, too. Do you get cold spots? That might be a sign."

"Oh. No," he said, and blushed suddenly, dropping his eyes. "No it's never cold in my office. That would be bad. I'm a chiropractor. Patients don't feel comfortable if it's cold. Cold makes the muscles tighten up and the patients get stressed and that's just what you don't want. Chiropractic aims to bring the whole body back in line, in harmony. Cold, unhappy patients don't have harmonious bodies."

He was babbling a little and I wondered why he'd gotten nervous. He looked uncomfortable and wiggled in his seat, casting his glance over his shoulder to search for his father. He was acting like a teenager on a date—

Oh. Right. This was the man who didn't date. And he was all alone in a room with a woman who wasn't a patient. He just wasn't sure what to do with me. Oh, boy . . .

"Dr. Arkmanian," I said, putting him back in his professional role—that seemed safer, "do you experience other phenomena? Things moving, changes in temperature, noises . . . ?"

"Oh," he replied, looking up again. "Yes, I do. But only in one area. It's not widespread."

"I see."

Sandros came into the room with three tumblers clutched between his hands. "Here we are. Plain Coke for you, Miss Harper, and the spiked kind for us."

I thanked him and looked back at Paul. "What part of your office is the phenomena confined to?"

"Treatment room two. It's on the back wall, near the window."

"Tell me what typically happens," I suggested.

He sipped his drink and shifted his gaze aside, thinking. "Usually it starts with a hot spot near the wall. It moves around, but it always sticks close to the wall. After a while the air just gets unbearably warm and I have to open the window, even if it's freezing outside. Then there's a loud noise. The first time I heard it I thought there had been a car accident outside, but there wasn't anything there. And then a sound like something really heavy being dropped on the floor—"

"Do your downstairs neighbors hear any of that?"

"No, and that's kind of strange, because they always hear the real things falling over."

"What things?"

"Oh. My towel cupboard fell over. It kept doing that. I even had it screwed to the floor for a while, but it still fell over. So I swapped it with a chair and now that falls over. Whatever's in that spot next to the wall always falls over or falls down about ten seconds after the crashing noise and then the sound of something invisible falling down."

"Have you tried leaving the space empty?"

"It's a pretty small room. I did try that, but things kept getting shoved over there to get them out of the way. And the noises happened anyway, even when there was nothing in the area."

That was a bit unusual.

"Is it the same noise every time?"

"Oh, yes. Identical. Like a car screeching to a violent halt, and then something being thrown on the floor."

"Does it generally happen at the same time of day?"

"No. It's not regular. It just . . . happens. It can be hard to work with. But it doesn't happen very often and sometimes it doesn't happen for weeks or months. Then it'll happen a lot for a while, and then stop again. Not predictable at all. It's been more active lately, so I'm hoping it will stop again soon."

Sounded like Dad had been kicking up a fuss. I wondered what else he got up to, why I hadn't been able to see him, and what Christelle was doing while all this went on. Except for my truncated conversation with Christelle, the office in the Grey had been silent.

"What other phenomena occur?" I asked, sticking to the immediate topic.

Paul thought and then shrugged. "Nothing. That's the whole thing. Just the hot spot, the noises, and the things falling down."

"Has anyone seen any shapes, unexplained shadows? Heard voices or other sounds in the area? Seen or thought they saw something move? Maybe in the dressing room mirror?"

He shook his head. "None of that. Just what I described."

He didn't take the prompt. A lot of people will say yes to such a list to make the investigator happy. It's a trick of frauds and true believers to suggest phenomena and then claim the description came spontaneously from the witness. Some people don't even realize they do it, so compelling is their desire for confirmation or justification. But it was strange that no one had observed any such manifestations; what Paul described and what I'd seen were more like half a haunting. It's unusual for such strong phenomena to have no accompanying features like corner-of-the-eye visions or voices. The falling objects was classic, but it was pretty small beer compared to the sound and its increasing frequency.

"I'd like to see the room for myself," I said.

Paul put down his drink and glanced at his father. Then he looked back at me. "We can go now, if you want. I can get back to the game later—the guild can do without me for a while."

I thought Sandros's jaw would detach and thump to the carpeted floor from shock along with his eyeballs, like something from a Depression-era Warner Brothers cartoon. "You want to go out? Now?"

Paul's shoulders hunched a little and his eyes widened, as if he were much younger. "Yeah . . . Is that OK, Dad? It's not that late, but I don't want to leave you all by yourself if you don't want—"

"No, no! I'm all right on my own. Go on, take the lady to the office." Then he caught himself and added, "But no hanky-panky, right?" He shot a look at me and nodded with his brows raised.

"Right, Dad," Paul replied, laughing.

I nodded, a little surprised myself. "It's fine with me if you two don't mind."

We left our drinks on the table and headed outside again within moments. Sandros stayed behind, but he did watch us from the doorway, like a protective father.

Paul looked a little embarrassed but said nothing as we headed for his haunted office.

TEN

The real office was creepy at night, more so than its Grey counterpart. There were no windows except on the back wall that faced an alley, and the dance studio had closed for the day, leaving a hollow sound in the shadow-drenched space. The Grey was still uncharacteristically silent.

Paul Arkmanian unlocked the front door and we walked into his reception area. Ghostly walls made a mist maze in the current space. We walked deeper into the chiropractic office and I searched both the Grey and the normal for any helpful signs. I'd have to be alone in the treatment room long enough to slip into the right bit of the past. I began looking for opportunities to send Paul in another direction the moment we were past the front desk.

We passed through a spectral wall—the memory of the wall that had once divided my father's office from his neighbor's. I felt cold sweep over me as we stepped through and then a blast of heat as we stopped at the current door marked "2." Paul glanced at me and then at the door.

"This is it. Are you sure you want to go in at night like this?" He glanced around and hunched his shoulders as if he were cold. "I never thought this was a spooky place before, but now it does seem haunted. I guess it's just the light. . . ."

I shivered, feeling something tremble at the edge of the Grey, sending ripples through the thin, silvery world. I hoped that wasn't what I thought. I looked at Paul and he seemed very far away, as if the mist of the Grey was a concave lens. Sweat formed in the small of my back from the strange heat coming out of the room.

"You might not want to go in with me. It might mess up the feel of the room to have two of us in there at once."

"I'd feel funny about that. Can you leave the door open?"

What a pain. "Sure." I'd have to maneuver into a place he couldn't observe from the doorway before I tried to get into the layers of history. I took my phone out of my pocket and started into the room.

"What's that for?"

"The cell phone antenna sometimes picks up electrical anomalies caused by ghosts. If I have the phone in the right mode, it will make noise when I'm near one." Not entirely untrue but generally useless. Ditto using the tiny camera to catch the lingering Grey impressions of ghosts passing through the glass; the rice-grain-sized lens was too low-quality to capture any images worth the effort. I didn't have any other props for my role as ghost hunter, but the phone would do if my line of fast talk was good enough.

Apparently it was, since Arkmanian nodded and stood back from the door to let me into the room. I stepped into my father's old office and halted with a jerk as the heat hit in earnest—it was like being swatted with a flaming bat. Then I heard the noise, like a runaway train rushing toward me. The layers of time heaved and rippled, a storm-racked sea of history battering the walls of the room as the screeching sound of something huge bearing down grew louder and closer.

"That's it! That's the sound!" Paul cried out, twitching back a couple of steps.

I bolted sideways into the blind side of the doorway, putting out my hand for the cold, slicing edges of the temporaclines. One of them stabbed at my fingers with fiery knives. I was shocked: Usually temporaclines feel cold as sheets of ice to me. I reached for it and shoved the layers open, sliding into the slice of history.

The room—Dad's personal office—hit me hard. It was a disaster of splattered blood and frenzy. Papers were thrown on the desk and strewn on the floor. Books, houseplants, furniture were all tossed about as if the room had been shaken by a giant hand and then drizzled with gore. The center of the room was nothing: a black void surrounded by a fence of flaming energy. Stars and lightning bolts of power shot through the space around the hole in history. Queasy and frightened, I walked toward it.

Hot knots of energy battered me back and the roaring noise rose to a hurricane shriek that ripped open the writhing mist of the Grey. A snarling monstrosity of spiderweb and bone poured out of the hole, snapping its dripping jaws at me and at the black void, flinching back as its fangs bit into the blazing energy around the nothingness. Bone spines rattled in the uncanny world as the creature shook its head in fury and screamed again.

I flinched away from its impossible mouthful of teeth. I'd run into the guardian beast before and still had the bite scars two years later. It turned its attention away from me as soon as I backed from the hole where the rest of the room's past should have been. Every time I moved toward it, trying to see any glimpse of my father, the beast snapped at me and drove me back. The beast's job was to keep non-Grey things out and protect the Grey from threats. It didn't like the thing that had blotted out or cordoned off this chunk of Grey. There would be no getting past the monster to get to my father, even if I could have gotten into the infernal void that seemed to have swallowed up all Grey trace of him.

I tried circling the hole in time, but there was nothing to see and nothing to touch when I beat the guardian's snapping jaws to the edge of the darkness where my father should have been. He was simply not there. Or not accessible even from the Grey. Whatever was causing that infuriated the beast.

Defeated, I fell back, sliding back into the normal, and sidling along the walls of the treatment room to the door. I checked the phone's clock and saw I'd been missing from the normal world for only a few minutes. Paul Arkmanian was peering into the room with his eyes wide.

"Did you hear it?" he demanded. "Where did you go?"

"I was right there, behind the door. And, yeah, I heard that noise. Is that the way it always sounds?"

"It was louder than usual this time."

"Huh," I grunted, closing my phone and putting it back into my pocket. There was a message icon on the screen, but I'd get to that later. "I guess I've upset your ghost."

"So . . . do you think the place is really haunted?"

"Yes. You have a ghost all right."

"Yeah?" He looked wary.

I nodded. "Yeah." The ghost of a ghost, I thought.

I excused myself from Paul Arkmanian as soon as I could without being suspiciously rude. He didn't say anything about my trip side-ways. He might not have allowed himself to notice it—most people didn't. I told him I'd be back in touch with him, though I privately doubted it would be soon and I felt a bit bad about the deception. He and his dad were friendly and deserved better than what I was serving them. I would be back, but not where normal people could see me. My dad's ghost seemed to be missing, but I wanted another shot at Christelle and what she might tell me about that hole and what had happened to her.

ELEVEN

I parted company from Paul Arkmanian outside and pretended to go on my way, waiting until he was out of sight before I ducked back into the building with the help of a pencil stub I'd jammed in the lock earlier. I made my way back up to the office and settled in to wait for another chance to talk to Christelle. I only hoped the security guard wouldn't come along while I was skulking in the corridor.

About ten o'clock I saw the slim shade of Christelle walking down the hall again, and I slipped deeper into the Grey to talk to her. She wasn't as friendly this time.

As I drew closer, she muttered something under her breath that I couldn't catch. Then she pasted on a fake smile and opened the phantom door to the waiting room. "Hi. Are you here for an appointment? You know Dr. Blaine isn't in, don't you?"

"Yes," I replied, following her into the ghost of the old office. "I wanted to talk to you."

She looked surprised as she sat behind her desk. "Me? Why?"

I stared at her, trying to catch her skittish gaze with mine. I knew she was capable of responding, of disengaging from the endless loop of memory in however fractured a fashion, and I needed her to speak outside the moment of history. "Do you know who I am?" I asked.

She peered back at me, pushing her glasses higher on her nose, her face pinched with suspicion. "No."

"I'm Harper. I'm Rob's daughter. Look close." I hoped the resemblance would be strong enough.

Christelle's ghost gazed hard at my face, her eyes flicking back and forth in restless study. Then she drew back. "Oh. Oh. It is Harper. I— But . . ."

"It's been more than twenty years since I last saw you."

"But it can't be. It's still Thursday!" she protested.

That made no sense to me at all. "Which Thursday? What's the date?" I demanded.

"September eighteenth."

"What year?"

"It's 1986. Why are you asking me such a crazy question?"

"Because it's not 1986 for me, Christelle. It's 2009."

Her expression puckered into confused fear. "I don't understand how that can be. . . ." she whispered. "That can't be right. . . ."

"I don't know, either. Christelle, is this the last date you can remember?"

"I don't know!" the spectral woman cried.

"Try to think. Just think about the appointment book. Think of each day you sat down and looked at the book. . . ."

She screwed her face up as she tried to force some kind of memory to come to her remnant mind. I wasn't sure a ghost could "remember" the way a living person did, but I hoped there was some way for her to fish up some information and give it to me. Finally she shook her head, upset and unhappy. "I can't remember anything after today. Today is all I remember!" She sounded a little panicked.

I felt like a therapist trying to coax a memory from an amnesia sufferer. "What happened today? What happened to you or to Rob? What can you remember?"

Christelle tried, but the memory was fragmented and she could only bring it back in shards. "I got up, I came to the office. Rob was already here. I don't think he went home. There was something wrong with the office. There was a man here—no, two men. I'd seen them with the albino man before. They left when I came in, but Rob wouldn't talk about them. He was angry at me. He said I should stay away from them. He said I should stay away from the office. He . . . he fired me. He told me to go home. He was angry. But he was scared. He had your picture! I remember! He had your picture in his hand, like he was trying to hide it. I went home. But I didn't go home. I don't know! I think I went home, but I don't remember being home. I only remember being here. But I remember walking. I remember walking toward home and the men came to talk to me. I ran away from them. I think I did. I—I don't know! I can't remember! I remember Rob. . . . I don't know what he was doing. He— No! It's just a big jumble! No! This isn't right! Keep him away! Keep him away!" she screamed.

Her screech turned into the roar of the guardian as it rushed into the room and pounced past us toward the source of its agitation in the back room. I couldn't hear Christelle screaming over the shriek of the beast, but I saw her thrashing at the air as if she were being attacked by unseen things. Then she sat down in a heap, landing in her chair as if broken.

I tried to grab her, shake her, but she had no more substance than a cloud, not even the electrical tingling of an entangled soul. There was no Christelle there, just a shape.

Then she looked up, her face composed and blank. "Do you have an appointment?" she asked.

"Christelle. Listen. Concentrate. Do you know what happened to you?"

"I couldn't say. Do you have an appointment?"

"No, Christelle. It's Harper. I want to talk to my dad. Do you know what happened to him? Do you know what happened to *you*?"

The bland, blank expression didn't flicker. "The doctor isn't in right now. Would you like to make an appointment?"

"No, Christelle. I want to know what happened to you."

"The doctor isn't in right now," she repeated. "Would you like—"

"No!" I shouted at her, but she didn't change her expression or her words; she just continued to ask her mindless question. I gave up, not sure if I'd destroyed whatever was left of Christelle's lingering memory or not, but quite sure she wasn't coming back for a while. Whatever intelligence had occupied the space that had been my father's office had fled, at least for now, and there was nothing I could do.

I left the building, taking care to restore the lock so it clicked closed behind me. A troubling weight of emotion dragged at me as I went: confusion, frustration, grief, and horror. I didn't know much more than I had when I arrived about what had befallen any of us: my father, Christelle, or me. I wasn't any closer to knowing why I was the way I was, either.

I tried to shake my mind clear and think hard as I headed back to my car and then onward to my hotel. Christelle's disconnection from events and her panic might mean she had ceased to exist—at least as a human—after that Thursday in 1986, but what had happened beyond that and who was responsible, I didn't know. The weird encapsulation of time in the office might account for the incomplete haunting phenomena and the odd silence in the Grey surrounding the time and place of my father's death. The anomalies—Christelle's shattered memory and Dad's lack of presence—had to be related, but what the relation was and how it might be connected to me and my being a Greywalker was still a mystery. Much as it might clear a few things up, it appeared that I wouldn't be talking to my dad anytime soon. The presence of the guardian beast and the way it had come rushing in each time I got close through the layers of history and connection was not good. I'd have to find another route to the information I wanted and I'd have to tread with care. I might be a Grey creature as far as the beast was concerned, but I'd seen it eat Grey things that misbehaved. I didn't want to be the next meal or a mindless loop like what remained of Christelle LaJeunesse.

My thoughts left me disturbed and I, childishly, couldn't face sleep with the chill of them in my mind. Even a long, hot shower couldn't dispel them after I returned to my hotel room. I paged Quinton and left a code on his pager. Quinton had an excusable paranoia about certain bits of technology, and though I'd upgraded to a cell phone, he never would. We'd worked out a set of codes that communicated volumes in only a few digits—the shorter the burst, the harder it was to trace or crack. I left a code that required a reply. He called back within minutes.

"Hi, it's me," he said.

I recognized the voice, of course, and drawled a pleased and tired, "Hey," feeling a small warmth kindle in my chest.

"How's the dead boyfriend?"

I bit my lip for a second before answering, "He's a jerk. And things are becoming stranger than I'd expected."

"Do you have any answers yet?"

"Not many. My dad—" I choked on the words.

"Honey? Harper? Are you all right?"

His endearment melted the ice block in my throat. "I'm . . . still confused by a lot of things. I don't want to discuss them now. I just wanted to hear your voice."

"I like hearing yours, too. I've been working on a ghost detector. I'm not sure I've got it right, but I'll show it to you when you get home."

"I'd rather not talk about ghosts right now."

"All right. Chaos has been chasing things around that I can't see and she runs over and tries to steal your shoes. But she only wants your shoes. I think she misses you."

"She just loves shoes," I said, imagining the crazy little ferret running manically around the condo or Quinton's bunker, chasing ghosts and giving her wicked chuckle of glee as they fled before her. She'd dived fearlessly into the Grey when we'd first encountered it and taken on the guardian beast single-handed. I'd had a little trouble getting her back. She was fearless, but she'd learned to pick her fights better after that. You can't win against an invincible force of the Grey, even if the battle is epic, at least to a fuzz-butt who weighed less than two pounds.

A pleasant silence fell between us and I closed my eyes, thinking I could almost see him.

"She's not the only one who misses you," Quinton said.

I smiled. "I miss you, too, and I'll be home soon." The conversation wandered and drew to a soft close as I dwindled toward sleep.

"I'll see you soon," he whispered before I reluctantly hung up and turned to roll into the covers, falling asleep with the comfort of his thoughts wrapped around me.

TWELVE

Will Novak screamed in my sleep. I jerked awake, twisting in my bed to spot the gruesome vision that had awakened me, so realistic was it that I had been sure I was present. I was sick of grim visions. First Cary, the office, Christelle, and now Will, the antiques auctioneer I'd met back when the whole Greywalking adventure started. He'd been in my nightmare of my death, too, but this was not the same dream at all. This was a hopeless, terrifying vision about Will himself.

We'd broken up over the ramifications of my incomprehensible life a year earlier, but I'd kept a soft spot for Will in my heart. He was in England now, working. And he was fine. Or he had been the last I'd heard from him. I didn't want to relive any of that, either, but it seemed my past—whether connected to my Greywalking ability or not—would not leave me alone.

To hell with it; it wasn't late over there. It was . . . I checked the clock and did the math . . . about 3:30 in the afternoon. I picked up my cell phone and poked the button for his number. In a minute, a male voice answered.

"Hello?"

"Hi. Michael? It's Harper Blaine." Michael was Will's much-younger brother. He was attending college somewhere in London since they'd moved there more or less permanently when Will and I broke up. Will worked researching provenances—the backgrounds of antiques—for Sotheby's. It had been a dream offer just when he'd needed it most. We'd tried to keep the relationship going, but the distance and my bizarre job had killed it.

"Oh. Hi, Harper. Umm . . . can I . . . help you?" I hadn't called since Will and I had broken up, and Michael sounded confused to hear from me.

"I just wanted to talk to Will. Is he home?"

"No. He's at work. He'll be home in about three hours, if you want to call back."

"How are you guys doing?"

He replied cautiously. "We're fine. I'm working on a bike for a motorcycle rally this summer and Will's OK, I guess. Works a lot. You know: the big brother thing."

"Yeah, I know that thing. Is he still on your case about school?"

"I'm out for the summer hols soon. He still doesn't like the bikes, but we get along OK if I don't cut class too much for them."

That sounded like the Novak brothers I knew. Michael plunging into his enthusiasms and Will watchdogging him.

So my harrowing dream had been only that—a dream—however disturbing and realistic. No one had chopped off his limbs or stuffed him in a box, and Michael wasn't a burned skeleton on a garage floor, either. I was still unsettled, but I took a long breath and made myself calm down.

"OK. Well. I guess I don't need to talk to him, after all. Thanks, Michael."

"No problem."

We both hung up in an awkward silence. I must have sounded nuts. I felt a bit nuts, too, for giving in to the need to check on them. The sense of something being out of joint lingered, although there seemed to be no reason for that feeling—just the aftereffect of the dream—and I chided myself for calling. Of course, I wouldn't have forgiven myself for not checking if there had turned out to be something wrong. Still . . . crazy ex-girlfriend was not a part I liked playing.

I left a string of numbers on Quinton's pager that meant I'd been thinking of him. It made me feel a bit like a clinging girlfriend, and yes, it was mushy, but it made me smile and that was a good trick after the fright that had awakened me.

It was too early to show up at my mother's house. I had no desire to intrude on any private moments between her and Damon. The thought of observing Mother setting another matrimonial trap made me gag, and the false friendliness her current prey displayed on meeting me was just as cloying. My reaction might be due to the contrast between reality and my now-ruined fantasy of what life had been with my father, but I still found Damon and his presence repulsive. Unfair and irrational of me, maybe, but that's how I felt.

I could just guess at the sorts of heavily varnished tales about me that my mother had been laying on him. Since he hadn't thrown me out of the house, I had to assume it was the Darling Daughter version and not the Ungrateful Spawn of Satan version—I'd been both before. Considering her performance the previous day, I figured I was probably growing horns in her mind right now. Yet another reason to hold off arriving until after the man du jour had gone and avoid any scenes.

A short workout and a shower didn't help mitigate the fact that it was the morning after a terrible day and night as much as I'd hoped. It still felt too early, and I hadn't even changed time zones. I called room service for a pot of expensive coffee and some food and sat down on the bed to prowl through my father's box again. If I couldn't talk to him or his no-doubt-dead receptionist directly, I could still try to get some sense of the real man from what he'd left behind. I knew I had romanticized him, just as I had romanticized Cary, but I needed truth now, not fantasies.

Most of the paper in the box was business files, which told me about his patients and his work habits but not much more. I noticed that his handwriting was very precise when in business mode, small and neat. The office as I'd seen it in the past had been wrecked, but the simple Grey memory of it had been squared away and orderly. The writing on his business correspondence didn't quite cross the line to fussy, but it was careful. In the journals it had been looser but still very legible, which I couldn't say for most people's casual writing.

All right: He'd been a bit type A, the sort of man who wore a button-down shirt even on his days off. I could remember him smiling and being silly with me, so he hadn't been too stiff, but if I was being honest, he hadn't been the life of the party, either. I had idolized him and built him up as an ideal parent in contrast to my demanding, peripatetic mother. I might not have been right about her, either, but that was not the issue of the moment.

I paused to eat and pour more coffee, and then I shuffled deeper into the box. At the bottom I found a couple of paperback books: *The Stars My Destination* by Alfred Bester and Chuck Yeager's autobiography. I'd never read either book, but I knew who Chuck Yeager was and, according to the blurb, the Bester was a sort of space-faring version of *The Count of Monte Cristo*. Space adventures, ordinary guys rising to heroism and glamour. I hadn't pegged my dad as fanciful, but it might have explained his marriage to my mother. They had both been starry-eyed, but his romanticism had turned inward while my mother's had turned outward. If I hadn't seen the hole where the end of his life should have been, I might have thought his visions had gone as sour as my mother's and written him off as merely crazy, but that void—whether it was caused by him or something else—and the terror that had poured out of Christelle changed everything. He might have been nuts—he sounded it near the end—but he hadn't been imagining that something uncanny and terrible had surrounded him.

Melancholy seemed to ooze from the box as I piled Dad's things back inside. I set the journals on top; I'd have to ask my mother if

I could keep them and the little metal puzzle, which I put into my pocket. By then it was nearly noon, so I called her.

"Hello, Mother."

"Oh, hi, sweetie!"

"Are you going to be home this afternoon? I want to bring the box of stuff back and take a look at those photos."

"Sure! Come right up."

There was one more thing I wanted to check; a last-ditch chance but I couldn't ignore it. "I want to drive past the old house first. What was our address when we lived in Glendale?"

"You mean the house on Louise?"

"Did we ever live in another house in Glendale?" How could she irritate me so much with so little effort? I wondered.

"Well, no, of course not!" she snapped.

"Then the house on Louise must be the one I want."

She sighed dramatically and rattled off the address. "When will you be done?" she asked.

"In a couple of hours. I'll bring the box by about . . . two."

"All right," she replied, her voice a little sharp. "We can have lunch."

I hoped it wouldn't be the same minuscule meal of fruit I'd seen abandoned on her breakfast plate the previous morning, but I didn't think I should refuse. "I'll see you then." Hanging up was a relief. She still made me feel unreasonable and clumsy even on the phone. I hoped I'd get the last of what I needed from her today, so I could go home as soon as possible. Any good feeling I'd had for my hometown was curdling fast.

The house on North Louise Street would be my last shot at finding any trace of my father's ghost, short of dumb luck. I couldn't think of any other places he might linger, and the house was a long shot as it was. The strangeness in his office made me think he wasn't going to be found just haunting around, but I might find a loop or some other trace that might tell me something.

I'd kind of expected something more . . . impressive, but once I got to it, it was just a house. Plain California stucco on a narrower lot than its neighbors, palm trees at the curb, a long driveway on one side to a garage in the back. It was only a few blocks, a short walk, from what was now Paul Arkmanian's office.

My memory saw the house as much larger than its narrow two stories. I sat and stared at it a moment, the house looking just the same in both the Grey and the normal so it seemed to be sitting in a pale shadow of itself. Wind chimes and shiny crystals hung from the porch rafters and in the windows. A rainbow-striped flag made a curtain for one pane on the upper floor. Subtle signals of the private life the residents kept quietly confined within the walls they'd cleaned of any trace of previous tenants. There weren't any particular lines of energy or gleams of residual emotion clinging to the house. No one loved it, or hated it, or lingered in it. It was just shelter, nothing more.

I got out of the car and walked across the street to look more closely at the house, but nothing changed. There were no ghosts here, no extraordinary extrusion of the grid or traces of more than passing emotional storms. It was as clear as scrubbed glass. Curtains twitched in nearby windows and I sighed, knowing it was only a matter of minutes before one neighbor or another called the cops to investigate me and my obsession with the house on Louise Street. I shrugged and went back to my car.

I wasn't any closer to talking to my father or figuring out what had tied us both to the Grey or when or how. I could almost understand, in a confused sort of way, why he'd written his suicide note to me—or at least not to my mother—but that didn't answer the questions I had. Disappointed, I turned the car around and headed back to Hollywood and up the hills to my mother's stormy white villa.

THIRTEEN

My mother was on the terrace, practicing a complex yoga pose when I arrived. She looked like a scarlet pretzel wrapped in green energy tissue. She untied herself as I entered with the box on my hip.

"I'll be done in just a minute, sweetie. You can put that on the kitchen counter and sit down out here." Then she wriggled into a more tortuous position than before and became very quiet.

I put the box down on one of the empty chairs—petty rebellion, that—and sat down on another, surveying the table for signs of lunch. It was just on two o'clock according to my watch, so her lack of preparation wasn't due to me. She just wasn't ready, which was no different from my childhood; if we had an appointment that furthered her ideas for my life, she'd be sure to have me dressed and prepped at least an hour before we needed to be gone. I would sit or stand, careful not to muss my audition clothes, until she was ready, which would always be in the nick of time, or just past it. We would rush to auditions and photo shoots in a flurry of shouting and speeding and narrowly missed traffic accidents. If we were too late, the drive home would be a misery of recrimination.

I shook off the urge to grind my teeth and put my booted feet up on the empty table while I waited. Ten minutes later, my mother unwound herself and trotted over to glare at me as she wiped her face on a designer towel.

"Really, Harper, I taught you better manners than that. Get your feet off the table. Now."

I left them where they were. "I thought we were having lunch."

"We certainly won't be having anything if your feet are on the table, Snippet."

I wanted the things from the box too much to tell her off. Narrowing my eyes in annoyance, I lowered my feet back to the ground.

My mother gave me a plastic smile and headed into the house. "Come on inside. Bring the box."

Shaking my head at myself in disgust, I picked up the box and carried it into the kitchen. She pointed to the end of the spotless granite counter.

"Just put it there. You can make a salad while I take a quick shower. Be right back, sweetie," she added, and whisked off, leaving me standing in the middle of the kitchen, too stunned to shoot her.

I was still trying to decide if I should make the salad or dump the entire contents of the fridge on her terrace when a round, black-haired woman about my age bustled into the room.

She stopped and blinked at me. "Oh. Hello. You're . . . Veronica's daughter, right?"

I blinked back. "Yes. Are you a friend of hers?"

The woman laughed. "No, I'm the maid! I'm Venezia—Vinny. She was in such a hurry to get me out of the house today, I left my bag, so I came back for it. I think she's too excited about you coming to see her."

"She doesn't act like it. She just told me to make salad while she takes a shower. . . ."

Vinny snorted. "Salad! Feh! Rabbits eat salad! Crazy woman . . . Here, I'll make the salad. You sit down."

"No, you're off duty. You shouldn't do that," I protested as she headed for the gleaming steel fridge. I followed her.

She turned to give me a deprecating snort over her shoulder and pointed at the dining table. "You're the guest. You don't make lunch! Sit down. Crazy woman . . ." she added, shaking her head and piling food on the counter. "Five years, I never see her eat anything but fruit and mineral water and crackers and drink wine. Today she has salad—proper damn salad." She flung the refrigerator door wide and pointed at the full racks. "You see all this? This is not for her. This is for that man," she added. She rolled her eyes. "Crazy!"

Vinny slammed the fridge door and grabbed a decorative glass bowl from the counter. She paused to wash it and her hands before shredding lettuce into the bowl and starting in with a knife on the fruit, cheese, and meat she'd pulled from the fridge, mincing it all furiously into tiny bits. "Salad," she muttered. "Crazy."

She finished up and doused the bowl with a hearty slosh of balsamic vinegar before putting it on the table. "There! Now, she'll have to eat."

"Oh, no, she won't. If she doesn't want it, she'll just push it around the plate and nibble on the lettuce," I said, remembering my mother's famous food avoidance routine. She'd rather eat the parsley garnish than gain an ounce by eating the actual food on a plate.

Vinny rolled her eyes and plopped down in a chair by the table. "She's so crazy! People have to eat!" She picked a bit of fruit out of the bowl and popped it into her mouth. "It's good—for salad."

I opened the fridge and peered in. "You want a drink, Vinny?"

"I don't want mineral water!"

"There's milk . . . and beer. . . ."

"Beer? That man might not be so bad. . . . But I'm not supposed to. . . ."

"Are you driving?" I asked, glancing back at her over my shoulder. Vinny shook her head. I grabbed one of the tall brown bottles and handed it to her. "I'm her guest. You're my guest. Here."

Vinny laughed and twisted off the bottle cap and then toasted me with the bottle. "Thank you! You have one, too."

"I am driving, so I'll stick to the mineral water."

She made a face. "Your choice . . ."

I sat down with one of the small green bottles of water and we both drank while the salad sat on the table and wilted. Mother was taking her time with the shower. My phone vibrated, but I poked it into silence, not willing to lose someone else's perspective on my mother.

"You're not the sort of woman I'd have expected my mother to employ as a housekeeper."

"I'm not the housekeeper. I'm the maid. I just clean once a week. I come with the house."

"With the house? I thought she owned it."

"Leased. The owner lives in Dubai right now. He wants the house taken care of properly, so the tenant gets me and my husband with the house. Tahn does the garden and fixes things. I keep it clean. And I keep an eye on the tenants." She shook her head. "Your mother . . . She's not a bad tenant, but she's so . . ."

"Crazy?"

"Yeah! If she doesn't have a man around, she's sad. When she does, she's scared he's going to leave." She shook her head. "Why a rich woman like her is worried about having a man, I don't know. I love my husband, but I wouldn't be worrying myself into a skeleton if I didn't have him."

Something she'd said earlier had just worked through my brain. "Vinny, what time did you leave here?" I asked.

"When I forgot my bag? About a quarter to two. She said you were coming at two and she needed to change."

"She wasn't doing her yoga when you left, was she?"

"I've never seen her do yoga. I think she goes to the studio down the hill."

"Oh," I replied, thinking. Mother hadn't been struggling with the moves, so she wasn't faking, but it sounded like her routine didn't normally include yoga at two p.m. And she didn't own the house, as she'd led me to believe. I wondered if she owned the car. How much of her facade was false?

"Has she ever . . . seemed in financial difficulty?" I asked.

"Your mother? No. She pays on time, in full. Never a problem. The lease term is up soon, but I don't think she's too worried about it, now that her man is making with the matrimony."

"They're engaged?"

Venezia would have answered, but we both heard my mother's clippy little heels approaching and turned our faces toward her as she entered the kitchen.

"Vinny. Dear. Did you forget something?" she asked, casually brushing her hair back from her face to hide a momentary scowl.

"Yes. My bag. When you chased me out. Your daughter was so nice," she added in a pointed tone, "that we just . . . got to talking. And there's salad. So now I'll get my things and get out of your way." She stood up and walked to the door, sweeping a tan Gucci purse off the tiles. She slung it over her shoulder and came back to offer me her hand. "I enjoyed meeting you. I hope you'll be back down for the wedding—it should be nice."

Then she bustled out past my mother, who glared at her, and disappeared toward the front door. I heard the door close and silence fell for a moment.

Then my mother said, "Well. I was hoping to surprise you with that little tidbit, but I guess I won't be doing that now."

"It's not that much of a surprise, Mother."

Mother made an aghast face I didn't buy for a minute. "Don't you like Damon?"

"That's irrelevant. Do you love him?"

"Marriage is not a matter of love—that's just a fairy-tale idea. It's about security. You may be perfectly content to gad about and take whatever comes, but when you're my age, you want to know you won't end up in some . . . old-folks ghetto."

I was rolling my eyes so frequently around her, they might as well have been marbles. "Please, Mother. Security I understand, but you're being melodramatic. You're not going to end up in a Medicare home. You're wealthy and you're only sixty years old."

"Fifty-nine!"

"Fifty-nine," I agreed, putting my hands up in a placating gesture. "I'm just saying, you're not old and you're not going to be cast into the street. You don't need to marry anyone. Unless there's something you haven't told me. I'd like to think that you're getting married to someone you actually like and want to spend time with, not someone you think you need for financial reasons."

"When did it become any of your business, Snippet?"

"You're my mother."

"That hasn't made you care what I want in the past."

I didn't want to argue with her. I just wanted to return the box, take a few things, look at the family photos, and leave. I didn't care to admit it, but I was feeling a little sorry for her. I'd always thought of her as mercenary, selfish, thoughtless, and pushy, and here she was challenging my prejudice. It was annoying.

"Let's try this again. You're getting married? Congratulations! I'm happy for you! Better?"

Mother pouted. "Yes."

"Then let's have lunch."

We ate the salad, which was tasty but not what either of us really wanted. Mother ate more than I'd expected, but she still ended up picking out the fruit and leaving most of the meat and cheese behind. Neither of us was satisfied, but we didn't say so.

Afterward I opened the box and asked to keep the Grey items—including the puzzle and the journals.

Mother waved them away. "Keep what you like. As you said, it's your father's junk and I realized I don't really want it. You might as well have it."

I put them aside and closed the box up before I glanced at her again.

"What happened to Dad's receptionist?"

"Who?"

"Christelle LaJeunesse. Dad had a note in his journal that you thought he was having an affair with her. Then she just seemed to disappear. What happened to her?"

"Oh. Her. She just took off one day out of the blue. I never really thought Rob was . . . up to anything with her, but I think I may have said so once when I was mad at him. When he . . . died it was a nine days' wonder, and the police did think he might have killed her, but they gave that idea up. It just didn't fit, so they dropped it."

"But what happened to Christelle?"

She shrugged. "I have no idea, nor do I care. I suppose she ran off with some man or changed her name and became a movie star—who knows? Does it matter?"

Only so far as determining if my father was a murderer. But I doubted that mattered to anyone but me. Was it better for him to have killed someone because he was deranged or for him to merely think he had, because he was slightly less deranged?

"No," I lied. "I guess it doesn't matter, really." I picked up the box and carried it back down to the storage room. Mother followed me downstairs and perched on her ladder again as I replaced the box and pulled out the two Grey twinkling cartons of photos. They weren't very large, but they were dense and heavy for their size, so I didn't want to take them far. I also noticed my jeans and T-shirt were smeared with dust. I swatted the worst of it away and sneezed. Then I looked up and caught Mother's eye.

"Is there someplace we can go through these that's more comfortable?" I asked. "And not so dusty?" I'd forgotten how irritating the pollen-laden dust of Los Angeles in spring could be.

She hopped down from the ladder with her face alight. "Let's take them to the living room! We can look at them on the coffee table."

Back up the stairs and through the kitchen, I slogged with the boxes. Mother trotted ahead of me and turned through an arch that led away from the carport end of the house. I followed, still sneezing and humping boxes.

The living room was filled with flattering, cool light filtered through pale aqua curtains. The sheer panels over the windows moved in the breeze entering through the open French doors and turned the blue canyon light into rippling motes of color on the white walls. The furniture was all light and soft-looking also, made of curling gray metal and puffy overflowing cushions in pale watery colors. The coffee table looked like a mermaid's forest of silver seaweed holding up a floating slab of sandblasted aquamarine glass. My mother scooped an arrangement of seashells and beach glass off the table and put it in the hearth of the small, white-plastered fireplace. It looked like a magical blaze of blue and green cold flames.

"Put the boxes here while I find a pencil and some towels," Mother ordered.

She scampered back to the kitchen and returned with a handful of writing implements and yet another pile of clean white hand towels. She didn't seem to own paper towels—at least I hadn't seen any in the kitchen. Maybe she held stock in a laundry. . . .

I had to give my mother credit: She wiped down the boxes herself to remove the dust and plunged into the project of shuffling through and identifying the photos with relish.

Most of the photos were just family and friends stuff that meant nothing to me or my current quest. Dad's family seemed to have no talent or luck with cameras. There were a lot of wedding and baby photos contributed by them with the tops of heads, hands, legs, or other bits out of frame, or with dust spots and lens flare, or with color problems as well as the usual lack of focus and composition. There was even one of me as an infant double-exposure, apparently the child of a headless mother.

She held a photo in front of my face. "I didn't know we had this! This is your father and your uncle Ron—his brother—when they were kids. Oh, my God, look at that hairstyle! Did we all have no taste at all?"

"Do most teenagers have any?"

She laughed. "Well, I did!"

I fished out a high school photo of her with an overteased Jackie Kennedy hairstyle lacquered into shape with enough hair spray to make a small hole in the ozone. She was wearing a horrendous striped dress that made even her Twiggy-thin figure look bloated. "Sure . . ."

"It was very trendy."

"My point, exactly."

But I wasn't paying as much attention to her and the photo as I seemed. I was peeking at the discarded photo of my father and uncle from the corner of my eye. There was an odd smear on the picture next to my dad. Most of his family's photos were bad, but this one was particularly messed up. I picked it up again and looked harder. There seemed to be a bit of light damage or water vapor right behind his shoulder. It wasn't on the photo, though; it was in it.

I pointed it out to Mother. "What's this?"

"I have no idea. Probably cigarette smoke—your uncle smoked like a chimney. Probably still does," she sniffed.

I put it down and went back to shuffling. Mother would identify anything I stopped at—I had to wonder how she knew or remembered all of those faces and details, especially when the photos were of Dad's family or her short-term second husband and his equally short-term friends. Once IDed, the photos were carefully marked on the back with soft pencil if they hadn't been marked before. Then she put them aside to rebox later.

We worked through the first box and got into the second, which seemed to have a lot more photos of me as a child and fewer of friends and family. There was one particularly funny picture of me at about three years old, wearing a white dress with a red sash and an incongruous brown cowboy hat and matching boots. My posture, with elbows bent and hands near my hips, seemed to imply I was challenging the photographer to a gunfight. My father was just in the corner of the picture, out of my sight, smothering a laugh. The photo was well-framed, but had been disfigured by a constellation of fingerprints and water spots on the lens.

"Which one of Dad's family took this and why am I wearing that silly outfit?"

Mother glanced at the photo. "Oh, I took that. You loved that ridiculous hat and boots your grandfather gave you for Christmas. He said you were a real little cowgirl and you decided to wear them all the time. I never could understand it: You hated the ranch—a girl after my own heart—but you loved that stupid cowhand hat."

"Cowboys are cool. Cows are not. At least when you're three."

"Trust me, sweetie. Cowboys may remain cool but cows never get better."

We both giggled, which was very odd to me; when you've gotten used to despising someone, sharing a joke with them feels weirder than bathing in gelatin.

A few pictures later I stopped and stared at a snapshot of a bunch of teenagers and younger kids goofing off in bathing suits on a riverbank. Yet another execrable Blaine family photo complete with spots and smears, except that this one showed me and a pretty blond girl with a long ponytail—longer than mine had been when it was caught in the doors of my fatal elevator—standing off to the side with our arms over each other's shoulders in the classic Best Friends Forever pose. We were thirteen or fourteen in the photo, and she was the girl whose watery specter had accused and harangued me through my flight to Los Angeles.

I held the photo out to my mother. "Who's this? With me?"

Mother took the photo and glanced at it. Then she put it face-down on the table and frowned at me. "That's your cousin Jill. You don't remember her?"

"No." Well, at least not from that photo or that age. I could recall a younger girl named Jilly who I'd liked, but not this living version of a dead teenager. And yet the photo indicated a close friendship. How could I forget that?

My mother sighed. "This is so painful. Jilly drowned. About three days after that picture."

"What happened?" I demanded.

Mother recoiled a little from my tone. "I just told you: She drowned."

"How?"

She put her hands over mine and squeezed a little. "Oh, baby, I know you don't want to remember this—maybe that's why you made yourself forget Jilly. Are you sure you want to hear this . . . ?"

"Yes, Mother. Tell me what happened."

She swallowed, looking down at the concealed picture. Then she licked her lips and drew a long, slow breath. "Well . . . You and Jill . . . wanted to swim in Danko Pond, down at the bottom of your uncle Ron's property. Do you remember that?"

"I think I remember the pond—it had a little dock someone had built for a sailboat no one ever sailed."

She looked up and met my gaze with hers, her brow puckered in concern and unhappiness. "Because the pond wasn't safe. There were snags and holes down there and current from the river that came in underground to feed it. But you girls wanted to prove to the boy cousins that you were as tough as they were, so you two wanted to swim in the pond. We all said no—the parents, I mean—so of course you and Jilly snuck off to do it anyway."

"And Jilly drowned."

"Baby. You almost drowned, too. If it hadn't been for Jilly's hair floating on the surface, they wouldn't have known where to look. Ron and your cousin Grant got you both out from under the snag, and you were both not breathing, and it was so horrible—" She started crying but she didn't take her eyes off me. "You started coughing up the water as soon as Grant picked you up, but Jilly . . . She didn't."

"Was it my fault?"

"Oh, no, baby! No! It was just a stupid, stupid accident. If we'd all just not made such a big deal about that stupid pond, you wouldn't have cared and the boys wouldn't have cared and it would never have happened. Now you see why I get so worried about you and your crazy job? You're my only baby and I almost lost you once!"

Under any other circumstances her melodramatic hypocrisy would have made me indignant—she hadn't shown any such concern while I was in the hospital after having my head knocked in—but right then I was too stunned. "How many times has this shit happened to me?" I muttered.

My mother stared back at me with tear-reddened eyes, her makeup running down her face. "Just the once, honey."

I grabbed the photo. She tried to resist my pulling for a moment. Then she gave up. I stared at the picture, studying it closer than I had the first time.

The spots and smears weren't all just dirt. Some of them looked like tiny blurred faces. Ghosts.

Cameras sometimes caught the images of ghosts as they literally passed through the thick material of the glass lens. Some odd property of glass slowed them down enough to make a kind of shadow on the film beyond. I'd learned this on a case almost two years earlier. The picture was busy with phantoms—although it was also just a plain crappy photo full of dust and sunspots.

I started pawing through the photos we'd already looked at, searching for more signs of ghosts. In the cowboy hat photo, I saw more of them, but they were clustered around my dad. The photo of Dad and Uncle Ron didn't have a wayward column of cigarette smoke: It had a ghost. Picture after picture showed something weird hanging around the Blaine family—mostly around my father and me. Or rather, I realized as I looked again, it hung around my father and only incidentally around me until after he died. Then it was all mine. Was my Greywalking ability some kind of . . . legacy? It still just didn't make sense, but it sent a chill through me.

I needed confirmation, evidence. "Do you have more pictures of me after Dad died? I mean just ordinary photos, not the pro head-shots from my resume."

"Well, of course, sweetie." She seemed happier that I wanted to indulge in some vanity and move off the subject of dead cousins.

We dug through the second box in haste, unearthing every photo we could find of me after age twelve. Every one had a spot, a smear, or an impossible streak of light at the least. Several had unexplainable faces peering from the edges. They had become more common as I'd gotten older. I felt sick. Only the professional photos were clear and I'd have bet large sums the photographers had spent a good deal of time in their darkrooms or computer suites removing inexplicable anomalies from my headshots and dance poses. Even candid photos of me at rehearsals and in shows had odd blurs and "tricks of the light" near my figure.

I'd been unwittingly haunted most of my life, and now those things from long ago—forcibly forgotten—were coming back.

FOURTEEN

A s if someone had drawn a cork from the bottle of memory, things flooded back. I did remember long-haired Jill, smiling and yelling and urging me into all sorts of trouble. Not that much urging had been needed. Rare holidays at Uncle Ron's had been some of the few times I'd spent whole days goofing off with other kids. During the school year my life had been nonstop classes—at school or dance studios—rehearsals, and performances, or exhaustion and hiding in my room to steal an hour reading my precious mystery novels.

In the midst of memory, there came a rising nausea, and a sharp pain cut through my left hand. The slicing sensation brought on a bright instant of vision, like a single frame of film flashed on a rough white wall: Will Novak, his left hand severed at the wrist, blood bright scarlet on plaster walls. I gasped and jerked reflexively toward the vision as if I could stop him bleeding.

"Sweetie? What? Are you OK?" my mother asked, startled.

"Fine," I snapped. Then I caught my breath properly and replied in a quieter voice, "It's nothing. Just some kind of muscle spasm. In my hand. Cramp, I guess."

She glanced at my hand clenched in my lap. "Are you sure? I have some warming gel if you want it. . . ."

I shuddered at the thought of the smelly companion of so many casual injuries in my youth. "No, thanks, Mother. I'll be fine. Really."

I was as startled by the vision as by the content. It wasn't quite identical to the previous night's bad dream, but it was close enough to be of the same moment. But I wasn't sleeping, and Michael had said there was nothing wrong with Will. Was this what had happened to my father? No. His visions seemed to come only after paranoia. I wasn't paranoid—just cynical. And I couldn't stop wondering what was happening to Will. Was this some kind of portent or just a fabulation? The logical part of my brain said he was fine, just as he'd been fine when I'd called before, but some terrified monkey part was screeching that he was dismembered and stuffed in trash bins spread across half of central London.

I forced the thought away, clenching my teeth at the mental effort. The horror wanted to stay. I'd never had visions before, and I'd been assured over and over that I wasn't psychic and didn't have the power to see anything beyond what was actually present in the Grey. Still, it gave me the creeps.

"Mother, have there been other . . . deaths in this family, like Dad's and Jill's?"

"Good heavens, sweetie, how ghoulish of you!"

"No, Mother, I just wonder if we have some . . . curse."

She tossed her head so her glossy hair flipped and swung. "No! We're not some family from a Southern Gothic novel, for goodness' sake!"

I nodded. I wasn't sure if I should believe her, but surely she wouldn't start hiding things now. She hadn't needed a lot of prompting to tell me about my father's suicide or Jill's accidental death. The frustrated actress in my mother relished the recitation of tragedy.

I'd have asked more questions, but my phone rang and without thinking, I answered it. I could see a message icon from earlier and reminded myself to check it when I was done with the current call.

"Harper Blaine."

"This is Carol, Mr. Kammerling's secretary. We're very anxious to have a meeting with you as soon as possible. Would you be available tonight?"

I wasn't sure if I was being ordered around or begged. I'd talked to Edward's various secretaries and assistants—both the mortal ones and the vampiric—and the tone from this one was a bit less imperious than usual. Of course, she might just be new and not yet used to being the daytime minion of Seattle's top vampire.

"I'm in Los Angeles at the moment," I replied. "Edward will have to wait until I get back. What is he so eager to meet with me about, anyhow?"

"I'm sorry; Mr. Kammerling's instructions don't say. It is extremely urgent, though. I can have a corporate jet bring you to Seattle this afternoon and return you to LA tomorrow, if you like."

Corporate jets aren't that big a deal to someone with Edward's fiscal standing, but the urgency was a bit unusual. Time has a different scale when you're three hundred years old, and while Edward Kammerling isn't known for his patience, he's gotten cagier since he's known me. Things in the vampire world rarely need to move at the speed of sound, but if his problem were a corporate, daylight-world one, he had a stable full of lawyers, assistants, runners, and two-legged sharks to deal with it. This must have been something of the nightsider kind, but putting his cards on the table was definitely not Edward's standard operating procedure in either realm.

I thought I'd test the waters before I committed to anything. "I should be done with my business here tomorrow," I told Carol. "Can't he wait that long?"

"No. He could come to you if it's necessary. . . ."

"He must be desperate."

She didn't reply to that.

I sighed. "All right. I'll wrap this up and come home today. If you can have the plane ready to go at Burbank airport by eight, I can be on it."

With the daylight lingering into the evening hours, Edward and his bloodsucking kind wouldn't even be moving until after nine p.m., so he wouldn't be much put out by my arrival at ten. And I wanted to see just how desperate he was.

"I can arrange that," Carol replied. I could hear her keyboard clicking in the background as she spoke. "The plane will be waiting for you at the executive terminal on Clybourn Avenue. I'll have a car meet you at Boeing Field when you land and bring you to the meeting."

Either Edward was very sure of himself and had already arranged the flight—somehow already aware of where I was—or his secretary had carte blanche to make it happen. Either way, I was impressed and a little worried.

My mother was glancing at me with suspicion as I hung up.

"Are you really leaving, just like that?"

"I have to. And I'm pretty well done here, anyway."

"But you just got here!"

"And I never meant to stay very long. I think I have most of what I wanted."

"I don't understand what it is you needed to know."

"I told you. I wanted to know if there was anything weird about my past—"

"It's not that weird," my mother objected.

"Oh, come on, Mother. Surely it's not normal to have a father who killed himself and a cousin who drowned with you, as well as a boyfriend who was killed in an accident and a near-death experience of your own in the first thirty years of your life. That's just a little too much death and devastation for one woman who isn't in the military or a Tennessee Williams play."

She heaved a dramatic sigh. "If you must dwell on the negative, I suppose it would seem that way."

I closed my eyes and breathed slowly before responding. "Yes, it does seem that way. Thanks for your help and understanding, Mother. It's not my choice, but I need to leave tonight. Let's finish up with these photos, all right?"

She stood up and flapped her hands over the table covered with pictures. "No, no. Don't worry about that. I'll finish them up. It's already five. If you have to go, you should get moving. Go, go, go."

Ah, the guilt trip . . . I guess my mother hadn't learned that I'd become immune. I took a few of the photos and tucked them in with my father's journals and the puzzle. Then I let my mother chivvy me toward the door. She was mad, but she'd be damned if she'd show it.

At the blue-painted front door—less conveniently located for the carport under which my rental was parked—we paused and stared at each other, already turning back into strangers as we stood. I bent down and kissed my mother's powdered cheek. She was so tiny I felt like a giant.

"Congratulations, Mom. Take care of yourself, OK? And gain some weight."

She bit her lip and smacked my arm. "Don't be fresh." I could see moisture gathering in her eyes. "I'll send you an invitation. And I'll be very upset if you don't come to this one."

"You mean that?"

"Of course! We're not best friends, but . . . I'm still your mother!"

"Undeniably." I nodded, reluctant, but feeling I had to. "I'll come if I can."

She didn't try to hug or kiss me. She just waved me away and watched me go.

FIFTEEN

I had a hell of a time arranging to return the car at Bob Hope Airport, rather than the larger rental stand at LA International, but the company finally agreed to let me leave the car at the smaller airport if I paid an additional fee. Getting out of LA was worth it. I packed up, checked out, and headed for Burbank by way of some more substantial food, since I wouldn't have any time for or interest in eating once I was in Edward's presence.

Sitting in a restaurant in Burbank, I paged Quinton again with a code that requested an immediate callback. I wanted to let him know I was heading back to Seattle as well as the how and why. In a few minutes, my phone rang from an unidentifiable number.

"Hi," I answered.

"Hey," Quinton replied. "What's up?"

"I'm on my way back. Edward's sending a plane for me."

Quinton was silent.

"Yeah," I said, filling in his thoughts. "I don't like that much, either."

"Be careful, Harper."

"I plan to. I'll be in touch as soon as I know anything, like where this meeting he's dragging me to is going to take place."

"How much time do you have before the plane?"

"An hour or so . . ."

"All right then, I doubt it's about me, but you should know before you go in that Edward is probably not my biggest fan right now."

"He's not your fan at the best of times. What happened?"

"Remember I said there'd been more vampire activity in the underground . . . ?"

"Yeah. And . . . ?"

"One of the vamps got a stunner."

"What? How?"

"I don't know. And I'm not sure it's one of mine. I mean, it looked odd, but it was slagged when I got to it, so that might account for why it looked funny."

I marshaled a calming breath before saying, "Give me details. I need to know, in case Edward brings it up."

"Well . . . I've been working on the ghost detector, right? So I was down in the underground with the ferret and the prototype, trying to measure changes wherever Chaos got excited and started doing that weird chasing-around thing she does. Last night the vampires were pretty quiet so I figured it was safe down there, but I heard one of the undergrounders freaking out, so I went that way. And you remember we wondered what happened if you electrocute a vampire with one of the stunners?"

"Yeah," I replied. Quinton had speculated that at a higher voltage the device might be capable of taking a vampire out permanently, but he'd been reluctant to incur Edward's wrath by trying it. "What happened?"

"They combust. Violently enough to suck the air out of a small room. It wasn't a problem for the bloodsucker who used it, since they don't need air, but I do. I thought I was next, but the discharge melted the device, and fangface wasn't interested in hanging around after that. I passed out for a minute until the bastard opened the door and let the air back in. But here's the freaky bit: There was no one else there. No undergrounder. Only the remains of the vamp who got shocked—they turn into piles of nasty, wet ash stuff that's pretty disgusting. I think I was lured there so I'd be found with the burned bloodsucker."

"You didn't mention this last night."

"You said you didn't want to talk about ghosts and that stuff and you seemed down, so I figured it could wait."

I thought about it. "You're right. Last night was a rough one for both of us and it can't matter that you didn't tell me then. I know about it now and that's good enough. Did you recognize either of the . . . guys?"

"I'm not so sure about the dirt pile, but the zapmeister looked like one of the uptown floaters—the guys from Queen Anne, not the ones who usually hang out down in the Square."

There were several factions within the Seattle vampire society, small as it was. Technically they all bowed to Edward, but there were always groups trying to undermine him or one of his favorites. The factions shifted constantly, but they tended to congregate by neighborhoods: Pioneer Square; lower Queen Anne near Seattle Center and the Space Needle; the University District; and over in the Central District and southern Capitol Hill.

By agreement, the downtown core was a free zone in which vampires were supposed to keep a low profile. If one of the Queen Anne faction was doing dirty deeds below Pioneer Square, Edward would not be pleased. He wasn't particular about his punishments or upon whom they fell, but he was swift—recently he'd learned to make retribution quickly rather than let situations fester into more trouble. Or give the appearance of weakness.

"What did Edward do about it?" I asked.

"Nothing. He'd love to say I did it and put the arm on me, but he hasn't. He's been very quiet."

"That doesn't sound right."

"No. It doesn't. And now he's bringing you back to Seattle on his personal express route, so . . . he's either a lot more upset than he let on, or there's something big distracting him."

"Edward wouldn't ask me to mediate between the two of you, so that can't be it. It's got to be something else."

"No idea what, though. Or why the Queen Anne bloodsuckers would be making trouble for me."

I hummed as I thought, but I didn't come up with an answer. "I guess we'll have to wait and see what he says tonight. Or what he does."

"I'll back you up if I can."

"I don't think that'll be necessary, but I'll let you know if I need it."

"And I'll take him out if he hurts you."

"Don't be ridiculous. I don't need martyrs, sweetheart."

"'Sweetheart'? Where did that come from?"

"You'd rather I called you 'babe'?"

He made a gagging sound. "No, thanks. It's just a funny kind of word."

"Like something from a Bogart movie."

"I thought he said 'kid.'"

"In *Casablanca*, yeah." I must have had Bogey on the brain, no thanks to Cary. "I could call you 'sweetie,' but that sounds like my mother."

"Then, please, don't do that. Ah, damn. I have to get off this phone. Call my pager and leave the address if you can."

"I will. Sweetheart."

He snorted and I laughed as we hung up.

But I didn't feel pleased for long. I didn't like Quinton's report and I was less enthusiastic about my meeting with Edward by the minute.

There are two civil aviation terminals at the Burbank airport. The smaller of the two is the swanker one, so naturally that was the one Edward's secretary had directed me to. The resident charter company didn't have a chance to woo me with their posh sitting area since there was already a TPM flunky awaiting me. He was standing near the doors. Judging by his military posture, I guessed he'd been standing just the same way in the same spot since he'd arrived, however long that had been. He knew me the moment I stepped through the sliding glass doors.

"Ms. Blaine," he said, stepping forward to take my bag, "the plane is waiting. Is there anything you require before we board?"

I looked him over, noting the close-clinging indigo of his aura—a color I'd rarely seen and wasn't sure of. Still, I didn't think turning around and leaving was an option. "I'm good to go."

He nodded and picked up my suitcase without effort, leading me out to the hot tarmac. A white jet with a green stripe on its tail stood just beyond the doors with a rolling staircase pushed up to it.

It was bigger than I'd expected, more a small jetliner than a sporty little executive jet, and clothed in a thin red haze from the frequent passage of vampires. Inside, my escort stowed my bag in a bin near the galley and led me back past a small work area to a seat that was more like an expensive Swedish lounger than an airline seat, except this had a seat belt. The cabin looked like a very posh living room. Aft past the wings, the cabin was cut off by an upholstered wall that showed a dull blackness in the Grey. It stretched from side to side and was pierced only by two large latched doors.

My escort noted my glance toward the wall. "That's Mr. Kammerling's private cabin. As he's not on board today, it's locked down."

"I see." I imagined that Edward's cabin was fitted for the needs of vampires—keeping the light of day and its noises out as well as any roving passengers who might not know his nature—and explained the bloody red energy clinging to the craft. From this side the area just looked a little more secure than the usual cabin. I raised one eyebrow a little, wondering how much the man with me knew about his employer.

"For safety's sake, you'll need to keep your seat belt on until we reach altitude, but after that, the cabin's yours. It's a short flight, but if there's anything you want, let me know."

"Well, there is one thing," I started, settling into the contoured chair.

He raised his eyebrows and waited.

"What's your name?"

He cracked a dazzling white smile and a tiny yellow flare of emotion that vanished again before he spoke. "I'm Bryson Goodall, Mr. Kammerling's head of security. You can call me Bryce."

He was not, I noted, TPM's security chief. Interesting. "Does Edward think I'm going to run out on him, or is he afraid I won't make it without you?"

"Pardon me? I don't follow your logic, Ms. Blaine."

"Head of security is a big man to send out as a cabin steward. So he's afraid of something, and I have to wonder, is it me or is it something else?"

"You'll have to ask Mr. Kammerling."

He smiled again and excused himself to let the pilot know I was seated and ready to go. In a few minutes, we were taxiing out for an uneventful flight to Seattle.

SIXTEEN

A blacked out sedan met us at Boeing Field just south of downtown Seattle, and Goodall settled me in the backseat. He rode with the driver. The sun was only just below the horizon, so Edward wasn't up to meet me, but the isolation in the big backseat made me nervous nonetheless. I was surprised when we passed through Pioneer Square without stopping at the After Dark club—Edward's audience chamber in his role as chief bloodsucker—and went on into downtown. I knew TPM owned quite a lot of real estate in Seattle and environs and that Edward used some of it for his personal business, but I hadn't ever met him outside the club. Finally, the darkened sedan pulled into the parking structure under TPM's headquarters building in downtown. Curiouser and curiouser.

Goodall stuck with me once we were out of the car, assuring me my luggage would be taken care of as he guided me into a locked elevator that he accessed with both a card and a standard key. But we didn't ride up; we went down.

The elevator opened onto a very plush lobby, but no amount of decoration could disguise from my practiced eyes that it was the antechamber to a secure bunker. Beyond the normal-world anti-intrusion measures, the room was wrapped and tied in layer upon layer of gleaming magic that burned with the deep red glow of things born of blood and darkness. There was no indication how long the wards had been in place, so I didn't know if it was a routine paranoia on Edward's part or something new. Either way, anyone stupid enough to make threatening moves in this place would die screaming. That was not going to be me.

Goodall crossed the room to a pair of double doors made of some dull gray metal inlaid with bronze panels pressed deep with complex geometric patterns. They were almost Art Moderne but not quite, and they, too, emitted the hungry red glow of blood magic.

Goodall waved me forward. "The inner doors won't open while the elevator doors are also open."

Drawing a deep breath against the stink of vampires, I complied. I stopped next to Goodall on the assumption that Edward wouldn't kill me after so much trouble to get me there, and especially not if it would take out his security chief at the same time. Edward had done some thoughtless things in the past, but he didn't generally waste useful people without reason.

Goodall pressed a button next to the door frame and I was glad it was him touching the black thing. I thought I saw an eye blink above it and the impression of tiny teeth gnashed at the air beneath Goodall's wrist. I knew these weren't spells laid by Edward—he didn't have any such power of his own—and his uneasy truce with Carlos wouldn't have persuaded the necromancer to lay them for his benefit. It worried me that such spells existed in Seattle; someone had to have set them and I had no idea who, but such power was dangerous and its source wouldn't be pleasant. I put that thought aside for later consideration and braced for whatever was next.

The big doors swung open with the hiss of hydraulics and we stepped through to Edward's private lair. The doors sighed closed behind us and I heard a faint click and a rattle in the Grey like the sound of insect wings. The bloody glow of the wards seeped though the walls into the room beyond and brushed over us like the touch of carnivorous vines. Then came the smell, the stomach-twisting psychic odor of vampires.

Edward entered the room through a door on the far side, bringing the heat and roil of his particular aura closer. Most of the bloodsucking fraternity seemed to exude a glamour of sexual attraction—prey attractor, I supposed, since if anyone could really see and smell them as I could, they'd never get close enough to get a bite in—and Edward's was thick enough to gag on. I eased half a step back without thinking. It had been a while since I'd had to deal face-to-face with the Prince of the City. I'd forgotten how hard it was to be in his presence.

He strolled up to me, his eyes, hooded from recent sleep—or feeding—were directed straight to mine as if Goodall didn't exist. Even freshly risen, he looked like a film star from Hollywood's golden age: dark haired, sloe eyed, and far too handsome for anyone's good. The spoiler was that he was short for a modern man—about five foot seven or so. He reached for my hand and caught it, stroking the palm with his fingertips. I wanted to shudder but didn't.

"My dear Harper. Good of you to come."

"As if I had a lot of choice."

He raised his eyebrows in question. "You are under no compulsion." He glanced at Goodall. "Is she? You've not got a gun to her back, have you, Bryce?"

"No, sir. Not that I think it would make a difference with this lady."

"Indeed. She'd tear your arm off and feed it to you if you offended her. Wouldn't you, my dear?"

I narrowed my eyes. "What do you want, Edward? Your secretary said it was urgent, not just an excuse to mess with me."

He sighed. "Blunt as always. Yes, all right. It is urgent. Bryson, you may go."

"I'd rather he didn't," I said.

"This one time, I'm afraid you have no choice," Edward replied, dropping my hand and lowering the temperature in the room with his scowl. "Much as I trust Mr. Goodall's discretion, this is not a discussion for his ears. Only yours. Stay or go as you choose, but choose now. I'm very busy."

I glanced at Bryson Goodall, who didn't move a muscle, not even to shift his eyes, which he kept fixed on his boss. The energy of his aura had expanded when Edward came near, and now it rippled in a dark blue corona shot with yellow lines and coils. There was something very odd going on between him and Edward, whose own red-and-black energy haze reached out toward Goodall's like the tongue of a snake.

"Why should I assume I'm safe with you, Edward?" I asked.

He closed his eyes as if he were too exhausted to bear it. When he opened them, they were darker than ever and infinitely tired. "If I wanted you dead, Ms. Blaine, you'd never have exited my plane alive."

"That's not a comfort with you."

He laughed. "True." Then he turned to Goodall. "Bryson, I believe Ms. Blaine will be staying, after all. Please retire until I call for you again."

Goodall gave a curt nod and left us alone, the door opening before him automatically.

"Neat trick," I said, watching the doors.

"Rather. It wasn't easy having them installed. The panels are ancient and powerful. I'm afraid I lost a few people getting it done."

So they were dark artifacts—objects that had been imbued with or accrued magical residue and, with it, power. That might explain the darkness of the spells around them. The wrong kind of magician would lust after them more than he would all the virgins of heaven.

I let Edward take my hand again and lead me deeper into his sanctum, resisting the urge to recoil from the hot/cold sensation that rushed up my arm at his touch. We went through a door and into a chamber—you couldn't call it a room—decorated in dark green.

All the better to conceal the blood, I thought, for this looked like a small board room and I imagined that any business done here carried the direst consequences for someone. A large black table dominated the center of the room with hard chairs ranged around it and audiovisual equipment hanging from the ceiling. Off to the side were several groupings of more comfortable chairs—no doubt for private conferences.

Edward led me to one of these and slid with his usual elegant bonelessness into one of the seats. There was already a drinks tray on the table between the chairs. I sat more carefully. He poured amber liquid into glasses and I didn't pick mine up.

"It's quite safe," he said, sipping at his own drink. "It's a rather rare whiskey and very nearly eighty years old. I wouldn't insult such a distillation with anything that would harm you."

"I'd rather know why you were in such a rush to see me."

"You really can be stubborn."

"It's one of my best traits, I think."

"Do me and my whiskey the honor of taking a sip, and we'll get down to business. Please."

Well . . . he wasn't going to kill me, and we'd long ago established that I'd be no use to him undead, either, so I took the risk and drank. It was, without doubt, the smoothest, mellowest whiskey I'd ever tasted in my life—not that I'm an expert. Once in my mouth, it went places and did things whiskey ought not to be allowed to get up to, and my fingertips tingled from the warmth of it. I could feel a flush on my face. Barrel strength. I narrowed my eyes at Edward.

"Don't," he said. "Appreciate it as it is. I'm not trying to get you drunk and take advantage of you."

"You won't." I put my glass down. "It is very good, but before the whiskey steals my sense, tell me what you want from me."

"I need you to go to London on my behalf."

"You could send Goodall. He's obviously in your good graces, competent, and aware of what you are as well as who."

"Mr. Goodall is only recently installed in his position, and anyway, he can't be allowed too far from my side yet—even if he wasn't known to be my employee. He won't do. I need someone horribly clever and not openly my friend. Which certainly fits you."

"I'm hardly thought to be your enemy, either."

He stood up, agitated. "You are a neutral party. They may think they can sway you, suborn you. I know they won't succeed." He started pacing on a short track across the space in front of the two chairs we occupied.

"Who? Who is this 'they'?"

"The London cabal. Possibly with the help of other factions and agitators, certainly with the help of my enemies there and here. You have seen us fractured and fighting here, but I assure you, Seattle is a tranquil sea of unity compared to the Old World."

I snorted, but Edward shook his head.

"It's the truth. I handled Seattle poorly—as you demonstrated—because I had grown used to the habits of England and its divisions and factionalism. They were an irritation but a constant in England that one simply accepted because the population is old and the territories and hatreds well-established. They could not be changed, only worked around. I have been trying to change that here. But it has not made my enemies into friends. I suspect my troubles on both sides of the pond are orchestrated by a single source, but among my unfortunately numerous enemies and evil-wishers, I don't know who it is. It's the sort of trouble old enemies stir up—people who've known you long enough to think they know your weaknesses."

"If these problems are connected, then why are you ignoring the destruction of vampires in the underground?"

His eyes narrowed. "Your friend is not in my best graces over that. . . ."

"He says he didn't do it."

"I'm aware of that. And of who did. There is much going on of which you are not aware, and I cannot simply do as I like. Still, I'm not best pleased to have lost one of my own. But I can address that myself. And I will, but that will require my attention here. I cannot go to London on this other matter. You can."

"What matter? You haven't said yet what's wrong."

"You haven't agreed to go."

"And I won't until you tell me what I'd be getting into."

He stopped over me, looming, his gaze trying to bore into mine. "You must agree first." His voice resonated, and ripples moved through the Grey. I felt the pressure of his insistence against me, weighing on my body like a physical thing.

I unfolded myself from the chair and stood, trying to shake it off. I towered over him, but that didn't help as much as I'd have liked. I felt weaker than I had in a long time, and Edward wasn't playing with me this time. He was deadly serious. He'd never put out so much effort to control me before. I felt hot and unwell. The combination of his blood-soaked presence and the blaze of his sexual glamour was sickening. I drew my breath with care and clenched my teeth.

He clutched my right wrist, pulling me down so my eyes were level with his. "You must agree."

"Go screw yourself," I growled. It wasn't the cleverest thing I'd ever said, but I was fighting, his will against mine. I squeezed my eyes shut to break the contact while I still could.

Edward, though shorter, was much stronger than I, and he yanked me into the nearest corner. I could feel something unearthly wash over us, but I kept my eyes closed, resisting his pulling and pushing with everything I had. His other hand came up to my throat. I felt it hovering, just brushing the fine hairs on my skin, waiting to wring the breath out of me.

"Say you will do it," he hissed, a note of desperation in his voice. "Say it, under the seal."

A seal, yes, now I could almost see it like an afterimage on my retinas. Some cold-fire sigil embedded in the ceiling and sending its icy power down over us both. I knew that promises made under the power of certain magics were binding even beyond death. The thought burst into my head that there could have been something similar acting on the ghosts of my father and Christelle, too. I'd bound and been bound myself by such magic. I wouldn't do it. I wouldn't let Edward bind me to whatever he pleased, no matter how distraught he was. I would not be a pawn, a living ghost with no will of my own.

His hand closed on my neck with just the slightest pressure. For an instant, panic surged in my system and I felt the knot of Grey embedded in my chest by another vampire twang and thrum, vibrating across the spectrum of the Grey in rainbow colors that danced on the inside of my eyelids. Wygan had tied me inexorably to the grid two years ago with that tangled strand. Now I forced every ounce of power, of thought, toward that singing in my chest and, bringing my free hand between us, I shoved. . . .

The world seemed to stretch and twist. . . .

Thunder shook the room and lightning coursed over my bones and out toward Edward.

"No!" I shouted, opening my eyes and giving one more desperate mental push.

The seal cracked, its power vanishing, and we both pitched away.

I landed hard on my back, rolling fast to my feet, drawing my pistol in one fluid movement and a sharp clack from the cocking lever. Unless I blew his head off, shooting him wouldn't stop Edward, but it might slow him down.

Edward was on the other side of the room, looking at me with narrowed eyes. "You're more formidable than I recalled."

I didn't know how I'd done it—I'd never pushed with that sort of energy before—but I didn't let on. "Don't flatter me. What do you want?"

"Would you please put the gun away?"

"I think I like it better in my hand and you on the other end of it."

He strolled across the room toward me. "It's really not that useful."

I kept the sights on him. "Call it a security blanket. You want me to go to London, and you're scared white of what might be going on or you wouldn't be trying to coerce me."

"I don't wish to coerce you. I want to hire you."

"Your negotiation skills suck. Give me a reason."

He was startled. "You would still go now?"

"I never said I wouldn't. You're the one who started the hardball tactics. Tell me why you need to send someone like me to look into your business—I assume it is your business—and I might consider it. If the money is good enough."

"I thought you weren't motivated by money, my dear." He was on more comfortable ground now that we were talking—especially talking money. He'd always preferred to solve problems with leverage and charm rather than getting his hands dirty. "It's not a matter of sending someone *like* you. There is only one Harper Blaine. I assure you that is no empty compliment but the truth of the matter—I need your skills and your ability to walk both the day and the night. This is a matter of my kind, and Mr. Goodall will not do."

"Tell me the situation and I'll tell you if I'll go."

"I . . . cannot risk telling you if you then don't choose to go. You would have the upper hand of me."

"Edward, I've got enough on you to wreck your unlife a dozen times over. But I don't have any reason to. I'm far better off with you, the devil I know, running this particular show. I've never rolled on you. What makes you think I would now?"

He turned away and slid down into his chair again. "Fear. My dear Ms. Blaine, I should trust you, but things that should not have happened have happened. Such things . . . don't just occur. They come to fruition through enemy action over time. I don't know whom I can trust."

"If you didn't think you could trust me in the first place, why call me at all?"

He drew down his brows in thought and picked up his whiskey

glass again. "That is a good question. So you would rather have me in control than, say . . . Carlos?"

"Carlos isn't likely to want your domain, only your head."

He raised an eyebrow and went back to his drink, waving at my gun with one lazy hand. "Do put that away and sit down. I swear by blood I won't attack you."

"So are we going to discuss your situation now or keep on fencing? Because I'm starting to lose interest in that."

"I shall tell you, but I prefer not to be literally under the gun. If you don't mind."

I let up on the cocking lever and the pistol clicked back into safe mode. I wasn't quite certain this was a good idea, but I reholstered it and sat back down.

"All right, spill it."

"Before I came to Seattle, I spent some years in London, where I discovered the importance of an economic base in the daylight world. Leverage to maintain control in the night half. When I left, considerable holdings remained, which also gave me considerable weight with certain people who worked for my interests both among the daylighters and the nightsiders. I was persona non grata, but my money and power were welcome to stay. I turned them over to the administration of a trust headed by a . . . friend."

"A flunky. You don't have friends, Edward. Only slaves and sycophants."

"On the contrary. I have cultivated a few relationships of trust. Maybe not friends but not enemies, either. You . . . perhaps."

Seeing Edward uncertain was disconcerting. As top dog in the vampire pack, such a sign of weakness would be an invitation to destruction, which was something I didn't want to be caught up in and surely would be if worse came to worst. If this was typical of his recent behavior, no wonder he was hiding in his bunker. I wanted to know more of what had spooked him, so for now I let it go and waved his comment off. "Whatever. Go on."

He nodded. "This friend, John Purcell, has vanished. As if he never existed—which is not entirely surprising for one of us. Silence has fallen all around what was John's. And around what was mine. Queries go unanswered, calls unreturned. I've tried to make contact with others in London, but they, too, return only silence. I don't know what's befallen Purcell or my assets. Or the others of my kind who controlled the darkness of London. I know they are still there, for the void left by their total destruction would be filled with notoriety and noise. But there is only silence. I must know what's happened! Have things fallen to another faction, been driven deeper under the ground, perhaps taken by the asetem—another species of my kind—or perhaps some other thing has risen . . . ? I must recover what I can or cover my tracks if nothing can be salvaged. And I want to know what's become of John Purcell. Is he the victim of some plot or is he the perpetrator? And of this, no one here must know. For each of my enemies in London, there are opposite numbers here. Do you see?"

It was a hell of a story but as plausible as anything coming from a living nightmare. "So what you want, in brief, is to find out why Purcell stopped talking and what's become of your stuff."

"Not exactly. I'm more concerned with the situation than the assets. It will hurt to lose them, but the greatest threat is what's made those assets inaccessible. I suspect a situation is developing in London that does not favor me at best and may threaten my position here as well, and I want that put to a stop."

"So . . . this is a search-and-destroy mission? I don't do that sort of thing."

"I shan't ask you to. Only to discover what is going on. After that, I can find suitable contractors for whatever may need doing." He shut up and looked at me, quiet and intense.

I didn't like the sound of it. But whenever he said "London," my thoughts flew to Will and my disturbing visions. It would be as good an excuse as any to check on him in person, and I felt an increasing need to do that and discover if there was any connection to the events of my death and the nightmares I'd been having about him. The job Edward was offering wasn't something I'd enjoy, but it would pay a lot of bills and serve my own ends at the same time.

"All right," I said.

He blinked, frowned. "Just like that?"

"You'd prefer to have to 'persuade' me some more?"

He turned up the heat. "You know how I'd like to persuade you. . . ."

I felt mildly unwell again at the thought. "Save it for someone without a pulse."

"They are considerably less interesting than you, my dear."

"I hear that's a problem with being dead—it's terminally boring."

He laughed and rose to his feet, putting out a hand to me. "It does pall. Come with me and I'll arrange everything."

I started to rise on my own, but he caught my hand, and this time he didn't crush it in his grip but brought it to his mouth and kissed the back. I recoiled but didn't pull my hand away, no matter how much I wanted to escape from the fire and ice that seared into me from his touch. I didn't have enough energy to fight him again right then, and insulting him wouldn't be my best move at that moment. Instead I stood up and smiled, taking my hand back as a matter of course.

He smiled back through slightly narrowed eyes, as if he knew I was faking something. Then he led me to the big table and revealed a computer under the surface, from which he extracted information and made various arrangements for my journey and my stay. Everything was to be at his expense, and he saw to it that no expense need be spared, either. I felt a bit mercenary for it all, but that is sometimes the nature of my job. We agreed on a price for my services that would clear my normal expenses for a long time.

"Do you have a passport?" he asked.

"Of course. I keep it up to date, just in case."

"Very good. When can you leave?"

"I may need to clear some things up, but that won't take long. Two days will be sufficient. That's not counting today."

"And you'll want to make arrangements about your home and pet, no doubt."

"No doubt."

He nodded to himself. "I'll have the tickets delivered to your office with the relevant information and paperwork."

"I'll be waiting."

He showed me to the door, pausing only to take my hand one more time. He seemed to enjoy my discomfort before letting me go.

In the outer chamber, Bryson Goodall was waiting for me. He didn't say much and his face didn't give away anything, but the nimbus of color around his head and body had turned a brighter blue. He saw me safely home and carried my luggage up the stairs to my condo. I didn't much like his presence as an adjunct of Edward on my literal doorstep, but there wasn't much I could do. He nodded to me as I turned back from entering my condo and then he left.

As I was unpacking, I realized someone had gone through my things. They hadn't taken anything or added anything, but that someone—probably Goodall and probably at Edward's direction—had snooped through my belongings at all was bizarre and disturbing. There couldn't be anything in my bags that told Edward anything he didn't know. But it left me unsettled and more anxious than ever to see Quinton.

SEVENTEEN

Quinton tucked me tighter against his body under the covers of his narrow bed. "You're not going to change your mind and stay home?" he asked.

"No," I replied. "I took the job; I'll do the job."

We'd discussed Edward's proposition twice by now, trying to suss out every possible pitfall and hidden agenda. Neither of us liked the situation and we were both convinced whatever was developing in Seattle's Grey world wasn't a coincidence, but if Edward felt the London situation took precedence, we'd have to take his word. Previous upheavals of the local vampire community didn't go unnoticed; they just got explained away. They hit the human population as crime waves, gang killings, and warehouse fires and took down both the agitators and the innocent. If a power struggle was violent and widespread enough, it would break out into open warfare between the vampire factions and no one would be safe. If the skullduggery in London was the key to the unrest Edward had hinted at in Seattle, then solving the London problem was priority one. I didn't know how the London vampire community worked or what the problems there might be. I'd have to trust Edward's assessment.

Quinton nuzzled his nose into my hair and murmured, "I have a bad feeling about this."

"I'm not exactly getting a vacation-at-the-beach vibe off it myself. And don't suggest you come with me. I need you to keep an eye on the situation here while I'm gone."

"And take care of Chaos. I know."

"Hey," I said, rolling over to face him, "you're not just the pet-sitter, you know."

He grinned and kissed me. "I know. The pet-sitter never gets the girl."

"The pet-sitter usually is the girl."

"Not in John Cusack films."

"Which film was that? The last one you saw, Cusack was an assassin trying to date his old high school sweetheart from Grosse Point, Michigan."

"Hey, I'd move to Michigan to date you."

"Does that mean there are still things I don't know about what you used to do for the government?" I asked, teasing.

"Well . . . yeah, but not that kind of thing."

"You're sure, now? Because if I get back and my condo has been used to stash the bodies of victims killed with ballpoint pens, I may be a tad upset."

"I promise: no bodies stabbed with ballpoints. Maybe just a Sharpie or two . . ."

"Quinton!" I yelled as he tickled me, grinning.

The conversation dissolved into amorous wrestling in the sheets for a while, until an alarm went off somewhere.

"What the—?" I started, jerking up out of the tangled sheets.

For a second, Quinton looked blank, trying to identify the sound. Then his eyes got wide and he pulled in a sharp breath. "It's the ghost detector. It works! Maybe . . ." He twitched his attention to me. "Do you . . . see anything?"

Not only did I see something, it was looming over the bed. Or rather, they were. The Grey was overwhelming my senses and a crowd of ghosts filled the tiny bedroom of Quinton's hidden home, leaving smudges of color like smoke in the silvery world around me, colors that ghosts shouldn't display. Some seemed familiar, others not at all, but they were all staring at me in the humming intensity of the Grey. I shivered.

"Umm . . . yeah . . . about fifty of them," I said, staring back. I feared to blink in case they rushed the bed. I don't know why I thought that, but the feeling of imminent motion pressed on me like an incoming storm front.

Quinton rolled out of bed and darted through the assemblage of specters to one of his workbenches. He didn't even twitch and I envied him that oblivion for an instant. He plucked a small LCD display out of a nest of wires that clung to it like fur and squeezed the rim, silencing the alarm while he studied the screen. Unconscious of his nudity, he turned slowly, treading the cold floor on bare feet as he swept the room with the ghost detector.

"They—" I started.

"Sh-h-h. I want to find them. Let's see if this works. . . ."

If he'd just looked at me I was pretty sure he couldn't miss the direction I was staring. I pulled the covers up to my neck. So long as the phantoms weren't moving I could stand to be patient with Quinton, but I didn't have to let them ogle me. Maybe clothes made no difference to them, but it made me feel better.

He pointed the messy hash of wires and readouts around the room until the wires were pulled too taut between the detector and a big box of mysterious purpose on the bench. He looked a little crestfallen. "Oh. It's you."

"No. Trust me. It's them."

"Are they . . . between us?"

"Oh, yes." I stared at the ghosts. "Stay right there," I told them. Then I crept out of the bed while keeping my eyes on them, reluctantly leaving the sheet behind, and backed to Quinton. The spectral mob turned as I went, tracking my movement like hunting hounds, but didn't come closer. That was strange; ghosts don't usually give much of a damn what I want, much less follow my orders. "Anything change?" I asked, still keeping my gaze on the ghosts.

"Only a little. The big reading is still by the bed."

"What is it measuring?"

"A low segment of the high-energy band—a little more energetic than photons, not as hot as neutrinos. I figured that's where the ghost energy had to lie. It's not very specific, though. I get a lot of interference."

"Oh." It didn't mean a lot to me but I trusted Quinton to have a handle on his subject. Either he was actually measuring ghosts or he'd found something else equally strange.

I strengthened my attention on the phantoms and slipped deeper into the Grey. "What do you want?" I demanded, feeling the cold of the magical world pierce my skin.

Most of them just stared. I had the feeling they weren't very strong willed, so something beyond their own desire was directing them to me.

A collective sigh replied and about half of the ghosts faded away into sparks and random swirls of mist.

"Reading's down to almost nothing . . . What's happening?" Quinton asked.

"They're leaving, but only about half are gone. I think your detector isn't sensitive enough to pick up a single ghost on its own."

He grunted and peered at the display. "That sucks."

"Uh-huh. You mind if I get rid of this bunch now? They're giving me more than the usual creeps."

Quinton cast a startled glance at me and noticed we were both still naked. He blushed. "Oh, God, I'm sorry."

He started to put an arm around me, but I shook him off. I was searching the remaining crowd of spirits for the cause of their bright colors. Aura energy is colored by emotion, habit, and magical associations, the trappings of life and action, which aren't exactly common traits among the memory shadows that are ghosts. Somewhere in the writhing soup of the phantom mob there had to be an emotional kernel that had drawn them together. That ghost would be the dangerous one—the one who'd dragged the rest to me for whatever purpose.

There: One hot, orange spike, like the stamen of an exotic flower, gleamed in the silver spirit fog. I fixed my eyes on it.

"You. You dragged your preternatural posse to see me for a reason, I presume. So what do you want?"

I hated it, but I stepped though the curtain of colored energy and into the depths of the swirling crowd of ghosts, shoving them aside with the edge of the Grey one by one as I advanced through them to their core. But there was nothing; only the burning orange glow of frustration from someone or something that couldn't come any closer, a shell of emotion with no apparent source. I pushed my left hand into it, trying to find any substance at all, Grey or real or merely transient, to clutch and confront. My fingers closed on nothing. The orange gleam flashed white and hot. I jerked my hand back with a yelp of pain.

Quinton dropped his gadget and leaped forward, throwing his arms around me. "Harper!"

"It's all right. It's OK," I panted. "I don't think it wants to hurt me. I . . . think I just startled it."

"What? What is it? What is it doing to you?" he asked, wrapping himself around me like a protective shield.

"Nothing," I said, amazed. "It reacted to my grabbing at it, but it's not doing anything. It's not a ghost; it's . . . just . . . some kind of emotional energy drawing other ghosts in like a magnet. I don't know what it wants or why it's here, though. It can't seem to communicate any better than this."

The energy around us faded to blue and pale yellow—colors I thought of as neutral or low-threat at least. It drew together and moved toward the workbench, leaving the ghosts huddling into a pale mass of cold steam and twisting into a tighter, denser rope of energy. It streamed toward the fallen detector, drawing the spirits into thin strands of silver within the elongating cable of power. The luminescent stream surged into the device and a squawk came from the alarm speaker.

The big black box on the bench rattled and steamed, the speaker pinging and squealing for a moment before it gave out a more coherent sound. "Not."

Quinton and I both stared at the box.

"What," the box croaked. "You." The bright rope of energy faded with every word. "Think. Why—" But there the message stopped in a fizz of sparks and the stink of burning wires as the rope flared and blinked out, leaving me coiled in Quinton's arms, naked in the darkness from which even the gleam of ghosts and the bright lines of the Grey power grid had momentarily faded as if all energy had been exhausted in the area. I could feel Quinton shuddering.

"You OK?" I asked.

"Yeah . . . for pretty loose values of OK. That felt . . . really nasty."

"I—I think your machine is toast." I'd almost apologized, but I hadn't done anything—had I?

"Probably." He squeezed me closer. "But I can make another one. How 'bout you? Are you all right?"

"As right as I ever am."

"Your skin feels cold." He kissed my cheek. "You want to get back in bed and warm up?" I could feel him smiling and a pink glow radiated from his body as the room's normal Grey presence began twinkling back.

"You are an adorable lunatic."

"I can go for adorable."

"Not so much the lunatic?"

"I think I prefer techno-geek. I know I prefer the bed over standing on this cold-ass floor."

The glimmer and gleam of the grid hummed back to normal as we scampered across the chilly floor to huddle under the blankets again.

Quinton kissed my temple. "That was pretty freaky."

"And I have no idea what it was in service to."

"That's the same message your dead boyfriend delivered: It's not what you think. Isn't it?"

I called that memory up. "Yeah, it is. But that . . . mob wasn't Cary."

"Someone wants you to get that message pretty desperately."

"Oh, I get it. But it's not very helpful. What is not what it seems? Me? Edward? His little business trip? That wasn't even on the table when Cary got in touch." The more I thought of it, the madder I got at the whole cipher-wrapped-in-an-enigma thing. "I'm not going to back out of this trip, even if that is what the ghosts are warning me about. I think I stand a better chance of finding answers in England than staying here and chasing my tail, not knowing which questions to ask whom and pissing Edward off in the bargain. I have a plane to catch in five hours and I'm not planning on wasting what's left of that time puzzling over the energetic missives of cryptic specters," I snapped.

"Hey, sweetheart . . . It's just me here now."

I closed my eyes, chagrined at my anger. "I'm sorry. I feel like I'm being played in some way. It makes me . . . short-tempered."

"Played by Edward?"

I shrugged dismissal. "Not really. Manipulation is Edward's stock-in-trade. There's something else. Ever since this started there's been something . . . lurking. I just have a bad feeling. . . ."

"I know."

I sighed. "I don't mean to take it out on you."

"I don't mind being your sounding board. Or your backup or whatever you need." He hesitated. "That's—you know . . . what you do for someone you love."

Something ridiculous and giddy swelled through me at the word. I could feel the fizz of it bursting out of my skin and igniting sparks in the writhing platinum mist, bouncing off the living, glowing streams of energy that powered magic, and the rippling knife edge of the Grey. After the devastation Cary had wreaked on the remnants of my juvenile romanticism, the gleaming evidence of Quinton's sincerity was intoxicating.

"Want me to prove it?" he whispered into my ear. His grip tightened just a little as his body temperature kicked up.

"You don't need to prove—"

He nipped at my neck below the ear. "I want to," he breathed against my skin. His hands slid up toward my breasts.

I turned in his arms and met his mouth with mine, passion heating the air until it baffled our lungs and fused us together, flesh to flesh. I forgot to say the words, but I did my best to show him that I felt the same way.

EIGHTEEN

E dward's idea of long-distance air travel for daylighters started at business class. Since he had, in his weird way, damn near begged me to take the job, I got first-class treatment—literally. Not the corporate jet—the opposition would catch on to me soon enough without that sort of red flag—but the cushiest seating British Airways offered to commercial travelers nonstop from Seattle to Heathrow. Nine hours in transit. It was the first time I'd ever slept comfortably on a plane and arrived feeling reasonably alert and uncramped.

Edward had run the reservations through a couple of corporate blinds so only an insider would know I was in London under TPM's aegis. The financial distance made for sufficient security to arrange for a car to pick me up and take me to my hotel without recourse to the Tube or my paying for a common cab myself. But the luxury of the car service—it was a huge step up from a cab, but you couldn't quite call it a limo—set me on edge; conspicuous consumption is just that: conspicuous. As I sat in the back of the black sedan cruising away from Heathrow on the freeway—no, motorway—I put my mind into undercover mode and thought about what I was heading into.

A tourist is one among thousands, but a first-class traveler is one of a hundred and, like any other undercover job, I'd had to look the part. Now I had to act it as well until I could shift into the next physical and mental disguise. I suspected that most of my investigations in London would require a less-affluent wardrobe and an attitude that wasn't as hard as my usual street armor. I already missed the convenience of my old, wrecked Rover with its cache of clothes and tools. The hotel would have to be my base of operations, so, first thing, I'd need to find an unobtrusive way in and out, or risk attracting attention. Vampires are a paranoid lot and if some local faction had moved against Edward as he seemed to suspect, they'd be on the alert for anything that indicated his eye was on them. Eventually, they'd connect me to Edward, but the longer I could keep that from happening, the better.

The car had just passed some kind of light industrial or office complex and the wide, multilane road descended from its protected cement embankments to run at street level as a highway when the preternatural world flooded over me. I hadn't noticed the Grey much before that; the area west of London along the M4 was a little more rural than the suburban mix between Seattle and our own airport at Sea-Tac and not quite as haunted—which isn't much to begin with. But leaving the motorway and entering the streetscape of western London was like stepping into a deep and turbulent sea of the Grey, even inside the damping barrier of the car's steel and chrome. I don't know why I hadn't given much thought to the weight and chaos of the unseen that would grow up along with a city over the course of two millennia, but it was as thick and opaque as a one of London's famous Victorian fogs and I shuddered with cold, although the sunny afternoon was pleasantly warm—hot by native standards.

"Would you like the air turned off?" the driver asked.

"Huh?" I coughed, the centuries choking and slamming through me.

"The air-conditioning. Would you like it turned down? You seem cold." His speech wasn't strict BBC bland but it was carefully correct.

I suspected he spoke with a broader accent at home but was supposed to present a bit more polish on the job.

"Yes. Please." If it would help me warm back up after the shock of sudden immersion in the icy sea of the past, I was in favor of it. I would have to gain some control and equilibrium before we reached the hotel or I might be completely useless—or at the least as sick and punch-drunk as I'd been the first few times I'd stepped into the Grey.

"Where are we?" I asked, groping for something to orient myself by.

"Just coming into Hammersmith. Not much farther."

"How much longer to London, then?"

He laughed. "Sorry, miss. We've been in Greater London since we left Heathrow. It's all London."

"But you said Hammersmith. . . ."

"It's one of the outer boroughs. London's like . . . a lot of little cities that grew together. I've a cousin in Queens, New York, says it's the same sort of thing there. One vast city made of a lot of bits. What you probably think of as London, that's really just a couple of the old cities—the City of London, and the City of Westminster—and the inner boroughs."

"Like most people think New York is just Manhattan," I suggested.

"That's what my cousin said!"

"So . . . how big is London?" I asked, realizing I'd bitten off a lot more than I'd imagined in agreeing to come with no idea which part to look in for Edward's answers or my own.

"Huge! But not to worry. Your hotel's central. You're almost in the Square Mile."

"What's that—the Square Mile?"

"Used to be the old City of London. Now it's business offices, banks, stock exchange, the Old Bailey, the Inns of Court, and the like. When your business associates say 'the City,' that's what they mean. Westminster is right next door. That's where the cathedral and the abbey and parliament are. You know: Big Ben and that sort of thing. Lots of sightseers round about, lots of one-way roads, narrow bits, alleys . . . Traffic'll be a bit thick. Far more agreeable to walk in than drive."

"So don't rent a car."

"Absolutely not. Stick to your feet when you can, cabs when you have to—even the Tube, buses, and so on, though they can be nasty— and you'll get round much quicker and slicker. A bicycle is useful if you have one, but walking's generally the thing."

I nodded, making vague noises of agreement as the car wormed its way deeper into the thick of London and its ghosts. I tightened my focus to the deepest levels of the Grey, where the magical energy grid of London blazed in polychrome lines and labyrinthine whorls that darted in and out of the earth we passed over. I hadn't been a good student of history, but I had heard that modern London was built on the wrack and ruin of earlier settlements and prior incarnations that had burned, or sunk, or been knocked down, and been built over again and again, rising higher on the delta of mud and memory. I concentrated on the hard power lines until I had a solid feel for the magical bones of the city and its layers of history before I let myself swim back up to a more normal level of vision.

As I drew a long, steadying breath and blinked around at the busy world of London's reality overlaid with the riotous layers of its ghosts, the driver pulled to a halt in a narrow road.

"Here you are, miss."

My hotel proved to be a modern, glass-and-steel-fronted tower on a tiny street just across a big road and a wide park from the Thames. I took a look up and down the lane from behind the sedan's tinted glass, trying to set the scene and location in my mind. There was a low Victorian stone building just across from the hotel with a strip of bright blue signage that identified it as TEMPLE STATION. A pair of other buildings flanked the hotel but faced the roads to each side, like bodyguards. No sign of a service or employees' entrance from the front of the elegantly stark facade, so I assumed there would be one on the side or a back alley where the public couldn't see the unglamorous aspects of hotel service without going out of their way. The small street wasn't very busy except for the people going in and out of the Underground station, but the wide boulevard running along the riverside was aswarm with all sorts of people from immaculately dressed men and women in business suits to tourists in jeans and T-shirts with sunglasses and hats protecting their eyes from the glitter of light off the waters of the Thames. Surging through it, layer on layer of ghosts. The mix, so close at hand, reassured me that I wouldn't find it hard to slip away from my glamorous pad and become anonymous.

A dark-coated doorman stood at the curb, wearing a top hat in defiance of the wind off the river. He stepped forward and opened my door as the driver fetched my suitcase from the trunk.

"Welcome to the Howard, miss."

I barely got out a "thank you," before I and my bags were whisked into the lobby. As I turned from the car, something near the Underground station gave a fractured glitter through the Grey like light tripping off a broken mirror. I turned around to catch it but saw only a white streak of movement that vanished into the shade of the station's doorway to roost among the steam-shapes of the Grey.

From my room I had a view of the Thames and the street below. The room was a bit too high for me to see the inside of the Underground station's doorway, but I could see the sidewalk in front of it. The layers of glass between me and the exterior filtered the Grey to a dim soup of mist and Saint Elmo's fire, but I could still detect something near the station's entrance that was more like a faceted void of Grey than the usual lingering energy colors. I observed it for about twenty minutes before it drifted deeper into the Tube station and disappeared. Something that wasn't quite there was watching my hotel.

NINETEEN

My hotel proved to have a rear courtyard and several service doors. As soon as I was sure there were no more watchers—at least none I could detect—I changed into more casual clothes and snuck off to the streets. I felt a little naked without my usual paraphernalia, but guns and my pocketknife were blatantly illegal in England for someone like me, and I'd left them in Seattle. I was at a distinct disadvantage against anything corporeal since I didn't know the lay of the land or have anything but my brains and my fists if I got into a jam. The wiser course was to case the streets and find routes in and out of the area as well as places I could disappear to if the hotel became untenable.

I moved away from the open areas along the river where dallying crowds were not always enough to hide in. A couple of blocks up I crossed the Strand, pausing on a curious island in the stream of traffic where a small church of weathered white stone stood under a rippling canopy of leafy branches. There was a sign with something on it about the RAF, but I didn't pause to read it so much as to catch my breath before I plunged back into the press of early summer tourists. An incredible range of voices and accents rang a complex peal on the air, and I was a little startled to notice how ethnically mixed the busy business folks and goggling tourists were. I had that American expectation that England was mainly peopled by white Anglo-Saxons, but London at least was more in the melting-pot mode. The city—its sounds, sights, smells—and the rippling effect of a thousand years' worth of ghosts made me dizzy and I had to concentrate to stay on task.

It took a bit of looking to find a newsagent. The shops were narrow and varied wildly, from specialists in arcane materials and curious arts that had been in business since William and Mary, to bustling little food stands selling everything from spicy kebabs and curry to bacon sandwiches and cups of steaming tea. There were also lots of pubs with contingents of smokers relegated to the sidewalks with their cigarettes in one hand and their pints in the other, talking nonstop and blocking the pavement, unable to hear my "excuse me" over the roar of traffic and the babble of voices.

I finally found what I was looking for. The small shop sat next to a post office and advertised newspapers, magazines, books, and maps on its sign. Like many of the small, street-level businesses I'd already passed, it was more like a deep stall than anything else and empty of people except me and the cashier. Local maps and other aids for travelers were prominently racked near the front, so I went in and bought several as well as a small bottle of water and an energy bar. I asked the very young woman behind the counter about the address Edward had given me for his missing agent, John Purcell.

She squinted, her brow creasing crookedly where a piercing had been removed, and tilted her mouth to one side as she thought. Her hair was patchwork brown over a previous dye job that had left it a bit brittle. Green and blue glints shot through her aura like tiny shy fish. If someone had asked, I'd have guessed she was coming out of a broken relationship with a bad boy and a bad crowd. Her accent was decidedly less posh than those I'd heard at my hotel and her demeanor a little nervous.

"Jerusalem Passage? Not sure. Here, let's look." She flipped open the map book I'd just purchased and riffled through the street index until she found it. Then she flipped back to the appropriate page. "Oh, that's Clerkenwell. Must be just north of the old priory gate. See," she added, pointing to a convoluted quirk of streets near Clerkenwell Road and St. John Street, about half a mile northeast of where we stood.

I peered at the page and had difficulty picking out the narrow wiggling line of Jerusalem Passage. "It must be a very narrow street," I thought aloud.

"It's not a proper street," the shopgirl said. "It's a passage."

I didn't know the difference. "Is that like an alley?" I asked.

"Sort of, but not. It's, umm . . . it's a walkway. Not a promenade— not wide like that—and not like a regular pavement on the edge of a road. Just a footpath, not very wide, say . . . three people wide—or two fat German tourists." She looked startled at what she'd said and lowered her head back to the map with a blush.

She studied the book for a moment and flipped it over to the Underground system map on the back before adding, "Not sure about the bus. The closest Tube station would be Farringdon, but you'd have to take the Circle line all the way round past Aldgate. Bloody pain that is." She winced a little and glanced at me to see if I'd noticed before going on. "Much shorter to walk if you don't mind it."

"I don't mind at all."

"Good. Weather's nice for it. Here, now . . . what's the best way . . . ?" she pondered.

Between us we worked out a route that was easy but not too ugly. "If you've a mind to, you could go up Hatton Garden to Clerkenwell Road instead of Charterhouse to St. John's. It's not so direct, but the jewelers are worth a glance."

I looked at the map again. Purcell's home was within a few minutes' walk of a lot of "points of interest," according to the map. Of course that was true for a lot of London addresses, but this one was old and close to a lot of economically important businesses that had been around since the city was young: the jewelers, the meat markets, the old business districts for cloth makers and brewers, and the hospital and medical school at St. Bartholomew's among others. An ideal place for a vampire who managed the long-term investments of other vampires.

Of course, if Purcell was there, he wasn't likely to be awake for hours, but he'd have to have some kind of daylight assistant I could track down. And if not, I'd look for records.

"Oh," I started, "where would I find records of titles and deeds and things like that?"

"For Clerkenwell? Parish records to start, maybe at Clerkenwell Heritage Centre if it's something old. They'd tell you where to go after that."

I thanked her and headed out toward Fleet Street and Clerkenwell.

I'd read a lot of British mystery novels in my time, but I didn't expect to see much that recalled the worlds of Christie or Sayers or Conan Doyle. But between the occasional high-rises, the roads were lined with buildings that hadn't changed in hundreds of years, and the routes blazed with a millennium of coming and going worn deep into the ground but still shining upward. And the city sang.

The Grey makes a noise composed of the murmuring of ghosts and the vibration of power. Each city sounds different: Seattle mutters and rattles; Mexico City hums like feedback. London raised a mighty chorus over the bass drone of the river Thames. The power lines of the Grey were not laid in a neat grid, like Seattle's wire-frame world, but in wild-hare directions and labyrinthine meanders that came together in knots of brilliant colored light. I couldn't see them all, but I knew there were layers of history as thick and striated as sandstone beneath my feet, just as they were at the street level. The ghosts of buildings glistened over the surfaces of present structures, and phantom traffic choked the streets with oxcarts, horses, trams, and pedestrians. Most of the visions were from the eighteenth century onward, after the city had recovered from its own Great Fire, but promontories of older times and buildings long gone thrust up from below or floated slightly displaced by the actions of history and nature. Glimpses of fire caught my eye again and again. I shied the first time I heard the whistle of a falling bomb from the city's memory of World War II.

I did not, in fact, dawdle through Hatton Garden, but took the more direct and higher-traffic way along Charterhouse to St. John, passing Smithfield Market's painted iron arcades where meat and poultry were still sold fresh in huge loads. From the outside it reminded me a bit of the cliffside buildings at Pike Place Market, though Seattle's famous produce markets didn't hold a candle to the meat markets of Smithfield's imposing quarter mile of whitewashed iron, brick, and glass, gleaming in the early summer sunshine. I turned up St. John, dodging cars, trucks, pedestrians apparently bent on suicide, and phantom herds of cattle swarming toward their historical demise. As I diverged from the hectic intersection into the upper part of St. John's Lane, the noise and traffic dropped to a distant babble.

Looking around as I walked, I thought Clerkenwell must have been a much quieter town before it was eaten by London. It was tall and narrow and had the feeling of age, layered as it was with phantom monks and people in rich, ancient clothes, struggling against a tide of newer ghosts from the rise of the Victorian middle class and the bombings during the Second World War, all threading through the busy spectral streets. If I'd thought the area I'd walked through earlier had a lot of pubs, lower Clerkenwell had it beat hollow, and the ghostly crowds of muscular men that gathered around the present pub doors were thick and well-worn into the neighborhood's history. As I walked up the road, getting closer to the dark squares on my map marked ST. JOHN'S PRIORY, the shades of history grew more pastoral and the dominance of the church felt like the chill of an open crypt.

The old priory gate at the top of St. John's Lane was a yellow brick and stone structure of arches and squat, square towers that cut across the road as if it might have once held massive turnstiles to control the traffic of people and beasts coming down from the fields to the north. The uprights and plaza stones of the gate glowed with a soft, red energy that rose from the ground like fog—vampires must have been in the neighborhood for a long time but without raising much notice, judging by the unusual form of the magical residue. That was interesting.

I passed a tall, narrow arch neatly wedged between two tall, thin buildings nearby. The words PASSING ALLEY were carved into the white plaster, and from the corner of my eye I caught the same colorless glitter I'd spotted near Temple Underground Station. I turned my head away, as if checking the address on the nearest building. Then I looked back, peering down the alley as my gaze passed over it. A bit of white floated back into the distant murk of the covered alleyway, but the shadows were persistent and the Grey remained a smear of silvery mist curiously impenetrable. Not a vampire, but there was something there—or more to the point, something pretending not to be there.

I turned and went on as if I'd noticed nothing. Whatever it was would have to come out into the sun and follow me through the open squares on each side of the priory gate if it wanted to keep up.

As I went through the arch of the old church, I pulled out my cell phone and held down the button that activated the camera in video mode. Keeping my hand down, I pointed the tiny lens behind me and kept walking through the narrowest part of the gate and across the square. I crossed Clerkenwell Road and stopped in a sunny plaza paved in bright white stone—some kind of marble maybe—with a dark circle laid around the edge as if there used to be some small building there that had long since vanished and left only its footprint in the road. A tall, dim hole in the old brick wall on the north of the open area was identified as JERUSALEM PASSAGE by a neat, tin sign. I brought the phone up to my face and took a quick look at the video capture.

The figure was difficult to see, not because of the low quality of the video but because it wasn't entirely present in the normal realm. It was also black and white where everything else was color and very vague around the edges. But there wasn't any doubt that the eerie thing was following me. I wasn't sure if anyone aside from myself could see it and I wondered what it would do once I entered the narrow confines of the walkway ahead. I didn't want to turn and confront it just yet. This was far too open and public a place for that to be wise if the thing wasn't corporeal.

Tense with anticipation, I entered Jerusalem Passage. But even turning back when I came to an unlighted corner, I saw and felt nothing behind me. I walked on, uphill through the twisted route. Occasional slashes of light came down through breaks between the overhanging roofs, spotlighting the low-ceilinged shops and tiny cafés tucked into the buildings along the narrow route.

Just at the bottom of a flight of stone steps, I found the address I was looking for. A bronze bellpull on a chain hung from a bracket beside the small, dark green door, which was adorned with a complementary knocker in the shape of a swan. The light was dim enough that looking round for trouble wouldn't seem strange, so I did. Still no sign of the glittering thing.

I used the knocker on the tarnished bronze plate attached to the door. Something rustled on the other side and the upper part of a phantom face pushed through the surface. It was unthreatening to me, just taking a look, and I took it for some kind of ghost-powered alarm or majordomo. Then it sank back, leaving a tiny ripple on the door's lingering Grey surface.

Clanking and scraping sounds came from inside, and in a moment, the door creaked open. I had to stoop to see into the low, dark opening. An odor like old gym socks and unwashed dishes wafted out. I clamped my teeth over an urge to gag and tried to smile.

A thin man with his back and shoulders permanently bent into a crouch peered out at me. His face was unlined, yet he seemed old, and the energy colors around him were scarlet and muddy blue-green.

"Whatcher want?" he demanded, his voice like the shrieking of unoiled iron hinges.

"I'm looking for John Purcell."

"Master Purcell's gone out." He pronounced the name "PURSE-el."

"When will he be back?"

"Don't know."

"Then, when did he leave?"

"What business is it of yourn?" he snapped, narrowing his eyes and showing sharp, yellow teeth.

"I have some business with Mr. Purcell on behalf of a friend in the US."

"We're not in trade with colonials," he declared, and moved to slam the door.

I ducked and put my shoulder into the opening, levering my weight against the carved planks and feeling the alarm-ghost imprisoned in the wood writhe away from the contact. The crooked man on the other side pushed back with considerable strength, but I dug in and shoved, forcing my body through the gap and bulling my way inside. The thin man plunged against my absence, unable to correct his drive to close the door, and ended up slamming it shut behind me. The bolts and latches clanked into place, locking me in the room with him.

The building must have dated from a time when anyone my height was a giant, and I could feel cobwebs from the ceiling snatching at my hair. The room was dark as the inside of Jonah's whale. But I had no time to study it before the man leapt at me, snarling.

TWENTY

"I'll devour you, witch!" the twisted man shrieked.

I had no idea what he was, but I wasn't stopping to ask. He sprang forward, his hands extended into black hooked talons. His eyes had gone huge and luminously pale, and the breath that gusted from his widened, sharklike mouth stank of rotting fish. He had way too many teeth and they wanted to meet in my flesh.

I didn't want him getting those claws or teeth into my hands or face. I sidled quickly and put my left shoulder against the wall, bracing while I drew up my right leg and kicked out sideways at his chest level. My foot met the triangular delta of his pecs with a wet thump and he spat sticky ivory phlegm as his breath was jarred from his lungs. His arms flew forward and those ebony claws pierced the denim of my pants legs, nicking the flesh below as they dragged back down toward my ankle.

The—whatever he was—collapsed backward, flipping onto his back and then up again, hissing. He whirled, his hands outflung, trying to flay me as he spun closer, herding me into a corner.

It was hard to see the material obstacles in the dim room, so I dropped out of the normal and threw myself down, rolling forward through the mist and light of the Grey. The room was still there and still cluttered, but at least I could see it. And the thing pursuing me.

Grey walls are thin, but they're solid enough for me when I'm deep in that world. I planted my foot against the nearest one as I ran toward it and took two long, driving steps up the wall, putting myself over the monster's head. I flipped and dropped back down behind him as gravity grabbed hold, landing on my feet. The misty floor bounced and groaned as I hit it. I pulled back to normal.

The creature turned, gaping, and I punched my left elbow into one of his staring fog-lamp eyes. He fell back again, but this time he rolled onto his belly and tried to squirm away. I dove on him, pinning his wriggling, slimy body to the ground facedown. I snatched for his flailing arms and yanked them behind him, feeling one pop from the shoulder socket. He gave a gurgling scream and thrashed before going limp under me.

I didn't trust him, so I didn't move off, in spite of the smell that came from him. "Where is John Purcell?" I demanded, pulling on his arms a little more.

He yowled, "Don't know!"

"Did you kill him, drive him away?"

"No! Master Purcell left me. He gone away and not come back," the creature panted. I could see the hint of gill slits under his jaw.

"How long ago?" I asked, letting the pressure on his arms ease.

The creature sighed in relief. "I don't know. Without the tide I can't tell."

"You're a river creature, then? From the Thames?"

"Yeah. Master Purcell caught me and kept me for his slave," he spat. "He paid a witch to give me this physog."

I caught myself frowning at the term. "Physog?"

"Face! She made me look like one of you, damn her."

I thought about that a moment. It had the pathetic ring of truth in anger. "What does Purcell call you?" I demanded, putting a little pressure on him through the Grey.

The thing fought against telling me, and I pushed harder on the magical compunction to answer until he made a bubbling sound and muttered, "Jakob."

"All right, Jakob. If I let you up, will you swear not to attack me again?"

"I protect my master and what's his."

"I'm not looking for your master to do him harm. We have a friend in common who's worried about him."

Jakob wiggled, testing my hold, but I didn't let go and he did himself pain wrenching at my grip on his arms. He gave up and flopped limp against the floor. "I swear. I won't attack you . . . this time."

I didn't let on that I'd noticed the situational clause of his promise. I'd just have to stay out of this thing's way if there was a next meeting—I had the strong impression he held grudges and didn't like being beaten.

I let go and moved off him, getting distance between myself and the creepy aquatic creature.

He rolled onto his back as I backed up to a chair and sat to watch him. One eye was shut and swollen purple, misshaping his face even as he morphed back to the seeming of human. He cupped one hand over the injured eye and glanced at me from the good one, showing his needle teeth as they slithered back into his human mouth. Looking at him in the Grey, there was nothing human about the mutant froglike monstrosity with its shark maw and spine-clawed, webbed hands. I preferred to look at it in a more normal plane—which also held the smell a bit at bay.

He crouched on the floor with his knees drawn up and his chin resting on them. His arms circled loosely around his shins, the one a little lower than the other due to the dislocated shoulder. He glowered at me.

"Who sent you for Master Purcell?"

"An old friend whose business he tends."

Jakob sniffed. "That's nothing."

"And that's all you need to know. I need to know what's become of Purcell and the business he was taking care of."

The creature shrugged. "Some of them blood drinkers came in the night—late, as the river sang of the rising tide—and took him."

"How long ago?"

"I can't count your time—s'meaningless."

Before I tried again, I considered: He was a creature from the tidal river. Sunrise and sunset meant little to him. But tides and moon phases would.

"How many high tides since Purcell was taken?"

He almost smiled. "Thirty-seven."

Unless the Thames was a freak of nature, it had two high and two low tides per day. . . . So Purcell had been missing for eighteen and a half days, give or take a bit. Financial investments and power rarely fall apart from a mere fortnight's absence, so someone had done something beyond just grabbing Edward's British comptroller. "Blood drinkers" Jakob had called them, so vampires were responsible; and since I'd rarely heard of the sanguinary brotherhood cooperating with humans willingly, it looked increasingly like the vampires of Clerkenwell had moved against Edward personally. "At whose instigation and why?" would be the next questions to answer, but that was going to be a lot tougher without tipping Edward's hand.

If it wasn't tipped already. There was still the matter of someone or something following me.

"Who sent them?" I asked, knowing vampires rarely acted on their own unless they were planning a coup, and even then they tended to gather cronies and work as a pack. I hoped Jakob would be able to tell me who was behind Edward's problem so I could get back to worrying about my own.

"I dunno! Their king or queen, the little one—or whatever they call it, I s'pose."

"Did the vampires take anything besides Purcell?" I asked.

"Papers." Jakob flung his good arm toward a doorway behind him. "From the table in there."

"What sort of papers?"

He giggled. "No idea. I can't read your scratchings."

"So you never did any paperwork for him, didn't carry any of those things to anyone else?"

Jakob nodded. "I've done, but only to fetch and carry and pay."

"To whom recently?"

He giggled again; it sounded like bubbles in an aquarium. "Y'think I know, or could say? One small-eyed, ugly face is very like another. Only the smell of your blood tells you apart." He leaned forward, showing his teeth again. "Can you smell living blood? Would y'know the scent of one or another of you if I told you? The blood drinkers, they smell of their meals and their death. And you, you smell of . . ." He took a deep breath through slitted nostrils. Then he pulled a face. "You smell . . . of water and gun smoke, death in steel, blood . . . and too much magic." Jakob scooted backward. "I don't care for your stink."

"I could do without yours, too, frog-boy."

He flashed his teeth but said nothing. A lot of magical bindings cease at death, but Purcell had been dead to begin with, so I wasn't sure how the magic would hold up if Purcell was dead in a more permanent way. Would Jakob keep on thinking he had a master long after Purcell was nothing but an empty coffin and a forgotten name? I wasn't sure.

I changed tack. "May I see the desk?"

Jakob shrugged. "Can't do more harm."

I took that for sufficient invitation and stood up to cross into the far room. Jakob took a desultory swipe at me as I passed and I kicked at him with equal interest.

The room must have started as a dining room. The tall narrow windows peered out at the next building with only the thinnest view of the sky above, but light still managed to find its way down the gap between the buildings and lend a wan illumination to the place. It was a clever security system for a vampire in its way, the daylight being a natural barrier to others and ensuring that the owner would always be awake when the room was habitable. Purcell had clearly not been having any dinner parties; the room was strewn with detritus, ripped paper, upended boxes and furniture, torn curtains, and general upheaval—and not all of it was recent. The table that must have served as a desk had been toppled onto one side, upsetting an old-fashioned ink bottle so it had stained the thick old Oriental rug below. A small pile of recent correspondence was neatly stacked on the one remaining intact chair—Jakob's concession to duty—but other than that, there wasn't much chance of finding anything useful in the heap.

I picked up the letters and shuffled through them. One was from TPM in Seattle; several others appeared to be advertising, or regular bills. I tore open the TPM letter, but it was only Edward asking after Purcell and what was going on with some import duty. There was a related note from Her Majesty's Revenue and Customs requesting payment of overdue duties on the import of half a dozen Greek amphorae, and another note about rents in someplace called Bishop's Stortford. Useless. I put the envelopes back on the chair and returned to the main room, where Jakob glowered at me but did nothing as I wandered around and took a look at the rest of the tall, shallow house.

In the basement were seventeenth-century kitchens, long abandoned, and a storage room that had been made over into Purcell's resting place far from the sun and difficult to storm. A wrecked safe stood ajar next to an ornate copper coffin and a massive double wardrobe filled with fashionable and expensive business clothes from several eras. The upper rooms were bedrooms and a tiny Victorian bathroom with an only slightly newer toilet and a massive claw-footed tub that appeared to be Jakob's sleeping place. A delicate French commode cabinet, wedged between the utilities, was filled with waterlogged trinkets and bits of jewelry. The attic was a wonderland of antiques and trunks filled with ancient odd and ends. My collector's sensibilities were overwhelmed, but judging by the dust, nothing had been disturbed in ages. I took nothing and put things back into their respective places, turning away to find Jakob silently watching me with his one good fog-lamp eye.

TWENTY-ONE

I looked back at Jakob with a bland face but keeping very still, just in case he was poised to leap at me again. "Nothing to say what's become of Purcell," I said, feeling the need to explain my snooping.

"Course not."

"Why do you think he was taken?"

Jakob made a face. "I don't know an' I don't care."

"I suppose you wouldn't be upset if he were dead."

He snorted. "I wouldn't care were he gone forever, though would he were floating in the river where I might find him and eat his heart—if he has one."

"Bloodthirsty little monster, aren't you?"

He smiled and bowed his head. "Are y'done now? There's naught else to see and naught to tell."

"I have one question. What was the last thing you did for your master? What job? Where did it take you?"

He made a coughing noise and scrambled down the narrow staircase ahead of me. "I carried a letter to a place what smelled of old things and sanctified theft. A big white shop with pots in the window and there was a black stone creature over the door—half a woman with a lion's head. She don't like me."

"I can't imagine why."

Jakob snorted again and led me down until we were back in the original sitting room I'd first entered. He scrambled to the door and held it open for me, stooped and inhuman now that I could better see him.

"Now go on your way. I've done with you."

I took the hint and left. I held my shudders until I was out in Jerusalem Passage again where the sunlight had slipped to an obtuse angle and long shadows had moved into the corners and overhangs. I looked around—more in reaction to Jakob than anything else—and started back toward St. John's Lane.

Traffic was much thicker and I realized I'd been in Purcell's house long enough for rush hour to overtake me. The clerk in the news-agent's had mentioned an Underground station nearby, and I paused near the priory gate to look at the system diagram on the back of my map book.

Farringdon. Right. I started off down St. John's Lane, thinking I would cross at Albion Place. But somehow I didn't find it.

The slanting light of afternoon played tricks on me in the Grey, and I turned onto a street much narrower than I'd expected. I seemed to be walking forever without finding any other large lane or roadway that crossed the street I was on. I turned south onto an even smaller lane, sure I'd become entirely turned around but would see a larger street soon if I kept going—I was still in the City of London and, as the driver had said, it was only one square mile. As I turned, the worlds quaked and the road jarred under my feet in a way I hadn't felt in nearly two years. Thick silver fog pressed close and receded to take misty shapes.

It reminded me so much of my first encounters with the Grey after I'd died for those two fateful minutes that I was disoriented and a bolt of unaccustomed fear shot through me. I stopped and looked around, trying to get my bearings for where or when in the Grey I was, slow-ing the racing of my heart and telling myself this was not the first time. There wasn't a monster waiting to snap me up in its grinding jaws or a vampire with an agenda waiting to plunge a knot of Grey into my chest and give me a "gift" I never wanted. Not this time.

The path ahead was very narrow—just about wide enough for two people to walk abreast, but no more—and the buildings loomed over the street in a drunken, tilted fashion. Some of them were brick and stone and others were faced with plaster over wood or something much rougher. The smell of horse droppings and garbage filled the air, and I could hear a chattering of distant voices coming from several directions.

I'd "slipped"—inadvertently stepped sideways through space and time to emerge someplace I had no control over because the Grey had wanted me so badly. I'd learned to control that slippage long ago, so I wondered why it was happening now. The narrow alley gave no clue.

I crept forward, noticing that my feet were just a little above the ground. I wasn't entirely in the visible plane of time but physically in another with a higher street level while I could only see this one. I moved down the alley, which opened a little into a small courtyard for about half a block. The court was lined with narrow, ramshackle houses on one side and a stable yard on the other—which explained the odor. Twilight already held sway in this slice of the past, and I could see a candlelit window at the end of the alley with the preternatural clarity of something magical afoot. It was so blatant that I had to assume something or someone wanted me to see whatever unearthly thing had happened by its long-ago light. I sighed and shuffled across the road I couldn't see to the tiny house on the south end of the darkened alley.

I looked in through the window and saw a young man and an older one sitting at a worktable in an old kitchen. Both the men were bearded and had dark hair that flowed from under close-fitting caps and hung over their collars. They wore robes of some kind that looked like daily clothes, not costumes or ceremonial vestments. An iron pot steamed on a hook over the fire in an open hearth. A third man slumped in a shadowy corner farther from the fire, looking either deeply asleep or dead drunk. A clutter of bottles sat on the table in front of him, so I was betting on the latter.

The oldest man put a slab of marble on the table between himself and the younger man, pushing aside a collection of bowls and bottles and what looked like surgical instruments. He stood up and fetched a ladleful of whatever was bubbling in the pot and poured it slowly onto the marble so it steamed off the cool stone.

"Quick, work it together," he ordered the younger man. "Don't let it run off the stone."

The younger man plunged his hands into the steaming mess and exclaimed in pain. "Ah! It burns, Master Simeon!"

"Of course, Ezra. It's just been boiling. It will cool swiftly, but it must be worked together first." Simeon returned the ladle to the pot and sat back down, helping Ezra keep the runny glop on the marble, scraping, turning, poking, and squeezing it together until it had cooled into a soft, steaming lump the color of shale.

"You must have all four elements to create life: earth and water, air and fire," the older man lectured, oblivious to the heat of the material they worked with.

"Is it not blasphemy to create life—to play at godhood?" Ezra asked, keeping his eyes on the stiffening pile of goo.

Simeon spit on the floor. "This for your blasphemy. Dabbling in magic is forbidden as it is. But this is not truly life, boy. Only a shadow that lasts a mere instant. A semblance."

Ezra scowled as he worked, not seeming satisfied with the excuse but not arguing, either. A vulpine intelligence gleamed in his eyes.

They rolled the lump into a cylinder and Simeon turned it over to Ezra. "Pinch it into form but leave openings in the chest and head."

Ezra, his hands reddened and blistered, formed the cylinder into a rough human shape about as big as his hand. He pushed his fingernails into the clay to create gaping wounds in the head and chest of the figure.

"This is the water and earth," the instructor said, watching his student work. Then he handed the young man a small knife. "Breath comes last, but for now we need the fire of life. I think a bit of ear will do."

Ezra looked startled. The older man pointed to the drunk at the end of the table. "His, you fool. Not yours."

Nervous, Ezra crept up on the sleeping man and pinched at his right ear.

"Don't shilly-shally! We must finish while the clay is hot! He shan't feel a thing—he's too gone in drink," his instructor chided. "Just nip off the lobe and have done!"

With a swift, guilty swipe, the younger man sliced off a chunk of the sleeping man's right earlobe. The drunk squalled like a branded calf. Then he shook himself, blinked, and dropped his head back onto his chest, unconscious again. Ezra scurried back with his prize, blood spattered on his hands and the sleeves of his robe.

His instructor pointed at the clay figure. "A drop or two in the head and the chest. Then your ring. And close it up quickly."

"What? My ring? Why?" Ezra objected.

His master pinched him on the arm with a vicious twist. "Do as I say! Quickly, quickly!"

Ezra did as he was bidden, squeezing the little bit of earlobe over the pits in the figurine's head and chest before wrenching the small silver ring from his pinkie and dropping it into the chest cavity. He pinched the clay closed, making the figure look as whole as possible.

"It needs a face, nincompoop," Simeon chided. "You can't breathe life into it if it hasn't got a mouth or nostrils."

Ezra shaped a rough face onto his doll, featuring an oversized nose and hollow eyes over a small slash of a mouth. The older man muttered some words and circled his finger counterclockwise over the little figure. In a moment the effigy turned brick red and a small white cloud of steam puffed from it.

"Ah, fire. Indeed. Well done," the teacher added offhand.

Ezra beamed.

Simeon looked at the little red figure. "You've made the nose big enough to breathe the whole stink of London into. Well, no matter—this shan't walk abroad for long. Now speak the words, breathe them into it."

"The . . . Name?"

"No, dunderhead!" the older man shouted, cuffing Ezra over the ear with a sharp clap of his hand. "You're the one who was so concerned about playing at God. You've far too filthy a soul to speak the Name and live. Call down a very apocalypse upon the lot of us, you would!" He pointed with the knife at something carved into the tabletop. "Those words, boy. Those. And only those! Don't get any bedamned ideas above yourself—talent or no, you're still only a bloody apprentice. Drink the wine there, then speak. And don't touch the golem with your muddy hands while you do it—you'll undo the stoking of the fire."

Ezra scowled, but he took a swig of wine from a nearby wooden cup—which made him sputter for a moment and turn a bit blue. Then he leaned forward and whispered into the little figure's face. His breath left his mouth as sparkling white vapor and wreathed around the inert little man of red clay before it seemed to be sucked into the figure's mouth and nose. Ezra leaned back, his eyes huge as he stared at the thing on the table. The golem had changed color and grown hair. Now it looked like a tiny version of the drunk at the end of the table, except this one had a complete right ear.

Master Simeon circled his finger over the homunculus again, clockwise this time, murmuring more words that froze in the air as crystalline shapes before they dissolved and spiraled down into the clay figure in a stream of blue smoke.

Ezra shuddered until he doubled over and heaved up the wine in a red mess that shattered on the packed dirt floor like thin glass. Icy mist rose off the shards while they melted in the heat of the fire and the wine soaked into the ground. The wine-red mud heaved and rippled with tiny stalagmites that fell away in a moment.

"Oh," the younger man moaned. "I don't feel well."

"That's because we used the blood of a drunkard. What the one feels the other feels." Simeon grinned like a wolf. "But as he's an accomplished souse and you're a blushing lily who barely tastes the seder wine, it's not surprising you feel wretched."

"How does it work? And when will it stop?" Ezra asked, swallowing hard.

"Your ring, boy. It is the channel. Your dear possession or your likeness joined in the clay to the blood or meat of the man knits together both your sensations in the golem. Watch."

The hand-high man on the table sat up and looked around. Simeon waved the knife in front of its face.

"What do you see, creature?"

The drunk at the other end muttered, "Knife."

Ezra drew a sharp breath, staring into the middle distance as if he, too, saw a knife where none could be.

The sorcerer poked the creature with the knife. "And what do you feel?"

Ezra yelped. The drunk whimpered in his sleep.

"Cold," said the golem.

"It—he doesn't feel pain?" Ezra stammered, rubbing his belly in the same spot where Simeon had stabbed the figurine.

"Of course not. It is not a man, only an homunculus of clay." He rose and walked to stand over the sleeping drunk, raising his eyebrows in speculation. Then he jabbed his knife point into the man's arm and jerked it away again.

Both the drunk and the student shouted in pain and alarm. Simeon eased the irritated souse back to the floor and sent him back to sleep with the soporific contents of another bottle. Then the sorcerer returned to the table and resumed his seat. "If I were to stab you, he would not notice—it's not *your* blood that ties you together, but the ring," Simeon said. "I can wield my knife against this little creature much more easily than torturing the real one—unless I wanted to. But if we removed the ring, you would feel nothing."

Ezra narrowed his eyes and looked speculative. "Without the ring I feel nothing and the golem is but a mindless slave who knows no pain. . . . We could raise an army of these things—"

Simeon gave a harsh laugh. "All the size of your fist. And they'd last no longer than an hour or the first rain. You need a great deal more material than a mere drop or two of blood to make one as large as a man that walked a week or more."

Ezra cut a glance at the drunk, his eyes gleaming.

"Do not think you can divide him up like a beeve at the market," the older man snapped. "You need the man living, for the image to live. Dead men power nothing, nor do they speak. You must be content with this."

"Surely, we can do better. . . . I can think of a way, I'm certain. . . ."

The worlds shuddered again and the light in the window faded as I fell through chilly layers of time.

TWENTY-TWO

Crashing out of the temporacline, I skidded into a small courtyard in the normal world, where the sun hadn't begun to set. I stumbled against a brick wall and into a short passageway to a street where, back in the sunshine of the normal, I stopped to catch my breath. A sign on the wall beside me read WHITE HORSE ALLEY on one corner and COWCROSS on the other. I remembered passing Cowcross. . . .

I looked right and left and glimpsed the grand entrance to Smithfield Market down to my left. The road nearby must have been St. John Street before it split and made St. John Lane by the priory gate. So the Underground station would be to my right and up Cowcross, according to my map. But there was no White Horse Alley on the map and the sign on the wall nearby seemed more of a historical marker than an active street sign. I suspected that White Horse Alley had been gone for a long time.

I walked on to Farringdon Underground Station and spent a while figuring out where in the layers of the station's platforms I needed to go to catch the right train going the right way. Having lived all my life on the West Coast of the United States where subways are a rarity, wrapping my brain around the overlapping complexities of the London Underground took a bit of faith and hope—two things I'm not that good with. I eventually sussed out that I needed to take a Circle line train towards Aldgate, which would go east for a while before it turned and went west closer to the Thames with a stop at Temple Underground—right across the street from my hotel. Confusing if you tried to reason it out, but plain enough if you just trusted the map.

As I stood studying the map and figuring out the fare, floods of commuters bustled in and out of the station while a public address system reminded them about long-distance trains to outlying parts of England. They weren't as pushy as Seattle commuters, but they were in just as much of a hurry. They paid me very little heed—almost like ghosts but much heavier when they stepped on my feet—swimming in a human tide as slick and rapid as salmon looking to spawn with the occasional "sorry" or "'scuse me" tossed into the air as they passed. I joined the swarm and went down to the Circle line platform.

The platform ceiling was a brick vault held up by painted iron columns, and even modern lighting left the ends a bit gloomy. So I wasn't surprised to see ghosts and squiggles of Grey energy wandering loose over the sizzling yellow lines of the electrified rails. Down at the far end a blur of white sent off a broken-mirror glitter. My mysterious shadow was here, too, and sick of creepy enigmas for one day, I fixed my gaze on it and strode down the length of the platform to catch up to whatever was making that freakish gleam.

As the station wall drew nearer, I could see only one source the gleam could have come from: a man, seated on the floor in the farthest corner. He wore old-fashioned trousers that had once been white under a vestlike thing and a long coat both made of some kind charcoal gray material that looked a bit like ratty crushed velvet. The light show was his aura, which, up close, looked like a wavering heat mirage. As I got within talking distance, he pushed back into the shadows a bit more—they seemed to ripple and close partway around him like a cloak—and kept his head down. Shoulder-length filthy blond hair streaked with white fell forward in clumped strings, hiding his face.

"I was expectin' a boy," he said.

"What?" I snapped, cocking my head to peer at him sideways, a trick I'd learned to filter out the chaff at the cusp of the Grey. Under my gaze he seemed to flicker and fall in and out of focus, and the curiously colorless energy around him looked like a hole in the world. My concentration narrowed to him alone and the ghost chorus of London I'd started to ignore swelled in my head like a forming wave.

"I expected someone stupider," he elucidated in an odd drawl. "More balls, less brain, considering the nature of this fool's errand. I'd have thought a girl'd have better sense."

"Who the hell are you?" It was pointless to pretend he wasn't something otherworldly and therefore ignorant of what I did. Nothing else in the Grey seemed to be, so why not this strange man, too? But I had no idea who or what he was.

"Marsden. Mole catcher, as used to be, but never chasin' moles for Edward Kammerling—as are you."

"You think I work for him."

"As you've come from seein' Jakob—and not many others would bother knockin' on his master's door as wasn't Kammerling's agent—yeah, I think you do, girl. The master's gone away and them as took 'im wouldn't have much cause to return for his menial wi'out laying that gruesome creature in a hot, dry grave. Jakob is still cursin' you for wrenchin' out 'is arm. That was a nifty trick you pulled comin' over off the wall like that."

"Yeah, everything I need to know I learned from Donald O'Connor," I sneered, instantly suspect of his flattery.

"Who?"

"Haven't you ever seen *Singin' in the Rain*? It's a movie. Gene Kelly, Debbie Reynolds, Donald O'Connor . . ."

He spat a laugh. "No," he said, and turned a little my way. "It's not the eyes, y'know. . . ."

Ineluctable fear lanced through me. I couldn't seem to breathe right and what air flowed into my lungs felt thickened with knives of frost. My head swam and my body chilled and burned by rapid turns as if with malarial fever. I eased back a step, poised to run.

He raised his head. The hair fell back and he turned his face to me—a once-beautiful, eyeless nightmare of a face. His skin was pale and powdery, stretched over exquisite bones that pressed forward as if they wanted to escape from the confining flesh. Reddened, flaccid eyelids hung over orbless sockets rimmed with ragged scars, one lid not quite closed and showing a hint of the gouged hollow behind it. Yet I felt his stare from those empty eyes, a phantom gaze as sharp as an ice pick. I jerked back, teetering at the edge of the platform.

Marsden sprang forward and snatched my hand into his cold, rawhide-hard grip, yanking me forward to safety as a train rushed into the station. The Grey rocked and swayed for a few moments, flashing disco lights around me.

"You're bloody naive, my girl," Marsden whispered into my face on a breath that smelled of lilies and ash. "Though you've more bottle than I'd have credited—damned if you don't." He chortled and let me go. "This is my train. I'll find you tomorrow where there aren't so many of the wrong eyes to see us."

I turned to watch him step onto the train. It was a phantom steam engine pulling a handful of old-style carriage cars, and though it looked too insubstantial to hold anything not already a wisp of smoke and memory, it lurched forward as Marsden got aboard and it started off. I jumped back from the platform edge as, with a blast of sound and wind, the normal train rushed in and displaced its ghostly predecessor.

I breathed in sharply, startled, and looked for any sign of the man, but he was gone. I waited through the next arrival just to be sure he hadn't been crushed by the multiple tons of electric subway train, but there was nothing to show he'd been there at all.

I felt a little queasy about stepping into the bright red train when it next arrived—just in case something else went Greywards in the next fifteen minutes—but I got aboard and hung on to a pole in the increasing crush of commuters all the way to Temple. I was relieved to finally step out into the fresh air and see my hotel standing there looking quite dully dignified and ordinary. The temptation to run in, repack my bags, and get the hell out of London was strong for a moment, but I backed off, went around the block, and checked for observers and tails before I finally headed inside through one of the side doors to the courtyard.

TWENTY-THREE

This had been one freakish day after a weird damned week even by my standards, and my mind was still trying to catch up to it all. The time difference had also left me a bit disoriented. I missed Quinton's easy ways and willingness to listen to my strange tales. I felt like a clinging idiot—or just a plain one—for thinking of him so often, and after the cold setdown I'd had from Cary, that was the last thing I wanted to be. I let go of my urge to page Quinton and told myself there was nothing he could say or do that would help and I didn't want him to worry about me. I'd been gone only a day, after all. What I wanted most after his sympathetic ear was a meal and a nap before I tried to make sense of the puzzles I'd been handed in Clerkenwell, but I thought I'd have to settle for just one or the other.

After I'd changed clothes and eaten, I returned to my room to make notes and call Bryson Goodall, who was acting as my contact to Edward for this trip. It would be dark here in a little while, but it was still daylight business hours back in Seattle, I thought.

Goodall answered his phone on the second ring. "Goodall. Go ahead."

"Mr. Goodall, Harper Blaine."

"How's England?"

"Mixed. I arrived at the hotel about six hours ago. Since then I've tried to contact Purcell, but he was abducted about eighteen days ago. Looks like some faction within the local branch of the fraternal order of bloodsuckers, but I don't know whose yet or where Purcell is now. Purcell's . . . assistant is still around, but he's not much use—he's homicidal and disinclined to help, to be blunt about it. The upside is that Purcell is still walking around somewhere. Or that's my guess based on the relationship between Purcell and his flunky."

I heard his thoughtful grunt and the sound of typing. "So no idea where Purcell is or who's got him. Any leads?"

"Not specifically. His office had been stripped of papers, except a few incomplete items. I'm following up on those tomorrow, since the business offices are closed here now."

"What sort of items?"

"Some bills and letters about taxes and rents. A lead from Jakob—the minion—that might be undevelopable. It comes off as gibberish, but he's not an idiot, so I'll have to see if I can make anything of it. It's not quite dark enough here yet, but I'll be going out again soon to see about Edward's other local contacts. No idea how that will go. So far, it's looking bad."

"Anything else?"

I didn't say I'd been followed. The sinister Mr. Marsden didn't seem to be part of the vampire community—quite the opposite—and I thought it was wiser to keep his presence to myself for now.

"That's all I've got at the moment."

"I'll report. Stay in touch."

"Planning to."

We disconnected and I took my map out again to plan my evening stalking vampires. Prep can make up for a lot when you're not familiar with an area and I was going to do my best to case the vampire neighborhoods before I hit the streets again. At least this time I might not walk down an alley that had ceased to exist unless I wanted to.

Funny thing about vampires: They're arrogant. Sometimes stupid-arrogant, and I've used that to my advantage in the past. This was tricky, however. I couldn't just say I was there on Edward's behalf, since something had gone against him and I couldn't risk bringing the wrong attention to myself.

I made the rounds of pubs and clubs, looking for signs of vampires on the prowl. Drunks and romantics were easy marks, and in the right kind of club, the herd would be especially pliable. Any place that catered to the emo and the fashionably disaffected would provide a preselected pool of easy, even willing, victims, but frankly any bar or club could do the same once the hour was late enough.

Clerkenwell hosted a lot of possibilities around Cowcross and across the road from Smithfield, as well as farther up St. John's Street, where another fairy ring of pubs and clubs had sprung up around Clerkenwell Green near the small church of St. James Clerkenwell. The rowdy workingmen's establishments were unlikely to be useful, and I quickly learned to recognize them from their traditional signs and loquacious crowds spilling onto the street. The more avant-garde and exclusive places with quiet frontages proved better stalking grounds.

As I poked about, I began to discern a pattern of local investment and caching that was interesting but not entirely clear. Several of the buildings that housed pubs heavily favored by vampires appeared to be in office blocks that were otherwise empty but very well-maintained. One of the pubs was located near the only gas station—petrol station, as the sign read—in the area. It also had a small, locked yard nearby where cars, motorcycles, scooters, and bicycles were stored. Remembering what my limo driver had said about the difficulty of negotiating traffic on anything bigger than a bike, this seemed to be a storage yard for a transportation pool. It looked like the vampires of Clerkenwell had collectivized a bit. Whether they could afford it as individuals or not, in such a close-packed environment owning a private car would be comment-worthy, and vampires don't like to draw comment. London's vampires were being discreet and careful. Centuries do that for you, I supposed.

I found a pale, pale woman in a club called Danse Noir. I'd never seen a vampire who looked so much like one—more than most—but I knew what she was by the gruesome red and black of her energy corona and the odor of things rotten and painfully dead. Her face was long and gaunt. Her skin was translucent, almost pearly, with the palest of blue lines suggesting veins and cold vessels in a vague reticulated pattern below. Her long hair was naturally colorless, a dead, icy shade of white that had been streaked with wide swaths of artificial black gleaming like an oil slick. I glanced at her eyes, not wanting to be caught in her stare, and found them a strange, flat brown. The color was like my own, but lifeless as paint. Then I realized they were contact lenses, dry from a lack of tears but seeming to gleam from some inner light the color of hellfire.

I started backing away, some instinct urging me to flee, though I'd backed away from only one vampire in my life. Then she stood up and lunged, grabbing my wrists and pulling me onto the bar stool beside her.

"No," she whispered. "Can't have you causing a scene. I'd like to stay a while longer. So you stay, too." Her fingernails bit into my skin like claws.

"I'll stay if you let go of my hands."

She looked surprised. "But if I hold on, you can't leave. Can you?"

I smirked at her—I had tried to smile but the still-panicking part of myself had twisted it a bit—and shifted aside through a cold ripple of temporaclines, wrenching my hands from her grasp as I slipped.

She twitched in surprise but didn't try for my hands again. "That's a wicked trick." Her voice was low and a little sibilant, with broad vowels. "You must be the American creature there's been so much talk of."

"Who's talking about me?" I asked.

"Can't you guess? I'd heard you were clever."

"I prefer not to make wild suppositions," I replied, still feeling a ridiculous urge to get away. She reminded me a bit of Wygan, and the fear and disgust that particular vampire engendered in me was welling up in the back of my mind as I sat next to this one.

"Oh, but I don't want to *tell* you. What fun would that be? It's so much more delightful to feel you fret. Let's play a game."

"No."

She snatched my hand again and twisted my wrist. "You'll be sorry if you don't," she hissed. "She won't like it. She wants it to be a surprise, but I think it's much more fun to build the fear a bit first. I'll be doing you a favor if I tell you."

"I don't know what you're talking about," I said, keeping my voice steady with effort. Was she schizophrenic and referring to herself or to some other "she"? I didn't know if vampires could be insane, since the human value for sanity wasn't applicable to them, being human only in their outer shape and pure monster at the core.

"Of course you don't. Not yet. And she won't know it was me that stopped her from wrecking the Pharaohn's plans. Oh, this will be fun! So much fun!" She was almost wiggling with excitement at whatever delight she anticipated. "Here's a clue: The deacon of Christ Church wrote her name up and down and side to side."

It meant nothing to me. I liked mysteries, but that sort of riddle had never been my fascination. I didn't know where to start with it.

"No?" the vampire said, disappointed. "Oh, here's another, then: She isn't small so much as little."

That was no better, but a feeling of dread was building in my guts as if some part of my brain had figured it out and wasn't telling the rest. She wanted me to guess something that would terrify. Toying with me brought a smile to her wide-cut mouth that made me queasy by its almost sexual excitement.

She chuckled and it rolled over me like the first wave of an Arctic storm. "Now you're thinking and you're scared. I like that. That's the difference between terror and horror."

She leaned very close and I could smell her breath of dust and carrion. "Terror is the instinct that tells you to run, dear God, run," she murmured. "Run for your life. But it just makes you into meat. Predators take the ones who run. Horror is the mind-thing, the worm of knowledge you can't stop turning over no matter how awful it is. It grows in your mind and destroys you by your own intelligence. That's why humans are the best prey. That is the thing that will drive you to despair if I tell you Mr. Dodgson's little heroine does not intend to let you go."

My heart lurched and stuttered in my chest. I wasn't a student of British literature and I had never been crazy for fantasy books or fairy tales, but even I knew the Reverend Mr. Dodgson had been Lewis Carroll. Alice Liddell had been the model for his "little heroine." I knew—had known—an Alice Liddell who'd looked just like the grown-up version of the photo by Dodgson in the front of *The Annotated Alice*. I'd seen it in a hundred bookstores. Not possible, I thought. She's just trying to scare me, though I don't know why—how—she'd know to pick that.

The Alice I'd known had been an ambitious vampire and tried to use me to break Edward's power and take control of Seattle herself. She'd interfered when a contingent of vampires and I, along with Mara Danziger and Quinton, had dismantled a dangerous magical artifact and accidentally set fire to a building. She'd spied on me for Wygan. Then she'd forced me into a magical binding that stopped me from helping Edward against her so she could grab the artifact for herself. In the struggle, I'd finally given in to the Grey and survived, sealing my fate as a Greywalker. But Alice had been staked to the floor of the burning building and left behind when the rest of us barely escaped alive.

It's not possible, I repeated to myself, but I had the awful feeling it might be. She could not have survived. But we'd never seen a body. And if anyone might hate Edward enough to come to England and ruin him, it was Alice—if she wasn't permanently dead. Alice had been good at grudges, good at hate. If she'd escaped from the flames of the doomed building, she would hate me with red passion and black spite.

I stood up slowly and stepped away, keeping my eyes on the pale monstrosity on the bar stool. She glanced over her shoulder toward a door at the back. Then she returned her gaze to mine. She smiled so wide her fangs seemed to grow over her lip—more like the venomous hooks of a viper than the usual vampire's. Behind her dull contact lenses, her eyes flared with orange fire.

I had to look. I raised my gaze over her shoulder and saw Alice stepping through the rear doorway. My lungs seized and I thought my heart had stopped.

Alice had changed; in the crowd and at such a distance, details were lost, but it was her. She was in the company of two men wrapped in the fire and darkness of her aura. But they couldn't be men. They were something magical, though in the mess of swirling energies between us, I couldn't tell what.

I backed to the front door, unable to keep the fear from rising in my chest like smoke that choked my lungs and made my head ring. Alice and her companions didn't see me, but the pale horror in front of me did and she laughed with sickening joy.

Outside in the street, I could still hear the white vampiress laughing, and the sound raked my spine and made me shudder. I steeled myself against it, but in the end, I ran. I dashed across Clerkenwell Green and down to the Tube station. I bolted away—anywhere away from that taunting laugh. Away from the impossible vision of Alice walking through the door.

TWENTY-FOUR

O nce again, bad dreams about Will roused me from sleep several times but they were amorphous things that couldn't keep my sleep-addled self up for long. Considering the state of my mind when I'd returned to my hotel, it wasn't surprising my sleep was disturbed. In the light of day, I told myself it was impossible for Alice to be walking around—she'd been burned to cinders—but I could not pretend I hadn't seen her, and the enraptured laughter of the vampire in the club at my horror drove a nail through the heart of any hope that it wasn't true.

How? Why? What was she doing? Was she responsible for what was happening or was it a coincidence? The questions chased each other through my mind in a debilitating circle until I forced them aside. Alice wasn't the solution to Edward's questions, only a new facet to the problem. Even if she was causing the problem, she wasn't doing it alone. I crawled out of bed to work out until my brain relinquished the useless panic and let me concentrate on other angles. I put my mind to the scanty information I'd gathered at Purcell's and turned it over and over, looking for patterns, for leads and clues. When I picked them out, I concentrated on seeing where they led, not worrying about a dead vampire.

The hotel's concierge was very helpful when it came to finding the right places to ask questions about the import duties and real estate issues I'd glimpsed at John Purcell's.

The rents turned out to be a group of terraced houses in the suburb of Bishop's Stortford that had been, as the agent said when I found him in his office, in the Purcell family for a donkey's age. In fact, he couldn't find a record of the land ever having belonged to anyone else. The same was true for the narrow house in Jerusalem Passage—land and building had been the property of a Purcell since the beginning of record keeping.

"Pro'ly back to the Romans," the estate agent joked. It wasn't impossible that it had been the same Purcell then, too, though it was unlikely. Vampires would have stood out a bit more back when the population was smaller. And whoever heard of a Roman named Purcell? So the land was Purcell's own little nest egg. His kidnappers wouldn't have cared about it if they were only interested in making trouble for Edward. They'd done nothing about his properties, which argued that Purcell's value to them was strictly as a lever against Edward.

The estate agent started rambling off on some tangent about what a lovely little town it was and he could find me another terrace or a semidetached in the area if I were interested. . . . I wasn't and had to shut him down rather harshly just to get out of his office. Clinging like a remora appeared to be a trait common to real estate agents on both sides of the Atlantic.

Having wasted a few hours with the real estate question, I then went after the remaining lead: Her Majesty's Revenue and Customs. I'd been advised that it would be easier to telephone than appear in person. Finding the correct office for the question you needed answered could be a right trial, the concierge had said. I paused for lunch in a prefab café sort of place called Pret before returning to my hotel to make the phone call at Edward's expense.

It was the sort of phone call that causes some people to go to the government bureau in question with fully automatic weapons and a duffel bag full of ammunition. I lost track of how many offices I was bounced through before anyone was willing to talk to me at all, and the person I got was, just like an IRS agent in the US, a recent immigrant whose English was heavily colored with an accent.

"Look," I said to the woman, who finally agreed to help, "we want to pay the duty, but I need to find out what my client is being billed for."

She sighed. "Importation of six amphorae from Greece. Not considered historically significant pieces. It's on your letter."

"Yeah, a letter that's been destroyed. When and where were these amphorae delivered? Because we don't have them." I certainly hadn't seen anything like that at Purcell's home.

"That might be because you're over a year delinquent in paying the duty."

"That was before my time, so fill me in. When were they delivered and to where?"

She heaved another sigh and I could hear her typing and shuffling papers before she answered. "On twelfth July 2007, the six amphorae were held in the Excise and Customs warehouse in the Docklands and shipped on later that week. As they weren't bonded goods, they weren't held pending duty. Your client was billed but never paid. I've notes indicating he challenged the billing several times—claimed they were not his goods. These challenges are still in the process of resolution. Although . . . this past April he agreed to pay, but he has not yet."

"Where were the amphorae moved to? You must have a record of who picked them up, at least."

"Oh, yes. I do have that. Sotheby's—the auction house, you know."

"Yeah. I know."

Will had told me Sotheby's moved a tremendous volume of goods from all over the world every year, so the coincidence of the amphorae being sent to the place he worked wasn't outrageous. And it wouldn't have anything to do with Will: He handled western European furniture, not Mediterranean antiquities. I did wonder why Purcell had suddenly decided to pay the duty after a year of contention. I still wasn't sure if he'd ever owed it or not.

I didn't get much more out of the woman and hung up feeling slightly trampled. A trip to Sotheby's was in order—the sooner the better—and it didn't hurt that I'd have an excuse to check in on Will. The increasing frequency of my bad dreams and my vision about him was worrying. I wanted to see for myself that he was all right, and I wanted to know if my sudden dreams of him were somehow connected to my search for my father and the truth about my own Grey past.

It took a bit of flipping back and forth in my maps to work out a route to Sotheby's on New Bond Street. It was longer than I could walk in a short time and I wanted to be there well before they closed up for the day. I'd have to take the Tube, and that seemed to mean walking to Embankment Station so I could get a train to Oxford Circus and walk on from there.

Since it was a classy business dealing in antiques and things most of us can't afford, I dressed up, but I didn't go out the front door. I was pretty certain that it had been Marsden who'd followed me the day before, but I wasn't sure that others couldn't find me now that I'd been rummaging about among Clerkenwell's vampires. I slipped out the side door again and around the block to the Strand so I could join the crowds of students at King's College next door before I exited the school on the water side.

The walk along the Embankment to the Underground station was lovely and busy enough to make losing a possible tail easy, though no one appeared to follow me. There were already plenty of students and workers heading for the trains, so I merged into the stream, just another businesswoman on the move.

The trip from Embankment to Oxford was hot and crowded, and I emerged into chaos.

Technically a circus in England is a traffic circle, but you could have thought of it as a big-top show just as well. The place was insanely busy, packed with workers, and tourists, and mothers chivvying children who had no interest in behaving, and I couldn't tell which direction I was facing. The pedestrians were a lot less polite than those I'd encountered in Farringdon Station, pushing and scurrying to get to the street crossings since most of the curbs were fenced away from the motorized traffic by chest-high iron railings. The openings in those railings were narrow, the walk signals were short, and the vehicles in the road were aggressively oblivious. I had to stop short of being shoved in front of a truck and then dash with a group of young men in bankers' suits to make it to the other side before the light changed. Then I wasn't sure where I was or which direction I was facing, and the other people on the sidewalk seemed to resent my stopping to look at my map while trying to orient myself.

People in more casual clothes stood in the middle of the sidewalks offering free newspapers from hip-high piles in plywood frames and further bottlenecking the foot traffic flow. I tried to work into the lee of one of these news pushers, but there was no lee. Rushing pedestrians, tourists, and commuters filled every space and I had to back up against a stone wall to get even a tiny relief from their pressure to keep moving at all cost.

I turned my back to the traffic circle and tried to find a street sign. The nearest building had a white placard on it that seemed to read "John Prince's Swallow." A closer look showed it was two streets: John Prince's Street to the right and Swallow Place to the left, which met as they joined Oxford Street. Regent Street was behind me, Oxford Street running past me. I looked at the map, twisted it around a few times, and finally got the gist of where I was: only three blocks from New Bond Street, straight ahead.

I walked, passing one shop after another jammed with clothes from the fashionable to the outrageous. The preoccupied commuters and the ogling sightseers were joined in their throng by shoppers weighted with bags that smacked into the legs and elbows of everyone nearby.

As soon as I turned onto New Bond, the foot traffic waned. Down a side street I saw a crowd gathering around the black-painted facade of a public house, the sidewalk and street choked impassably by their numbers. At first I thought the crowd was waiting for the pub to open, but then I noticed the glasses in hands, the clink and rattle of post-work social drinkers chattering like starlings and raising a fog of cigarette smoke.

The farther I walked, the lighter all traffic became until I could see little sign of the bustle at Oxford Circus and even the pubs had disappeared. The buildings were dignified and sat right at the edge of the wide sidewalks with no greenbelt or setbacks, putting up their predominately white fronts in an aloof row. The numbering system was not the orderly odds-on-one-side, evens-on-the-other of most US cities, and as I walked south I kept glancing across the street to be sure I hadn't passed the building I sought on the wrong side.

A blue banner hanging over the sidewalk let me know when I'd found my destination. I stopped in front of the wide cream-colored building and looked it over. Two arch-topped plate glass windows flanked an arch-and-column doorway. In one window there was a photo display of Chinese ceramics and a sign giving information on their auction date. The other window showcased an upcoming auction of Asian metalware. Over the door a basalt bust of Sekhmet, an Egyptian goddess of something, looked out at the street from her small shelf. The figure radiated spokes of white and red light.

Then it moved.

TWENTY-FIVE

I n the Grey Sekhmet turned her lion head and stared at me. "What are you?"

For a moment I just blinked at her. She was a lion-headed woman—half a woman, really, since the statue was only a bust—and the window below her had in it what someone uneducated might well refer to as "pots." Sotheby's was the last place Jakob had ever run an errand for Purcell. Sotheby's, where the amphorae that Purcell said weren't his had been delivered and where my ex-boyfriend worked when he wasn't turning up tortured and murdered in my sleep.

A shape of light moved away from the carved black stone bust above the doorway and trickled to the pavement beside me, manifesting as the misty image of the goddess—a thin, bronze-skinned woman with the head of a lioness and a false mane created by her heavy, braided wig. She wore a thin dress of crimson linen that left her small breasts bare. Her hands were slim and graceful, but the fingernails were black claws. A sword and a knife were loosely belted at her hips. Gold bracelets and bands decorated her muscled arms and she had a bow slung on her back. A golden cobra sat on her head, holding up a disk that was as red as the sun seen through clouds of battle smoke. The cobra moved restlessly side to side, making the small sun sizzle.

Sekhmet looked me over with kohl-darkened eyes in her leonine face and licked her chops. "I have seen something like you before. . . ." she said. "Speak up: What are you?" she commanded. Her voice was an angry growl in my head, without substance in the air. "I may have to kill you."

"You'd be the second in as many days to try," I replied. She spooked me, but I wasn't going to let her know that. Lionesses are the ones that do the killing, after all, and last night I'd done all the running from predators I intended to do for a while.

She turned her head a little and looked at me from the corner of her eyes. "Have you an enemy? Are you a hunter that your prey turned upon? Speak!"

"I guess I'm a sort of hunter," I replied, glancing at the few people passing on the street. They pretended not to notice my conversation apparently with myself, but hurried on. Maybe they thought I was using a cell phone with one of those ear widgets. "I look for things, for people, for answers."

"And you come to my house on what business?"

"Your house?"

She sniffed in disdain. "They are soft and care not for bloodshed and war—they prefer gold as their weapon and baubles as their love—but they have taken me as their own for these past years when others had forgotten me. I do not let them suffer if it is in my power to stop it. You touch darkness and death. I shall not let you spread them here. What brings you? And do not prevaricate. My patience thins."

"A man—a sort of frog-man—named Jakob came here a few weeks ago on an errand. I want to know what it was."

"The river spawn. He brought a charmed letter for one of my people within. He had a stink to him I did not care for. I made him leave it and go."

"He's the servant of a vampire."

"Ah! The asetem-ankh-astet."

"The what?" I asked, wincing internally at having interrupted a goddess—they tend to be cranky about that.

She showed her teeth but forbore from attacking me. "The tribe that are the life of Astet—the priest who died, yet lived. They are numerous here, but not like the kind of my home. Those—the true asetem—are few, and you can tell them from the common blood drinkers by their fine white skins and cobra forms. They do not feed on blood, but on the ka—the soul. Once they helped me, but now . . . even they do not honor my name! Ambitious fools! I did not think your river spawn reeked of their habits, but perhaps his own odor and that strange charm confused me. . . ." Sekhmet scowled. "I should have sent him away the first time with an arrow in his spine. He would have been better as a frog on a pike, roasting in the sun for crocodiles."

My mind was spinning and I felt a sense of doom rising in me. Some shrieking, distant voice in my mind was insisting that something horrible from the past was repeating itself, swelling out of history into the present like poison gas. The vampiress in the club—surely she was one of the asetem-ankh-astet? The description fit. It rang another bell as well: Hadn't my father described his "white worm-man" in similar terms? The thought made me queasy and I wanted to ask her about it, but I knew she wouldn't have much patience. And what about Alice? The white vampire I'd spoken with last night hadn't even liked her, so what was the connection? If the asetem were responsible for Purcell's disappearance, how was Alice connected? Or was she? She hadn't been connected to my father or she'd have taunted me with that information long ago.

I chided myself. I wasn't seeing something. I was letting myself be distracted by my fear and incredulity. I needed to stick to the most immediate question. "Jakob was here before?" I asked.

"I say it; it is so! He has been here several times in two cycles. He did not stink so badly at first, but he began to rot once he touched the wine jars. The corruption sealed in those vessels offends me even yet. What waste of blood! The asetem took them away, but the smell lingered."

"These wine jars . . . were they Greek ones? Amphorae?"

"They were the Greek style, but they never came from the clay of Greece. No Greek stores blood in jars such as those."

"There was blood in the jars? Old blood?"

"No! Corrupted with death and magic but fresh enough. I should have slaughtered them all!" And she gave a roar of fury, snatching at her blades to clang them together over her head. She whirled back to face me, menacing and enraged. "Now you say you seek these things?"

"I don't. I wanted to know what was in them. I have a bad feeling they're meant for something terrible, that they have something to do with my past and my father's, but I don't know what. And I have a friend here I'm worried about. Someone who shouldn't have had anything to do with these jars, but I'm starting to wonder. . . ."

"Who? Which of mine do you care for?"

"His name is Will."

She shook her dreadlocked mane and growled. "Describe him to me!"

"Tall, talks like me, has silver hair, but he's young—"

"Gone! He has not come here since he took the letter your Jakob creature brought."

"The charmed letter? Was for Will?" Cold clutched my chest, strangling the breath in my lungs. My dreams weren't just dreams: Will was in trouble and it was Purcell who was behind it—Edward's agent, Edward's "friend." Or the asetem who seemed to know Alice and Wygan and white worm-men who'd probably killed Christelle and driven my father to suicide.

I started to bolt, to find Will wherever he was. The goddess snatched my arm, jerking me back around. I should have been able to pull free, but I couldn't. Sekhmet sliced the palm of my left hand with the tip of her knife, releasing a fine bead of blood. She bent her head and lapped the wound, which closed again as she touched it. Then she narrowed her eyes at me.

"I taste life and death in you, hunter. You are of my charge—a warrior—but you shall have to choose your course yourself. I will not help you this time. You must first prove your worth. I charge you to choose justice. Or I shall see you at the gates of hell and Anubis shall eat your heart. Do not betray me—I am a forgotten god, but not powerless where you go."

She threw down my hand, spinning me back to face Oxford Street. "Now. Run," she commanded.

I ran, twisting back only once to look for her, but she'd returned to her plinth above the door, cold stone, black and patient. It wasn't fear of a god that made me go, or even fear of the past that chilled my bones, but fear for the living. I didn't understand how it had come about. I was here on Edward's business and it was Edward's broken empire that had been used to set this up, I had no doubt. Alice had tried to topple Edward before and it seemed she ought to be the one I found at the core, but the leads somehow came back to me and my father and whatever had happened to him. This was the cycle again, whatever it led to: The asetem had wanted something from my father, so they took Christelle. Now they may have taken Will. . . .

TWENTY-SIX

I knew the address of Will's flat but I didn't know where it was in this rabbit-warren city. The tail end of rush hour clogged the streets and I fought for every step toward Oxford Circus. I'd find a place to search my map once I was in the station's ticket lobby—I'd make one if I had to. There were eddies near the big maps on the wall that I could stand in long enough to find his street, people I could ask to direct me, poor befuddled American that I was. I'd even play the helpless female if I had to. I'm not religious but I do take the words of gods seriously these days. It's safer.

Will's flat was on Whitcomb Street, which my map showed as northwest of Trafalgar Square. Two Underground stations were nearby on a line directly from Oxford Circus and another on a different line. Of the three, I chose Piccadilly Circus, since it was only one stop away. I assumed a famous tourist site like Trafalgar Square would be a madhouse at rush hour on a sunny Friday afternoon, so I hoped I was making the right choice by avoiding it to start at the north end of Whitcomb.

I had no idea what the distance was—my maps didn't seem quite to scale sometimes, though I knew they must be. The twists and turns of London's thoroughfares and byways made every street seem longer and farther from the previous one. I ground my teeth impatiently while waiting for the train and then standing in the crush.

I shoved my way out of the train on arrival and dashed up the stairs heedless of others and raising a commotion in my wake. I didn't care. I ran on, two long blocks down Coventry to Whitcomb and south on Whitcomb. . . .

I was nearly all the way to Pall Mall, almost to Trafalgar Square after all, before I spotted the number I wanted and had to turn sharply, cutting across the street, dancing between cars and trucks as irate drivers honked at me, to dive into a gated courtyard on the other side.

The fact that it was commuter hour and I was wearing business clothes worked in my favor; a man in a business suit was just unlocking the gate as I dodged up, panting, "Lost my key."

He held the gate, smiling. "S'all right. I'm on my third—flatmates keep takin' 'em."

"Thank you," I said, catching my breath. Now I just had to shake him while I looked for Will's flat. "I just can't seem to keep track of things," I added with an inane giggle.

His smile got a little cooler. "Ah. You're American."

I nodded.

"I suppose you know the fellas up on the second floor, then?" he asked, looking a little hopeful, but of what I wasn't sure. Conversation? A date? Maybe it was just his natural expression, but I really didn't want him to take too much interest in me, since I was sneaking in. "They seem quite nice."

"You mean Will and Mikey? Oh, yeah. They're sweet! It's so nice to hear a voice from home, y'know?" I scratched my nose, then inspected my nails. "Eww! I can't believe how dirty I get here!" There's nothing like offhand insults and bad personal hygiene to make someone wish they'd never seen you. Cary used to say the easiest way to get someone to stop looking at you was to pick your nose in public. I hoped I wouldn't have to go that far.

The man coughed and picked up his briefcase before turning away. "Umm . . . yes. Gets a bit filthy during tourist season . . ."

Left on my own just inside the gate, I only needed to get up to the second floor to reach the Novaks' flat. I'd gone up one flight and along the corridor for a few feet before I remembered that the British start numbering above the ground floor. What I thought of as the second floor, they called the first. I hurried back to the stairs and up another flight. Then down the hall to number twenty-two.

There was no bell, so I pounded on the door.

The building was old but recently renovated, and the doors were thick so I didn't hear anything until the sound of the locks scraping back.

Michael Novak, shaggy flaxen hair hanging in his eyes, opened the door, saying, "Jeez, Will, can't you just use the key?" He stopped and stared at me. "Umm . . . Hi, Harper."

I knew I was mussed and out of breath but the awkward effect of my phone call from LA apparently lingered, as he tucked himself back behind the door and peeked out through a narrow opening.

"Will's not here."

"I got that, Michael. Do you know where he is? He hasn't been at Sotheby's for days." I believed Sekhmet and I'd look a fool if she'd deceived me, but I'd take the chance.

"What? No. He goes to work every day, even part-time on Saturdays."

"Not recently. I think he's in trouble. Please let me in." I held out my empty hands. "I don't mean either of you any harm. I'm just worried about Will."

"I don't know. . . ."

"Oh, come on, Michael! Call Sotheby's and ask! If I wanted to hurt him, don't you think I'd be the one who took him?"

"Will isn't gone! He's— Hey! There he is!"

I didn't look immediately but shoved my foot into the open doorway and turned my shoulder into the opening as I glanced back down the hall. But Michael didn't try to shove the door closed; he pulled it farther open and I found myself inside the flat, looking back out at Will Novak.

Tall, thin Will with his prematurely silver hair and small rimless glasses blinked at me. Then he smiled.

"Harper." Something funny about his voice . . .

I narrowed my eyes and stared at him as he stepped into the flat.

A large dark blot wrapped in bands of energy—blue, yellow, red, and green—moved where Will should have been. It moved toward the kitchen. Michael and I followed him.

"Will," Michael said. "What's going on? Harper says you haven't been going to work."

"OK," Will said.

"No, not OK," Michael objected, going through the kitchen doorway after Will—if it was Will.

"Michael, I don't think that's Will," I warned him.

He scowled at me over his shoulder and turned his back.

A sandwich sat on the counter by the sink, resting on a paper towel with the knife and makings piled beside it. Will trailed a hand along the counter edge, knocking the knife onto the floor. He walked past it.

"Will? Hello?" Michael said. "What's with you lately? Are you mad at me?"

"No."

I went into the kitchen right behind Michael, stooping to pick up the knife.

Will stopped and turned sharply around. "Harper," he said again, but the voice was worse than before. Not angry or upset, but just wrong, like the chorus of the city's Grey energy was funneling through his mouth. His eyes gleamed, both in the normal and the Grey, with a red glitter. He reached out and grabbed my arm—I was getting damned tired of that—and yanked me toward him, knocking Michael aside.

"Will!" Michael shouted, dismayed at his brother's violence. "What—?"

"It's not Will!" I shouted back as the thing occupying Will's shape dug its fingers into my arm. It opened its mouth and let out a shriek of red and black light that struck at me like a cobra.

I slammed my other fist into the Will-thing's chest, cutting off the magical scream and nicking its flesh with the knife. The thing rocked backward. Then it raised its other hand, clawed, toward my eyes, grimacing.

From behind us Michael yelled, "You're crazy! Get away from him!" He lurched forward, grabbing me around the waist and hauling backward.

I dug in my heels, reversing the kitchen knife with a flip and driving it into the hand descending toward my face. The blade cut into the flesh with a damp shushing sound. The hand kept coming. I pushed on the knife and twisted. Then I yanked sideways, cutting through the fingers of its right hand. They pattered to the floor and lay twitching there as I wrenched my other arm free.

"No!" Michael screamed, jerking me back.

We fell down in a pile between the sink and the serving island. The thing that wasn't William Novak came forward, flailing and silent, with its mouth gaping. Light in ugly colors started to pour out of its mouth, flowing toward me and Michael.

I shoved Michael backward along the slick floor and scrabbled back myself, shouting, "It's not Will! Run, Michael!"

Michael lay where I'd pushed him, staring in horror at the unbleeding, mutilated hand. A hand made of something dark and solid and definitely not human flesh.

Stuck between Michael and the not-Will thing, I took another swipe with the knife at the creature. It ignored the blade once again, stabbing a handful of light at me that jammed into my shoulder. I jumped back, right into Michael as he struggled to his feet, clutching the counter for support.

I stumbled and ducked, using the maneuver to scoop my purse up from the floor where it had fallen. Then I swung around fast and smacked the heavy leather bag into the creature's face.

It stumbled back a step.

I grabbed Michael's shoulder and hauled him all the way to his feet. "Get the hell out of here!"

Dazed, he lumbered out of the kitchen as I turned back to the monstrous thing, which was now coming forward again. My shoulder burned and I dug my fingers into the ache, not taking my eyes off the not-Will, and hooked my fingers into the energy that had lodged there like a broken blade. I yanked it out and felt it ravel away. Then the thing lurched at me.

I slashed the knife at the first thing that came toward me and saw one forearm fall away. But that didn't slow it any more than losing the fingers had. It wasn't losing blood, just substance, and it didn't seem to care. The arm on the floor writhed, though the chopped fingers had stopped wriggling and were turning a chalky brick red color.

It was some kind of golem—like the thing I'd seen in White Horse Alley but full-sized—and it would keep on coming for me so long as it held together. So I'd have to take it apart and hope the smaller pieces would die off faster. I chopped at the other arm, at the neck and face. Bits fell away. I jammed the knife into its chest and ripped a hollow in the unreal flesh. Something fluttered to the ground. I stooped and swung at the legs, taking a chunk out near one knee as I scooped up the fallen object.

The thing lurched sideways and kept coming. But it was slower. I rose, threw the knife into the wreck of its face, and whirled to bolt.

Right into Michael's chest as he stared from the hallway. I grabbed his arm and propelled him around. "Run, damn it!"

"It's—it's . . . it's not bleeding!"

"Damn right it isn't! It's a golem. It doesn't bleed! It just keeps coming until it falls down! Go!" I added, shoving him forward.

He stumbled and began running down the corridor to the stairs. I was right behind him, stuffing the stiff bit of paper I'd snatched from the kitchen floor into my pocket.

We raced down the two flights to the ground floor and burst out into the courtyard. I heard someone scream behind us and looked back to see the shambling horror that had counterfeited Will Novak pursuing us as one of the neighbors stared after it.

"It's still coming!" Michael gasped.

"And we're still running!"

But the golem wasn't the only problem.

As we dashed out onto the street, hot columns of red energy erupted along the street and the ghosts of London turned to look at us. Then they screamed.

I remembered that whatever the golem saw, the man at the other end saw, too. And that man was Will. . . . If he were under duress he'd tell whoever had him exactly what he saw. So whoever controlled the golem knew where we were right now. I forced my mind into escape mode: We'd gotten out of the flat, but we still had to lose the backup crew. Or I had to. They could have had Michael anytime, so it wasn't him they wanted—but I wasn't going to abandon Will's brother to whatever force was chasing us, and not just because dumping Michael would give them another lever to use against me. I liked Michael and I wanted both Novak brothers safe.

As we ran down the road toward the teeming bustle of Trafalgar Square, spikes of vampiric color darted from the buildings nearby and sped toward us: cat's-paws and demi-vampires—the daylight assistants and slaves to things like Edward. And they were coming after us.

"Who are those guys?" Michael panted.

"Villains," I shouted, grabbing his hand and pulling him along. I kept more than half my sight tuned to the Grey, looking for holes in their net and bolting through them, twisting through their perimeter. I hauled Michael along, not sure which way to turn as I saw another group of red flares go up among the crowds below Nelson's Column, between the fountains in the open plaza of Trafalgar Square.

I spat a curse.

"What?"

"More. In the square, around the fountains," I panted.

"How do you know?"

"I just do!"

"C'mon," he yelled, jerking me sideways.

We paralleled the square and dodged through a tribe of red buses, bumping through tourists to cross the next street, jinking into a wide alley and across another open courtyard. Steps. We leapt down them and flew across another wide avenue with a huge building—a columned horseshoe of white marble—on our left and another open space ahead.

"Where are we going?" I shouted.

"Horse Guards. St. James's Park."

"Parks aren't good! Too open!"

"Crowds, museums on the other side. Westminster Abbey, the Tube, the bridges, lots of ways out . . ."

I followed Michael's lead and we sprinted down into Horse Guards Parade, an open, paved area between the road and another big white building on the left with some kind of soldiers' memorial and the ponds of St. James's Park on the right.

A large group of ghostly horsemen cantered along the road in an orderly square while a milling crowd of tourists wandered obliviously around the green. We cut across the park, through the thick stands of trees along the southern edge. Our pursuers were falling behind. But the ghosts among the trees turned to follow us with their eyes, and those that had any will at all screamed as we passed. The vampire minions shifted to follow the sound.

"They're still coming!" I yelled, running across a bridge over a swan-dotted pond with Michael now in tow.

"Who? How?"

We dashed off the bridge, and Michael started left as I started right. The ghosts turned toward him and shouted.

I grabbed him and hauled him toward the gurgling song of the Thames. I couldn't see it, but I could feel its rolling presence in the Grey.

"It's you," I panted. "They're tracking you. You have something . . . on you. . . ."

"I've got nothing!"

"Keys, pocket change, bus tokens! Anything Will gave you in the past week!"

We dove out of the park, crossing a road with wide sidewalks and into a narrow defile of stairs.

"St. James's Tube!" Michael shouted, pointing diagonally right through the buildings beside us.

We stumbled out of the stairs and down a street. I yanked Michael to a stop near a statue of Queen Anne at the intersection, our trackers momentarily behind and blinded by the buildings.

"Empty your pockets."

Wide eyed, winded, Michael turned the pockets of his jeans inside out, letting everything fall to the pavement. In the pile was a gleaming rectangle of blue and white plastic. I kicked it with my toe.

"Get the rest. Leave that."

"But—"

"Now!"

He snatched the keys, his wallet, and change from the ground and shoved them back in his pockets, staring at me as if I'd just confirmed I was totally insane.

"C'mon!" I ordered, pulling him around the corner and into the nearest doorway. I pressed him back and we both peered out.

The local spirits stared toward the lonely bit of plastic and screeched as if in pain. A pair of red-crowned men ran down into the intersection and stopped below Anne's statue, stymied, looking around until one of them spotted the thing on the pavement. I would have sworn the statue glowered at him, though it didn't move an inch.

"Bloody hell!" he yelled.

The other one had kept on scanning the area, and he spotted our peeking faces. We were much too close—I should have pulled back farther.

"There!" he shouted, pointing.

I jerked Michael out of the doorway and plunged into the street, dodging people and cars to cross the road. We ran into the first street and down the block. Then I tugged him around the corner back toward the intersection we'd just left the tracking device on.

TWENTY-SEVEN

"We're going the wrong way!" Michael objected. "The Tube's to the right!"

"Hush!" I snapped.

I dragged him up a street, slowing the pace a little as a stream of red flares came toward us, and then turned away into the road we'd been last spotted on. I pulled Michael across the way and through a break between two buildings that left us in an alley lined with parked cars. I let our pace drop to a trot.

"What the hell . . . ?" Michael panted, jogging beside me.

"They can't track us now, so they'll head for the Underground station—it must be obvious that's where we were going. We'll find another while we still have the lead. They'll spread out soon and come looking, so we have . . . maybe ten minutes to get to something else," I explained.

"We can get a bus at Westminster Abbey," he suggested. "That'll take us to a Tube, one direction or another."

"Good. What was that thing?"

"That you made me leave on the street? My Oyster card—thanks a lot!"

"What's an Oyster card?"

"Transit card—like a MetroPass in Seattle. Bus, Tube, whatever."

I nodded and conserved my breath as we jogged on. I let Michael lead while I kept an eye out for random vampire minions who might get smart enough to head for the same place we were. I had to pull Michael aside twice to let some pass us.

"I still don't know how you can spot them," he whispered.

"Good eyes."

We caught a bus on Victoria Street that eventually dropped us at Victoria Station. The place was massive, made of stone and iron, and the last stragglers of rush hour going out were meeting the crowds coming into town for the weekend. There were plenty of ghosts, but none of them turned and shrieked in alarm at us, and the only magical things I saw were slinking by quietly, neither wanting attention nor paying any to us.

I called a halt long enough to get some fast food and to clean up from our flight before we carried on.

We both slumped over cups of tea and Cornish pasties by the long-distance train platforms.

"So . . . I mean . . . what the hell?" Michael asked, staring at his food. "I don't know what just happened. Can I go home now?"

"I think that might be a bad idea," I replied. "They know you know something's wrong and they'll come looking for you—if they aren't waiting at the flat right now."

"Why would they do that? They aren't after me!" he added, glaring at me.

I gave him back a hard look. "Because you're the guy who thinks I'm a psycho ex who just murdered your brother—that's why. And they can use that, like they used Will. I don't leave friends behind. I won't leave you with them any more than I'm going to leave Will with them. I think they know that."

Michael bowed his head again, his shaggy hair hiding his face. His shoulders heaved and I wasn't sure if he was just breathing heavily, trying to control a fit of temper or nerves, or if he was crying. After what we had just been through, he was entitled to either. I left him to it, rooting about in my pockets for the object I'd snatched from the golem.

It was a photo of me. The usual ghost-laden image, but I stared at it, barely recognizing myself with my waist-length ponytail of straight brown hair. It had been a long time since my hair had been so long. . . . I'd sliced it off to save my life in the elevator when I'd been beaten . . . to death. I felt strangled and I shuddered: The picture had been taken two years ago, a few minutes before I'd gone inside the building in the photo and upstairs to confront the man who killed me. I stared at the photo, trying to understand why it had been in the golem, in Will's kitchen in London two years later. Where had it come from? What was it doing there? Could that be Alice's connection? I was just turning that idea over when I heard Michael snuffle and blow his nose into his napkin.

I put the photo down on the table and looked up at Michael, who was swiping moisture from his face and trying to look less like he'd been crying.

I poked the photo toward him. "Is this Will's?" I asked.

He shook his head and pushed the photo away, his mouth still a bit shaky and his eyes not meeting mine. "I don't get it," he rasped, a little teary but putting his man face back on. "What was that . . . thing?"

"Can't say I'm an expert, but I'm guessing some kind of golem. A kind of magical automaton."

"I know what a golem is," he snapped. "Rabbi Loeb and the Jews of Prague and all that stuff. I do read books."

I pressed my lips together. He wasn't mad at me; he was just mad, and there wasn't any point in taking it personally. At least not yet. I put the photo back into my pocket and tried to steer the conversation in a more useful direction.

"Michael. Do you know why your brother and I broke up?"

He shook his head. "Not really. He said you guys just came from different worlds. He said you had to do things he couldn't live with. I thought he meant . . . like . . . your job was too weird for him. I still don't get that. What's so weird about what you do? You follow people, you look into records, you tap phones—"

"I don't tap phones. That's a federal crime. The rest . . . yeah, that's what I do, but . . . umm . . . that different worlds thing . . ."

"What?" he scoffed, leaning back in his flimsy seat and crossing his arms over his chest. "You saying you're an alien or something?" He snorted.

I laughed, though it wasn't my best laugh. It came out weak and shaken. "No. I'm not from outer space. I just end up working around a lot of things most people would call magic or myths. Things like that golem." The golem was creeping me out even more now that I'd seen the photo. That was a channel . . . like Ezra's ring. I tried not to go any farther in that mental direction. I'd scare Michael as much as myself if I let on what I was thinking.

Michael scowled. "You're saying you're a witch or something?"

"Not even remotely. I just see things most people don't. And they see me."

He still looked very skeptical.

I sighed. "OK, try this. For the sake of argument, say ghosts exist. Just as a supposition."

He nodded reluctantly. Most people do believe there are things they can't see—whether they call it "magic" or "God" or "quantum physics." They have some belief in an unseen force that does things they can't control.

"So, if there are ghosts and monsters and witches, isn't it possible they have problems, conflicts that need resolving?"

I waited to see if he was buying in at all. He gave another nod, a little less incredulous this time. "Okaaaay, maybe."

"I solve problems for people. That's really what my job is: finding answers. Sometimes the answers or the problems—or even the clients—just happen to be ghosts or monsters or magical weirdness.

That's what your brother meant when he said we came from different worlds. Now the worlds are colliding, and Will got caught in the middle."

"So, that . . . back there—that's your fault?"

"Yeah. I'm afraid so."

"Why!" Michael demanded. "Why would anyone do that?"

"I don't know. I only got here yesterday, but that golem's at least a few days old, maybe a week. Someone knew I'd come looking for Will, but not when. And they didn't want anyone else looking—not the cops, not you—so they made the golem. If I didn't come straight to them, I'd come to see Will and then they'd get me."

"Why would you come all the way here to see your ex-boyfriend? And why did you? And that phone call—"

"Bad dreams."

"Huh?"

"I had some awful dreams about your brother—and sometimes you, too—being in danger, hurt, or killed. I don't have dreams like that; I'm not psychic. But they freaked me out and I had to check in to be sure they were just dreams. So I called."

I couldn't bring myself to tell him how the golem was probably the channel that sent the dreams and what they meant about what must be happening to Will. It was bad enough to think someone had kidnapped him and substituted a fake Will. But why Will, the ex-boyfriend? Why not Quinton? I had to stuff down an instant's panic and desire to call and be reassured that he was all right. I had to believe he was fine, or I wouldn't be able to do anything to help Will or Michael or myself. I was sure this was about me, about my father and whatever had started twenty-two years before. How any of it connected to Edward and his problem—if he really had one—I didn't know, but I'd find out.

"But I told you everything was all right," Michael said. He looked distressed.

I nodded. "You did, but the dreams kept coming, and then I had a chance to come here on business and it seemed too good to pass up—way too good, not just a coincidence. My case had a connection to Sotheby's, so I thought I'd check on Will while I was there. But I found out he hadn't been there in a while. That didn't jibe with what you'd told me, and other information about the case tied up to Will. So I knew he was in trouble and I went to your place. . . ."

Michael frowned. "Would they have brought Will back if you hadn't come around?"

"I don't know."

"But you don't think so, do you?" he demanded. He screwed his face up against the emotional pain my nonresponse brought. We were both silent for a while until he said, "Now what?"

"We find you a safe place to stay while I finish up this case and get Will back."

Michael shook his head. "I'm not going to be warehoused somewhere. I'm sticking with you."

There was no way I'd include Michael in the further investigation of whatever was going on, but I knew I had no power to order him around. I'd have to convince him to keep out of it in some other way, later. I cut him an irritated glance. "Let's find a safer place to have this discussion."

We picked ourselves up and made our way down to the Underground station. I paid the fare and in spite of Michael's annoyance we didn't replace his Oyster card. I wasn't sure what the nature of the tracking spell had been and it was always better in these situations to leave as little trace as possible. However else the card could be tracked, I was certain the Underground authorities kept tabs on the cards themselves. Every attachment is a potential point of weakness for an enemy to attack, even a piece of plastic with a chip in it. Or a photo, or a loved one.

TWENTY-EIGHT

We started to come up at Temple Station, but the crowds in the lobby had an unpleasant smell and aura to them. Before we'd reached the upper level, I turned around and pulled Michael along behind me, back to the train platforms.

"What's going on?" he asked, bewildered but following without a struggle.

"More bad guys. I recognized a face or two. We'll go on to the next station and walk back."

The next train gusted into the platform and a familiar figure in a long dark coat and white trousers stepped off, carrying a white cane held out in front of himself. It was Marsden, the unpleasant and uncanny man I'd met in Farringdon Station. He seemed to have an affection for dramatic entrances on Underground platforms.

Marsden turned his head back and forth as if scenting for me. Then he headed directly for us and hooked his arms through each of ours, turning us around.

"C'mon, you two. Not safe above."

"I had figured that out on my own," I said.

"Who's this guy?" Michael asked.

"That's a good question," I replied as we stepped aboard the next train into the platform.

Rush hour had faded to a thick trickle and we found some seats at the far end of a car. Michael stared at the blind man and his strange outfit for a moment, making a crooked face. Then he leaned in closer.

"They're little pelts!" Michael exclaimed, pointing at the uneven texture of Marsden's coat.

"Moleskins," Marsden replied, spreading his coattails out. "They little gentlemen in velvet weren't in need of 'em any longer. Not once I'd done with 'em." He grinned, showing crooked yellow teeth that seemed unusually pointed, and his odd, colorless aura flashed and moved like a kaleidoscope of clear glass. He turned his attention to me. "I'd a feeling I'd find you at that platform, and there you were with a bloody great lot of Red Guard upstairs."

"Soviets?" Michael questioned.

"Vampires' servants," Marsden corrected.

Michael quirked his eyebrows and twisted his face in incredulous disbelief. "Get away."

"God's truth, boy." Marsden fixed his eyeless gaze on me. "Do I lie?"

I didn't want to admit it in front of Michael, but I said, "No." The crowd that had tried to herd us in Trafalgar hadn't wasted much time once they realized they'd lost us but had come straight to my hotel and the nearest Underground station. I had no doubt they'd be stationed all around the block and probably at each Tube station nearby. They knew where I was staying. As did Marsden, it seemed.

"How did you know where to find me?" I asked.

"As I said, I had a feeling. I always heed those impressions. I imagine you're much the same, aren't ya?"

Michael was watching us both with a wary expression.

"I don't take hunches for granted, no."

"Your instincts are fine-tuned to the mysterious. Your father wasn't so good at that."

Now I was glaring at Marsden with suspicion. "You knew my father?"

"Not in person, but we had some enemies in common. Those same as were lying in wait upstairs at Temple. Not that lot specifically, but the same cut of crypt robbers."

The speakers in the car blared with the news we were approaching the next station. I stood up. "My father was a paranoid who thought things were watching him. He thought his receptionist was a monster. And right now my instincts aren't urging me to believe that the enemy of my enemy is my friend."

I beckoned to Michael and started for the doors. I didn't like speaking so harshly of my dad, but I didn't trust this creepy man and his coincidental appearances. He had been watching my hotel and now there were others staking it out who didn't have my best interests or Michael's in mind. I may have tripped up and been careless shaking off watchers and tails, but I thought it more likely someone else had tipped them off.

As we stepped off, Marsden's whisper carried to my ears. "Your father did you no favors in blowing his brains out and making *you* the Greywalker in the family. Nor did he do any favors for the rest of us, the bleedin' coward. May he rot in whatever damned hole he's been locked in."

Michael looked at me with wide eyes as I stopped and spun back toward the train car. Had he heard that?

The doors hissed closed and the train hummed before it swept away, leaving us on the platform with the fast-dissipating crowd.

"Second thoughts?" came Marsden's voice from a shadowed corner.

"This is seriously wigging me out," Michael muttered to me.

"Just stick with me," I replied.

Marsden was lurking in his corner, gleams of ghostly white the only sign of him in the darkness. "You and me, we're the same ruddy thing," he hissed, furious. "Should have been your dad's job, but he bunked it and that left you. That monster what's been stalking one of us for his own all these years, he's coming for you now. I can see his marks on you—and yes, I see. Clear as you do in this half-a-place." He stepped forward into a slice of light that silvered his face as if it were made of ice. He folded his cane and tucked it into a pocket of his long moleskin coat. Then he closed the distance between us, growing misty and indistinct as he did.

Implications and connections rushed together in my head. His shattered aura, his almost ghostly appearance on my phone camera, ". . . one of us," "same ruddy thing . . ." Marsden was a Greywalker.

Michael jerked beside me and I put my hand on his arm to stop him bolting. "You've seen worse today. Don't let him scare you." Immersed in the Grey as he was, Marsden was no physical threat to us so long as we stayed on the corporeal side of the line.

"Your father thought he'd gone mad—as do we all at first. I gouged me own eyes out, thinking it was them what made me see things that couldn't be. But it's not these eyes," he added, jabbing a phantom finger at my face, "that sees this place. It's another set entirely, and I didn't stop seeing monsters, no more shall you, girl. At least you're not runnin', but you're trailing your coat and you don't even know what manner of thing may be stalking you or what it means to do. You are in enemy territory. It called you here, it forced you, it dangled bait. And you came. Now what will you do? Pitch yourself into its arms?"

He stepped through me, giving a bitter laugh and sending bone-deep cold through my body. My chest ached, and I choked on some frozen terror that exploded through me and then passed as quickly as Marsden stepped away.

"You are a babe in the woods."

I would not give him the satisfaction of fear or even anger. I turned with deliberate care to face Marsden's new position. Michael shook beside me and I held his arm in a tight grip at my side. I hoped it reassured him, but more than that, I couldn't risk him running.

"Do you practice to be such an asshole? Or does it come naturally?" I sneered.

Michael giggled without sounding hysterical. Good: I was defusing the situation. He'd had more than enough freak show for one day.

"Marsden, you want to talk to me, do it like a human."

The man firmed up, sliding back out of the Grey. "Are you ready to listen, then?"

I nodded. "After I put this kid somewhere safe."

"Hey!" Michael objected, squirming in my grasp. "I'm eighteen!"

"Old enough to drink doesn't make you adult, boy," Marsden said.

Michael bridled in my grip. "Don't argue," I advised. "This is not the time to split hairs." He grumbled under his breath but stopped wriggling, and I let go of his arm. "Where can we go?"

Marsden shrugged. "It's not me they're after and I doubt you'd feel safe enough in my abode. You're not entirely sure about me, are you?"

"You got that right."

"Where are we?" Michael asked, looking around. No more trains or passengers had come through since we'd stepped onto the platform, which seemed a little odd until I looked around.

The platform hadn't been in use in ages. The only lights were safety lights in the tunnel and an occasional gleam from something above us. I could hear trains nearby, but when one did finally rush though, it didn't even slow. The station had an arched roof and sides that were tiled in soft greens and brown. The signs were all tiled in place, too, but they'd faded badly with time. It looked like something from a WWII movie, and the ghosts in it were dressed in the clothing of the early twentieth century, ignoring us without a care.

"Oh, wow," Michael started, answering his own question, "it's a ghost station."

"A what?" I asked, startled.

"An abandoned station on the Underground. I've heard of them. How—?"

"You're in the company of two people for whom the paranormal is the normal, and you can ask a cloth-eared question like that?" Marsden hooted.

"Back off him, Marsden," I started, but Michael closed with the older man and glared at him.

"Step off, sunshine. I thought I saw my brother hacked to pieces today. Then I found out he was a golem. Then I got chased by creep-azoids, and now you want to rag me for being a little freaked? Well, bugger you!"

Marsden gave him a feral grin. "You'll do," he said.

"Fine," I said. "Now, where can we go from here? I doubt there's going to be another train stopping for us."

TWENTY-NINE

Michael had been looking around while Marsden and I talked and now said, "This says Down Street Station." He pointed to a sign tiled into the wall. "The only Down Street I know is near Green Park. But . . . that's the Piccadilly line. We were on the Circle line. . . ."

"Weirder things have happened today than that," I reminded him. "Do you think we can get out of here?"

"Yeah, I think so. . . . There's a sign for an emergency exit. We can try it."

We headed for the steel mesh door Michael indicated at the end of the platform and pushed. It opened with a mild complaint of hinges onto a steep staircase that looked a lot newer than the station. We started up and kept climbing for what seemed a very long time. Finally we came to another door and had to push very hard. It creaked open reluctantly, and I poked my head out first, scanning for vampires and other things that might lie in wait.

Just the usual ghosts, Grey, and humans lay beyond the door, and we emerged onto Piccadilly with the door clanking locked behind us. Michael pointed to our right.

"That's Hyde Park Corner! Hey, we're close to my garage!"

"Garage?" I questioned. I knew most people didn't have private cars in London, except for the collection I'd seen in Clerkenwell that the vampires shared.

"Yeah, where I keep the bikes—well, it's Loren's, really. It's just an old horse stall, but he might have left the key to his boat there. We can borrow it—he won't care."

"A boat," I said doubtfully.

"On Regent's Canal. No one would look for us on a narrow boat!"

Marsden and I had to agree that it was unlikely anyone would stumble upon us in such a place—especially since it was on water, which vampires tend to dislike and ghosts rarely haunt unless they are on the shore or on a boat themselves.

Michael led the way north and a bit west.

Marsden turned his head toward him as we went, as if he were peering at the boy with his empty eyes. "Your mate has a horse stall in Mayfair?"

"It's his sister's place." Michael blushed, keeping his eyes averted from the disconcerting face beside him. "Loren's family has money— like the kind of money even rich people think is a lot of money."

We went a few more blocks into a very nice, old residential neighborhood until Michael stopped in front of a long row of connected houses with tiny yards in front. Then he led the way up a short alley to a green-painted door in what looked more like a shed than a stable. The door certainly wasn't wide enough for any sort of car. Michael dug his keys from his pocket and used one on the padlock attached to the door's hasp and handle assembly. The door swung open to show a tiny space packed full of motorcycles and repair gear. There was barely room to step in and move the bikes.

"The Ducatis and the Enfield are his. Mine are the BSAs," Michael said, rummaging through a rack of keys on the wall. "I meant to take the Comet to a rally in a couple of weeks, but I'm guessing that's not going to happen."

"Why not?" I asked. "This should resolve in a day or two. It's not the end of the world. At least not yet."

Michael goggled at me. "If Will's skipped work for a week, they can deport us both. I mean, they might not, but who's to say? He's on work contract and he has to show up for work at the job that brought him here or he has to leave. Keeps people from coming at an employer's expense and then ducking out for some other job or just slacking around on the dole." He found the key he wanted and held it up with a shout. "Got it!"

"Where's the boat?" I asked.

"Last time he left it in St. Pancras Basin. It'll have to be somewhere between there and Islington. That's only a mile or so to walk on the towpath, and we can take the Tube to Pankers to start."

"St. Pancras will do quite nicely," Marsden said.

"Nicely for what?" I asked.

"Oh, you'll see, girl. You'll see."

Michael looked at me and rolled his eyes. "Do we have to keep him around?"

"Safer to keep him where we can see him," I replied. But it wasn't just that.

Someone had wanted me here in London. There'd been no guarantee Edward would talk me into coming, so I was guessing that the bad dreams sent through the golem had been an additional goad to force my hand—was that Alice's part? Whoever it was had tricked Purcell or gained some kind of hold over him so he'd stopped disputing the customs bill and used the charmed note Jakob took to Sotheby's to help snatch Will. They had to have Will to control the golem, and they hadn't wanted anyone but me to come looking for him, so they'd left the golem in Will's place.

I wasn't sure what connection there was to Edward's problems, except that with Alice in the mix there had to be one. I knew she wouldn't want to let that grudge go, but I was also certain she wasn't the key player. I liked that part better for the asetem-ankh-astet, the

Egyptian vampires Sekhmet had described. They were involved in this and in my father's fate and my own. I still hadn't figured that angle completely; I didn't know what they wanted or how Wygan—who I was sure was also asetem—fit in, but so far, things were connecting and I thought they'd all come together when I could figure out what Alice was doing and what the asetem wanted with me.

Several things still bugged me. I didn't know why they'd snatched Will instead of Quinton if they were trying to get a lever on me, unless it was simply that he was here and so were they. In addition, Marsden may have spilled the beans to the vampires about where I was, but then he'd shown up to detour me and Michael away from them. He didn't seem to be their friend any more than they were mine. Greywalker or not, he wasn't my friend either, but I didn't know where he really stood or what he was up to. He did know something about my father, though, and I wanted that information, even if it meant playing with fire. I wasn't going to let Marsden slip away—he had answers or he could lead me to them, of that I was sure. I thought about these problems as we made our way north and east toward the canal.

Another ride on the Underground got us up to St. Pancras Train Station. It was a massive, echoing pile of Victorian Gothic architecture—looking more like a red brick cathedral than a train station—that was being rehabilitated and partially renovated into expensive flats. We had to thread our way through leggy forests of scaffolding to get out of the building and around the back, up several industrial blocks to Regent's Canal.

We passed a sign directing us to ST. PANCRAS OLD CHURCH as we detoured around some construction and the rail yards, looking for a way down to the canal. I noticed that the train rails cut right up against the churchyard walls before they crossed the canal on a low bridge. The rail yard was deep with ghosts and blurry with a mess of disrupted ley lines. The canal, being older than the rail yard and full of water, had bent the energy lines of the Grey gently into its own shape so the magical supply lines curved with its bends and crossed them without a hash and noise of magical strife. It was a relief to get down to the water's edge and walk across a small park to find the towpath, away from the growl of furious magic.

Along the canal wall, several long, skinny boats were moored to iron mushrooms or stakes driven into the grass. Upstream stood the brick piers and wooden doors of a small lock. Michael led the way toward the lock and around a sharp corner in the path to the sudden appearance of a boat basin. The St. Pancras Cruising Club building stood on the landward side, overlooking a rectangular body of water cut from the canal that was filled with more of the long, thin boats.

The sun was dipping toward the horizon, turning the sky a watercolor pink, but the boats were magnificent even in the waning light, all painted in bright colors and many sporting designs of stylized flowers, castles, and ribbons, with touches of gilding, polished brass and bronze, and gleaming, varnished wood panels on the hatches. Some of the boats had louvered or shuttered windows along the sides while others had names painted on colored panels on the sides that looked a lot like old-style advertising. Some had tillers of curved and tapered poles covered in rope and ribbon for grip, sticking out of oversized rudders that looked like half a Dutch door, while others had stern rails and tiller poles of slender painted iron. Tin smokestacks poked up from the flat roofs of the low, slope-sided cabins. It was a riotous display but still oddly uniform. All the boats were about the same width and height, and most looked between forty and sixty feet long with flat roofs and very narrow side decks. None had lifelines or stanchions on the outside but seemed to rely on fingerholds on their roofs to keep the crew on board when they scampered along the deck—and scamper was what you'd have to do if you couldn't traverse the boat inside.

Michael trotted down along the basin path and pointed at a primrose yellow boat with green and red trim. "There it is!" The big side board had been lettered "Morning Glory, St. John's Wood" with curlicues of green filling the corners and trailing around the edges of the rectangle, evocative of the boat's namesake vine. He stepped aboard at the stern, pulling from his pocket the padlock key he'd taken from the garage, and opened up the boat.

I stepped aboard and down into the aft cabin. Marsden made a face and chose to stay on the land. I found I had stepped down into a utility room with a tiny washing machine tucked under a counter and a number of foul-weather coats and fluffy towels hanging on pegs nearby. I looked forward, into the boat, following Michael's progress inside. The interior was like a very long and luxurious camper trailer that had been cut down to about seven feet wide. Compact and efficient, it had more than enough headroom for my five-foot-ten frame even in heeled boots. It wouldn't be much fun if you were claustrophobic, but it was fine for our purposes. Michael pointed out that the boat had one large bedroom and a dining area that could be made into another bed, so we'd each have a place to sleep—except for Marsden. That gave Michael pause.

"Don't worry about him," I said. "I suspect he's not going to stay."

"I could stand that—the guy gives me the creeps—but how do you know?"

"He didn't come aboard and he looks like the very idea of a boat makes him queasy. I think it's just you and me, Michael. Right after I have a little chat with Mr. Marsden. Will you be OK alone for a while? Don't go anywhere while I'm gone."

"I can manage. Although . . . we're going to need food. . . ."

"We'll figure it out. I'll be back soon."

I ducked back out and collared Marsden, who was still standing on the quayside, scowling.

"Seasick?" I asked.

"Not a bit of it. I don't like them closed-up things—like floating metal coffins."

"Then you're not staying with us?"

"I should say not. Two of us in the same space for long might attract the wrong sort of attention, and we're not the only things what can see into the Grey and talk back to those hunting you."

"I'd like to talk to you a bit more about that—" I started, but he cut me off.

"Good, because there's a few things you need to know. But here is not such a grand idea. Come with me."

"Why and where?"

"Where is old St. Pankers, and why is that the presence of a lot of ghosts may mask the presence of the pair of us. And there's something you should see. Come on."

THIRTY

He turned and started briskly out of the boat basin, his white cane out but obviously more for show than use. I followed and caught up quickly with my long stride.

We went around the railroad tracks and under part of the new train station and came up in front of a broad flight of steps that led to an elaborate iron and gilt gate with a small church visible through its arch. SP had been worked into the black-painted iron filigree above the locked gates and picked out in gold leaf. A plaque mounted beside them identified the building beyond as ST. PANCRAS OLD CHURCH. Marsden stopped close to the gates. Then he shimmered, went thin, and walked through.

"Come in, girl. They'll be waking up soon to do their own dirty work."

I looked into the graveyard. The shadows were growing long as dusk fell, but the cemetery in my sight was a field of colored lights, close packed and spiking upward like searchlights reaching for the sky while a tangle of Grey power lines surged beneath it. For a place of the dead, it was one of the liveliest in London. Reluctant, I sank into the Grey and found a temporacline where the gates stood open and rusted. I stepped through and pulled back from the Grey.

The churchyard was busy with ghosts. They pressed in closer than the rush-hour commuters on the Tube had. Marsden led me deeper into the cemetery to a large stone tomb that stood in its own little oval of lawn behind its own iron fence. Marsden slipped through it and crossed the lawn toward the tomb, which looked a lot like an oversized stone phone booth with a tiny Grecian temple in it and a big stone block inside that. Feeling like a trespasser, I followed him until we were both standing beside the memorial stone of one Sir John Soane, an architect with rather odd taste in monuments, and his family. The silence under the stone roof was profound—even the Grey chorus of the city was distant—and it was empty of everything but the two of us.

"Hundred years ago," Marsden started in a low voice, "this churchyard was three times the size it is now. Reached near to the Euston Road. Then they built a railroad and exhumed the bodies—well, some of 'em. They moved the stones from the lower churchyard to the inner churchyard. There weren't enough room for 'em all, and a lot of the coffins was rotten or they had none to begin with, so they lined 'em up in trenches or mass excavations or just dumped 'em all in one big hole and made the memorial stones look as nice as they could. Some of them dead was nigh to fifteen hundred years in the ground, and they did not take well to the move. They're restless. Just look out there; look at 'em movin' about. You see how they're clustered like prisoners round that tree and up that rise? Them's the places that fool Hardy stuck 'em, pilin' up the ghosts in batteries that could light half of England. This fella here, he wanted his rest quiet. So he built this. Grand and mad, isn't it?"

I nodded.

"I doubt he quite knew what he was doing, but the way he had it made and the way it's laid, the shape of it as it lies across the leys, makes a sort of eddy in the Grey. We're surrounded by a fence of the supernatural but immune to its touch until we step out. The ghosts don't even know we're here, so they can't grass on us to any snooping mages or sorcerers. So, what made Edward send you?"

"I don't breach client confidentiality without a damned good reason."

"Don't play games with me, girl."

"I think a game is exactly what you want. You keep alluding to my father and to answers, but you're not giving any. What game are you up to? You show up from nowhere and you know too much. Then you vanish and suddenly there are demi-vamps on my tail."

"'Twasn't my work as done that."

"Really? How did you know where to find me today? Or yesterday?"

"I told you—I had a premonition. That's one of my particular talents. Yours seems to be giving offense."

"And here I thought it was attracting pains in the ass like you."

Marsden's pale, eyeless face was smooth and cool as the stones we stood on. For once I couldn't see someone grinding ideas and lies into a response, but he was thinking. After a moment, he spoke again, chuckling a bit.

"He's lost his control."

"Excuse me?"

"Edward. He sent you to Purcell. But Purcell's not there. The empire is failing—he's been pulling strings in London for a dog's age, but they've been cut, haven't they? Edward's panicking. He hasn't any more idea what's going on than you do."

"And you do?"

"In no wise."

"Then how do you propose to help me?"

He laughed. "I'm not here to help you, girl. I'm here to stop you."

THIRTY-ONE

"Stop me from doing what? How can you possibly stop me when you don't even know what I'm doing?" I spoke boldly enough, but I didn't know the answer, either, and I was afraid of him. I pushed myself back two silent steps. Whatever else Marsden was, he was a Greywalker and one with more experience than I had. It would only take a step out of our charmed circle by the tomb to be back in the churning power of the Grey. I wanted a head start.

"I don't give a tinker's damn what you're up to for Kammerling. It's what you may become that cannot be allowed. That is what I must put a stop to."

"I don't know what you're talking about."

He cocked his head and adjusted his stance a little to face the sound of my voice. It hit me that in this Grey-free pocket, he was truly blind; he couldn't see me at all so long as I stuck close to the Soanes' tomb.

"You're meant to take up where your dad wouldn't go," Marsden whispered. "He didn't hop the stick because he could see ghosts, and he wasn't mad, neither. He tried to put a stop to the Pharaohn's plans by destroying the tool: himself. He didn't know about me before him or that you'd be next in line."

"Next in line for what? You make it sound like this runs in the family." I wasn't sure it didn't, but I hoped that wasn't true.

"Not exactly, but the possibility was strong in your case, and what your dad did made it stronger. It only needed a bit of pushing in the right direction and you'd be perfect for the job. And he's pushed you ever since your dad blew his own head off. You're knees deep in death, tangled up in the Grey since you was a child. He just needed you to die a little. Then he could shape you a bit while you were out of this armor of flesh." He whipped out the cane and struck me on the shoulder. "Ah, there you are."

"Ow! Who? Shape me into what? A Greywalker? I think it's too late to put a stop to that." I stopped talking and eased aside, keeping on my toes to make less noise on the stonework and get a little closer to the steps.

"The Pharaohn-ankh-astet. The king of worms. He has a plan. Has had since he and Edward first faced off here . . . two, three hundred years ago or more. I can't tell you what it is—I don't know—but whatever it is, you can be assured it is terrible. And he needs a Greywalker. A particular type. And as he couldn't find one, he thought he'd make one."

"Make one?" That rang an uncomfortable bell for me. I paused and stepped back to where I'd stood a moment earlier. "Sekhmet said something about the asetem-ankh-astet. Who's this Pharaohn?" I hoped it wasn't who I thought. . . .

Surprise reshaped his face. "You've talked to the Lady of Dread?"

"You didn't know that? I thought you knew everything I did and everywhere I went."

"I have the curse of premonition, but it's not a bloody crystal ball, my girl," he spat. "When and where did you converse with her?"

"Today. In front of Sotheby's. She told me Will was missing, that the asetem were involved. That's why I went to see Michael, which was where the Red Guard picked us up after I chopped up the golem standing in for Will."

He stopped and tapped his chin with the handle of his cane, thinking. "She let you live. And the asetem . . . No, that can't be right. It can't. That's how the trouble started." He flicked the cane back up and jabbed me in the chest, shoving me back over the low parapet surrounding the sunken tomb.

I rolled aside on the grass, kicking the cane out of his hands. Then I tucked up my knees and flipped myself to my feet. Marsden was more spry than I'd have thought and hopped up onto the wall after me, his hands scrabbling like spiders for the missing cane.

"Damn you. I'm sorry to do this, but I have to." He pounced in my direction and I danced farther back, but I moved too far, and the roaring song of London and the gasping mutters of the churchyard's ghosts deafened me for an instant. Marsden could see me like I was spotlit and rushed forward, shoving me hard against and then through the fence in a flash of cold and a tearing of temporaclines across my back. He propelled me backward, toward the large old tree he'd pointed at earlier.

Several hundred tombstones had been arranged around Hardy's tree in a spreading sunburst; rank after rank of grave markers, their memento mori animated into chattering skulls with gleaming golden eye sockets by the tangled and knotted threads of a thousand displaced ghosts. The shrieking of them rose in pitch as Marsden pushed me back. I whipped a look over my shoulder. Where the tree stood in the normal, the Grey showed only a howling void—a hole where the energy around it had twisted up into a vortex. The hole was more than big enough to swallow me and the sound it made was like the baying of starving hounds.

Primal fear ripped through me at the sound. I did not want to be forced into that hungry void. I knew with bone-certainty that what went in never came out. I dug my feet into the grass and ducked, toppling Marsden over my back.

Something rustled and groaned, tipping out of a crypt with the cry of stone crumbling against stone. I glanced around and saw a pair of something tall and skeletal rushing toward me from the direction of the tiny stone building of St. Pancras Old Church.

Marsden pushed me again toward the sucking void of the old tree. "Bloody hell, they're on to us. Got to . . . get rid . . . of . . . you."

The white things, looking like undead famine survivors as they finally closed the gap between us, grabbed at Marsden and me. Marsden spun around, smashing his fists into the thing that had grabbed him.

"Gi'roff, y'soulless bastard!" he yelled.

The thing's ribs collapsed where he struck it, but it kept on struggling, trying to throw him into the vortex. The other clutched me, keeping me away from the void.

I didn't want its help, sure that whatever it was saving me for was worse than Marsden. I struggled with it, kicking it with the heels of my boots. I felt the brittle bones beneath its stretched white skin shatter and it fell against me, not letting go its grip on my arms.

I spun and stopped short and hard, the creature slingshotting off one arm to flail wildly at me, trying to reassert its hold. I ran toward the vortex, bashing at its remaining fingers until it lost its grip and fell away. I kicked it and it tumbled into the whirling hole in the Grey, vanishing with its empty mouth agape as if it would scream if it only could. The vacuum of magic tugged at me and I fought my arm free, feeling the edges of the thing bend and flex like rubber as they clung to me. I struggled and twisted my hand loose, feeling a tiny bit of the emptiness break away and spin off into another sucking black hole the size of a pinhead. But the original hole was no smaller. Instead it had grown ragged around the edges and seemed to be reaching for more substance to swallow. I had to crawl across the tombstones, digging in with my fingers and toes against the magical tide, to get out of its pull.

Once out of the maelstrom, I turned back toward Marsden, who was having a rougher time with his monster. He tore off its remaining hand and shoved it away, battering it to pieces with his cane until it fell to the ground in a pile of grave dust.

In the shriek of the vortex, even the chorus of the city was hard to hear, so I was sure Marsden wouldn't hear me as I crept up and snatched his cane away again. Then I used it to poke him backward toward the hole as he'd done with me.

"What the hell were those things?" I demanded, watching him slip on the tiny hole and fight the edge of the Grey whirlpool's grasp.

"Lych wights," he panted. "Animated corpses."

"What did they want?"

"How the bloody hell should I know?"

I poked him again and he stumbled a little, grabbing at a fence railing near the tree to keep himself from being sucked backward.

"They're probably the advance guard!" he shouted over the scream of the vortex. "Now we're out in the Grey, someone can feel us moving around. Whoever sent those Red Guard after you and the lad, most like. They'd have killed us both, no doubt."

"I don't think so," I snapped. "They could have just let you push me in that thing and then tossed you in, too, but they attacked you. They only tried to hold on to me."

"They must be working for the Pharaohn-ankh-astet, then. He'd want you alive—such as you are. I can't believe it—the asetem working with the brotherhood . . ."

"What are you talking about?" I screamed against the storm of noise at the vortex's edge.

"Egyptian vampires," Marsden panted. "The asetem are the commoners; the Pharaohn is the king—like the word 'pharaoh,' y'see? He's the one what's after you for his own. He's the one what tormented your father till he killed himself. That's why I have to get rid of you. So he can't use you, like he's been trying to use one of us for centuries."

"You were going to kill me!"

"I can't bloody well kill you, you stupid git! You have a limited number of deaths—it's like a damned reset button for our sort."

"What? You mean like a cat's got nine lives? Are you insane?"

"It's true! We bounce back from death—you've done it! For a while afterward, you're malleable. If I killed you, they'd rush in and grab you in limbo and reshape you for whatever he's got in mind! It's only a few minutes but that's all they need here—we're in the middle of the biggest magical well in southern England and they're looking for you. The moment your body was shut down, they'd be on you like jackals! I was just going to put you somewhere else for a while. Someplace safe."

"Safe? Where does that . . . hole lead?"

"I don't know."

"Then you don't know if I would have survived it!"

"I don't care! I only care that they couldn't have got at you. I don't mean it's safe for you! I mean safe for the rest of the world. You need to stay out of the Pharaohn's clutches and you ain't got a lot of choices, girl. I couldn't do it on the Tube—there weren't nowhere to put you. I had to get you here, to the tree. But you couldn't just fall in. No! Now they're looking for us again—for you."

His hair whipped in the preternatural wind around the shrieking hole of the Hardy tree. His hands were locked on the protective fence around it like the claws of some dead white bird.

"My choices are not yours to make! Why doesn't this Pharaohn come after you? You're a Greywalker, too."

"I'm damaged goods. He's tried with me already and failed. He's sent ghosts and monsters to kill me and shape me, but he made a mistake with me he can't unmake. I'm at my limit. Next death's for good and all."

"What?"

"I told you: We got a limited number of deaths. It's more than one, but it's not infinite. I'm at my last."

"How do you know?"

"I just do! You will, too. It's like . . . gravity. You get close enough to final mortality and it grabs on. You can feel it holding you to the earth."

"Then what happened to my dad?" I asked, poking him again. He was getting too comfortable and I didn't trust him to keep on spilling his guts if he wasn't afraid I'd topple him into the sucking hole in magic. I knew there wasn't a lot of time, but I thought I was probably risking his life more than mine.

"He tricked 'em. A clever man was your father—though not half clever enough to save you. He diverted their attention to his nurse—"

"She was his receptionist, Christelle. She died. I think your asetem killed her."

He shrugged it off, but he couldn't hide his fear of the hungry void behind him. "As you like! I'm not sure what he did—and I'm not sure how she died neither—but he got them chasing after her, dividing their attention, and then he shot himself, made his brains into pudding. They didn't see it coming, so they couldn't stop him and they couldn't put him back together. The Pharaohn punished him for that, but he couldn't use him for his . . . whatever it is he means t'do. Whatever he's been shaping you for since then. Whatever he put that . . . thing into your chest for."

"What?" I was too shocked to keep pressure on him and dropped the cane. He'd confirmed my worst fear and the implication fell like a blow.

Marsden dropped to the ground and scrambled away from the Hardy tree and its aurora of shackled ghosts and blurring, shining energy. He whipped back around, but even shocked as I was, I wasn't falling for his tricks. I dropped and swept his legs out from under him with a low, round kick.

He fell on his back and I knelt down next to him, furious, grabbing a handful of the velvety moleskin coat. I resisted the urge to beat him into the ground. Barely. "Don't try it. I'm not as soft as you think I am and I won't hesitate to throw you in there this time."

"I tell you—"

"Save it. As you say, we're out of time here." I hauled him back to his feet. "There is one way they can't follow us. I know you can manipulate the temporaclines, so shuffle up the right one and we'll go back to the canal. Water's a good barrier. We can take the boat out and they'll have a heck of a time getting to us. Now, do it."

"It's not that easy, girl—"

"Bullshit. But I can leave you here if you prefer. . . ."

THIRTY-TWO

The trip back to the boat basin was faster than the walk to the churchyard had been, but exhausting. We pushed our way through the Grey the whole time, and I at least hadn't eaten for hours and felt wretched by the time we emerged into the normal on the canal side. It might have been less dreadful if I hadn't kept thinking of Wygan and everything that spun out from that.

Wygan was the Pharaohn-ankh-astet. He had to be. He'd tied a bit of Grey into my chest. He'd pushed me. He'd . . . shaped me. He'd tried again and again to make me a bit more dead—I knew this, but I'd never thought there was a plan behind it all. That it had been going on since . . . forever. Since my dad died. Since before that. It hadn't occurred to me. What a fool I'd been.

And now what was he up to? If the asetem had influenced Purcell and that had resulted in Jakob delivering the charmed note to Will, then it was the asetem—and Wygan—who were behind Purcell's disappearance and the destabilization of Edward's control in London as well as the kidnapping of Will. But why? How did any of that fit with Wygan's plans for me? It seemed too elaborate just for a ruse to get me out of Seattle. . . .

Seattle. I felt sick as I wondered what was happening in Pioneer Square, down in the dark where the dead are. And Quinton. It was where Edward held power, but things were falling apart and vampires were attacking one another with tools built to look like Quinton's. I couldn't breathe; my chest felt crushed in a grip of icy steel, squeezing my heart. I wanted to cry with fear for Quinton and my home, but I couldn't let Marsden see me fall apart. I didn't think he was completely on my side and he'd take advantage of any weakness.

My impulse was to flee back home and save my lover and my friends if I could. But I didn't know what was happening or even if my fears were grounded. I knew there was something happening here, in London, but I didn't know how it connected to Wygan or to Seattle, except that it had to and Alice had to be involved. She'd worked for Wygan before. If he'd saved her from the fire, then she owed him everything, and Wygan being what he was, he'd make sure she paid him back.

There was a link between Seattle and London, between my father and me, and the vampires of both kinds—and they all came together in a single plan of Wygan's. Before I could stop it, I'd have to know what it was. I couldn't just run back to Seattle half-cocked with hostages left in London, business left undone, and Alice walking the night. I had to move faster, but I couldn't be stupid about it.

What was I supposed to do for Wygan that Marsden couldn't—that my father was supposed to have done but hadn't? And what was I going to do about Will? I had to get him back—the rest be damned.

It was a nightmare. Wygan running the asetem, who seemed to be central to the whole puzzle of who and what I was and what was happening now. Alice in Wygan's debt. Alice who hated Edward and hated me more. If she had Will, I'd have to negotiate with her or find a way around her. . . . It all whirled in my head and left me fatigued and unquiet.

Michael had the boat warm and lit when we arrived. The sun hadn't been down long, though it felt like hours to me.

"Sorry," Michael said. "There's no food. And I'm starved." He looked me over. "You look awful."

"Thanks."

"Umm . . . no, I mean . . . ummm . . ." He gave me a significant look and touched the corner of his mouth. I touched mine and felt something sticky. Blood. I didn't recall having bit my lip or been hit in the mouth, but there it was.

He pointed the way to the "head" when I asked: a compact little room—cabin, I guess—with a small toilet and a shower and a sink with a metal mirror over it. I looked like I'd been dragged backward through a wood chipper, and I had no idea how I'd gotten so filthy, cut, rumpled, and bruised. The shower was very tempting, but I put a hold on that and settled for washing my face and finger combing the worst of the rats' nests from my hair.

When I'd washed and brushed enough dirt and anxiety off, I snuck out into the kitchen, listening to the lap of water on the hull and the mutter of Michael and Marsden outside, and paged Quinton. I left an urgent reply code and hoped he'd call soon. I waited but no call came.

I forced my fears down and rejoined Michael on the aft deck. Marsden was sitting on the edge of the railing as if he'd jump off and vanish any second. He might at that, I thought. I put one hand on his nearest forearm to keep him still. His skin was cold and felt like paper.

"Michael, do you think you can get this boat moving?"

He gave me a puzzled look. "Sure . . . but why?"

"Some things don't like water. I'd like to reduce the number of things that might show up unannounced. I think we've had enough for one day." The gods knew I had.

"Oh. OK. Yeah. The fuel gauges show full, so I suppose we could go a while if you want."

"Any place we could tie up and buy food?"

"Umm . . . I think there are a couple of inns and pubs that have docks in both directions, but it's a bit late for the shops."

I glanced at Marsden.

"Head for Little Venice—we shan't have to go through the lock," he said, his eyes darting about and not meeting anyone's.

Michael pottered around and had the boat ticking happily away within ten minutes. I helped cast off, forcing Marsden to stay aboard. I still had a lot to discuss with him, and I didn't trust him, but he seemed disinclined to swim for it.

Sailing in the dark on the unlighted canal was eerie. Only our quiet chuffing and the lap of our wake bounded from the brick embankments. Light reflected off the water's surface from buildings and distant sources, and streamers of colored Grey power lines drifted, distorted by the waves, just beneath us. Occasionally, eyes peeped at us from corners of the towpath or within the water itself. I told myself they were cats and fish and reflections, not the luminous saucer eyes of Jakob's kin.

The boat moved along the canal for less than an hour before Michael spotted a lighted building above the dark jut of a small dock. As we drew near, it became obvious that the restaurant was floating on the water, moored to the canal side, on a long barge. Another narrow boat and a small motor cruiser were tied up to the water side, but Michael reversed the engine and our yellow vessel stopped a foot or two from the float. I grabbed a mooring line and jumped across the gap as someone trotted out from the restaurant and offered to help tie us in. With his help, we were safely docked within minutes.

We were in luck: since it was Friday, the place was busy and not inclined to close any earlier than it had to. I sent Michael in with the stranger to get a table and order some food. I hooked my hand into Marsden's collar and kept him beside me on the boat's stern.

"Now," I started as soon as Michael and our assistant had gone inside, "tell me more about my dad and the Pharaohn-ankh-astet and his followers."

He heaved a disgusted sigh. "You'd be better off out of it."

"I like to know what I'm into before I bail out. So start talking and I'll make up my own mind. Or I can pitch you in the canal and see how well you swim."

THIRTY-THREE

In the darkness of Regent's Canal on that cricket-serenaded summer night, Marsden chose to talk rather than let me teach him to swim. I guess he knew my technique would involve a lot of holding him under. "The asetem-ankh-astet are a type of vampire," he started.

"I figured that out from what Sekhmet said. What makes them special? Why do you seem a bit more freaked out about them than Edward's kind?" Not that I wasn't, but I wanted to know if my heightened fear near them was just my problem or if it was their effect on everyone.

"They have a glamour of terror. And they feed on more than blood."

"All of them do. Sekhmet said these feed on souls—the ka, she called it."

"Not that I've seen, but I suppose you could think of it that way. They dine on emotional energy—on the psychic component."

"Isn't that just another kind of Grey power?"

He scoffed. "That's an *expression* of the energy. Blood's just a . . . a fuel source, so t'speak. What makes the Pharaohn so hideous is he eats, he breathes, he lives chaos. It gives him power beyond the ordinary vampire sort of guff. He breeds mayhem, havoc, and destruction. He uses his people to create it through devastation, death, pain, terror . . . whatever it takes. Y'can imagine other vampires don't care for that."

"Yeah. So what?"

"The current Pharaohn seems to have some longer-range plan in mind that involves the Grey itself. Something that either breeds chaos or feeds on it to do something else. He's been looking for a tool that'll make the Grey . . . flow the way he needs it to—a Greywalker with a special ability plying it as he directs, in the right place. We're a rare enough bird as it is that he decided not to wait until the right one come along but to grab a few and see what he could do by force. You could say he's been working on his technique awhile at our expense.

"Your father was a particularly favored experiment of his. Fortunately he ruined the Pharaohn's plans, but he left you behind for the bastard to try again."

"And the Pharaohn punished him for escaping. So you said. What did you mean by that?"

"You ever talked to your dad? To his ghost, I mean?"

"No. I tried but it's like there's a hole where the ghost ought to be."

Marsden nodded, his lank hair swinging. "Because the Pharaohn's got 'im bottled up somewhere. He's got a hole like that Hardy tree and stuck 'im in it."

I narrowed my eyes at him. "He *made* a hole like that? I thought vampires didn't have any magic."

"He didn't make it. They just happen. He found it, or moved it. And he shackled your dad's ghost with torments and stuck him in it to scream and suffer till he's got something better to do with him."

I tightened my grip in anger without thinking, pressing Marsden against the boat's stern rail. "How come I didn't see the guardian beast around the tree then?"

"What?"

"When I got near where my dad should have been, the beast turned up. You know it?"

"Course! Rattling thing of bones and ghost-sinew. Nasty temper." His mouth quirked at one corner. "I don't like that."

"It's not high on my hit parade, either."

"What did this hole look like? Like the tree or different?"

"Very different. It was more like a fire around a core of emptiness. It was a million colors and it was completely silent. The guardian beast didn't want me to go near it."

"Colors. That is trouble. Means the white worm's figured out the beast's weakness. The guardian's got a bit of a vision problem, see? Sequences of certain colors cause it confusion and blindness. Whatever he's up to, the king of worms doesn't want the beast anywhere near it."

"Because the beast would destroy it?" I remembered my first meeting with Wygan as he sat in his broadcast booth, a rack of colored lightbulbs flashing randomly. Now I knew they'd kept the guardian beast at bay; Wygan was already a threat to the Grey and had to hide from the monster that patrolled its borders. Whatever he was planning had to be pretty bad.

Marsden nodded again. "I'd bet my life."

"Then why doesn't the beast come after me?"

"Think it reads minds, do ya?" He scoffed. "Got no reason to until you do something to threaten the Grey. So long as you're not doing nothing, it's not interested in you, no matter how weird your psychic shape is."

"My what?"

"What do I look like to you? In the Grey?"

"Like broken glass and mirrors—colorless, moving shards."

"As I should—I'm neutral to the Grey, as most Greywalkers are. But you are bright white to me—all the colors at once. You're active to the Grey—you're tied up in the living Grey itself because he tied you to it, didn't he?"

I nodded while saying, "Wygan is the Pharaohn—the 'white worm-man' my dad wrote about. What's he up to?" My voice sounded like poison.

"I've no idea, but it will affect the Grey—else why would he need a Greywalker for his dirty work?—and he'll move heaven and hell to get it. He'll burn you out like a candle."

"As if you care what happens to me."

His face twisted into a fearsome expression. "I care what becomes of us all, girl. You've a lot of brass, but that's not enough—he's three thousand years old and a lot more cunning than you. You're a bit of flash paper—a fuse—for his bomb. You may have that gift of persuasion, but it's not going to work on him. You can't fast-talk him into changing his mind."

I shook my head as if flinging water from my ears. "What the hell are you talking about now?"

Marsden growled and whipped his head side to side as if he were looking for watchers. "You think it's just something everyone does? Do you?"

Now he had me frowning. I didn't know what he meant, but I was annoyed by his tone.

"It's your particular talent," he went on. "We've all got one or two—us in the Grey. You are unnaturally persuasive. Didn't you ever notice that everyone answers your bloody damned questions more readily than most people's?"

"If I was any good at persuasion, why didn't I get my mother off my back a lot earlier, hm?"

"Maybe y'didn't really want to."

"And maybe you're really full of shit. It's just a psychological trick. I was taught it in college," I growled. "It's not some kind of magic—"

"Bollocks. You got better at it; you learned a new way to pretend it wasn't special. You learned how to endure, how to act like everyone else, how to blend in, how to lie to yourself so you could lie to others. That's what you're good at. And look at what you use it for: snoopin', pryin', doin' other people's dirty work—"

I grabbed his shoulders and shook him. "Shut up!"

"You should be home. You should be putting paid to that bastard Wygan and whatever he's up to, not chasing after Edward Kammerling's blasted fantasies—that is, if you really think you can."

"It's all connected, you blind idiot! You're such a know-it-all and you can't see that? I don't know how it all fits together, but I won't leave until I do! And I'm not willing to sacrifice others to save my own skin!" I shouted, shoving him over the rail. I startled myself with what I'd said and the heat of the anger that had forced it out.

Marsden flipped over and sprawled on the dock, slowly rolling onto his back, laughing at me. "You're madder than what I am. You think you need to stay on Kammerling's good side? Need to keep on with your charade of an investigation? Or are you afraid—"

"I want my friend back!" I spat. I leapt off the boat and squatted down beside him, holding him down on the dock with one hand. He didn't try to rise but skewered me with his eyeless glance. I met it and didn't flinch at the eerie sense of vision from those scarred hollows. "I don't give a crap about Edward's business except how it might be part of Wygan's plan. I *know* it's all connected: Vampires took Will Novak and I want him back. I will leave when I have him or when whoever took him is back in their grave forever. And I don't care about your warnings, or the Pharaohn's lackeys, or the threats of stone goddesses. Do you understand?"

Marsden just lay still and said nothing, his empty eye sockets gleaming a transient blue. "It's a key."

THIRTY-FOUR

I jerked Marsden up to me from the surface of the creaking, darkened pier. "What?"

"It's a puzzle," he replied in a distant voice. "That is a key. A key to an enigma. That is the way. A . . . door at the center of a labyrinth." He shook himself and sagged onto the dock. "Will you bloody well unhand me, girl? You've got the damned thing in your pocket. I'd like to see it for myself."

"What damned thing?" I asked, eyes slitted.

"The puzzle. It belonged to your dad, yeah? It's in your pocket. Show it me!"

That was when Michael stepped back out onto the dock and stared at us, lit from behind by the lamps of the floating restaurant. "What are you two doing? If you're going to kill each other, can you do it later? There's food in here and I, for one, want to eat it. Are you coming in or not?"

"Lad's got a better head than either of us, I think," Marsden mumbled. "Food first, eh? Fight later."

"Don't tempt me. . . ." I muttered, letting him up.

Marsden brushed at his moleskin collection and straightened his clothes. "I shall still want to see that puzzle."

He started into the restaurant and I followed him as he followed Michael. "What's it got to do with saving Will?" I hissed under my breath.

"Nothing. It's for later. If you insist on being a bloody heroine."

"Don't start."

He cackled and ignored me until we reached the table. We eased into our seats and kept an ugly silence while we fell on the food Michael had ordered. Meat pies, salad, bread, and beer vanished and I didn't even taste it. Marsden and Michael did theirs in with equal speed, though they seemed to enjoy it more. Marsden finally leaned back and patted his mouth with his napkin before holding up his glass for a refill.

As we waited for the new round, Marsden put his hand out on the table palm up. "C'mon, girl. Show it me."

Glowering, I brought the little metal puzzle out of my pocket and put it on Marsden's palm.

"What's that?" Michael asked.

"It's a puzzle my dad used to carry around. This guy seems to think it's important."

"It is," Marsden said, fidgeting with the puzzle. He didn't bend his head to look at it. It wouldn't have done any good, but the effect of him scrambling the puzzle with deft fingers while he kept his head tipped back and his wrecked eyes turned toward the ceiling was still unsettling.

He grunted and scowled. "Here," he said, forcing it back into my hands. "You'll have to do it—it only likes you." He put his hands over mine.

I wasn't sure why he said it liked me—objects rarely have any "feelings" about people one way or another—but this one did seem to . . . fit me better than it had him. Maybe because it had been my dad's, but I doubted that was the only reason. Where or when had my father gotten it? Somewhere in the Grey? But he couldn't have. He would have said something about it in his journal. And it seemed to me he'd always had it, as far back as I could remember.

Marsden's cold, dry touch guided my fingers. I repressed a frisson as the metal links slid into positions I'd never seen before, making low, sure clicks with every change. The little puzzle gleamed pale blue until something fell into place. Then it blazed gold and settled down to a dull humming in my hand that felt like a fistful of bees. Yet another strange link between my past and the present.

It didn't look like a key—actually it looked more like a mutant fork or a lock pick—but the satisfied sensation it gave off left me with the conclusion that it was pleased with its current shape and ready to do something. I wouldn't call it alive or sentient, but the odd, flat prong I now held did seem . . . ready for something, even eager.

The thought left me uncomfortable. My dad had never made such a configuration with the puzzle that I'd seen. If it was something only I could do . . . was that a sign of the direction in which Wygan was pushing me, of the purpose to which he'd already bent me? I didn't like that. It stunk of Fate and Destiny and a lack of free will.

I pressed on the last puzzle piece that I'd moved and bent it back until it clicked again. The golden glow drained away, and the whole thing faded back to an inert collection of metal parts as I shuffled the surfaces around and wondered what it was meant to do. Or I with it. Besides the useless drivel Marsden had spouted on the dock, that is.

Michael had watched it like a hawk does a mouse.

"Did you see something?" I asked.

He hesitated. Then admitted with a drooping head, "No. I was hoping . . ."

"Haven't you seen enough uncanny stuff for one day?"

Michael shrugged. "Not so much, really. I mean . . . there was Will—that thing that wasn't Will—and the Tube station. . . . Everything else is just creepy stuff you and this guy have told me."

He was trying to forget the extent of the weirdness and I wasn't sure that was wise just yet. "That's not enough to convince you some-thing strange is going on?"

"Oh, I'm convinced! It's just . . . y'know . . . if there's vampires and witches and stuff, it might be fun to see—"

"Don't think it, boy. That lot's fun like being thrown off a cliff," Marsden said.

The waiter brought our drinks and we set to them for a moment, each in our own thoughts. Or at least Michael and I were. Marsden somehow gave the impression of watching us both.

Michael shot him a nervous glance. "Why do I feel like you're star-ing at me . . . ?"

Marsden snickered. "More perceptive than I'd have credited. I'm wondering what we shall do about you."

"We who?" Michael demanded. "Do what about me?" He turned a furious expression toward me. "Who is this guy, anyhow? How do we know he's not with them?"

Marsden patted at the air with one lazy hand. "We've been through that already."

"Not with me you haven't!" Michael snapped.

I sighed. "He's not with the enemy. But that doesn't mean he's trustworthy, either," I added, giving Marsden a sharp look.

Marsden almost smiled. "You're getting smarter. But I am not going to do you any harm, boy. You're a bystander in this—like your brother."

I almost choked on my beer. "You two-faced rat bastard," I muttered.

He made a little shrugging motion on one side. "All right. I admit I don't give a tinker's about this missin' brother, but the lady here says she ain't leaving without 'im. The sooner she's gone and out of reach of certain people, the safer we all are. So. I'm for finding that brother quick and gettin' shut of the lot of you."

"Yeah? Well, isn't that lovely of you?" Michael sneered.

"Michael," I started, "he's a lying, manipulative, sneaky—"

"Rat bastard," Michael reminded me.

"Yes. But he knows the lay of the land and I don't. I don't know where to start looking for Will."

Michael glowered at Marsden. "He does?"

"Probably."

"Of course I do. Mind, I don't say I know where he is or who's got 'im, so don't get shirty 'bout that. But I have an idea where to start lookin'."

I hated having to cooperate with Marsden. I knew I couldn't trust him; he had an agenda and I wasn't sure it had changed since we'd left St. Pancras churchyard. But he was the only resource I had left.

"Where should we start?" I asked.

"The Greek sisters," Marsden said.

THIRTY-FIVE

Michael had, of course, wanted to go see these mysterious sisters at once but as it was growing later—and deeper into the most active part of any vampire's evening—both Marsden and I quashed that idea. The sisters, Marsden assured us, would be as easy to find and interrogate in daylight as night and far safer. Michael found a place along the canal to moor the boat after dinner and the two of us readied for bed. Marsden slipped away during our inexperienced scrambling about in the dark, but much as I didn't trust him, he'd had ample opportunity to rat us out to the vampires and hadn't. So whether he was telling the truth about Wygan or not, he was at least not working against me at the moment.

I slept worse than I had in years. Quinton never did return my call, and that along with the exertions and revelations of the previous days made me miserable and woke me in a foul mood at an ungodly hour. I went up on deck to get a break from the tiny, shared space of the boat.

A couple of hours later, as I'd hoped, Marsden turned up at the canal side, alone. Unexpectedly, he was carrying a canvas sack that clanked. He stopped at the edge of the towpath and tapped on the side of the boat with his cane. "Here," he called to me as I sat on the stern rail, watching him. "I need a hand with this."

"What is it?"

"Hospitality, my girl. As we're likely to be keeping to this . . . floating cigar tin for a while, it occurred to me we might be in need of food."

"And you brought some?" I asked, surprised. Unalloyed generosity didn't strike me as a Marsden trait. So far, when he'd offered anything, it had been for his own reasons and advantage. Even keeping me and Michael out of the hands of the demi-vamps had been in service to his plan to bottle me up somewhere until whenever he felt it was safe for me to rejoin the world of the living—or semi-living—whether I'd liked it or not.

"Yes, I did, Miss Skeptic. Now come take it or I'll toss it in the canal and you can do for yourself."

I swung over the rail and stepped onto the towpath to take the bag from him. He didn't look any better in the daylight than he had in the dimness of the Underground or the screaming ghost-light of the graveyard. His pallor was more obvious with the morning sun on him—the color of someone who's been very ill for a long time—and the scars around his eye sockets were livid and sickening, stretching into his hair and down his cheek on one side as if made with filthy claws. I couldn't look at his face without considering the state of mind that would allow him to deal himself such damage. I felt queasy at the thought. I wondered for a moment why it hadn't happened to me. Even in the best light, my dad had been a bit over the edge, and Marsden had apparently gone several miles into insanity before he'd come back out. If he had.

With the sack in my arms, I climbed back onto the narrow boat. Marsden followed, wary of every step. I couldn't decide if it was the motion or the mere fact that it was a boat that upset him.

Michael stuck his tousled head out of the hatch. "What's going on? Oh. You're back," he added in a cold voice when he saw Marsden.

"And bearing gifts," Marsden replied. "So shut it if you want brekkie."

Michael drew his head back in, muttering, "You're a cranky old bastard in the morning. . . ."

"I am a cranky old bastard all the time, boy. As would you be were you a hundred and fifty," Marsden added.

"I wouldn't have pegged you a day over a hundred and twelve," Michael snarked back.

I followed them down into the cabin and through to the kitchen—galley, whatever—to unpack the bag on the counter. Among the assorted largesse I found coffee and bacon, though I couldn't say it looked like any bacon I'd ever had—more like a thinly sliced section of a large, boneless pork chop. But it tasted delicious once Michael had cooked it up with a half dozen eggs.

Michael withheld Marsden's plate. "A hundred and fifty, huh?"

"Give or take a few decades."

"Don't look it."

Marsden turned his head without raising his face toward the younger man. "Time moves very slowly when you're spendin' it in the comp'ny of the livin' dead."

"You mean vampires?"

"I mean all of 'em. Ghosts, vampires, lyches, banshees, wights, zombies, darkwalkers—things what ain't quite dead but ought to be."

Michael sent a skittish glance at me, and while he looked away, Marsden snatched the plate from his hands and cackled in horrible glee.

"Hey!"

"It's unwise to get between a cunning man and his breakfast, boy."

"A cunning man? Isn't that another word for warlock?" Michael shot back.

"Hardly," Marsden replied around a mouthful of food. "Warlock means 'oath breaker.' That I am not. Nor any sort of mage—which is what the cunning folk are. Mind your terminology or you're likely to bollocks up our job today. The sisters are empty heads, but if you give offense they're as like as any to trap up and turn a cold shoulder. So guard your mouth."

"Just who are these sisters?" Michael demanded.

"Oh, you shall see. . . ."

"How do we know this isn't some trap or game of yours?" the boy snapped.

I rolled my eyes. "How 'bout you both shut up and eat? I want to get this over with as quickly as possible. I assume you guys do, too."

Michael looked abashed while Marsden just kept his face down over his food. I didn't think the other Greywalker was embarrassed; he just didn't care. I wondered if he really was as old as he claimed.

Once we were done eating and had started walking under his directions, I asked him.

"I've given up countin'," he answered. "I meant what I told the lad, though—time's different when you walk in the Grey. When you're in the thick, y'don't age like normal. After a while, people start to notice you ain't as old as y'ought to be. Had to leave me village and come here to the Smoke when they noticed. Hadn't given it any heed till then—couldn't see me own face anyhow." He made a dismissive hacking sound in the back of his throat and went on. "You'd ha' thought they'd take more umbrage at my going mad and tearing me eyes out, but that they took in stride. That I wasn't as old as what I ought to be frightened 'em more than all the raving I'd ever done about the things in the fen and the battalions of dead tommies. There's more ghosts and creatures of the Grey here, but at least they ain't no one I knew." His face had gone hard, the expression rigid as a wall to hide behind.

I broke his mood by scoffing. "You're saying we're immortal?"

"Not a bit. We age and we die, but time does what it pleases round us and we've very little say in it. More I don't know, but I know that bloody well."

I thought a moment. "You said you were gifted with premonition—"

"Cursed with it. No sort of bloody gift. All me life. When it began to get worse—when it all started coming clear rather than hintin' and dreamin' and disappearin' when I reached for it—that's when the worst started."

"That's a function of time, though, isn't it? Premonition? A glimpse forward."

"Perhaps."

"And you have a way with the temporaclines that I certainly don't. Maybe it's the same thing. Maybe your . . . curse isn't premonition, but something to do with time in the Grey. That's why you look . . . seventy or so, not however old you really are."

He grunted and walked on. Michael shot a curious glance at me and started to say something. I put a finger over my lips, shook my head, and caught up to Marsden again.

"I take it back," he said.

"What?" I asked.

"You might actually be clever enough to trip up that white-scaled bastard."

"Who?" I wasn't on board the same train of thought, apparently.

"Wygan. You might do very well after all."

"So you're glad you didn't shove me into that tree?"

"We'll have to see. You're still too naive by half. Still . . ." he added, but said no more, shrugging one shoulder and continuing in silence.

Now I got it: Marsden was as bad at saying he was sorry as I was. The food and this odd admission were as close to an apology as I was likely to get. I wasn't sure what to think of it. I still wasn't sure how much I trusted him, though it might have been a bit more than I had the night before.

I could tell Michael wanted to ask what was going on, what we'd been talking about, but he took a good look at my face and kept his mouth shut. He was dealing with these inflections of strangeness much better than his brother ever had. I hoped Will was all right, wherever he was. And Quinton, too. My sense of impending crisis was growing.

We crossed a road and passed by a large terra-cotta-colored building that turned out to be part of the British Library, according to the sign. It wasn't what I'd have expected, except for a glimpse of a much older building through the straight angles of the gate and the big red building. A little farther on, we crossed the large street we'd been following that ran from King's Cross past Euston Station. I could see the big war memorials and remains of the first train station's driveway just across the road as Marsden came to a stop in front of a wrought iron fence that stretched the whole block. A discreet sign mounted on the fence noted that the building's architectural details were under renovation, and thanked some public trust and a list of donors in the name of the St. Pancras parish for their generosity. I guessed this must be the new St. Pancras church, though it certainly wasn't less than two hundred years old to my eyes.

"Here they are." Marsden waved at the soot-streaked building on the other side of the fence. A long, tall wall of once-white stone pushed up from the lawn around the building. Greek revival and very Georgian in design. A couple of bright red doors punctuated the wall. The nearest was just in front of us in a jutting corner under a sort of porch roof that was held up by three Grecian-style statues and one lump swathed in white Tyvek instead of pillars.

"The caryatids?" Michael squeaked.

Marsden humphed. "My Greek sisters. Or at least they look it. Very popular, the Greek look, when they was installed. Bit too short, mind—cut 'em off in the middle so they'd fit. Just mouthpieces, though. Not a decent thought in any of their own heads. They mostly let the dead speak through them, but they do have some personality of their own. You'd best be nice to 'em or they won't say nowt."

"But they're statues!"

"Empty iron pillars, actually. The statue part's just clay. But y'see, the pillars reach down into the crypt. What the dead know, they know."

It sounded as likely as anything I'd encountered in the Grey, though it had to sound crazy to most people. I wasn't going to recount my conversation with Sekhmet to Michael, who was still staring in frustration at the rank of caryatids, so I only said, "Things are often more than they seem. Especially old things that have been hanging around a while."

"Most especially old things what have been hanging about over a crypt and across the road from a train station. We should go inside the fence so we don't have to yell at 'em," Marsden suggested.

Bewildered, Michael followed us around the corner and into the church's entryway. We started up the stairs so we could jump down into the small side yard but got no farther as a woman emerged from the church and called out to us.

We all turned.

She was a round, middle-aged woman with muddy red hair, dressed in a bland, conservative dress and low-heeled shoes. "Hullo! Come to see the church?"

Michael was the quickest of us. He turned to face the woman, nodding. "Hi! I'm at university down the street," he said, pointing south. "We wanted to take a look at the caryatids."

"Oh. The one's under renovation, I'm afraid. Would you prefer the south porch? They're all four there."

Michael cast a querying glance at us, and Marsden shook his head. "No. It's the renovations we're interested in."

"Can't see much with the shroud on her," the woman said in doubtful tones. "Should be much more interesting once they've got the work further along."

"That's all right—we want to see the contrast. Y'know. Track the progress over time. Is it all right if we go look at them a little closer? Take some sketches and photos, make some notes about the progress?"

"Oh. Well. Of course. Yes. You can't get up to the porch at the moment to take a really good look—ladder's away for the weekend to discourage children from climbing about—but if you're satisfied looking from the ground . . ."

"That'll be fine. Thanks!" Michael added, waving the woman away with a smile. It was the same sort of reassuring blather his brother used with nervous customers, and hearing Michael do it made me sad and roused my worry over Will anew.

We hopped down and hurried around the building out of the woman's sight.

"Nice work," I said.

Michael grinned and took the lead to the crypt. Once in front of its red door, Marsden resumed command.

"That was cleverly done, boy. Care to be the lookout while we see who's home?"

"Lookout for what?"

"Anyone as might think it odd that we're talking to statues."

Michael nodded and agreed to keep his eyes peeled. Marsden told me to lean back against the fence so I could keep an eye on the three uncovered statues while he tried to get their attention.

I put my weight on the fence and looked up. The three statues were identical except that one was the mirror image of the other two. They were all long-haired women wearing some kind of Grecian dress—not a toga, since I knew only men wore those—and each had an extinguished torch of reeds resting on the ground in one hand and a jug dangling from the other hand. They looked rather odd from my angle; like their legs were too long and heavy for their bodies. And the faces and hair didn't seem like the ones I'd seen in museums; they were somehow more Western and smooth than I remembered.

Marsden spoke quietly. "Good morning. Anyone care to talk? We're in need of some help." I wouldn't have expected such a deferential tone from him, but I suppose when you're dealing with a potential cryptful of ghosts, you don't start out by pissing them off.

Nothing happened for a while. The air around the crypt seemed a bit brighter than the air farther away, but it didn't seem particularly energized and there was no sign of specific ghosts, only a single hot line of blue energy that struck through the crypt from the east side. Then something pale white seeped up from the dirty stones and wreathed around the three statues. The plastic sheeting billowed in opposition to the prevailing wind of passing traffic. A second flush of colored mist and spiderweb light crept up the figures and played over their faces, casting shadows that made them seem alive.

"Go away," one of the statues moaned.

"It's much too early to get up," another groused. "Can't you come back later?"

A girl giggled, a slightly cracked sound like someone on the verge of a breakdown, while the covered one muttered unintelligible word gravel.

None of them were actually moving at all, yet the voices seemed to come from them into my ears, not straight into my head the way some ghosts did. Michael was staring at them with eyes wider than the church doors. I motioned him to get back to his job. If he could make out the presence of whatever animated the caryatids, it was a safe bet others might, too, and that wouldn't do.

"Mornin', my dears," Marsden said.

A muffled voice spoke from somewhere inside the crypt, rising upward, "Is that my Peter?"

"Of course it's Peter. No one else bothers to come talk to us."

"I can't see him. Could you move aside, please?"

Someone scoffed, and the Grey pall over the second caryatid from the left rippled and turned pink, giving the statue a startling semblance of life. The eyes of the statue seemed to blink and the shadow of a smile played across the mouth. The caryatid next to it frowned.

"Good morning, Peter," the pink one trilled in a voice so excessively sweet it could have given diabetes to abstemious sheep. "It's so lovely to see you again. It's been a very long time since you visited."

"Gad," the darker one in the middle muttered in a surprisingly deep voice. "I may be unwell if she keeps on."

"Don't be snippy," the one on the far end chastised. "We don't get so many visitors who actually listen anymore."

"But do we have to put up with that for it?"

"Do they have to be so loud?" I asked, casting a glance at the passersby on the sidewalk.

"I 'spect it's the iron column inside 'em," Marsden said in a low voice. "Resonates." He turned back to the pink caryatid. "Good morning, Hope, and you, too, Temperance, Prudence." I guessed that was the dark, grumpy one and the pale, cautious one, in order.

The Tyvek rattled and deflated.

"What are you doing?" the statue in the middle snapped—Temperance, I thought.

"I can't see anything—there's a bag on my head!" a new voice whined.

"Chastity!" Prudence, the one at the open end, called. "Come over here and share with me. Leave Tempe alone. You know how she gets."

The fourth voice muttered something that might have been "old bat," and moved to the far end, making the shape and visage of the caryatid's face blur and ripple.

They were like the caricatures of their names. "Don't tell me," I muttered. "The four on the south side are the other virtues: Faith, Justice, Fortitude, and Charity."

"No idea. Them four don't talk." Marsden turned back to the masonry sisters. "I am havin' a problem, so naturally I come to you for help."

"Oh? What sort of problem?" Prudence asked.

"Something unsavory, I've no doubt," Temperance added with a sniff.

"Do you suppose it's very unsavory?" Chastity's voice asked, giggling a little.

"Oh, I'm sure not!" Hope twittered. "And of course we'll help. Of course we will!"

"Let us hear what it is he wants first, Hope," Prudence cautioned. "Don't be so, so . . ."

"Intemperate?" Temperance supplied.

"Well . . . yes. What is it that you want of us, Peter?"

"You see the lad there? He's lost his brother—taken away by the vampires and their kin. This . . . young woman is lookin' for him, but we don't know which of the clans might have taken the fella or where."

"It might have something to do with some amphorae—or not," I added.

"You mean the jars . . . with the blood?" Chastity asked with a hint of avidity.

"Ewww!" Hope squealed.

Marsden turned his eyeless face toward me. I shrugged. "They keep coming up. Jakob and Purcell were connected to them and Sekhmet wasn't happy about them. They were kept at Sotheby's for a while, which is the last place anyone seems to have seen Will. Whoever has the amphorae knows something about all this."

He grunted.

"They've been broken," Chastity mourned.

"Good," said Temperance. "They sound entirely unsavory."

"How do you know that?" I asked.

"Barnaby told me."

I glanced at Marsden again. He hadn't turned his face away and seemed to know I was looking at him. "Probably one of the dead in the crypt," he said.

I turned my attention back to the caryatids. "How would Barnaby know anything about them? How do you, if you don't mind my asking?"

"How indeed!" Prudence declared, rippling a bit as if she were trying to glare at the other spirit sharing her statue.

"Barnaby Smith is a drunkard and a liar for all that he kept the church records at St. James's," Tempe stated. "You should consider his every word with suspicion."

"I like him!" Chastity flared, turning the statue she shared with Prudence shocking red. "He's not a prig like you!"

"Oh, Chassy, please!" Hope twittered.

"My dears, we've no time for this," Marsden cut in. "There's a fella gone missing and the longer he's among their kind . . . Well, you know what might happen."

The arguing statues fell silent.

Marsden waved at me to continue.

"Chastity, how did you know about the amphorae?" I asked.

"They passed this way in the Underground. I was just . . . I was bored. I just thought I'd take a look in the tunnel. . . . There's so many funny little bits of tunnel and sometimes I can catch someone staring at me. It's fun to see their faces! Oo! A haunt!" She giggled the same slightly unbalanced laugh I'd heard when we arrived. Time was not being easy on her.

"Who had them and what were they doing with them?"

"Oh. Some lot of Red Guard. But they didn't notice me. Dull old duffers, the lot of them—no fun at all. They just wanted to carry their boxes off, never mind me. They were taking them toward Islington. I could smell that the jars had blood in them and it was so wonderfully gothic—just like a novel!—and I so wanted to know what they were going to do. Some kind of ritual or something, I thought. But no. They just carried them off and broke them, Barnaby said." The disappointment of her ghoulish hopes was palpable as a settling green fog around the farthest caryatid.

I hid my disgust. "How did Barnaby know?" I inquired.

"Oh. I asked him and some of the others if they'd go a-haunting for me, keep an eye out and all. And Barnaby said he'd seen the jars down under the old priory and then they were all smashed up the next night. It was so disappointing."

"Which priory was that?"

She sighed as if she thought me very stupid. "The priory of St. John, of course, in the parish of St. James Clerkenwell. Barnaby used to keep the parish records at St. James's. And since St. James's is near one of the Underground stops, I thought he might be able to watch for me. I asked some of the others, but they didn't see anything."

All roads lead to Clerkenwell, I thought. "Why didn't you go yourself?"

"I can't go far from the church here, can I?" she snapped. "I'm not a proper ghost at all. It's so unfair!"

"There's no need for that sort of histrionics, my girl," Temperance chided. "Things could be quite a bit worse for you."

"Worse! You haven't got a bag over your head day and night!"

"Chastity, really. It's just temporary," said Prudence.

Hope chimed in. "And you'll be the prettiest of us all when they're done!"

Chastity made a dismissive noise. "Phooey."

"Chastity," I interrupted. "Could I talk to Barnaby for a few minutes?"

"No," she replied in a petulant tone. "I would have to go fetch him and who knows what I'd miss?"

"I promise we won't say anything while you're gone. Would you please fetch Barnaby?"

"Don't be contrary," Prudence said.

"Well . . . I shall, but only if the handsome one asks me to."

"Excuse me?"

"That lad you brought. He hasn't even looked at me. I want him to ask me."

"Chastity, don't be such a goose. The lad doesn't even know you're here," Prudence said.

"He is rather nice-looking, though," Hope added.

"I shall be decidedly ill if this continues," Temperance muttered.

Nothing like playing matchmaker to a ghost—or not-quite-ghost. I turned and tapped Michael on the shoulder.

"Hey, I need a favor."

"What?"

"Have you been following any of this?"

"Only you and creepy-face."

Marsden snorted.

"OK, a little, but not much," Michael admitted. "Why?"

"This is nuts . . ." I said.

"Well, yeah. It's all been pretty nuts for a while. What nutty thing are we doing now?"

"There's this . . . spirit here in one of the caryatids. We need her to go get another ghost named Barnaby for us to talk to. But she says she wants you to ask her. She thinks you're cute."

"Me? What? She what? OK, that is absolutely the biggest chunk in the fruitcake so far. She wants me to ask her to get this Barnaby?"

"Because she thinks you're handsome," I added, nodding.

He raised his eyebrows and blew a silent whistle. "Well . . . all right . . ."

I pointed him toward the right statue. "Her name's Chastity," I whispered.

Michael turned pink and looked up at the statue. He tried to smile, but it was a nervous grimace. "Umm . . . Chastity . . . would you please— oh, man this is so freakin' weird." He cleared his throat and restarted. "Chastity, would you please get Barnaby for us? Umm . . . please?"

He looked at me, wrinkling his face into an unspoken question.

I put up a finger to tell him to wait while I listened for the caryatid's response.

"He doesn't seem very sincere," Chastity complained.

"Give over, my girl! Surely you're satisfied that the lad's made the effort at all? Gad, he probably can't even hear you! I say take what you've got and be happy with it, you silly little chit!"

"Tempe!" Hope gasped.

"Oh, dear . . ." sighed Prudence.

"Oh . . . all right! He is very pretty. And he did ask. Though I wish he'd cut his hair so I could see his eyes. . . ."

"What's going on?" Michael murmured, looking uncomfortable.

"They're arguing about how well you did. And if you should cut your hair," I said.

"Oh, for God's sake!" Michael stared back up at the caryatids. "Please, you guys, just help us out! Harper says she needs to talk to Barnaby so we can find my brother. Please get Barnaby. Please? I just want my brother back. . . ."

Temperance sniffed, no doubt put off by Michael's taking the Lord's name in vain, but Prudence and Hope both glittered and smiled.

The changeable shadow of Chastity wavered. "Oh . . . all right," she said. "I'll fetch him." She flickered away, drawing down into the crypt.

THIRTY-SIX

"She's going," I whispered to Michael as Chastity slipped away into the crypt.

He breathed a sigh of relief. "I hate this."

"None of us are thrilled, believe me."

"I wish I could hear them or see them or something. All I get is mumbling and flashes of light in the corners of my eyes. This is . . . I don't know. It's crazy. I mean, maybe they aren't there at all and you and Marsden are just—"

"We're not. I swear there are ghosts and vampires and we are doing what we can with one to stop the other and get Will back. I know you don't have a good reason to trust me, but try. I do care what happens to your brother and I'm not messing with you."

His shoulders slumped. "It's just so crazy. . . ."

"I know." I'd have said more, but a misty figure pushed its way out of the crypt through the red doors so it stood on the grass with us.

He was a tall man who stooped horribly and had a small potbelly, so he looked like a numeral six. His hair had thinned into a monk's tonsure and the bags under his eyes were heavier than those in an industrial laundry. Even pale in death, his nose, cheeks, and ears were reddened by the spiderweb veins of alcohol abuse. He shifted back and forth, as if constantly shuffling his feet.

He addressed himself to Marsden. "I am . . . I am Barnaby Smith. Of . . . umm . . . St. James's in Clerkenwell. Miss Chastity said you wished to . . . talk to me?" His voice rose to a squeak at the end.

No wonder he'd been a drunk: The world scared him senseless.

Marsden pointed at me. "She'll ask the questions."

"Oh. I . . . well. All right. I'm at your service Miss . . . umm . . . Miss . . . ?"

"Blaine," I said.

"Blaine? Are you by chance related to Anselm Blaine of Peartree Court?"

"Not that I'm aware of," I replied.

"Oh. Pity. I always thought him a fine fellow. I . . . you must pardon me; I find it rather hard to hear you."

I shifted a little closer to the Grey, watching the colors of the grid and the shapes of ghostly things grow brighter and more solid. Smith looked a bit more like a person in the mist-world, but not so much that I could forget he was long dead. "Is that better?"

"Oh, yes! Quite improved. Thank you."

This was going to take forever at this rate. I kept my impatience under control and turned my gaze full on Barnaby Smith.

"Mr. Smith, Chastity said you'd seen some Greek amphorae under St. John's priory. Can you tell me more about them and when you saw them last?"

"Oh. Those. Umm . . . well. Nasty business. They contained blood and body parts—gruesome, to say the least. I did see them in the old catacomb. That's under the current crypt—very old, quite probably part of the original foundations from the twelfth century. Terrible condition. Terrible."

I gave him a stern glance.

"Oh! I am sorry. I— Oh. Ha-ha," he laughed nervously. "Yes, not to the point. I am sorry. Umm . . . I'm not sure what they were up to, but the Red Guard who brought them left them for a . . . ah . . . a sorcerer," he whispered. "And some of the Red Brothers—"

"I'm sorry, Mr. Smith. I don't know who you mean. Could you fill me in?"

He blinked at me. "Oh! I just assumed. . . . You're with . . . him. I thought you knew."

"I don't. I'm not from the area. I don't know all the players."

"'Players.' Ah, that is a fine description. But, oh my . . . if you don't know—"

"I assume they're vampires, but what else?"

"Oh! Yes, you do know! What a relief. I found my life a nightmare when I realized— Oh, but that's not what you want to know."

"Yes. I need to know about the amphorae, who had them, what happened to them, and if you know anything about a man called William Novak. Or John Purcell."

"Purcell!" He raised a silvery hand and pressed it to his chest. "My—my stars. Mr. Purcell. I believe he's a prisoner! I can't say I have much pity for them, but it's cruel to see what they do to one another. They don't die easily, you know. Would that I had been a stronger man in life—but no. I suppose it wouldn't have changed anything."

He noticed me crinkling my brow.

"Oh. I do apologize. Here, let me explain."

"Go right ahead," I invited. I knew he'd dither less if allowed to tell his tale his own way and I sat on my impatience as he did.

THIRTY-SEVEN

"I really had no idea," Smith began, "when I came to St. James's of what a horror was below the surface of our fine parish. It's a very old parish, you know. The well and the baths had been there a very long time and it had been quite the pastoral spa once—where the gentry would go to escape the city. There was always some friction between priory and parish. But I didn't know that . . . among our parishioners there were so many . . . of them."

"Them?" I asked.

"The . . . vampires," Smith whispered, and it came out on a cold breath that chilled the warm summer morning. Even Michael shivered, though he plainly hadn't heard a word. "Once I realized what they were, I was shocked! I was outraged. I—I told the vicar, the rector, the prior. . . . They all laughed at me. Well, in our modern age, who wouldn't? But the word got out. They knew that I knew and they took delight in tormenting me with the powerlessness of my position. I was just a lay clerk; not a priest or even an assistant curate who could go to the bishop. Oh, my . . ."

"What's wrong?" I asked.

"Oh. I . . . I find it distressing still. I'm afraid . . . I took to drink.

Weakness. Terrible weakness." He shook his head for such a long time I thought he'd given up until he said, "I suppose, in its way, the drink saved me. I lost my position and was asked to leave the parish. I could have stayed in Clerkenwell—even a bishop can't really force you to leave your home—but I ran from it. Oh, not far. This pleasant green here is not too far removed in miles, but a world away to me.

"I made a pleasant life for myself. I married a widow who had a small bit of money and we were not unhappy. But I could not forget what I saw. It haunted me. And . . . I suppose, that is why . . . I still feel drawn there."

I looked expectantly at him, waiting for the rest of the story.

"The . . . uh . . . Red Brothers—that is what they termed themselves—had come from the priory originally. I don't know how they came into being, they were just . . . there, but there was a falling-out among them. A bloody thing, played out beneath the streets in secret places carved out by the old rivers and the Romans long before the priory was raised there. The slaughter was immense among the servants of the Brothers. The Brothers themselves were too hard to kill, and most escaped unscathed. When they had done with their battle, they broke into two parties and mockingly named themselves after the houses of God below which they had rampaged. They still call themselves St. James and St. John—the Red Brotherhood of St. James or St. John, as they please. The others, the white creatures from the docks, they had no part of it—or none I could see."

Marsden leaned close to my ear and murmured, "He means the asetem. The docks and south of the river is their haunt."

"Then what happened recently?" I asked Smith.

"Oh. I . . . I didn't see it all. It began a month ago or so . . . I think. Time . . . is so hard to tell now. The white ones started showing up and the strife between the Jameses and Johns increased—I feared there might be bloodletting again. But they quieted. Until the Greek jars arrived. I hadn't paid them much attention at first—I didn't want to know what they might contain. But I had to investigate when Miss Chastity asked it of me. I can hardly say no to a charming lady."

He gave me a quick, nervous smile before lowering his head to watch his invisible feet a moment.

"So, you went to see what had happened. . . ." I prompted.

"Oh, yes. I went back to where I'd first seen the amphorae. It was very hard as it was the same place beneath the priory where so much carnage had been wreaked during my time. But the jars had been broken already and it seemed something must have happened of which I could not guess. And then Mr. Purcell appeared in that place. The Red Brothers were very cruel to him and they taunted him horribly. About what I couldn't understand. I never have figured it out. . . . But from what they said, this I believe to be true: The creature that was in the amphorae was taken out and reassembled into . . . whatever it was, and it is still there, somewhere."

That was startling. Sekhmet hadn't mentioned anything in the jars except blood, magic, and corruption. "A creature?" I questioned. Maybe that had been the corruption. . . . "What sort?"

"I have no idea, nor do I want one! Please, don't ask it of me. It was chopped into pieces and reassembled from those horrible jars. When I saw what they were doing, their sorcerer making it whole again . . . I—I am not a brave man and I could not bear to look. . . ."

I nodded. "I understand." But I didn't understand it all. A sorcerer? What had it made from the parts? Did the vampires have a spellbinder working with them? Or was it one of the asetem? Of the vampires I knew, only Carlos had any magical powers. Edward had told me most of them didn't, but maybe that wasn't true for the Egyptians. Or maybe there was another player in the mix.

By his quivering and translucence, I knew I couldn't press Smith any further on that. It was frustrating, but it would do me no good to let it show, so I changed tack and hoped I wouldn't regret my noble ignorance later. "Which of the factions has Purcell?" I asked. "St. James or St. John?"

"St. James. I don't know why they chose to store the jars beneath the priory of St. John—perhaps to work some magic against their enemies? I don't know. I feel for Mr. Purcell—I knew him in my time. He . . . was like a . . . go-between. He did business for both parties and they agreed to let him alone. But now the Jameses do him great harm. He is . . . not a good man—he is not a man, indeed—but none deserve the tortures to which they put him, poor soulless thing."

"What about William Novak? Do you know anything about him?"

"Who? I don't know the name. . . ."

"He's the missing man, this young man's brother," I clarified, waving my hand toward Michael, who was holding back with an anxious frown on his face. "He's a young man, too, but he has white hair, like an old man. He's very tall and thin. Have you seen—"

"Oh! That one! Oh . . . no." His voice was freighted with dread.

I restrained an urge to lean forward, to grab for the dithering ghost and shake information out of him, but with Michael looking on, I didn't dare make a move that might upset the boy. I didn't know how much he was picking up but he was observant and smart, and if I acted distressed just after using Will's name, he'd know something bad was in the works.

"Go on."

"I have seen him. I have. But they move him about. And . . . they . . . they torment him most horribly. He cries— Oh, my soul. It's too much to bear," the ghost said, covering his face with his hand.

"Please," I asked. "Could you tell me where he is right now?"

"I don't know that. As I said, they move him."

"Could you go look?"

"No! No. I . . . I couldn't. I can't. I— No. No, no, no," Smith whispered, aghast.

Barnaby Smith stepped back from us, staring at each of us in turn as if we would leap on him and rend him to bits in a moment. He gasped, clasping his hands over his heart as he backed away. "I'm sorry. . . . I cannot. I cannot. . . ." And he vanished back through the red crypt doors.

"What appalling manners," Temperance muttered from above.

"I think he's distraught," said Prudence. "Poor fellow. He must have seen something truly nasty down there."

"But don't you think he'll reconsider and come back?" Hope asked. "Really, it would be the right thing to do. . . ."

"Which is why he won't," Tempe said.

"Oh, Tempe . . ."

"Do use what little brain Inwood gave you, my girl."

"Tempe!" Prudence gasped.

"Oh, you're just horrid!" Hope shouted, and vanished with the sound of a lightbulb exploding, leaving her statue blank and cold.

"Whatever is the matter with the chit?" Tempe grumbled. "It's true. Mr. Inwood wasn't overly generous in what he gave us. He even cut us short in the middle!"

"And you are not overly generous in anything," Prudence retorted. "Now I shall have to go after her. Oh, dear." Her statue also went dark.

"I hope you got what you were after, Peter. I doubt they'll any of them come back."

"It will do or we'll make do," Marsden replied.

"Yes. Well," Temperance said. "I shall go and look after them. Mr. Smith is an upsetting presence. It's quite a pity his wife, Rosemary, has left him on his own, but I suppose one can't grumble about another's passing on. Now I must go. Good luck to you, Peter—and your friends."

Given the inflection she gave to "friends," I was pretty sure she didn't care for me and Michael. I wasn't entirely sure she liked Marsden, either. Temperance's caryatid also went dark, leaving us alone between the crypt and the iron fence.

We waited a few minutes in case Chastity returned, but didn't get lucky. Marsden and I gave up. I stepped back from the Grey to what passes for normal to me and turned toward Michael. He looked everywhere but at me.

"Michael. Are you all right?" I asked.

"Yeah. Yeah, I'm fine," he replied too quickly.

I hadn't had a chance to prep him for what happened when I submerged into the Grey and got a bit see-through in the normal, and he'd said he saw and heard a little. Anyone would find such things disconcerting; for a kid who'd been through what he had in the past day, it must have been staggering.

"Michael—" I started, turning up one hand and reaching for him.

He waved me off. "No. I'm fine. Just. Fine."

It was better than his brother's reaction, but it still left me frustrated. Doing my job had always caused problems for someone, and it had gotten worse after I become a Greywalker. I didn't have the luxury of making other people comfortable about what I did or how I did it most of the time. Usually, I didn't have to worry about people seeing me do something strange; most people ignore the majority of what goes on around them, especially when it's weird or upsetting. But Michael had had this dumped on him with no mitigation or preparation. I felt rotten about it, but what was I supposed to do? If I went at it with kid gloves, what was already bad would have turned worse—if it hadn't already, and I feared it had.

"Time for tea and discussion," Marsden stated. "Keep up, you two."

He headed off through the church gates, cane out in front and confident that we were trailing him like ducklings.

I made a rueful face at Michael.

He gave a self-conscious shrug and took off after the blind Greywalker.

THIRTY-EIGHT

"St. James's," Marsden said over tea. "Very odd, that."

Marsden had led us to a grubby little shop on a side street near the British Museum, which turned out to serve good, cheap tea and sandwiches that had no resemblance to delicate bits of thin bread and watercress. We'd spent a quarter of an hour bringing Michael up to speed, though he was thinking and watching more than talking while Marsden and I tried to make a plan. Michael seemed to getting his mind around it, though.

"What's so odd? I mean, aside from ghosts and vampires and talking statues . . ." he snarked, swallowing a mouthful of bread and meat.

"What's odd, boy, is that the Red Brothers of St. James is the faction what Harper's employer used to run with. Purcell was his man of business. But he doesn't know what's happened to Purcell, so the conclusion I draw is that either the rift is mended between the Brotherhoods—which I doubt—or someone's suborned the whole lot. That would be a rather good trick. And if it's done, it's the asetem what have done it. That could be worse, but not a whole bloody lot."

"What's the asetem?" Michael asked.

"A different type of vampire altogether—"

Before Marsden could get started, my cell phone rang. I'd almost forgotten I had it until it started jiggling around and making my purse rattle on the tile floor. I answered it and let Marsden explain the Egyptian vampires.

It was Quinton. "Hi," he started, breathless and sounding strained. "I'm sorry I couldn't call you back last time. Things are getting scary here. I'm not at my place; I'm at yours—it's safer, if that tells you anything."

"What's happening? Is it . . . a vampire thing?"

"Right in one. It hasn't moved up from the shadows yet, but it's bad. The dark places are not safe. And there's a lot of new creeps around making a whole lot of trouble. I'm not sure if it's better for you to come home right away or stay out of it."

My heart seemed to be tap dancing and my stomach twisted. "I've only been gone . . . what? Three days? When did this start?"

"Pretty much as soon as you left. It's like they were waiting for you to be gone."

"Oh, no," I said, feeling that sense of doom hanging over me again like the Sword of Damocles. "I think it's connected to my case here. Or rather, it's all part of the same thing."

"Damn it. I was afraid of that. Edward's in this, isn't he?"

"Somehow, yeah. But I don't know exactly how. Keep a very low profile, and especially keep away from Wygan."

"The DJ?"

"Yeah, that one. He's not your average bloodsucker. He's something special and very nasty." Just thinking of the feast for the asetem that massive destruction and unrest among Seattle's vampires would provide nauseated me, and from what Marsden had said about Wygan's known plans, that was just the icing on the cake.

"Oh?" Quinton prompted.

"Yeah. He's like . . ." And I stopped, not sure I could explain it succinctly and still include the shades of suspicion, implication, and intuition that were holding it all together in my mind. "Damn it. It's complicated. He's got very big plans that include me and the Grey and something about Edward, too. He's been pulling strings and causing trouble since I was kid. I still need to find one more big piece of the puzzle and I think I'll know what I am and what he has in mind."

"What you are? You're Harper Blaine. You're what you make of you, not what some megalomaniac vampire wants."

I could have reached through the phone and kissed him for that. It reminded me that no matter what Wygan had in mind, the decisions weren't all his.

I grinned for the first time in days. "Yeah. I'll give you the whole messy story when I get back, but I have to finish up a few things here first. I'm not sure if Edward is playing me or if he's really a victim, but whatever else is happening, the local vampires have William Novak and it looks like they've been using him to get to me. For Wygan. Why is still a mystery, though."

The pause grew very long. "Novak. Your ex."

"Yes."

"I guess the ghosts were right."

"Sorry. I'm not sure what you mean."

"They said it wasn't what you thought. All this stuff that's been going on isn't about the vampires; this is about you."

"Not all of it. Some of it's a plan of Wygan's—"

"That needs you to make it work and needs Edward or something of Edward's. Whatever's going on there is all about you. Or they wouldn't have taken your ex."

He went on as I fell silent, thinking about what he'd said. "The stuff that's going on here has the feeling of clearing the decks. It's dangerous, but it's not concentrated yet. It started when you left. And I think it'll shift into higher gear when you get back. Or whenever they find Edward."

"Every vampire in Seattle knows where to find Edward."

"No, they don't and neither do a lot of other people. That's what I needed to tell you: Edward's missing. It's on the news."

"What?" I hoped that Edward had only pulled back to hide in his bunker if handbaskets were indeed hell bound. If Edward was gone, I might be in a lot of trouble when I got back to Seattle—or even before, if the things I was thinking were true.

"They're hinting he's been kidnapped," Quinton said. "The vampires are going nuts. They're all over the place and they're all over each other. The new ones—"

"Creepy white bastards that seem a little . . . snakelike?"

"Yeah."

"The asetem-ankh-astet. They're Wygan's people. They might be magic users, so stay away from them."

"I'm already staying away. They resist the stunners and they scare the crap out of me. They seem to scare the other vamps, too. I don't know if it'll get worse before you get here, but it's not pretty now. It might be better if you don't come home."

"You don't want me to come back?"

"I want you, but I think, given what you've said, that things will get worse when you do. You don't have to play whatever game Wygan is up to."

"I'm afraid I do, but I don't have to play it his way if I know how to avoid it. And I can't leave here without getting Will out first. Even if they didn't try to use him against me again . . ."

"No. You can't leave a friend behind. Not even an ex-boyfriend. I'll hold on here. Let me know if you're coming back to Seattle or if I should bail out with Chaos and meet you elsewhere."

I bit my lip, worried and conflicted. "How—how is the furball?"

"Crazed. She zooms around the floor like she's chasing things, and she makes that chittering sound and dances around with her mouth open like she's just killed the biggest rat in history."

"You getting anything on your detectors?"

"Yes, I am. But without you to confirm it, I'm not sure I've got a good calibration. It could be stray cell phone signals or it could be the Loch Ness monster for all I can tell. Harper . . . God, I wish you were here."

Something hard knotted up in my throat and made it difficult to talk. "Me, too. I'll finish up as fast as I can," I promised.

My companions were both watching me as I disconnected. I swallowed a few times to clear the emotion that choked me. "Change of plan," I said. "We have to move faster than I'd hoped."

Marsden pursed his mouth. "So it's startin', is it?"

I just nodded. Michael looked grim.

Marsden grinned, a terrifying and feral thing with his yellowed teeth and gouged eye sockets. "Right then. We'll be after the Primate of St. James tonight."

"The what?" I queried.

Michael looked startled.

"I don't mean the Archbishop of Canterbury, boy," Marsden said. Then he turned back to me. "It's their little joke, y'see. They're taking the piss by calling the head of their cabal the 'Primate' as if he were the equal of the Archbishop of All England."

"Seattle's only got one community of vampires. . . ." I said, though it appeared that wasn't strictly true anymore.

"London's older, more factionalized. Some of the Brothers go back to the founding of the city under the Romans. They're playing by a different set of rules than what your lot is. You could approach the Primate of St. John and hope to get him on your side, but you haven't got that time. You'll have to go straight for St. James."

"No."

"And why not, may I ask?"

"St. James is in the Pharaohn's pocket."

"Hark at her. The expert!"

Annoyed now, I shook my head and snapped at him, "Listen. Two years ago in Seattle the Pharaohn used another vampire to watch me. Her name was Alice Liddell—"

"Like *Alice in Wonderland* Alice?" Michael asked, wide-eyed.

"Yes, but I'm not sure she's that Alice Liddell, not really. Anyhow. She tried to use me to take Edward out so she could be top dog, but it didn't work. She attacked us and we killed her. Or I thought we had—we left her staked down in a burning building. We assumed she was dust. But I saw her two nights ago in a club in Clerkenwell. It was less than two blocks from St. James's church and she didn't look like she was having any trouble with the locals."

"Are you sure she's got St. James's for the Pharaohn?" Marsden questioned. "She could just be playing her game against Edward again on her own."

I gave some thought before I opened my mouth again. Edward was a common enough name, but Wygan wasn't, so I'd have to speak with care. Michael didn't need to know that one of Seattle's favorite late-night radio personalities and one of its richest citizens were vampires with a deadly grudge that had tangled both himself and his brother in its uncaring coils. "There was an asetem in the club—"

Marsden interrupted me. "'Asete' for just one. 'Asetem' is the plural."

I gave him a sharp nod. "Asete. This asete talked to me, taunting me. She knew Alice, knew who I was, and said something about Alice and the Pharaohn's plans as if I ought to know. She said it would be more fun if I was afraid. Alice is working for the Pharaohn-ankh-astet, and I think it's safe to assume she now controls St. James's or they wouldn't have let her in the place.

"Edward used to have a line on things in St. James's," I continued, "but he lost it when Purcell disappeared. Sekhmet said Purcell's lackey, Jakob, had—" I stopped myself from mentioning the charmed letter that had been sent to Will. "Had got the amphorae for the asetem. I thought she meant the vampires in general then, but now I think she meant the Egyptians. Barnaby said they were the Brothers of St. James, even though they took the jars under the priory of St. John. If anyone would know the difference between the Brotherhoods, I'd imagine it's him. I think they used the priory basement for whatever ritual they did with the jars of blood to raise the creature Barnaby Smith mentioned, and they chose that location to intimidate the Brotherhood of St. John. The timing's right for that skullduggery with the amphorae to be connected to Alice's takeover of St. James's."

"One problem with that," Marsden drawled. "The Brotherhoods both hate the asetem. They've had an agreement for ages to divide London up at the river and not interfere with one another. That's how Edward got hisself run out: He tried to bring the asetem into the Brotherhood of St. James by pulling some jiggery-pokery with the Pharaohn."

"The same Pharaohn?" I asked.

"Yeah. He and Edward is mortal enemies because of that."

"Enemies united . . . Alice, St. James, and the asetem against Edward," I said, fitting the pieces together. Wygan hated Edward for whatever had happened in London. He was running Alice now as he had when we met. "Alice is denying Edward his control in England. Keeping him trapped in Seattle while the Pharaohn starts his ball rolling . . ."

"If you say so."

"Educated guess. My friend on the phone said things are going nuts back home, and there are asetem stirring the pot."

"You should pray he exaggerates, girl."

"I don't think he does. What's happening there is connected to what's happening here. The big players are all in Seattle."

"Except you," Marsden reminded me.

"I'm not a player, according to you. I'm a tool waiting to be shaped and used. I think that's why I was lured to London."

He shrugged. "You say so. Why is St. John not objecting to the asetem in Clerkenwell?" Marsden demanded.

"I'm not sure, but I'd bet whatever they did with the jars under the priory has something to do with it. Probably some kind of intimidation. If I can get to the Primate of St. John, he might help me get past Alice and get Will out."

"You'd have to break St. James. That'll mean breaking this Alice and whatever asetem she's got with her."

"I don't think she's very popular with them. The asete in the club didn't like Alice. She acted like she was working under orders with which she disagreed. Once Alice is gone, I don't think St. James will continue to work with the asetem. But I don't give a damn what becomes of the Red Brotherhoods. I don't care if Edward's empire crumbles and they all kill each other so long as I get Will out alive." And avoid whatever nasty tricks Alice has in store for me, I thought.

THIRTY-NINE

As a result of that conversation, I stood in the basement of a restaurant just off Clerkenwell Road at about ten o'clock that evening. I'd been there for more than ninety minutes. The priory of St. John was a block away and St. James's church was about five blocks away. I'd walked past the clerk's well for which the area was named, tucked behind its window in an office block, as I'd come down from Angel Tube station. I hadn't wanted to run into any guards at Farringdon, even though the walk was a long one and it took me past enemy territory first; a calculated risk. Now deep in the earth, I thought I could hear the water gurgling somewhere nearby and wondered if the well's source lay below St. John's. The lines of the grid were a curiously placid blue with an unhealthy tinge of green from the contaminants in the aquifer. The room I was standing in, however, was charged with red and yellow energy that buzzed around the room like a swarm of bees and thick with the shades of medieval plague victims gasping and dying in forgotten corners, cast out from the clean confines of the priory. They didn't make me feel any better about what I was about to do.

Between us, Marsden and I had concluded that the restaurant housed the nighttime office of Henry Glick, the Primate of the Red

Brotherhood of St. John. My unannounced arrival had thrown the local bloodsuckers into a visible tizzy that had so far worked to my advantage. It was the same reason I'd crossed through St. James's territory on the way: I'd hoped to breed a little confusion and chatter and keep the attention of any snooping vampires on me while Marsden and Michael scouted for the location of Will's imprisonment. I doubted they'd be able to rescue him on their own, but they'd signal me when they found him and we'd carry on from there, depending on what happened with the Primate of St. John.

So I was standing in the dim cellar among the smells of damp wood and spilled beer, waiting for an audience. It didn't feel like the first time I'd met with Edward at the After Dark club in Seattle. I'd been naive and lucky then, however scared and ballsy. This time I knew better and I was a lot more frightened. I hoped the delay wasn't an indication of bad things and I camouflaged my fears in boredom and the discomfort of being in the same clothes I'd been wearing for two days. At least the shower and washer in the boat worked well enough, but I still missed my suitcase and figured I'd never see it again.

Idly staring around the room, I could detect the Grey outline of a door in the stone foundation wall, charmed to appear solid to most people. I pretended not to notice. I sat on a stack of beer kegs and rolled my eyes, yawning for the benefit of my single "escort," a demi-vamp who seemed to be named Dez and who didn't quite ignore me but didn't say much, either. He boiled with unfocused anger and frustration that seemed to have nothing to do with me. Not all demi-vamps are thrilled about their station in life or addicted to the rush I'm told they get from whatever it is that keeps them hovering halfway between one state and the next. The unsure ones, like Dez, don't survive very long.

The restless energy of the room shifted, steadied, and flushed a bloody crimson, reeking of carnage. The suffering ghosts moaned and flickered out, washed away by the influx. Dez stiffened and turned his attention toward the magic doorway as it sparkled and faded to let someone in.

The sound of shoes on stone stairs preceded the appearance of another male vampire. At least, I assumed he was a vampire, since he presented himself with authority, though he didn't have the same aura or look as any vampire I'd met before—even the asetem. He had the strangest eyes I'd ever encountered: silver, pupilless discs that seemed to float in the sclera like coins on a sheen of oil. He was whippet thin and wore a long brick red coat over a dark suit that seemed to have come from some other time and place, though in the glimpse I had of it, I couldn't tell where or when. He had a double aura I'd never seen before: one pure black, relieved by jagged sparks of red; the other a shifting maze of silver planes.

He glanced at me and then at Dez and pointed at me with a jabbing motion. "Search her. Then you come downstairs with us." His was a strange accent with stretched vowels and soft consonants.

He made an ironic little bow to me and then stepped back into the darkness of the concealed doorway. But I could see his unearthly eyes gleaming in the shadow as Dez stepped close to me.

I raised my arms and let Dez pat me down. He was just short of overly familiar in his thoroughness and stiffened as his hand fell on the hard object I'd tucked into the back of my waistband. He yanked it out and brought it out in front of us.

"It's my cell phone," I stated, a bit snappish for effect.

Which it was. Closed and quiet, hardly a threat.

Dez held it toward the vampire in the doorway. I saw the dismissive flap of his hand in the dark. I rolled my eyes and took it back.

"Thanks so much," I said, tucking the phone back into the place I normally holstered my pistol. It felt comfortable there and it was out of the way.

Dez finished the pat down, leaving my wallet and my father's puzzle unmolested in my pockets, and then escorted me toward the concealed stairs. The eerie-eyed vampire preceded us down the steep stone steps. It felt like we were descending a tilted well. Once again I had a sense of water nearby that rose as we went down below its unseen surface, and the sounds I'd thought came from the clerk's well swelled as we continued. We passed through layer on layer of ghosts, descending by centuries until even the Roman soldiers patrolling a phantom riverside were far above our heads. By the time we reached the bottom, the sound was much too loud to be another well, but there was no sign of real water other than some clinging moisture and moss on the walls.

We went down a twisted, arched passage and stepped out into a large, vaulted stone chamber that was lit entirely by candles as long and wide as my arm. I wondered if it was the same place where Barnaby had seen the broken amphorae. Energy seemed to lie at its edges like a live thing held leashed and ready. The room had the intense feel of a place meant for rituals that shouldn't see the light of day.

The room, shrouded with the roiling stink of vampires and their restless red-and-black auras, was unevenly five-sided, and arched doorways cut the walls on all sides. We'd entered on the shortest wall, and directly opposite, in the apex of the crooked pentagon's crown, was a low wooden platform. One of the other arches looked onto the back of the platform at one end. A handful of vampires, demi-vamps, and Red Guard assistants stood around the edges of the room, watching us with a coil of eldritch yellow light beneath their feet. Within the darkened arches, eyes gleamed orange like hellfire from pale smudges.

Two male vampires were waiting for us on the dais, one seated and smiling just a touch, the other standing back a little, his expression one of panic barely held in check. He was bowed down by something, and I could see a bend of yellow light around his body. I wondered who he was and why he seemed to be held prisoner there. I knew I'd interrupted the usual flow of business and I hoped the strange tableau indicated nothing sinister to my purpose, but I wouldn't have bet on it.

The seated vampire stood up as we drew near. He looked more like someone you'd expect to be running the local stevedores' union than a film vampire—stocky, heavy featured, scarred on face and hands, self-conscious in his tailored suit. My unsettling escort stopped at the edge of the platform and glared at Dez and then stepped aside while Dez faded back to the wall.

The husky one from the chair shot an uneasy glance at the silver-eyed vampire. Then he gave me a hollow smile and took half a step forward, closing the distance between us to a couple of feet. With the platform giving him added height, I was still tall enough to see the frightened vampire over his shoulder, but just barely.

"Miss Blaine," the one nearest me started. "Pleased you've come round. We all hoped as you'd be here sooner. I'm Henry Glick." He emphasized "hope" as if I'd disappointed him. His accent was working-class, with the Hs softened almost to silence.

I took Glick's proffered hand with reluctance. I was under no illusion that this was a social visit, but I needed to be polite if I was petitioning his aid. I hated the touch of vampires, though his was much cooler and less nauseating than most. I still took my hand back as quickly as good manners allowed and stepped away a little.

I glanced at the cowering creature behind him. "Have I interrupted something?"

"Not so much. Don't pay that any mind." But as he said it, his gaze slipped to the side and his mouth was stiff, like someone telling an uncomfortable lie.

"Mr. Glick," I started. "I came here on behalf of a . . . former Brother of St. James. I know there's no great love between St. John and St. James's, but I think we may be of use to each other."

"How's that?" Glick asked, licking his lips. A nervous gesture.

"I'm a stranger here, so I'm not entirely sure of the situation, but I suspect there's been a change of management up the street at St. James. Is that true?"

"Ah. Yeah. Clever way o' putting it."

So we'd guessed right about a power grab at St. James's. That didn't cheer me, since it was probably Alice who'd snatched the reins. I felt eyes on me and a chill that pushed through my body, sharp as a knife. A frown creased my face and I tried to clear it away, not wanting to offend the man I was going to ask for help. The resulting expression must have been stiff.

"I believe your rival up the street," I continued, slower, trying to feel my way through the shoals of the situation, "has taken a friend of my employer and a friend of mine prisoner. I'd like to get them back and I think the only way to do it will be to take the current Primate of St. James down."

"Why would you think I'd help you?"

I felt as if I were dragging every syllable from him.

I used the information Marsden had provided. "Because I believe the Primate of St. James has brought the asetem-ankh-astet to your doorstep. She's violated the covenant set long ago among the three clans of London. Asetem are supposed to stay south of the Thames, aren't they? Yet I saw them only a couple of nights ago not a hundred feet from the doors of St. James's church."

"True it is, Miss Blaine. That was the covenant. And the asetem do roam in Clerkenwell, but we—"

"Then why haven't you done anything about it?" I asked, losing a bit of my patience.

The apparently trapped vampire behind Glick writhed and looked down at the floor and then back up at me as if he were trying to direct my eyes to something, but I couldn't risk pulling my attention away from Glick long enough to study the slick-looking patch of stone he stared at.

Glick sighed, his shoulders sagging. "Because I'm no longer the Primate of St. John." He shot a glance over his shoulder, and something stirred in the shadows of the nearest arch. "She is."

"Harper, dear. You were just a day too late," said a female voice, and then it giggled with a greater measure of madness than Chastity's unbalanced laughter had contained.

Most of the arches filled with the pale white presence of the asetem-ankh-astet as they stepped into the verges of the light, their orange-glowing eyes dimming in the room's illumination. The coil of yellow power around the edge of the room shivered and crept higher up the walls, closing the room in a protective circle. I looked toward the empty arch behind the platform where the voice came from.

A slender female strolled out of the darkness, dragging it with her like a train. Alice. She wore some kind of skintight black stuff that looked more like bandages or a winding sheet than clothing, leaving only her head, forearms, and feet uncovered. A bright red choker circled her throat, dangling ruby beads on glowing white skin. Her eyes burned from shadowed sockets above lips stained the deep wine color of a fresh bruise. Wine: that had been the color of her hair when last I'd seen her in Seattle—staked through the chest on the floor of the burning house. Now her hair had gone the dark auburn of dried blood.

"Imagine, trying to suborn my underlings like that," she said. "Naughty, naughty," she added, her voice resonant with pressure against the old geas between us. The geas was a magical compulsion between us; one I'd forced her into so she'd let me live if I let her get to Edward. It bound us both equally. I should have wondered harder about the lingering effect of the geas that kept me from speaking of certain things, or doing them, after I'd presumed her dead. But I hadn't, and now I was going to pay for that.

A dark-haired, bearded man stepped out of the arch behind her and stopped a few paces back, watching the show. A phantom black strand of magic unreeled between him and Alice while another reached out to touch the spooky-eyed creature beside me. A third strand, white and heavier than the others, stretched between the creature and Alice, closing the unnatural triangle. The new man seemed familiar. . . . He carried his own cloud of ugliness that boiled with glimpses of tormented, crying faces. Then I remembered where I'd seen him before. "Ezra?" I asked.

He gave a small, crooked smile and tilted his head. "Ah, no. But how would you know? I am Simeon. My apprentice left this world

long ago. But he was useful in making me as you see me now. Before
he died, we discovered a great deal about the making of clay men and
the binding of souls, which has been invaluable in my work here. I'm
wroth with you for destroying my golem. It was a masterpiece."

He'd made the golem of Will. I cringed, thinking of what must
have been done to make it so big, strong, and real. Real enough to fool
Michael; strong enough to walk around for a week or more.

My stomach curdled and I tasted bile in the back of my mouth as
more pieces fell into place. Blood and bandages, a sorcerer below St.
John's, and Alice up and walking where she shouldn't have been. Alice
must have been the creature in the jars filled with blood. I wondered
how he'd done it, how he'd stitched her back together, and how—

The word slipped out. "How?"

Alice had strolled to Glick's side and then half a step past him,
eclipsing him. She raised one hand toward the silver-eyed creature
beside me. "Kreanou," she murmured. "Very good."

Kreanou—was that a name or a title?—made a sound a lot like a
growl and pinned his spooky gaze on her as if he would devour her in
a single bite if he had the chance. But he didn't move.

Alice smirked. She was on the dais, several steps above me, so she
could look down at me. It was barely enough extra height: We were
almost eye to eye.

"How did I survive the fire? The Pharaohn, of course. Wygan followed me to the house. But not for me, Harper. For you." A minute
sharpness in her voice gave her fury and bitterness away. "He wanted
to be sure you'd survive whatever happened. You have no idea how
often he's looked over your shoulder, or for how long. Like a guardian
angel." She gave her mad giggle once again, her eyes glittering. "Or
maybe I should say, 'like a guardian beast'?"

I narrowed my eyes and kept my mouth shut over the urge to spit.
Or vomit. Her aura had never been pleasant but it was a vile thing
now. Twice dead, twice resurrected, blood-soaked, mad, and burning
with her own fury, she was Hate walking.

"He took me from the fire. You and the others almost destroyed me, but he saved me. He bathed me in blood, soaked me in it, drowned me in it."

I could see it as she spoke, like a film blazoned in fire on the glimmering, cold air. He dragged her from the house as Cameron had dragged Carlos and hid her in a place of cold stone and salt water. He did murder and let blood run like a brook. Her body, cracked and blackened like a cinder, drank the blood, swelling with it and healing itself, the pores of her skin like a million tiny mouths. For months he nurtured her on blood and the poison of his mind. Then, beneath the surface of a swelling pool of gore, he cut her into pieces. . . .

". . . and he put me into the jars, filled with the blood that kept me alive, healing my burns. I was just too . . . large to heal in a single piece, he said. But the blood would keep me and mend my flesh. He promised me Simeon's help when I rose. How was I to know it would take so long? What could I do?" she added, her hand curled elegantly as she made a small shrug. Her black bandages rippled and hitched over her still-raw joints. "He owned me then. And I owe him. And what he wants is you."

The mood was broken as I felt my phone vibrate in the small of my back. It stopped after one buzz. Then it started up again in a moment and went on for three more cycles. Michael's signal at last. They'd located Will and were coming to meet me. I didn't know if they had Will or not and I hoped they wouldn't get too close or do anything stupid if I wasn't at the rendezvous when they arrived. They may have had what they'd gone for, but I didn't and I couldn't just leave, not with Alice preening and purring in front of me.

"You didn't have to take Will to get me. I was coming anyway," I ground out as my guts churned and settled again slowly.

She made a pout. "Oh, you don't think I believe that, do you? That you would come just for Edward? Oh, no. The Pharaohn-ankh-astet said to take the thing most dear to you. And here he was! I already had your picture from when I first watched you for Wygan and seduced that silly man to beat you. Simeon knew just how to use the photo to make you desperate to come here. Nightmares are so much more persuasive than pleas, aren't they? How could I resist? When I'm done, I get Edward's domain in London with the help of the asetem and Simeon, and all I had to do was take Purcell," she said, waving dismissively at the trapped vampire behind Glick, "and your William. This great fool," she added, flicking a scarlet-tipped finger toward Glick, "has been the last little cherry on my cake. And I'll have done what Edward failed to do—hold all of London in my hand, all the vampires beneath my rule. Mine. Not his."

I felt weak and dizzy. She hadn't just followed me; she'd helped to kill me and she would push me farther into death for the sake of the debt she owed Wygan. I wondered what had become of my assailant once he'd left the courtroom the last time I saw him. Yet another thing I'd have to discover if I wanted to put my mind at ease or at least shut down the mental screaming that was threatening to overwhelm me.

Alice laughed, the sound purely insane and dangerous, rolling across the still room like an earthquake.

Glick stiffened. "For the Pharaohn? That filthy white bastard? You said they was breaking from the Pharaohn. You said it was for our advantage. Knew I shouldn't have caved to the likes of you! You brought the asetem among us, you brought him—that Jew," he spat with a glare at Simeon, "and you turned us on ourselves."

Alice gave him a pitying glance with a lifted brow. Simeon didn't react at all.

Glick took a step away from her, glancing at Simeon and picking a route far from either of them. "You lied to us," he said, amazed. "A thing like you? Deceived me? Deceived the Brotherhood?"

Alice's expression turned to a slow sneer of disgust. "Weak, useless fool." She flicked her scarlet-tipped claw at him. "Kreanou. Relieve me of this . . . thing."

A low hiss rose on my other side. I whipped my head to look at the silver-eyed monster beside me, but it was already moving. I shifted my glance toward Glick, Alice, and Simeon.

A look of terror flashed across Glick's face. All eyes watched as he spun around and bolted with the unnatural speed and strength of his kind, streaking for the nearest open doorway. A black wind raced after him, edged in brick red, and blocked the door, congealing into the shape of the silver-eyed vampire—or whatever it was—with saber fangs curving from its impossibly gaping mouth. Simeon and Alice turned as one and walked a few steps toward them, Alice laughing with maniacal glee.

I heard a noise from Purcell and I dashed to him, hoping to get him out of the inevitable line of fire.

"No," he gasped.

The room shivered in the Grey, flashing silver and red by turns. Something shrieked and Purcell collapsed to his knees as if he'd been scythed down. I closed the distance, but a rushing cold sprang up from the floor and gripped me like an icy fist. I was trapped as surely as if I'd been caged in steel bars.

"I tried to warn you," Purcell whispered near my feet. "You stepped on the switch. Now you're stuck in one of these damnable spell cages, like me! Another of Simeon's horrid inventions. Don't try anything magical or they freeze you like a fly in amber."

"What about you?"

"It just crushes me if I move. I shouldn't have flinched. But poor Henry . . ."

Glick screamed, and under the sound of Alice's laughter, I could hear something tearing wetly apart. Glick's screams stopped abruptly and the smell of blood thickened the air. Purcell whimpered as the spell squeezed down on him.

"Why, John," Alice said, returning to our side of the dais, "you've got our guest stuck." Her smile was sickening.

She turned and swept the room with her glittering stare. "There will be no more resistance from any of you! The kreanou has no mercy.

He listens only to me and he only wishes to destroy." She pointed back toward the arch where Glick had met his quick and gruesome end. "*That* is what happens to fools who try to cross me."

My Greyness made movement into torture, and every degree of rotation ripped into me as if I were bound in barbed wire. Turning back to face Alice felt like I was being flayed alive, but I managed it.

Alice was watching me. "How nice of you to truss yourself up. Now all I have to do is deliver you and it's all mine." Then she added, her voice not much louder than a whisper, but piercing and clear as shattering crystal, "You should know. You should *want* to know, what it is you're going to do."

"I'm not going to do anything for you or the Pharaohn." That didn't sound as commanding as I'd hoped; more a pathetic whimper.

She just smiled back and purred words as sickening as venom. "It's going to be lovely. He's been trying for so long and now he finally has you here, alone, and Edward where he can't run. It's all been so very perfect. He said you're a gate." She tilted her head back and forth as she gave her tiny, evil smile, and I thought of my father's puzzle, tucked into my pocket. It was a key. . . . "I don't see it. A gate. Well"—she twitched her eyebrows, dismissing the incongruity—"I suppose you will be when we're done. I am disappointed, however. I hoped you'd make more trouble. He says you have to die just a bit more. I wouldn't mind if it were a lot more, but . . . well. He wouldn't like it. And I have my demesne to look after now."

She turned and beckoned. The kreanou, glowering, blood splashed, and ravenous, prowled over to her. "The House of Detention," she said, her voice taking on the strange blue shiver of command. I could see the strand connecting her to the kreanou shimmer with it. "We'll see what the butcher makes of her. And if not him, your turn." Alice glanced at me again. "It would be a pity if the kreanou gives in to his nature. Dez!"

I didn't have time to wonder about the kreanou's nature and the connection between the creature, Alice, and her sorcerer. I was pretty sure someone was going to kill me—or do their best impression—in a few minutes, and I wasn't quite sure I believed that Greywalkers always bounced back. It hadn't worked that way for Dad. I preferred not to test Marsden's theories if possible, and I just plain didn't want to die!

The wavering demi-vamp dragged his steps to the dais. It was obvious he didn't like what had happened to Glick, but he didn't have a lot of options other than following the orders of his new Primate or being the next stress test for the kreanou.

"Take them to the House of Detention. You can dispose of Purcell there and leave her for the ghost. It's really very poetic, don't you think? Letting the ghost have a chance at killing the ghost killer?" She looked me in the eye with a red gleam of hate. "It wouldn't work if you weren't what you are. And don't worry: I'll take such good care of your dear William."

FORTY

She couldn't kill me, so she'd do something worse to Will. I prayed that Michael and Marsden had found an opportunity to grab Will without waiting for me.

As Purcell and I were prodded out of the room by Dez with the glowering kreanou in his wake, I tried to think of a new way to thwart Wygan's plans. I didn't have my dad's option—and I wouldn't have taken it if I had. I'd come close when I'd been new to Greywalking but I didn't think giving up was a good idea anymore. Marsden had seemed to think just getting me out of the way would stymie whatever Wygan was up to, which meant there wasn't a new Greywalker around with similar talents. But that wouldn't stop Wygan from trying to make another like he'd pushed to make my father and then me into the shape he wanted. If it came to a fight, I might not survive.

I wasn't sure, specifically, what the kreanou was, but the term "killing machine" fit it in general pretty well. I didn't want to tangle with it if I hoped to live and save Will.

I kept Will in the front of my mind, even through the torturing jolts the cage stabbed into me with every step, even when my thoughts tried to wander to Quinton and whatever terrors were building back home, even when I wondered about the strange little puzzle in my pocket and what a gate might do with its own key. I focused on the one immediate thing: I had to get Will out.

We passed through the magical barrier around the room in a haze of pain. Once outside of the ceremonial chamber, the cages dropped off and Purcell and I could move easier, but we were both drained from the agony of the short walk. It was wretched going with Dez and the kreanou prodding us along through the buried catacombs.

"What's this place?" I muttered to Purcell.

"We're in the bones of the city. The catacombs and old tunnels. Down where the rivers used to flow until they covered 'em over and made 'em into sewers. You can hear the Fleet muttering its old songs if you listen," he murmured back, misunderstanding what I'd meant to ask.

"No, I mean what's this House of Detention?"

"Used to be the holding jail—where they kept prisoners until they could send 'em to another place. Or hang 'em. Miserable, it was. It's a ruin now. Breeds ghosts like a battlefield. Most of 'em nasty."

I tried to see into the darkness that descended as we went farther into the tunnels, but the ghost light was uneven and I kept catching glimmers of white and reflections of forgotten illumination that caught in my eye like dust. Things moved in the distance and sounds echoed and rattled strangely.

The last of the candlelight from the chamber beneath the priory had long faded, when I saw something flicker down a connecting tunnel like a distant mirror in the sun.

Then came a silver-white flash behind us that went up to the ceiling with a concussion that threw us forward. The roar and scream of the explosion came right behind it and my ears rang, but I could still hear a mad cackle in my head. Marsden's cackle.

Fast footsteps pattered like a distant storm on my right and a clammy hand grasped my upper arm, wrenching me upright. I jerked my head to look at the hand's owner.

Michael Novak yanked me toward the nearest black branch of the tunnel. "Come on!" he rasped in a low, panicky voice.

Screaming and rending sounds came from behind and the iron smell of blood mixed with the nauseating corruption of vampire curdled the air.

I didn't look back. Whatever Marsden was doing, I didn't want to waste the time he was buying us by watching it. I started to go with Michael, but Purcell threw himself between us onto my other arm. He stared into my eyes and clapped his hands around mine, pressing something rigid and toothed into my palms. "Edward's vault. Tell him I am sorry."

The kreanou shrieked its victory as Dez's screams cut off short. Purcell shoved me after Michael before turning to run toward the carnage.

The younger Novak hauled me along, twisting my arm near to dislocation in his rush. "Run, run, run," he chanted.

I gathered my wits, closed my fist around the hard, biting thing Purcell had entrusted to me, and sprinted with Michael through the opening and into the darkness of a passageway that plunged downward into the earth and the smell of sewers. I could hear scuffling and growls behind us but not a single cry. I hoped Purcell was made of tougher stuff than Dez and Glick had been. Never thought I'd root for the vampire . . . I hoped all this wasn't in vain.

"Will?" I asked as we ran.

"Couldn't get to him," Michael replied, gasping the words. "Got worried . . . waiting for you . . ."

"You know . . . where?"

He grunted, "Uh-huh." Then he shut up and we charged on.

I was lost, not knowing what direction we were going or where we were in the twisting tunnels and dry, ancient sewers below Clerkenwell. I just tore along in Michael's wake. We flashed past a silvery line on the floor and I heard a crack of thunder as another blur of white light shot up behind us, leaving a barrier of sparking magic and acrid smoke. The shape of the spell reminded me of the tangles and traps Mara had made for me once—little bits of hedge magic woven into rings of thorns and grass. It wasn't the same but it was similar, and I assumed it was something Marsden had done to cover our escape. I didn't really care so long as the kreanou didn't follow us.

Michael jagged to the right and into another tunnel. A pale smear detached from the wall and hurried beside us.

"That should send 'im whimperin' back to his mother," Marsden crowed as he fell in with us. "Round the left—we'll be able to hop over there."

"Over . . . what?" I panted, adrenaline shortening my breath and making me stagger.

"Time. To the House of Detention when it was still standin'. There's a way out back then."

"No!" I objected. "That's . . . where—"

"I heard the plan," he snapped. "But we shan't be going through the bit that bloodsucking bitch had in mind, and they can't follow us my way. The only other way out from this end takes us through St. James's. You don't want that!"

"No," I agreed.

"Then bleedin' trust me!"

Around the next bend in the passage we came to the fragment of an ancient wall and threw ourselves over it. Marsden scrambled up first, clutched at the thickly silvered air, and wrenched. . . .

The world jerked sideways.

We rolled to the ground and up against the wall at a new angle. Or possibly a different wall.

Marsden picked himself up and brushed dirt from his trousers and coat. He turned back to us, whispering, "Been a prison for three hundred years. Lots of bad things floatin' about." Then he put his finger over his lips. We followed him in silence.

FORTY-ONE

I wasn't sure how or where we entered the prison itself. The walls just gave way to rooms and proper corridors crossed at strange intervals by low tunnels for ventilation or sewage. The cells at our end were the dankest and foulest confinement I'd ever seen outside the "hole" at Alcatraz. Most of them were empty in the time we'd tumbled into, but even in the past, the place boiled with ghosts and the gelid air stank of waste and water and human despair. The song of London's Grey had become a dirge.

We scrambled through the labyrinth of the prison's lowest pit, where real, solid brick vaults and ghostly doubles stood in the earth to hold up a structure soaked in the uncanny and the horrifying. Low brickwork doorways led to low-ceilinged cell blocks of white-washed brick. Marsden motioned us forward at every turning with frantic gestures and the cocking of his head this way and that, listening.

Explosions and screams rocked the building, and we found ourselves rushing through panicking crowds of prisoners. The impression was so thick and strong, even Michael responded to their press and their terror. The memory of fire broke out behind us.

"It's burning!" Michael yelped, his own exhaustion and fear

pulling him into the verges of hysteria where the Grey flickers into the visible like campfire smoke images.

Marsden turned back to him with a furious expression. "Hush!"

The warning came too late; something had heard and filtered itself from the murk of history and the memory of smoke, flowing fast across the teeming vault of the cell block toward us as it solidified into the shape of a gaunt man. The stink intensified as he came closer—not just the stench of the prison but of corruption and bodily rot—homing in on us like a hunting hound.

"Bloody hell," Marsden breathed. "It's the wraith. Bloody butcher Norrin. We're in it now."

The wraith cut through the crowd of ghosts like a sword. It wasn't quite like them but something more eternal and horrible with a greater solidity in its accumulated bulk of evil. So this was what Alice had been sending me to: a spirit old, solid, and wicked enough to do someone like me serious hurt. Anyone with a hint of sensitivity would feel it, whether they were touched with the Grey or not. Someone descending into it by close association with the likes of Marsden and me couldn't help but know it was there. Michael retched in the swirling darkness beside me and stumbled back. I put myself between him and the barely corporate monster that approached.

But it wasn't interested in me. It fixed its attention on the other Greywalker, blocking our path—unless we wanted to go through it and I certainly didn't.

"Peter, Peter," the wraith sang in a voice that chilled my spine. "I knew ye'd come back, y'lyin' pig swiver. Ah, but what happened to yer pretty blue eyes, eh? I told ye I'd pluck 'em out for ye if y'didn't care for the sight o' me. But y'did for yerself, didn't ye? I should punish ye for that. But ye've brought me some other pretties, too? Ah. That'll keep yer lying throat uncut a while longer."

The wraith turned burning eyes on Michael and me, picking us from the crowd of alarmed ghosts who ran from the memory of flames. An unearthly gleam danced along the fine edge of a blade in his hand. His thumb brushed lightly across the tang, and the reflection of light turned scarlet as his face stretched into something lupine and horrible.

"Keep yer distance, Norrin," Marsden spat back at him. His lank white hair swung over his face as he turned, making shadows dance in his ravaged eye sockets. "They're not for the likes of you."

"No? But y'know I like a bit of fun whether ye will or no, Peter."

The knife flashed as Norrin lashed out sideways, never shifting his gaze. I dodged back, shoving Michael away. The boy grunted and stumbled sideways, coming clear of my body. Norrin sprang at him, mouth gaping into a black chasm lined with rows of ripsaw teeth.

Michael rolled.

The blade glinted red and rang a quivering crystal note on the firelit mist of the Grey for a moment, slicing through the fabric of magic like a razor as the unearthly Norrin snapped and howled.

The keen edge nicked through Michael's sleeve near the shoulder. Michael gasped and clapped his other hand over the shoulder. His eyes were wide with shock.

Marsden and I both jumped for the wraith as the phantoms of panicked prisoners rushed through us with the feel of an ice storm. Norrin twisted in our grasp, slippery and lithe as an oiled snake. Looking deeper into the Grey, I saw him as a hollow frame of bright energy lines without the usual tangled core of a soul. He was difficult to hook my fingers into as his apparent surface sparked and fizzed like an overloaded electrical circuit.

I glanced at Marsden as we struggled to hold the thing, but he didn't seem to have any better grip on it than I did. Norrin swore and stabbed at us with his knife, his face oozing into the shapes of eldritch beasts and monsters.

The eerie blade bit in like the real thing. I could feel blood running down my chest where the eldritch knife had sliced me. It really was a ghost that could kill me! Or at least enough to make whatever tweaking and shaping Wygan had in mind possible. That chilled me, but I dug in and tried to get my fingers into the weave of the wraith's energy shape, which resisted like callused flesh.

Marsden wrapped his arms around the writhing form and squeezed. The ghost shape compressed a little and Norrin shouted, "I'll have yer liver, y'bastard!" as he fought to escape.

"We can't break it. You'll have to run. Go on!" Marsden urged me. "Get to the door and get out. Take the boy!"

I let go of Norrin and turned back to haul Michael to his feet. He came along, dazed and stumble-footed as I dashed for the nearest door that looked to lead out. But the door was locked and the terrified prisoners who had escaped their cells—or never been confined at all—swarmed around it, clawing at it frantically. The heavy iron-bound portal wouldn't yield to me, either.

I looked back over my shoulder toward Marsden.

The other Greywalker doubled over and twitched as Norrin drove a blow into his gut.

"Marsden!" I shouted, alarmed; if the ghost's knife could draw my blood, what did it do to him? They seemed to have prior history and maybe there was a connection the wraith could use against him.

"Key," he gasped, the sound carrying to mortal ears through the cacophony of phantom horrors.

I scowled, closing my hand in my pocket on the hard metal thing Purcell had pressed on me. But I had no chance to question as Michael grabbed my hand, forcing me to look at him.

"The key. That puzzle thing. Maybe it works here."

My dad's— No, my key. How many gates could it open? Was it some kind of lock pick after all? I rifled through my pockets in haste, stabbing my fingers on sharp odds and ends until the cool, bent shape of my father's puzzle came to my grip. Casting anxious glances over my shoulder, I scrambled through the puzzle's solution, but it didn't click into place and glow. I tried it again, shaking, trying to breathe steadily and not give in to my own exhaustion and the fear that rose off the ghostly crowd like a stench.

I could feel the flutter of temporaclines at the door. I could have simply slipped away on one, leaving Michael and Marsden to their own devices. The boy might be safe enough without two Greywalkers nearby to warp the thin veil between the worlds into a hellish reality around him. But Marsden had brought us to the slice of horror we found ourselves in, and I wasn't sure that my disappearance would drop Michael back into the normal. If not, he'd be helpless in the memory of the burning prison and alone with Norrin once Marsden couldn't hold the phantasm back anymore—and he was failing fast.

I shuffled the puzzle again, shooting another anxious look back at Marsden and Norrin in time to see the other Greywalker collapse to the floor. Norrin wheeled toward us, grinning and letting the unearthly blade catch the firelight.

Michael and I both swore. I started to push the key at him and head back to Norrin, but he refused it. He rubbed at his shoulder and looked at his hand, unsmeared by blood or gore.

"It hurts but . . . I'm not really bleeding. I'll get Marsden. You open the door," he added, dashing across the floor to meet the savage monstrosity that approached like a stalking tiger.

Michael ran all the way to Marsden's side, dragging Norrin's attention to him as he went.

I slid the puzzle through its paces with frantic fingers once again and felt it click into shape, humming its satisfaction. I jammed the glowing prong into the lock of the ghostly doors and twisted. The latch squealed and resisted the strange key for a moment. Then it gave up and clicked open. I almost cried in relief.

I turned back, running for Michael and Marsden. The old man was halfway to his knees as Michael hauled him up. Norrin pounced on the boy and Michael stumbled, knocking Marsden back down.

"No, y'don't, y'bloody bastard," Marsden muttered, scrabbling something from the ground. He flicked it out and the white cane unfolded from his hand, giving off a strange blue luminescence that snapped through Norrin and wrenched the specter's attention back to him.

Norrin roared and dove for Marsden as if goaded with a hot iron.

"C'mon, y'murderin' pig. Lost your strength, have ya? Y'cut me and held me to the Grey for that white snake but y'couldn't break me enough, not even then. But y'came fer me a man full-growed when I were prisoner here. Have to go after youngsters now, do ya? Y'always were an effin' coward," Marsden panted, hunching onto his knees and elbows. He took another swipe at the lunging monster, knocking the knife from the phantom's hand. As it fell away, it glimmered for an instant in a tangle of energy strands.

I dove for it, snatching it from the enclosing mist before it dissolved back into ghost stuff. I felt it firm up in my hand, burning like a live wire and holding the menacing shape Norrin had made of it: a blade that cut into the energy shapes of the Grey and left pain and ragged edges in its wake. I rolled to my feet and dashed two steps toward Norrin as the prison's butchering wraith raked clawed hands into Marsden's tucked head.

Marsden stifled a scream as the hands passed through his face, dragging an illusion of gore and the memory of an eye with them. I plunged the knife into Norrin's back, ripping downward along the nonexistent spine and feeling the mirage of human form rend into frayed wisps of fury and hate.

The shape that had been Norrin shrieked and whirled into a cloud of bloody smoke and the stink of slaughterhouses.

Only the roar of the phantom flames and the cries of the terrified prisoners remained. I flung away the cruel knife of Norrin's energy and saw it unravel and settle back into the grid as glimmering strands of magic, but I could already see the edges of Norrin's form knitting back into shape in the Grey world. We had half an hour at most to get the hell out of the House of Detention, and I had no idea how far we had to go.

Michael and I put our shoulders under Marsden's arms and levered

him up. His legs were wobbly and the white cane collapsed as he put
weight on it.

"Damn," he muttered. "Relyin' on sprats and women . . ."

"Shut up and say thank you," I suggested as we lurched forward
like a bad entry in a three-legged race.

Head hanging so we couldn't see his face, Marsden mumbled an
ungracious thanks.

Michael snorted, shaking a bit. "Let's just get out of here. I'm really hating this place."

We stumbled out the door, open only to us, through the crowd of
trapped prisoners, and up into the memory of a courtyard filled with
rushing jailers and shouting constables trying to douse the flames at
one corner of the building with buckets of water. By the time we'd
walked out the unguarded prison gate and around the corner, past
phantom crowds and more bucket brigades, Marsden was able to support his own weight.

We stopped around the corner and Marsden leaned against the
nearest wall. "Pray there's no one out for a late walk," he said. Then
he pushed history aside and the world shifted with a grinding feel and
a scream of friction.

Ordinary streetlights and city haze lit the urban night. No sign of
flames as cars grumbled along Rosebery Avenue.

Michael threw up.

"There, boy. Y'lived through Norrin and the Fenian bombing,"
Marsden mumbled, still unsteady on his feet and paler than normal—
which is to say he nearly glowed in the dark.

"Eff you," Michael gasped back, wiping his mouth on the un-
tucked hem of his shirt. "I felt that thing cut me! And the place was
on fire—I could smell smoke!"

"But y'couldn't feel the heat, could ya?"

"No, but who cares? It was on fucking fire! I could see shadows
running around like there were people in there running from the
flames. And then that . . . thing cut me!"

"Did y'see him? Norrin? Did y'see that bloody monster?" Marsden asked, grinding his teeth into the words.

Michael hesitated, looking away, breathing too fast and sweating. "I . . . saw eyes. A shape. And I smelled something . . . rotting. And a flash like light off a knife blade. And . . . something . . . cut me," he added, clutching his shoulder again.

"How is it?" I asked in as gentle a voice as I could muster with my own heart beating triple time.

Michael turned his face to mine, seeming grateful to look away from Marsden. "It hurts, but it's not bleeding. Feels like it's cut to the bone, though."

"That'll fade in a few days," Marsden said, rubbing his hands over his face, "but I shan't say it'll be pleasant. Hurts like merry hell, it does."

I glanced down at the blotched front of my shirt and jacket. The fabric wasn't cut, but I could feel the stickiness of blood that stained my shirt from the inside. I wished I could go back to the hotel, take the longest shower in history, and fall into my expensive bed for the next twenty hours. My knees shook a little: a post-stress reaction to burning up more adrenaline than I normally expended in a month. I didn't feel much better than Michael looked, but I didn't have the luxury of puking.

"We have to get off the street. The vampires will still be looking for us," I reminded them.

Michael straightened up, making a face at me. Then he glanced around the street and pointed to a bus stop nearby. "There's a bus coming. We can take that and then change when we're far away from here."

FORTY-TWO

s we stood at the bus stop, rain began, just pattering down, but it helped to wash the filth and the stink of vampires off us. Michael chivvied us onto the first bus that came along Rosebery and made us change to another closer to the middle of town. We collapsed into our seats as if we'd been thrown.

The bus rambled the wrong way for a while until it turned near Marble Arch. Beside the arch stood a spectral three-sided gallows from which hundreds of hanged corpses swung in the night wind, their superimposed shades so thick they seemed like a moving blackness filled with bones.

"Tyburn Tree," Marsden muttered, not raising his head.

From there the bus trundled up past Regent's Park toward the canal where we'd left the boat.

"Bleedin' lucky we was. The Pharaohn don't know I'm with you or he wouldn't have tried the same trick twice."

"I don't know what you mean. What trick?" I asked.

"Butcher Norrin. When he tried to shape me, the Pharaohn had me taken up on a thievin' charge in Clerkenwell and put in the House of Detention where Norrin could get at me."

"He trumped up a charge just to get you into the right prison?"

"He didn't trump up nothin'. I stole the things as I was accused of. That I done it by his leave—that wasn't allowed to come out. It was all done proper and quick, and I were put in the very block we walked through. I thought Norrin wouldn't be there tonight when we passed through, as he'd not been down the pit when the Fenians bombed the building in 1867 to rescue their man. But someone caught his attention," he added, turning a bit toward Michael, who cringed.

I put my hand on the boy's shoulder. "It's not your fault. Alice must have had some way to wake him up or she couldn't have been sure he'd come after me."

Marsden snorted, but I could feel Michael loosen with relief.

"So. All of this, like what happened to my father, is just a replay of what the Pharaohn's trying to do to me," I said.

"Looks it."

"We'll have to break that pattern. He used Christelle against my father. Now he's trying to use Will against me. We have to get Will back before . . ."

I realized I'd already said too much when Michael frowned at me. "Before what?"

"Before they kill him," Marsden supplied. "Be glad it's not my decision, boy. I'd leave him to his chances. This softhearted fool means to save your brother even if it ruins her own chances of staying sane and whole. And it will. She's worth ten of any normal fella."

Michael growled under his breath. "Why did we save you? We should have left you there for him to . . . to . . ."

"Rend to pieces? Drive mad? He's had his chance to do both. My term at Clerkenwell's when I thought I'd gone mad for certain—when I started seein' butcher Norrin, when—" He faltered, his fingers curling over his gouged orbits, twitching. He took a long, shaking breath and went on. "I learned the trick of falling through the cracks of time there, and it saved my life, so it did. They tore it down in 1890 and I thought that was the end of bloody Norrin. He's among the worst of the things that haunt that wretched place. He's not even a proper ghost—he's a wraith, a hollow remnant of an evil man filled with hate and a love of violence till he's nearly solid with it. I'd hopes we could pass through without attracting anything's attention so long as we went where there was so much confusion already. Should have known better. Things like Norrin don't die. He's not gone yet, I'd wager."

"I saw him re-forming as we left," I confirmed.

Marsden made a hacking sound. "Still, you did well, girl. That trick with the knife—wicked clever. How did you guess it could cut him?"

"Because it cut me."

Michael and Marsden both turned toward me, but their expressions weren't the same. Marsden only dropped his hands and seemed a bit surprised, but Michael looked shocked.

"Are you OK?" he whispered, choking on the question.

"I'm fine. It's uncomfortable but shallow."

"But . . . you don't look hurt. . . ."

I lifted the edge of my jacket so the bloodstain on my shirt showed. "It only cut my skin, not my clothes. I'm not like you as far as ghosts go. I see them and they see me. If I can hurt them, they can hurt me—we're part of the same fabric. That's how I figured I could use the knife. It cut me, so I could use it to cut Norrin."

"Could—could I have . . . done that?"

I shook my head, but it was Marsden who answered him.

"No, boy, y'couldn't. Nor could I, I imagine. Just her. She's got a bit of the same stuff in her—part magic, she is."

"But you're—"

"Not like that, I'm not. She can hold on to that stuff. All I can do is walk through it. You just float around the surface like everyone else that's normal." He turned his sightless gaze on me. "That must be why he wants you."

I knew he meant Wygan and things were making sense in a horrible way. "I can't do it for long," I objected. "It's like holding on to a live electric cable—it burns all through me. He can't—"

"I doubt he cares about your comfort."

"It doesn't matter. A few seconds feels like an eternity in the electric chair! I couldn't do much."

"Maybe there's more to come. . . ."

That was what I feared. I wasn't so sure I was a gate, as Alice had said, as the thing that could build one. I remembered the way the bit of the vortex had clipped off under my tearing hands and spun off into its own tiny black hole. Marsden had said they weren't made; they just happened. But maybe a Greywalker who could grab on to the power lines and tangled threads of the Grey could do something more with it, with the right nudge. And the right key. I wanted to throw my father's puzzle out the bus window and never see it again—except that it was my dad's and it had opened the door at the House of Detention for me. I had a feeling it was my key, not Wygan's and not part of his plan, or he'd have taken it when Dad died.

I shook myself out of my conjectures and tuned back in to the conversation Michael and Marsden were having.

"More what? What are you talking about?" Michael demanded.

Marsden and I both shook our heads. "I can't explain it," I started, unable to say more. A mental block I'd never been able to fathom stopped my speaking of the living nature of the Grey. It wasn't just power; it was a live thing, a collective of energy that almost touched sentience. And it didn't want me to say so. Not even to Marsden. Another oddity specific to me . . .

Real horror took hold of me. What would happen if the magic did start to "know" and what would it do to . . . everything? It was no wonder the guardian beast hated the living prison Wygan had erected around the hole where my father's ghost was captive—that was magic in the control of havoc and mayhem. I thought of that on a larger scale—whatever Wygan was up to would have to involve more of that hungry, chaotic fire—and I felt sick to the core. I had to get home. I had to stop it. . . .

"Harper?" Michael quavered. "You all right?"

I shook off my panic, but the disquiet and desperation remained. "Fine. No," I corrected myself. "I'm scared. But I can't do anything if I let the fear own me."

"You didn't seem scared, before."

I felt so wretched I wanted to cry, but I swallowed it, closing my eyes against the burn. "I fake sangfroid really well. Just close your eyes and think of ice cream."

Michael let out a nervous giggle. Marsden snorted. Three injured, crazy people dreaming of dessert. Yeah, we were tough all right. . . .

FORTY-THREE

Once back in the relative safety of the *Morning Glory*, afloat on the waters of the canal where no vampire would come, we began to plan how to save Will. We knew where he was being held and it was doubtful they'd move him. Alice would want another shot at me and that was an obvious place to take it, but we'd have to make her window as small as possible, force her to come after us with minimal planning and support. We'd have to get in just before darkness when she wasn't awake to command Simeon or any vampires who might be a lot tougher.

"What about that kreanou thing?" Michael asked. "Is that a vampire or what?"

"That, boy, is the vampire to end all vampires. It hates and it thirsts and it don't care about pain."

"Wonderful," I snarked.

"What's funny is, they normally go after the vampire what made 'em—driven to it no matter what stands between. That Alice must be controlling it through her sorcerer, Simeon. . . ." He twitched with unpleasant revelation. "She made it on purpose!"

"Made?" Michael asked.

"They're usually mistakes. No vampire wants a kreanou coming for them," Marsden explained. "The rage of death incarnate. Faster, meaner than any of 'em, and it bends magic—it reshapes itself."

Michael said, "It's a shape-shifter, like a . . . a lycanthrope?"

"Not that sort, but they can make some changes to their bodies. It don't last long, it takes a bit o' power, and it must hurt like merry hell, but what do they care? They need longer legs? They get taller. They need a bigger mouth? They unhinge their jaw. They don't usually last long, so they don't conserve their strength or care for their bodies. Remember that, girl. It's their strength, but it's also a weakness you can use against it."

"And that thing's going to be prowling around down there?" Michael asked.

"No, it won't," Marsden answered. "It's still a vampire and it still sleeps during daylight. Alice will make sure of that, since she can't exert control while *she* sleeps. She's probably got that Simeon laying sleeping spells on it every morning. And that's another reason to go after your brother in the late afternoon, before the vampires wake—during the changing of the guard, so to speak—when everyone's a bit sleepy and off their stride. The kreanou won't be up and about until Alice is, and Simeon will be tired; the summer daylight lasts longer than his sleep spells can, so he'll have been up at least once while everyone else was kippin'. But the timing's tricky, since we'll be coming at the catacombs from the sewers where we can't see the sun."

"Marsden . . . " I asked, "how do you kill it? I thought I knew how to kill a vampire, but . . . Alice is up and walking. . . ."

"The kreanou's easy so long as you keep away from him—he'll do himself in once he's had the prey he's after. Let him get at Alice or Simeon and he'll burn out on his own—he's tied to their power. If we can break their control, he'll take out the nearest one and we take the other. The sorcerer's powerful, but he's still just a man at heart and she's not as tough as you think. Stakes just hold 'em down. Decapitation works wonders. As does fire."

"But she survived both of those before."

"In special circumstances. The Pharaohn chopped her up while she was immersed in blood. Then he put her into jars full of blood—and probably just the right kind. Everything lived, though plainly she's madder than a March hare. But if she'd not had the blood or if he'd just cut her head off and left it, she'd have died for good. Once they bleed out, that's the end of 'em. Or burn 'em up till there's nowt but ash, or leave 'em for the sun to finish off if you've a vicious streak to ya. That'll turn the trick, though you'll have the devil's time getting it done. Panic makes 'em stronger and they're fly ones to begin with. But you chop her up until the blood's all gone and she won't be getting back up. You get her head off and put it where she can't stop the bleeding. That'll do the trick."

"How am I supposed to take her head off? It's not like a pumpkin on a stick—"

"She's still healin'. Wounds are weak spots. I'm not saying it's going to be easy—it's not—but that's your only chance."

Did I say it wasn't a great plan? It was a desperate plan, but it was what we had right now and we didn't have time to wait and hope for better opportunities. I sighed. "We're going to need supplies," I said. "Some kind of . . . protective clothes against the water—"

"A boat would be better," Marsden said.

"How?" I asked. "It's also a lot bigger."

"You'll be glad of it once we're down there. In case you hadn't noticed, it's started to rain. And it's been raining in the north for a few days. All that water'll be running downhill toward the Thames fast as a flood. We could try with waders and Wellies, but I doubt we'd make it far before we was bowled over like a leaf in the gutter. What we need's one o' them little boats like a coracle or them Eskimo things."

"A kayak?"

"Yeah. . . ."

"And the bikes—"

Marsden interrupted me. He looked nervous, though I wouldn't have thought it possible. "You sure about them things?"

"Yes," I snapped back. "The traffic's too thick to make it in a car and we're too slow on foot. It'll have to be the motorcycles. The Red Brothers have transportation, but a bike's small and nimble and we should be able to get a lead. We don't want to lose them; we just want to stay ahead of them."

"You really know how to ride one o' them things?"

"For the gods' sakes! Yes!" Not in quite a while, but I wasn't going to tell doubting Marsden that. "Michael, can you get two of the motorcycles to the meeting point in time?" I asked. "It'll be somewhere near Farringdon Tube, probably on the west side of the road."

"Yeah. I'll have to shuttle them, but it's not too bad a trip. They'll be there. We'll need some kind of safety straps, in case . . ." He swallowed hard, worried. "In case Will can't hold on."

I nodded.

We made a list of the things we'd need and where Michael and Marsden thought we could find them. Clothing was on the top.

I'd left the hotel in my business suit two days earlier and had only the contents of my purse, some paperwork, a passport, and TPM's credit card with me. Since then I'd escaped from the Red Guard, scrambled through abandoned Underground stations, hidden out on a boat, been captured and led toward certain death, evaded vampires by scuttling through temporaclines, and fought a vicious ghost in the ruins of an old prison. I looked a bit rough to go out on business. And I imagined Will would look even worse when we got to him. It's much easier to evade pursuit if you don't look like you're running away. Even once we were clear of the immediate threat in Clerkenwell, we'd have to get Will on a plane for home or into a doctor's, depending on his condition when we found him. We could fake a lot, but four-day-old clothes that had been worn hard would stand out.

There was also the matter of Edward's stolen property. I might not be able to reclaim his control in London, but I could salvage as much as possible and give Edward options to fight back against Wygan once

Alice was out of the picture. Right now, Edward was in a corner—wherever he actually was.

Wygan would pull the plug on Alice as soon as he knew she'd lost me. I had no doubt the nasty piece of work I'd met in that Clerkenwell club would lose no time telling him, but I didn't intend to let Alice survive long enough to be a problem for Wygan or his white-skinned kin. And I thought I knew right where to lure her to make sure she didn't come back from this death.

"I shall meet you tomorrow noon at Angel," Marsden reminded me as we finished our plans. "Be sharpish."

He had no idea how "sharpish" I felt already. . . .

FORTY-FOUR

After we'd agreed on our plan and used up all the water in the *Morning Glory*'s tanks trying to wash away the sense of filth that clung to us after our brush with Norrin, Michael and I slept on it and started out in the morning to see if Edward's credit was any good outside of Clerkenwell. Marsden had taken off to tend to his own mysterious needs as we went shopping.

Michael had directed me on and off buses and now we were strolling along a section of Oxford Street I hadn't seen on my last trip to the area, looking for a building called the Pantheon. Traffic was a little lighter due to the intermittent rain, but we still had to dodge a few unneeded umbrellas, and the pedestrians were grumpier to make up for their sparseness.

"Are you sure shopping with this guy's credit card is safe?" Michael asked. "I mean . . . y'know . . . these guys are dangerous company."

"Agreed, but it's a simple test without much risk," I replied. "They either accept the card or they don't. And if the use gets reported, I don't think we're going to be mobbed by vampires in Marks and Spencer. If they don't take the card, then I'll know I was set up right from the start."

Michael had been the one to suggest "Marks and Sparks" on the grounds that it had nearly everything we needed, but it wasn't anything special—just a chain store, really, no matter how nice. Opulent Harrods, on the other hand, seemed far too likely to be observed by exactly the people we didn't want to tangle with.

"Oh. You know, you—you don't have to . . . do this. I could go to the cops."

I didn't stop walking down the sidewalk, which was gently speckled with rain and lined with tall, broad buildings—some older than my home state—but I did slow down a bit to match Michael's suddenly dawdling stride. I glanced at him but didn't stare; I could see he was wrestling with his thoughts.

"Do you want to?" I asked. "We can alter the plan if you've changed your mind." I doubted that would work out well for the Novaks or myself, but I didn't want to give Michael the impression I was pushing him. It seemed unfair after all the weirdness he'd had to endure that he should also be coerced by someone like me, someone he was inclined to trust, but probably shouldn't even know. I was coercing him a bit and I knew it. I needed Alice dead in a permanent way and I had to get Will out of her clutches. I didn't mention the difficulty of getting the police involved, or explaining the problem to them in a way that didn't make Michael sound crazy. It wasn't likely to happen that way. I let him argue himself out.

"We . . . could ask Sekhmet. . . ." Now, that was a pretty crazy suggestion. Suicidal even.

"Sekhmet? Where did you come up with that name?"

"You and Marsden talked about her. I know who she is—she's the Egyptian goddess of war and justice and women."

"Do you believe in goddesses now, Michael?"

He glanced away. "I don't know. I didn't think I believed in ghosts or vampires . . . or talking statues. But if she's real . . . wouldn't she be more powerful than we are? Couldn't she just . . . fix it?"

"I wish. I don't think that's how she works, though. She's kind of fierce and . . . well, I don't think it would be a good idea to ask. She told me to go solve my own problems and do it right or she'd be angry. Angry goddesses are a lot of trouble. They usually break more than they fix." And I didn't want my heart to be dinner for Anubis.

Michael looked pensive, nodding. "Hm. Yeah. I guess she might not be a good choice."

"Do you want to back out?"

"No. I guess not. I'm just worried. I mean . . . what's going to happen . . . ?" Michael looked small and scared.

"To you and Will?" I finished.

He nodded, mute and keeping his head down as he walked on.

"Once we're out of this, I think you're safe. Alice is the only person interested in hurting you two to get at me. One of us will not be walking away from this. I intend for it to be Alice."

"I feel creepy when you say that. I mean . . ." He dropped his voice to a harsh whisper. "We're talking about killing someone."

"Yeah. It creeps me out, too."

The buildings of stone and brick kept reeling by and it seemed surreal that we were having this conversation on a civilized street in London with a mist-fine rain touching our faces and dewing our hair with tiny lights and jewels. A dank bar in some abandoned, dark place would have been more appropriate. We walked for a while without speaking, our pace more normal, but our thoughts bleak.

"We're going to do it. Aren't we?"

"I'm going to do it," I said. "Because I have to. You're going to stay out of it, wait with the bikes, and then take Will and run like hell."

"They'll be waiting for you—they know you'll come after my brother."

"I'm counting on it. We've got a plan, remember? And if that doesn't work, I'll wing it."

"Do you need ice cream for that, too?" He snorted a sudden laugh, breaking the uncomfortable tension with a blow of the improbable.

"I hope not. I barely fit in these pants as it is."

We found the big department store and went inside to test the legitimacy of my job through retail therapy. In the end, the card worked like a magic wand and nothing bad happened. Knowing Edward hadn't hung me out to dry was more reassuring than I'd expected, but I thought I'd better make the rest of my arrangements without getting back in contact with him, just in case. Michael split to drop off supplies and start moving the motorcycles. I watched him go and then doubled back to the ladies' washroom to change into my new clothes before I went on about my end of the business.

A little restored and dressed in clean, inconspicuous clothes and practical shoes, I set out to do something about the key Purcell had given me. Marsden had identified it as a very old-fashioned safe-deposit box key—the sort banks had stopped using decades ago. But a few strange little companies still maintained private vaults the key would fit. He'd suggested the most likely one, given the age and financial connections in the case, and I headed there.

My destination proved to be one of four dozen near-identical shop fronts located in an elegant Georgian arcade—a sort of eighteenth-century shopping mall—behind a tragically grandiose facade from a much later era. Ironically, it wasn't very far from Will's flat, just north of Piccadilly Circus. The arcade was sandwiched between the Royal Academy and a red-and-white masonry building from the late Victorian era that might have been right at home in Seattle's Pioneer Square.

A gentleman wearing a vest and a top hat decorated with gold braid asked, "May I assist you, madam?" as he saw me peering at my directions.

I wasn't sure how I felt about being "madam," but I wasn't too proud to ask after the business Marsden had suggested. The long, sky-lighted row of shops was rather more upscale than I'd expected when Marsden had called the shop "an old silversmith's," and while I'm not easily intimidated, I know better than to stand out if I can avoid it. But the beadle, as he called himself—which I guessed was a kind of private policeman in a Victorian suit—didn't mind. His accent was the kind of upper-grade working-class you'd expect of his job—not too posh for the position, but not too dirty, either.

"Ah," he said, smiling a bit. "That would be down the other end, on the right as you go. The sign's quite discreet, so you shall have to look sharpish just above the door, but you'll know it by the silver angel in the window. Percy's rather fond of that shop." He gave the merest wink as he said it.

"Percy?" I asked.

"He's our poltergeist. Don't mind him and he won't cause any bother."

I had the impression that the beadle wasn't entirely serious, but if he'd met some of the poltergeists I've known, he wouldn't take it so lightly. I thanked him and headed into Burlington Arcade, moving through a throng of ghostly shoppers dressed in clothes from the Regency to the modern. There was also a number of older ghosts doing somewhat less savory things, such as flinging garbage over the former garden wall against which the shops had been built. I imagined that the current row of shops was roofed over to put paid to that sort of shenanigans.

As I walked through the phantom crowd, something blinked and twinkled at me from the surfaces of glass panes and around the corners of doors. When I reached the silversmith's I was looking for, my eye was drawn to the window where a silver figure about a foot high gleamed in the show lights. It was an angel standing on top of a box carved of cloudy crystal, its wings spread like a cape in the wind while streams of small, flat rectangles fell from its hands. I leaned closer, narrowing my eyes to study the odd figure, and saw that the wings were fletched in oblongs identical to the objects that fell from its hands. I tilted my head and got a better look at one: It was a letter, complete with a tiny chased stamp. The angel's wings were made of letters. As I stared at it, the silver figure glimmered blue and gold and then turned its head and seemed to wink at me before returning to its normal state.

Something giggled.

"Percy, I presume," I muttered, opening the shop door.

The interior glowed with light off the polished surfaces of hundreds of silver objects and sparkling glass cases under discreet white lights. A young woman in a stylish pantsuit turned to look at me as I entered. "Good morning," she said. "How can I assist you today?" She sounded as if she saw me regularly and was delighted I'd dropped by. I was delighted myself to be talking to a perfectly ordinary human with nothing sinister in her energy corona and no otherworldly minions lurking about. I didn't count Percy.

"I'm not sure," I answered. "I have a key. . . ." I added, taking Purcell's gift from my pocket and holding it up.

She blinked and looked a bit surprised. "Oh. The vault. You'll want Mrs. Jabril, then. I'll ring her. Which box?"

"Pardon me?"

"Which box did you come to open? I should let her know which key to fetch."

"I'm afraid I don't know. I have a power of attorney and a key, but I don't know which box it opens."

"Whose box is it, then?"

"It was kept by John Purcell for Edward Kammerling."

"Ah. Right, then. I'll ring Mrs. Jabril. She'll know."

She turned away and used an old-fashioned phone that sat on the counter. "Mrs. J, there's someone here for Mr. Purcell's vault." She listened a moment and then replied. "No, it's not the same fellow as last time. It's a woman with legal papers." Another pause to listen and then: "Yes, ma'am."

She turned back to me. "Mrs. Jabril will be right down to help you. Would you care to look around while you wait or would you prefer a chair?"

I wanted to ask something else, but instead I said, "Could you tell me about your angel?"

"In the window? Everyone asks about him. He's not for sale, I'm afraid—the first owner made him and he's become a bit of a mascot. It's the angel Gabriel. He's a messenger, you know, which is why he has letters. Rather clever that, don't you think?"

"Very," I replied, not remarking that Gabriel is also thought by some to be the angel of death. So far, I'd found the silversmith's to be an interesting choice for whatever Purcell had hidden.

A door opened at the back of the shop and a tiny, elderly woman in a restrained designer suit passed into the room. She was thin and her skin was brown and wrinkled like a mummy's. Her round head was accentuated by a mass of frizzy amber curls that defied attempts to tame them into something more fashionable. Sharp, emerald eyes glittered in her hollowed face and sought me out like a hawk looking for mice. She stepped through a break in the counters and walked toward us with a firm tread, concentrating on me as if she could read my history and intentions by looking at my face. Her demeanor was no more disconcerting than her aura, which was pure gold and lay close to her shape as if she were gleaming with light borrowed from a roomful of bullion.

She stopped next to the clerk and folded her hands in front of herself—the left one was heavy with big brass keys. "Good morning," she said, her vowels as round and dark as plums.

The shopgirl jumped as if she hadn't noticed the other woman's approach, though I didn't know how anyone could have missed her. "Oh, Mrs. Jabril! You caught me unaware."

Mrs. Jabril barely turned her head and gave her a cat smile. "Keep your wits about you, Ivy, or I may catch more than your 'unaware' someday." She retrained her piercing gaze on me. "You have paperwork to prove you should have access to Mr. Purcell's vault, miss?" She also pronounced it "PURSE-el" like Jakob had.

I offered her Edward's limited power of attorney, which I took from my bag. "I'm Mr. Kammerling's agent. Mr. Purcell gave me the key. He's unable to come himself."

She chuckled, and it sounded like the rolling of well-oiled but very old gears. "Of course he is." She took the pages and read through them rapidly. "Have you identification proving you are Ms. Blaine?"

I handed her my passport, which she studied for a moment before looking up again. "This will do," she added, returning the papers and passport to me. "I see you have the key with you. Come. We shall go down. Ivy, I shall let you know when we are done."

"Yes, Mrs. Jabril," the younger woman replied, relieved. I had the impression the older woman made her nervous.

Mrs. Jabril led me back the way she'd come, through the door and into a small office at the back of the building. An odd sort of platform lift formed the floor in one corner and we stepped onto it. My guide pulled a safety cage down around us, put one of her keys into a slot on the nearest upright, turned it, and trod on a button with her foot. The lift lurched and then sank smoothly below the floor. "There is only the one key and no other entrance," she assured me. "Our vaults are very secure."

"Why does a silversmith need a vault?" I asked as the platform continued down into a cold stone cellar.

"Before the rise of the great banks," said Mrs. Jabril, pausing to raise the platform's gates as we bumped to a halt, "goldsmiths were often the bankers and moneylenders of the day. But there was no place to store your valuables outside your own home or to get a small amount of cash for a short term. Silversmiths would occasionally act as . . . pawnbrokers of a sort to the gentry. It was not unusual for a bachelor to put the family silver into storage with a silversmith until he married and had a use for it again. If his pockets were to let, he might borrow against the weight value of the silver and pay it back when he was in brass again. The British pound sterling was tied to the value per weight of silver at the time, of course, so it was like you were trading commodities for cash. Not a word of gossip would attach to a gentleman, or lady, who paused on occasion to visit their family silversmith."

She stepped down from the platform and made a directing wave at the stone-walled room and its ranks of metal-doored lockers of all sizes, lit by dim electric bulbs that were strung somewhat sloppily from the ceiling. "The first owner of the shop built these to store his patrons' articles. Steel doors were fitted to replace the old iron ones in the nineteen thirties. They withstood the Blitz without so much as a buckle."

"It's impressive."

"I shall not say it is as secure as the Bank of England, but unlike the Old Lady of Threadneedle Street, we have never been robbed." When she smiled, her teeth gleamed like sharp pearls.

I could see why any thief assaying this place might think twice. The stone walls supported a collection of mechanical contrivances that looked, at first glance, like a fantastic Rube Goldberg device for catching mice or fetching objects from the tops of the vaults. But as I studied the brass gears and levers and trails of tubes and wiring, the shape of the machine emerged as a gigantic, moving guillotine that could probably make a party of robbers into hash in seconds—after securing all the vault doors with supplementary grids and bars, of course.

The rather grim mechanical marvel glinted with polish and oil, but even looking as deep into the Grey as I dared, I saw no sign it had ever fulfilled its deadly purpose. The vault was remarkably quiet in the Grey, except for the occasional flicker of Percy the poltergeist, though I supposed that shouldn't have surprised me: Magic and technology have an uncomfortable relationship.

Mrs. Jabril smiled again as she saw me figure it out. "Mr. Jabril was fascinated with mechanics and clockworks. Had his father not been a silversmith, he would no doubt have become a watchmaker. Come along," she added, walking forward into the stone embrace of the vaults.

I wondered exactly how distant was the relation between Mrs. Jabril and her mechanically inclined namesake. Given the sinister oddities I'd already encountered in London, I thought it might be healthier not to inquire.

"When was the last time anyone accessed this vault?" I asked as she stopped before one of the larger doors.

There was a tiny pause before she spoke again.

"You have all the right papers and you do not appear to be . . . malign in any way. You are not like Mr. Purcell and Mr. Kammerling, but I can see you are not . . . like other people." She paused again before she added, "I shall answer your questions."

She went still as she thought about my query, her eyes looking off to the side and I imagined—no, I was sure—I could hear the muted whirring of minuscule gears. "Just over three weeks ago, Mr. Purcell sent his assistant, Jakob, to place a few things in the vault. An unpleasant creature, that one. He also left a letter for me which asked that I open the vault for him later that week at half an hour before closing time. I did so. Mr. Purcell arrived exactly on time and replaced several objects as well as adding a box of papers and a letter that I believe is intended for you."

"Me?"

Mrs. Jabril nodded. "For whoever might come to open the vault after him, that is. He said that he might not return to open it again. And he forbade me to open it to Jakob without his presence."

Purcell had been twisted to Alice's purposes, but he hadn't been entirely in the dark about the dangers. He had anticipated trouble and done what he could. I hoped the letter would give some indication of why he hadn't spoken directly to Edward about it, though with the asetem in the picture, that may have been enough.

Mrs. Jabril cut short my mental wandering by opening the iron grille in front of the vault door. It looked too heavy for such a tiny woman to move, but I was becoming quite sure she wasn't at all a normal person. She pointed to one of two keyholes—there was one on the top and one on the bottom of the door, an uncomfortable span for anyone other than an ape—and told me to put my key into the one on top. She slid hers into the keyhole on the bottom and we turned them together. The door loosened in its frame and sighed a little as a gust of air cooler than the air in the cellar leaked out. Mrs. Jabril took hold of the door's handle and turned it with the sound of metal rolling on metal. The hinges made a whisper of protest as she opened the door.

Given the production of opening it, I expected the treasure of King Solomon's mines, but the interior of the small vault was packed with various crates and wooden cases with a pile of plastic file boxes near the front. A large envelope had been taped to the top of the nearest file box and an open carton sat beside it.

"I shall return to the office above, if you like," Mrs. Jabril offered. "There is a bell near the lift which you can ring for me."

There was no way I had the time or temptation to go through the whole vault. I suspected that Purcell had left everything I needed in the box on top, and I was certain I could trust Mrs. Jabril. "I don't think that's necessary. If you don't mind waiting while I read the letter, I'm sure I won't be much longer than that," I said, looking into the vault.

Mrs. Jabril said nothing and stood silently by as I reached for the envelope, which was addressed, "Edward, or his Agent." A curious little symbol near the bottom of the address glowed red and then blue as I picked up the letter, and I thought it was probably some kind of ward. I wondered what would have happened to the letter if I wasn't in possession of Edward's power of attorney. Bursting into flames seemed likely. A gold wafer and two small blobs of blue wax held the flap closed. A little nervous, I broke them and opened the letter.

Dear Ned,

> *I have fallen to the twin follies of complacency and arrogance which led me to betray your trust and lose our security to your enemies. I can only say I did not realize what I had done until it was too late, did not know there was a cuckoo in our nest. I cannot say who works for them—I don't know which of our friends*

and servants have taken their coin—but the asetem-ankh-astet are among us, and destruction already rules the day. I hope you will forgive me.

I have done what I can to mitigate your losses, converted as much as possible to negotiable forms, made transfers of deed and title, and moved assets as swiftly as possible to those safe places of which we spoke long ago. I have collected copies of those papers into the boxes attached to this letter as well as certain articles which I know to be of great importance to you. I have left them to the care of the clockwork, she, of all things, being unassailable. Once the proper forms are filed, your property will be restored, as much as it can be, but the power that held St. James's is gone, taken by that abomination that called herself Alice and that black monster, Simeon.

Beware of them and even of your own shadow. There is a traitor among your close circle who comes from the Pharaohn himself and will be dangerous beyond description and subtle as a serpent. You must be most careful if you are to escape the Pharaohn's machinations. More so than I have been.

I regret that my foolishness has cost you so much and that I shall not see you again to say that I am sorry.

Your friend, as ever,
John Purcell

I refolded the letter, feeling a little sad once again for Purcell even if he was a vampire, and returned it to its envelope. Then I peeked into the box next to the file case. A clutter of objects had been thrown into it, including a handful of animal teeth, an oddly shaped knife with a missing point, a single ornate garnet earring, and a black silk scarf, lumpy with the masked shapes of other things below it. Something about the contents made me shiver and I set that aside to open the plastic file box.

The sheer volume of paper was staggering for such a small container. Packed into the box were records of stock transactions, transfers of title to dozens of properties, records of deed and incorporations, bank account records, recordings of probate, and dozens of other legal documents. From the dates, it appeared Purcell had done it all himself in a whirlwind of activity during the shortening spring twilight of the two weeks before he was taken by Alice's minions. No wonder he hadn't replied to Edward's messages; he'd spent all the available time trying to fix what had gone wrong and he didn't trust anyone to make replies for him—not once he'd realized that Jakob was tainted by the asetem, as he must have been. I put the letter into the front of the file case and picked up both that and the small carton of odds and ends. Then I carried them out of the vault and shut the door.

"I'm ready to go," I said to the patient Mrs. Jabril.

She hadn't moved or complained while I looked through the boxes. Now she stepped forward and helped me relock the door before closing the grille back over it.

I watched her through the deepest layer of the Grey as she finished her job. Her eyes really were emeralds and her teeth truly were pearls: she was "the clockwork" that Purcell had mentioned, a thing of metal and machinery beneath her sagging skin, animated by that pure golden magic I had observed in her corona and by a spark of something human tangled at the heart of her gears and pinions. But beyond that, the only sign of humanity was the lingering trace of the man who'd built her, though she faked it well.

I surmised it was her job to care for the vault—maybe it always had been—and her charge to answer if asked the right questions. Jabril, the silversmith who'd wanted to be a clockmaker, must have built her. I'd never seen anything like her before, but she was a thing of laws and mechanisms, and one thing I knew was that creatures like her did not lie or deviate from their programming. She must have been nearly two hundred years old, but she would mind the shop and the vault and carry out her maker's intentions until she fell to bits, however long she lasted.

She turned and looked at me as she finished. "Is there anything else?"

"Only that you shouldn't allow anyone access to that vault except Edward Kammerling or his agent."

"You?"

"Gods, I hope not," I replied, shuddering at the thought.

"Shall I see Mr. Purcell again?"

"I don't know."

She nodded and started back to the lift. I caught up to her in a few strides.

"Mrs. Jabril," I started, a little reluctant to ask but compelled to the question and knowing she would be equally compelled to answer, "have you ever met a man called Simeon? A . . . wizard?"

"A sorcerer," she corrected. "I met him once, when Mr. Jabril was still alive. An evil man. He had raised up an apprentice of great talent—a distant cousin of Mr. Jabril's named Ezra—nurtured his power, and used him to learn great things. Then he slew him and drank Ezra's soul. Only I knew, and I could say nothing against him. I do not care to see Simeon bin Salah again. Has he something to do with Mr. Purcell's going away?"

"Yes."

"I see." She said not another word until I was leaving the shop, and then she shook my hand with her cold, hard one in which I felt the cables and cogs moving under the skin. She said, "I shall look after the vault. As we always have." She had a significant gleam in her emerald eyes as she nodded to me. I pitied anyone or anything fool enough to try to get past Mrs. Jabril and her mechanical cousin below.

On my way back down the arcade, Percy tried to trip me, giggling in a chorus of ghostly voices. I stumbled and caught myself, muttering, "Damn you. Don't make me come after you, you pain in the butt."

The collective mean spirit of Percy whispered in my ear, "It wasn't at all what you thought, was it, little girl?"

"What?" I barked, turning in a circle to catch a glimpse of the poltergeist.

"It's not over," the chorus whispered.

One of the beadles strolled over and steadied me by the elbow. "Are you all right, madam?"

"I'm fine. I slipped but I'm OK." It wasn't just what the poltergeist had said but how that flipped me out. "Little girl," it had called me—my father's pet term, again. I'd always supposed that he'd have continued to call me that, had he lived to see me at my current five foot ten, and I was shaken by the poltergeist's use of it. Had all these communications really been from my father? Was Dad somehow reaching through the wards around him? Why—or how—after so much time . . . unless he was making a desperate effort to help me before it was too late. . . . The thought added urgency to my plans and a terrible weight to the future.

"Do you require assistance?" the beadle asked.

I started to refuse but thought I'd be better off without another visit from Percy. "Yes, please. I seem to be managing poorly with these boxes." With a very good grace, he took the biggest box from me and escorted me to the nearest street door to hail a cab and wave me on my way. There were no other little tricks from the resident poltergeist.

I asked for the nearest place I could pack and ship the boxes, and the cabby obliged with alacrity while I worried at the question of what the poltergeist meant. It was obvious this was a continuation of the messages I'd been getting since this whole kerfuffle started, but they'd dropped off once I'd left the States and I'd been happy to be shut of them for a while. Now here was another message and much clearer than before. The question I'd started out with had been answered to a degree: I was a Greywalker because my father had dumped the job and Wygan, the Pharaohn of the asetem-ankh-astet, had a purpose for one, a special one, so he'd pushed us to be that tool. But, as the ghosts had warned, that answer wasn't the answer at all. The real question wasn't so much "why" as "what next?" and the answers seemed to be coming, in a way, from my dad, if the telltale endearment meant anything. Obviously, I had a lot of unfinished business back in Seattle, which included finding out what had become of my killer and what Wygan was doing with the ghost of my father. Yet another reason to get home as soon as possible. The job I'd come for was almost done and the one remaining loomed like a tidal wave.

FORTY-FIVE

Once the packages were on their way to my place in Seattle—I figured that even the collective powers of the Red Brotherhoods of St. James and St. John couldn't subvert FedEx—I called Quinton. It was about eight in the evening there, so it only took a few minutes for him to call me back as I was walking toward the nearest Underground station.

"Hey, beautiful," he said.

"Hey, yourself. You still at my place?"

"Yeah. It's still crazy under the streets. Crazier, even. And Edward is still missing or incognito."

I made a face. "I hate to say that's what I was expecting."

"So, you're not coming back?"

"No, I *am* coming back. Tomorrow in fact. So long as things go as planned. If not, well . . . send flowers."

"It can't be that bad."

"It is all of that bad. Do you remember Alice, the vampire who crashed our party at the museum two years ago?"

"I thought she was dead," Quinton answered slowly.

"Join the club. She fooled us all. She was hooked up with Wygan and he somehow kept her going long enough to ship her here and start pulling the rug out from under Edward. Once she was in control, she lured me here under his orders and tried to make me a little more dead so I'd be a better fit for whatever Wygan has in mind. That's what this has been about since I was a little kid, even before I was born. My dad was supposed to be the Greywalker, but he quit with a .38-caliber resignation." I was amazed how angry I felt as I recited it. I was furious at how I'd been used, how my father had been pushed until he broke, how our friends and family had been hurt and killed and used as levers against us.

I continued, "Alice was Wygan's cat's-paw from the start. She got me killed the first time, too—or the second, I guess, but who's counting—so I could be the right kind of Greywalker for Wygan's purpose. Once I have Will back, I'm done here, because what's going on at home is apparently just the start of Wygan's endgame, and I'm going to stop him. At least now I know. I know what I am: I'm a tool to build some kind of gateway—but I'm not going to do it."

"You don't have to. Sweetheart, we could run—"

"No. *You* can run. Wygan will just keep coming after me until he gets what he wants or he gets stopped."

"I'm not going anywhere without you, unless I'm running toward you."

I smiled and felt warm for the first time all day. "I'll be the one running toward you. Will you come get me from the airport?"

"Sure."

"I may have the Novaks with me, but I'm hoping they can travel alone and attract less attention. I'll page you with more info. Then I'll call the condo when the plane touches down. You should be able to get to the airport by the time I'm through customs. The car keys are on the—"

"Floor. Chaos has them."

I laughed. "She's such a little thief."

"She's not a very good thief. She never tries to fence anything that's worth a damn. Just old squeaky toys and buttons—which were mostly mine to begin with."

We both laughed a little more, but the next breath brought back our worries and Quinton said, "You are coming back. Right?"

"I am coming back. Yes. Because the alternative is not an option. And I love you." It was the hardest thing I'd ever said, especially after the casual blow Cary's ghost had delivered about those words, and I waited in torment during the silence that followed.

Very quietly, Quinton responded, "I love you, too. And I will see you soon. Once I get the keys back from the ferret."

I hung up, smiling, even though the prospect ahead was grim, and headed for my meeting with Marsden at Angel Station.

The platform was busy, and I looked through the Grey for Marsden's slippery aura of colorless shapes rather than try to sort the crowd by eye for him. It took a bit of walking and a ride up the nearly endless escalator to find him on a bench in the intermittent sunshine that was breaking through the clouds.

A girl and her mother were sharing the bench with the blind man, who was keeping his head down, his long hair masking the disfigurement of his face, as he talked to them. The woman looked a bit wary, but the girl was smiling and holding something out to him. He took it and stroked the thing with remarkable gentleness. I got a little closer but stopped to watch, rather than interrupt the scene.

Marsden must have sensed my proximity; I saw him stiffen a bit and turn his head a little in my direction. He passed his gnarled hands over the furry little thing. "Magic, he is," he murmured. "Just magic. I had a hob just like him once—noble fella and a fine mole catcher, too. Quick as thought, he was, and clever with it. He'll do well with you, I think."

Then he held the fluff ball out for the girl: It was a young sable ferret with a little bandit mask and bright eyes. The sight of it made tears sting in my eyes as I thought of Chaos living in Quinton's pockets, and I hoped she would stay safe. "I've got to move along now,"

Marsden continued. "Thank you, my dear, for introducing me to your Dexter. You'll take good care of him, eh?"

"Yes, sir," the girl replied, cuddling the little animal to her chest.

He nodded at her mother before tapping his way across the busy cement apron around the station's mouth to where I stood.

"You're late," he said.

"And you are a big fake, you grumpy old man. I didn't have you pegged for a ferret fancier."

He snorted and began walking on, expecting me to follow. "Clever little beggars. Excellent at flushin' moles from holes. And ghosts from buildings—they can't resist chasing 'em. Not trying to kill 'em, mind you; they just like to rout 'em out. They'll dance and chatter like a mad thing and drive the haunts bloody bonkers. They'll zoom along a ley line and pounce on anything Grey as gets in their way. Fearless, they are. Charm the socks right off ya, too."

"Yes, they do," I replied, thinking of Chaos's wild behavior around anything ghostly, like the first time she'd dived headfirst into the Grey to take on the guardian beast on her own. She hadn't won that fight, but she hadn't lost it, either. "I have a ferret at home."

"Do you, now? P'raps your dad didn't father as big a fool as I thought."

I rolled my eyes. Back to the same old Marsden.

"So what are we looking for?" I asked.

"The right sort of sewer opening. Did you have any luck with the silversmith?"

"Did you know she's some kind of machine?"

"Is she indeed? I take it she was the one."

"She was. I found a lot of papers that should repair most of the financial damage. They might not give Edward any leverage back into St. James's, but they should give him some options. I shipped the important ones home."

"And what will happen to them if you do not return?"

"I have a friend who'll deal with it."

He nodded. "You've surprised me."

"Really? How?"

"You carried through. Y'didn't have to, y'know. Good chance this will go pear-shaped, and then what's in it for you, eh?"

"Integrity?"

"What's that matter to a dead woman? Which is what you had best be if this goes wrong."

"It seems to matter to some of them. And who says I'm going to die?"

"If you misplay Alice, if you don't win, you'll have given them what they're after—a chance to shape you how the Pharaohn wants. You'd be better off down that hole in the Hardy tree or splattered across the landscape like your dad."

"You don't know what's best for me, Marsden. Even if we foul it up and he does make me the Greywalker he's after, tools don't always work they way you think they will. You can use a knife for a screwdriver, but that doesn't mean it can't cut you."

He chuckled and said nothing, continuing west and south until we came to the turning of Penton Rise away from Pentonville Road. I looked around, seeing the mismatched buildings from a century of construction and renewal; the neon sign of a Travelodge hotel poked out above a lion-guarded Victorian facade in one direction and a steel-fronted car repair shop lurked in the other. The road was loud with traffic and filthy even in the middle of the day.

"Can y'feel the river yet?" he asked. "Under all this muck and steel?"

"No. Which river are we after again?"

"The Fleet. What was the grandest tributary of London before the Great Stink. Still comes to the Thames under Blackfriars Bridge, but we daren't start there. Stretch for it. We can't just guess at this."

"What about you?"

"Two heads are better than one, they say. . . ."

Putting our two heads together and quartering the area like

hunting dogs on a scent, we finally found the cold, blue trace of the Fleet River buried beneath the streets and buildings south of King's Cross, just a few blocks south and west of where we'd started.

We walked south, sunk in the Grey, along the onetime banks of the Fleet until we reached Holborn Bridge, coming perilously close to the memory of the priory of St. John as it stood across the phantom stream, solitary stone among a scatter of wood-and-plaster buildings in a rolling meadow. Beyond the bridge, the river vanished in a haze of broken Grey and a sharp wall of shattered temporaclines. Reluctant to step into the normal in such a place, we retraced our steps until we could come back to the modern surface safely.

We slipped out of the Grey and stood on the street, looking around for our bearings and the nearest sewer cover. A large building rose behind a brick wall topped with razor wire just across the road from us. The other buildings nearby were a mix of very old and very new housing.

"This should be close enough for Michael's motorbikes. Are y'certain y'know how—"

"For the last time, yes!" I snapped. They were Michael's bikes, yet he had been less worried about possible wrecks than Marsden, but then, he would be carrying his brother and didn't have much anxiety to spare for anything else. Marsden would be stuck with me and my riding skills, of which he was obviously in doubt.

Now we only needed to know where we were, and it would be up to Michael to bring the bikes to the right place. I walked up the road a bit, noting the utility access cover in the road near the intersection, until I found a sign screwed to the brick wall. It read PHOENIX PLACE. Another beside it identified the building as the Royal Mail sorting facility of Mount Pleasant. We were in luck; I couldn't imagine a better place to keep monsters at bay than the staid and secure environs of the Royal Mail.

I pulled my map book out of my bag and found the location and nearest major streets. So long as Michael didn't get picked up for loitering, it would be a pretty good spot. I called him and left the information on his voice mail—he didn't answer and I figured he was too busy with his own arrangements to bother with the phone. I didn't mind. He seemed to be holding up, and so long as he didn't stop to think too hard about what we were doing, he would be fine.

Marsden and I retraced the route of the river Fleet upstream through the Grey, passing through the chilly film-flicker of its submerged history until we found a place we both recognized. We were back at St. Pancras Old Church, but this time it stood on a rise above the banks.

"Blast," he muttered. "The stream's subsided more than I remembered." He didn't turn his head to look at me. "I suppose you could make a boat. . . ."

"What? I don't know a thing about boats and we don't have time—"

"I meant a boat like Norrin's knife—a Grey construct."

"No."

"That's bald of you."

"That's not how I work. I can't make anything. I'm only any good at tearing things apart, and even if I had the ability, we don't have the time for me to learn. Nor would it be wise to make our approach through the Grey," I added.

"Oh, yeah?" he challenged me, turning toward me at last.

I noticed the gouging in his flesh then. Deep in the Grey as we were, the damage he'd taken from Norrin was plain. He stood more stooped than usual, hunching over the place he'd been stabbed in the gut, and the marks around his eyes seeped glimmering tears of uncanny blood. I knew he didn't want sympathy, so I didn't offer any, or any indication that I saw anything amiss. My objection would have been the same regardless.

"It's too exhausting. If we want to get in through the rivers that exist now, we need to start in them. And we'll need everything we've got to fight through to Will and get out again. Pushing through the

Grey the whole way and hoping the river hasn't changed course from the temporacline we picked is too risky."

He grunted grudging assent.

A waft of blinking energy fragments drifted through us with a touch of frost and reminded me by my discomfort that I wanted out of the Grey as soon as possible. I climbed the hill toward the stubby square tower of St. Pancras Old Church as it had been when it was the only St. Pancras church. Assuming that Marsden would follow me into the ghost-thick graveyard, I shifted back to the normal. I looked back down the now-smaller hill as Marsden showed up beside me, scanning the road for another manhole cover.

"Then we'll have to take the boat in the same way we mean to get out—through the holes in the street. At least we shan't have to carry the boat far," Marsden said, "once we find one slim enough to fit through one o' them holes."

We found the right sewer cover in the bend below the church where the train station loomed up to arch over the street. It was only a few blocks from where we'd originally found *Morning Glory*. We walked into the street to get a general idea of how large the hole would be, and then headed off in search of a small boat for our journey along the bricked-over remains of the river Fleet.

FORTY-SIX

I t was already six o'clock by the time we returned with a two-man plastic canoe we'd bought from a boathouse near Regent's Park Zoo. I only wished we'd been able to find one sooner, as we now had just over two hours before sunset and our plan only worked if we could reach Will before then.

I'd left my bag at the *Morning Glory* and now packed the contents of my pockets into a couple of zip-top plastic bags. Then I helped Marsden open the sewer access and slip the boat in. Once we had the skinny vessel down the manhole, I was glad we'd gone for the tippy little boat and its stumpy paddles: the headroom in the brick vault of the lost river was too low for the long pole of a kayak paddle to have fit. The rain had stopped, but the river was halfway up the curving sides.

"Water's a bit swifter than what I'd expected, but we'll do well enough. At least we shan't be wadin' in muck all the way to Clerken-well."

"Wonderful," I muttered, hoping we'd get downstream before the vampires woke up. The rain had another compensation, though: The freshwater from the north was diluting the glutinous sludge the City of London poured into its ancient sewer, and the smell, while un-pleasant, wasn't overwhelming.

As I scrambled around, getting into the canoe without ending up in the water, Marsden lashed a waterproof flashlight to the front post through the mooring ring. It wasn't much light, but it would have to do.

"Why do I have the feeling you've done this before?" I asked in a whisper as we paddled along the dark waters of the hidden Fleet.

"How'd y'think I ended up in the House of Detention, girl?" Marsden muttered back.

"You said the Pharaohn set you up."

"Fer the nick, not fer the thievin'. Not like I'd never done it afore; I'd just not been caught. If you were desperate enough, you could go right up the drains in some o' the fine houses, skinny as I am. And I were bloody desperate. I suppose I could have got a regular job as a flusher—that's them as clears the sewers—but I was already half-mad by then and even the Board of Works wouldn't take on a fella who sees haunts and monsters."

"You told me you were a mole catcher."

"So I was, but I've done whatever would turn a coin at times and not all of it's been clean nor kind."

My stomach rolled a little with the stink of the stream and at the ideas that rose with his words, so I didn't notice the rocking of our little boat or the odd ripples on the black water until something exploded from the river.

Pale webbed hands with long, spatulate fingers sporting black spinelike claws grabbed at me as a gurgling scream of rage echoed through the tunnel: "Die!"

I slapped at the hands with my paddle, but they only moved to clutch the side of the boat and jerk downward. Then they shoved upward, spilling us out of the canoe and into the rank waters of the Fleet.

I couldn't see in the churned-up water and I kept my mouth and eyes shut tight against the filth, thrashing to keep my head above the chest-high surface of the moving water and gasp for air. I broke the surface for a moment and, in the bobbling illumination from the canoe's makeshift headlight, I spotted a steel ladder rung in the wall. I struggled toward it.

Marsden had climbed onto the overturned canoe, clutching his paddle. "What the hell—?"

"Don't know," I gasped, grabbing for the rung.

Sharp points dug into my leg and something tried to drag me below the water again. I caught a flash of needle teeth and luminous eyes as wide as saucers below the surface. I swore and kicked off the bottom harder, snatching at the rung in desperation.

"Jakob!" I shouted. A thread of horror spawned in the back of my mind: Jakob wouldn't be on the loose in the sewer unless Purcell was truly dead. I felt a sting of remorse for the vampire who'd sacrificed himself.

"River spawn. Bloody hell!" Marsden swore, smacking at a pair of hands on impossibly long, spindly arms that reached for him from below the canoe.

There were only two of them and smaller than us, to boot, but they were quick as fish in the water and we'd only been lucky to get to the surface again at all. I didn't doubt that they'd pull us down and hold us till we drowned in the sewage if they got a good hold of either of us. I shoved my left arm through the rung and bent my elbow to hang on. I kicked viciously into the place I'd seen the eyes while hoping to find a purchase on a submerged rung for my feet. I'd lost my paddle when the boat turned turtle, so I had no tools but a bagged cell phone and my father's puzzle; it was a fine lock pick for Grey doors, but I doubted that was going to help this time.

Marsden was still battling the reaching hands from the back of the canoe, but he called out, "They're fast, but they're fragile as eggshells—go for the gills if you can or break their nasty arms, and they'll give up soon enough! And they don't care for light or cats!"

"I don't see any cats down here!" I shouted back.

Jakob lunged out of the water, hissing, and slashed at my eyes. I jerked back, pulling up one foot to boot him in the face. He twitched aside and my waterlogged shoe connected with the side of his head. By blind luck, my water-heavy foot slid down his slimy skin and jammed against the gill slits beneath his jaw. The feeling of my toe sinking into the delicate structure was sickening. Repelled, I whipped away and felt the tissues rip apart like wet cardboard.

Jakob let out a terrible gurgle and blood gushed from the hole in his neck. He made one more swipe at me, his glowing eyes glaring malice, and fell back into the water, bubbling and thrashing. He was drowning and I stared in horror as he writhed.

In the bobbing, shivering light from the flashlight, I saw the other river spawn leave off snatching at Marsden to dart through the water to Jakob. But it didn't try to help him; it sank its claws into the injured monster and held the struggling creature fast while it bit into the bleeding flesh of its neck.

In my Grey core I could feel echoes of his distress and pain. Feel the life rushing out of his body on the tide of his blood. I had never been so close to something living as it died before. Just the shock in a shadow of someone's death hurt, but this. . . . I gagged and flung myself away from the sight, falling into the stream of filthy water as I tried not to vomit. Marsden grabbed my arm and hauled me toward the canoe.

Chest deep in the sewage and ice water of the Fleet, he flipped the canoe right way up and heaved me into it. Then he flung his paddle and himself back in and pushed us away from the bubbling, thrashing sounds of Jakob's death. I hung my head over the side and threw up, heaving until my gut ached.

My gods, I'd killed something. A living thing—not a ghost or a zombie, not a thing already dead and needing to be let go—but a living, thinking creature. The shock of death was bad enough, but I had never killed anything before, never ended its existence like pinching out a candle—nothing alive, at least—and I hadn't thought I ever would. Ghosts and vampires were different—they weren't really alive and they didn't send out the wrenching shock of death. Jakob hadn't been a human, but . . . he had been alive. He hated me and wanted me dead—it was self-defense!—but I couldn't stop retching, knowing I'd killed him.

In a few minutes I noticed we were no longer moving. I raised my head and saw Marsden squatting on a narrow ledge nearby, holding the canoe's mooring lines.

"Done?" he asked.

"I think so," I choked, my throat raw from heaving up the contents of my stomach. I wanted to rinse my mouth but there was no clean water and I didn't dare to even wipe my lips on my sleeve, soaked as it was in the disease-infested tide of Fleet Ditch.

"Y'mustn't take it on yourself like that. He'd have done you worse, if he had the chance."

I croaked and spat.

"Horrible as it was," Marsden continued, his voice low and vehement, "the other one did him a favor. Killed him quick. I should have remembered as they were cannibal. If they'd got you, they'd have ripped into you as you drowned and taken pleasure in your bubbling screams. They'd have plucked out your eyes and saved 'em as treasures. Unpleasant, grudge-carrying fiends, the river spawn. Legend says they're the bastard get of sirens and fae lords, cast out for their ugliness and hateful toward the whole world because of it. The stories say they devour children and drown sailors in the Thames for the shiny baubles they make of their bones. Right lucky you were."

I didn't feel lucky; I felt wretched and damned and sickened. It wasn't logical or reasonable, but the feel of something . . . dying by my hand, not just falling apart, disturbed me deeply.

Marsden turned his head back and forth, as if listening for something I was missing.

"They're gone. The other one must've swum away—we're no business of his. We'd best get on. Before the vampires wake and decide to torture your friend a bit."

For a moment I didn't move, and Marsden growled in his throat. "C'mon, girl! You've more bottle than this! Get up!" He kicked my leg ungently.

"Bastard," I muttered.

"Bloody well right. Off your jacksy, girl."

"What?" I questioned, sitting up, stung, annoyed, and generally pissed off now. Have I mentioned that I don't do self-pity as well as I do anger?

"I said get off your arse and do the job. You want that young man back, you'll have to go fetch 'im and time is short."

FORTY-SEVEN

I did not know where we were going. Marsden had been there with Michael while I was getting captured by Alice, and the last bend of the river into an even older bit of waterway was unknown to me. The walls of the watercourse were white here—or once had been—rather than the red brick and Portland cement of the Victorian sewers we had just left. The lichen-pocked stone glowed with some odd luminescence and the tunnel widened into a reservoir with a spiraling staircase built into its wall.

Marsden paddled us to the stair and tied off the canoe to a rusted iron ring that I suspected was meant for just that purpose. As we started up the stairs, we passed dozens of pairs of eyes that gleamed in the darkness.

"What are those?" I whispered, unable to see more than a humped shape, even in the Grey.

"Cats. Vampires don't care for 'em much more than river spawn, but they know it keeps the fish men away. Shows we've found their back door."

"Why aren't they doing anything? We must smell just like the river spawn by now."

"Not to the cats. We're warm-blooded. We've got to move, though. It's coming on for sunset."

Marsden pocketed the flashlight and we crept up the stairs in the dark, relying on our senses in the Grey and the dim limning of stones by the weirdly glowing lichen to see us up the steps.

At the top a spiderweb of arched corridors stretched into the darkness below Clerkenwell. Marsden led me along one of the tunnels and I could hear the water of the Fleet gurgling in the distance. Now I knew that was the sound I'd heard when I followed the kreanou to meet Glick.

We went through a door into what turned out to be a storeroom. Marsden huffed in annoyance and started out again immediately, but I stopped when I spotted a pile of water containers in the far corner. It appeared that someone had stocked the area as a shelter sometime in the past, and it seemed likely, given the disarray of the boxes and cans, that the vampires used the goods as food and supplies for prisoners and henchmen and anyone else they needed to hide from the daylight world.

I found a few clean rags and wet them from the water containers so I could wipe off my face and hands. I rinsed the sludge from my mouth. The water tasted of old plastic, but it was a big improvement over the filth from the Fleet. I wished I had the luxury of time to look at the itching wounds on my leg where Jakob's claws had pierced my skin, but I let that be, hoping I'd be able to do something about the infection later. Marsden shook his head in exasperation, but I noticed he used one of the rags to wipe his own face and hands before leading us again into the maze of corridors.

The hall we walked down next was thick with cold Grey fog that sparked with random shots of energy and eddied into the shapes of oblivious ghosts. I imagined it was used once in a while but not with any frequency, which was good for us; we'd be able to escape along it with little chance of being intercepted. Marsden stopped at a crossing, tilting his head to concentrate on sounds ahead.

"Four," he muttered. "Red Guard, all humans; no Brothers or demi-guard. We're in luck, but we'll have to take them out fast."

I reached into my pocket and got the puzzle out of its plastic bag—I didn't want to fumble for it when we needed it to unlock Will's cell. As I looked up, I saw Marsden reach under his moleskin coat and pull out two gleaming knives. He flipped one of them around and offered it to me, underhand and without turning his head back in my direction.

"No," I whispered. I didn't want to kill anyone else; what I'd done to Jakob was terrible and still sat like a weight, regardless of any justification.

"Don't be daft," he hissed back. "They'll kill you quick as look at you—or take you prisoner again for that mad harpy, Alice, to play with. Clever as you are with your hands and feet, girl, it won't be enough against them, and that does your man no good."

Reluctantly, I took the knife.

"Look sharpish," he warned as we started forward.

I kept my vision turned more toward the Grey, looking for any sign of magical traps. This time we weren't unexpected, and I doubted that Alice and her pet sorcerer wouldn't have beefed up the security where they could. They'd probably laid a lot of different traps to cover all the bases. The upside was, making and laying any magical traps would have worn Simeon down, which was definitely in our favor. We'd just have to be clever about looking for them and hope they'd relied on magic more than technology.

I had long ago realized that vampires didn't really know what a Greywalker's capabilities were; it wasn't until I'd met Marsden that I understood that we were each different, which certainly threw a wrench into most magical plans. Magic is strongest when specific. Loose, general spells are usually weak or short-lived, according to Mara. But the vampires wouldn't need anything powerful down here; just something strong enough to hold us or slow us down until reinforcements could arrive.

The first guard we came across was looking down the hall the opposite way. An ordinary-looking man, except for his blood-tainted aura and the small submachine gun—entirely illegal in England—slung high under his arm. He had his back to the wall quite a few feet away.

"Here, can you get round him through the Grey?" Marsden whispered.

I nodded. I'd look like a ghost and there would be nothing I could do to the guard while I went, but if I popped out fast enough and hit him hard enough, it should work. I only wished I could go behind him, but he'd left no room and I didn't want to try walking through him.

I eased deeper into the Grey and the catacombs sprang up in fiery lines through the silver mist. Knots and tangles of power that looked like messy coils of barbed wire dotted the hallway—traps. I skirted the nearest one, hoping Marsden could see it, too, and glided to the other side of the guard, who looked like a red-and-yellow smear as I passed him, the gun a cold, dark block swinging by his side.

The guard stiffened and turned his head toward me as I slipped back to normal. He yanked the gun up, bracing against the sling as I punched him just below the sternum. He grunted as his breath was driven from his lungs, and Marsden pounced on him from behind, forcing him to the ground. The guard's finger must have tightened on the trigger as he collapsed, but his body muffled the short burst of gunfire. I felt a sharp tearing sensation in my chest and head as he died, and I clamped down on a cry of shock and agony, biting my tongue.

The guard lay in a clumsy heap as a thread of blood oozed out from beneath him. A furious haze of red energy rose off the downed guard and resolved into a ghost that glared at me and spat a few vile words before the heat of his ire was sucked away into the grid. The memory shape of the dead man dissipated with the odor of rotten eggs.

Marsden picked himself up, pulling his knife from between the corpse's ribs. "Next time, just cut his ruddy throat," he growled, side-stepping to avoid the magical trap on the floor.

"Don't you . . . feel them?" I asked, still aching.

"Yeah, but you learn to turn it down after a while. You'll get used to it."

I hoped not. I didn't want to have cause to get used to the sensation of fresh death.

We slipped back into the Grey and stalked the next one, who was turning to see what the noise had been. Marsden slipped, jumping over time and space, to exit the Grey next to the guard. I had to run the distance through the mist, over the hot lines of the grid and around the cold bulk of stone walls toward the bright, living shape of the guard. Marsden cut the man's throat before I could reach them, and the knife of pain and shock ripped through me again. The blood ran across the stone floor, blazing with white light that flashed away like a magician's trick smoke.

Marsden reached through the thin barrier between normal and Grey and hauled me out. "Quicker."

"What are you—?" I started, furious and disgusted and hurting, but he clapped a hard hand over my mouth.

"We have minutes. Only minutes. You'll have to bear it and save your man. I'll manage the guards."

He nodded toward a heavy wooden door in the wall—the portal to an ancient cell. A metal observation plate hung slightly open in the door's surface. I peeped in, checking for other humans. I could have slipped through, but I couldn't leave with Will that way, and I was willing to bet there was no keyhole on the other side.

The room within was dark except for the shaft of dusty light that fell through the observation door. I shifted around, trying to see into the gloom without obscuring the light. "Will?" I whispered.

I could hear a shuffling noise beyond the door. I pulled back and studied the door for further traps. A blue gleam shone though the planks between the ancient bulks of wood. There was something magical on the other side. Another shock hit and I slipped painfully into the Grey, trying to get a better look at the spell in the cell.

It was a tangle, meant to hold someone or something in place for a few minutes. Just like one of Mara's, the heart of the spell was a braided ring of thorny bramble. The whole mess was tied to the foot of the door, so anyone sneaking in or sidling to the door for a peek outside would be stuck to the door itself. Admirable ingenuity, but I cursed Simeon bin Salah nonetheless. The working zone of the spell was almost a foot wide, which would make it hard to open the door with it in place. I fell back into normal, feeling the pressure of time and the stabbing aches of the dying, wondering how I was going to get past this.

Down the hall I heard a thump and a slithering sound as another death-shock hit me. It wasn't as bad this time—it was farther away—but it still doubled me up. I didn't want to look, but I cast a quick glance over my shoulder. I couldn't see any bodies on the ground but I could see stains that shone with the same bright white light and liquid red as the second guard's blood. My stomach rolled, but I pushed my sense of horror aside. When the vampires woke, they'd smell the blood and be on us like hounds on a rabbit. And I wouldn't have been surprised if some of the lower ranks and demi-vamps slept down here in the catacombs. I had to move faster no matter how it hurt, but I also had to be careful.

I couldn't use tools well in the Grey—normal things became difficult to hold—so I had to do it like a normal person. I knelt down on the floor and passed the knife under the door, hooking the threads that held the tangle in place and slicing through them. I felt a tiny electric jolt as each one parted. Not sure where Will was in the room, I didn't want to move the tangle until I had the door open.

I shuffled Dad's puzzle until a key shape clicked into place that buzzed happily. I looked around as I put the key into the lock and saw Marsden trotting back to me.

"What're you dawdlin' for?" Marsden demanded. "Get 'im and get a move on!"

"There's a spell tangle on the inside of the door. Give me your cane."

His face creased into a scowl, but he pulled the cane out and flicked it straight. I unlocked the door, the mechanism rolling freely to my odd key. Then we both heaved on the heavy door, pulling it open to its widest.

I took the cane and probed for the tangle, not sure if the magic would be conducted by the stick or if the cane might become gripped in the trap. I felt the trap bloom and clutch the cane, which yanked away from my grip and stood upright in the middle of the doorway. But the trap was sprung, and Marsden and I rushed into the cell and stopped short.

Will cowered in the farthest corner, the watery light from the corridor barely glinting off his filthy hair. His clothes were dirty, torn, and bloodied and he'd lost his glasses. The smell in the tiny, unventilated space was worse than the sewer: blood and waste and unwashed clothes stiff with fear sweat and dirt. I took a step toward Will as Marsden turned back toward the door—the blind man standing lookout.

Will turned and scrabbled at the wall with his bandaged right hand as if he could claw his way out, muttering, "No, no . . . please, no more . . ."

"Will, it's Harper. I'm getting you out of here," I said, walking closer, relieved that I could see the bulk of his left hand swathed in a startling white bandage—they hadn't cut it off. The visions I'd had in Los Angeles must have been exaggerated by Simeon's "new techniques." At least I hoped so, hoped that the odd shape under the bandage was indeed his own whole, living hand.

"Harper?" he questioned, peering in my direction against the light, which made me a black blot in the doorway. Then Will panicked, throwing himself against the wall and cringing into a ball, covering his face with both unwieldy hands, wrappings extending up his arms as far as I could see. The sight of those bandages almost brought me to my knees, but the worst was when he started crying. "Get away, get away! How can you do this? Just kill me and get it over with. . . . Dear God, please . . ."

I threw myself down on the icy floor beside him and grabbed his face between my hands, brushing his weakly flailing arms away. I didn't know what they'd done to him to make him so hysterical, but it must have been awful. He battered at my arms and head without strength, trying to rear away, but stopped by the unyielding stones of the cell.

"It really is me," I said, my voice low and calm as I could manage as I held him, willing him to look at me, to hear me and believe me. I pushed on every compulsion I could think of, on every bit of persuasion and hope. "And I really am here to save you from this place. I'm not going to kill you. I'm not going to hurt you. I'm going to take you back to Michael. We're going to get you out of here."

"No! No! You're that . . . witch. That . . . monster! You can't trick me anymore. I know Harper's not coming."

I thought fast and talked faster. "We met at an auction at the Ingstrom Shipwrights warehouse. You sold me a cabinet and a chair. We had dinner at Dan's Beach House. I got arrested. You got mad. Do you remember that?"

Marsden hissed, "Get a move on!"

I ignored him and kept my attention on Will.

Will whipped his head back and forth in my grasp. He didn't quite believe me, but there was a submerged gleam of hope in his eyes and his cold, shut-down aura flickered with a pale green and blue flame like a will-o'-the-wisp. I had to feed that hope or he'd never come willingly, and we couldn't possibly carry him.

"On our next-to-last date you gave me a puzzle ball that used to be on a newel post in an old house," I reminded him. I knew Alice wouldn't have told him such things—she'd been hacked up in her jars by then. "The last time we met was at Endolyne Joe's. We broke up because I'm not like you—because I'm broken and I see monsters."

He sobbed for breath and collapsed into my arms, his head falling hard onto my chest. "I . . . saw them. I should have believed you."

"It's OK. You don't have to believe any of it, but you do have to come with me. We're taking you to Michael and you'll be safe. Now get up and come with us. We have to go fast."

"I can't."

"You'll have to."

He cringed tighter against me. I shot a look at Marsden and hoped he could figure out that I needed his help.

"I can't walk," Will cried.

Marsden came over to us, his neck bent so his hair covered his face. "They've cut the bottoms of his feet," he muttered to me. "Done worse to his hands and arms. Bled him like a pig. We'll have to support 'im. And we must go. I can hear something coming."

FORTY-EIGHT

I could hear it when I concentrated: a storm of rapid footsteps from several directions and the wind-rush of leathery wings beating the air. Ignoring his fears and injuries, I hoisted Will up and supported his left shoulder with my right. Marsden took his other side. Will whimpered but did his best to move with us as we hauled him toward the door.

Marsden snatched at his cane just as it started to fall from the trap, and we burst out of the cell, into the stone-built corridor. And into another figure running toward us in the dimness. We jerked to a halt. The other person, obscured in shadows, skidded and stopped. Then he breathed, "Will!" and launched himself the last few feet into us.

"Michael!" I hissed. "What are you doing here? You're supposed to wait by the bikes! You could have been captured!" I wanted to yell at him, but that angry whisper was all I could risk. The stupid boy! If he'd have been caught . . .

Michael ignored me and wrapped his arms around his brother's waist, not noticing the stench or bandages. "Will! Thank God. You're all right?"

"Not in the least," Marsden snapped. "Nor shall we be if we linger for family reunions. You got in so tidily, you lead us out of here, boy, and the faster the better."

Startled by his rough tone, Michael backed off and spun around, jogging ahead. "C'mon! I couldn't stand waiting for you. I found a tunnel from Hatton Garden—it's faster than the sewer route."

We went forward, hauling the emaciated and staggering Will between us as quickly as we could, but our speed was still only a bit better than a jog.

As we plunged into a section of unlit corridor that arched over the grumbling passage of the buried river, a whiff of its effluence leaking through the masonry, Marsden let out a chuckle. "Good thing we smell of sewer, girl," he mumbled. "They'll have a harder time following us with the odor of the Fleet below."

Michael, ahead of us, didn't hear, but Will did and he made a noise that might have been a cough—or not—and tried to move faster. Every step hurt him—I could see it in the bright red strobing of his energy corona—but he kept on and I saw the white gleam of his teeth as he bit into his lower lip.

"It's just a few blocks," I whispered to him. "Not far."

He nodded in the dark.

We staggered through the murk—we didn't dare to use the flashlight—with the sounds of pursuit growing closer by the moment. Michael stopped to glance back at us over and over, even though most of the route was too dark for him to see much but our shambling shapes. I began to feel the cold-hot press of blood rage and insanity far behind, like the blast from an explosion bearing down on us in slow motion.

"Harper!" Far away, I could hear Alice shriek my name like a swearword.

"Catching up," Marsden muttered, voicing my fears.

Michael whipped around a corner and dashed a few feet ahead to a set of steel loops set in the wall. He scrambled up them and pushed the iron manhole cover aside with his back. We could hear it scrape across the road above, and the sound echoed into the tunnels below as if the earth itself had groaned. Behind us, the scrambling and rushing noises paused and changed direction, coming straight for us.

Marsden and I started shoving Will up the steps, using our backs as braces to support him as he tried to pull himself up. I heard a whimper of pain escape as he struggled upward, tangling his mangled feet in the loops and hauling with his injured hands. Michael whispered encouragement from above and, when he was close enough, grabbed his brother's wrists and hauled steadily. Will's weight eased off our shoulders and then vanished as he climbed clear of the hole.

"You next," Marsden said. "I have some more tricks to hold 'em off while you get that infernal motorbike running. But don't dawdle!"

I scrambled up the rungs and levered myself into the street. A dozen yards away, I saw Michael fussing with Will, who was leaning against a wall and sinking slowly. I ran to them and helped with Will's helmet while Michael got the small motorcycle started.

Will tried to smile at me, but it was weak and faded away under tears, pain, and exhaustion. "What now?" he asked as I pushed him onto the bike behind his brother and grabbed the webbing straps we'd bought earlier.

"Now you go to the doctor. After that, Michael will take you someplace safe."

Will was shaking as Michael pulled his arms around his own waist. I strapped the two men together and patted Michael's helmet to let him know I was done. I hopped back as the small bike zoomed away.

From the open manhole came a flash and a roar. I swung my attention to the other motorcycle: It looked like Michael had borrowed one of the Italian bikes from his buddy, and I was grateful I wouldn't have to remember the oddities of old British motorcycles as well as how to ride one at all.

The bright yellow bike roared on the first press of the starter. I threw my leg over, tucked my hair down my collar, and jammed the helmet on as I felt Marsden's weight hit the back.

"Go!"

"Hold on!" I yelled back. As his arms locked around my waist, I kicked the bike off the center stand. It leapt forward and bit into the road with both tires, chirping as it bolted. Even over the engine, I heard something more of flesh and rage roar behind us with an eruption of wing beats and a howl of fury.

I could hear Alice's screeches of wrath among the howling and the voice of something that nearly jellied my spine, raking at some lizard-brain part of my mind that contained primal fear. My grip on the throttle slacked and the bike gurgled quieter, slowing. . . .

Marsden jabbed me in the ribs. "I'll kill you first if you drop us," he hissed. The ridiculousness of the threat struck through the terror and I clamped back down on the throttle, twisting it hard. The Ducati jumped forward, screaming.

We were the only prey left to follow, but we had a lead. They'd have to go back for their own bikes if they wanted to follow. Too bad there hadn't been time to hobble them.

The streets were busy and narrow and they twisted into each other at odd angles, reducing the maximum speed I could put into negotiating a path away from Clerkenwell. Our pace was still excessively fast, but something seemed to be close behind, something that breathed the stink of death down our necks and jinked through the traffic as nimbly as a gazelle. We were ahead of it, but I didn't imagine that would last long. Distantly I heard the throaty sound of other bikes and knew it was Alice and her cohort—I only hoped it was a small one, that her wanton slaughter of Glick and the loss of me had driven a wedge into her control of the Brotherhoods and the support of the local asetem.

I raced the bike northwest, toward King's Cross and St. Pancras. I was fine on the one-way streets, but I dreaded the bigger roads and had to concentrate on sticking to the left side of the line. At the first opportunity, I moved, even though it meant using smaller streets where there were fewer witnesses to anything the vampires might try if they caught up. I twitched the bike into a right turn across traf-fic, shooting through a hole in the pattern to race into a new route, dragging our pursuers away from the main streets. If I'd been a more experienced rider, I might not have made the move, but as it was I relied on the luck of fools.

We made it. I turned twice more, up into Pentonville and then west, dropping to a smaller road and flashing past the boat basins on the south shore of Regent's Canal. Then a hard right-left jink at York, staying south of the canal and sprinting the bike through the empti-ness of Goods Way, which sliced between the back of King's Cross and the cement banks of the canal. We drove past the skeletal ring of a Victorian gas regulator that stuck its black iron fingers into the sky and under the S-turn at the back of St. Pancras Station.

I skidded the bike to a stop on the sidewalk in front of St. Pancras Old Church and we left it, with my helmet thrown to the ground beside it, like a signpost gleaming yellow and rippling the night air with its heat, as we scrambled for the only magical place in England I was familiar with: the graveyard. It wasn't ideal, but I knew the dead spots and the hazards, and the vampires would have to take bigger risks than Marsden and I would. If we were lucky, they'd already left Alice to sink or swim on her own.

Marsden and I slipped through the Grey and into the cemetery.

The first thing to come at us was neither Alice nor her pet sorcerer, but the kreanou, the black streak of fury that had pursued us from the start. We turned back to look from our vantage near the Soanes' tomb and saw it throw itself against the fence. It stopped when the gates didn't budge, revealing the silver-eyed man-thing that had attacked Glick and escorted me toward death and doom. It let out a shriek that sent an icy frisson up my spine.

"Holy hell," Marsden murmured. "At least it's alone. . . ."

The kreanou found an angle it liked, stepped back, and vaulted the churchyard wall beside the gate as if it were no more challenging than a beginner's long-jump competition. Then it charged at us.

We dodged in two directions, Marsden toward the tomb, I toward the Hardy tree and its well of void. The kreanou swerved to track me. I cut behind the tree, hoping the monster was stupid enough to run in a straight line. It jinked right, trying to intercept my path on the other side of the tree. I dodged back, feeling hopeless as it corrected and closed. . . .

"Stop!"

Alice stepped delicately down from the nearest wall, assisted by Simeon and holding one hand up to stay the kreanou. Her black wrappings fluttered and trailed around her like wisps of smoke. She dropped down to the grass near the parade of gravestones in the corner south of Mr. Hardy's tree. Simeon followed her, but otherwise they were alone. My heart leapt with hope that we might survive after all.

"I want to kill her myself," Alice continued, stalking closer. Simeon seemed to glide over the grass behind her.

The kreanou growled but held still. In the Grey I could see the magical leash between the three as well as if it were a rope in the sun, holding the kreanou equidistant from both Alice and Simeon. I wondered what would happen if I could break that leash. . . .

"I thought you were going to hand me over to the Pharaohn," I replied. "Oh, but you let me get away, didn't you? After the way you screwed up in Seattle, too, I guess you don't get to be Primate of all London after all. And Wygan's so very unforgiving. . . ." I edged as close to the tree as I dared. I hated the proximity, but my discomfort wasn't important; Alice's was. I wanted her angry enough to kill and not think what it would mean.

"To hell with him!" she screamed. I'd struck the right nerve. "You've been the ruin of my plans too often! I should have torn out your throat in Seattle. I should have gutted you when I had a chance. I should have tortured you and feasted on your blood while your lover and the shivering shade of your father watched. But now I'm just going to kill you and let the kreanou scatter your bones like sticks!" She caught her breath and what passed for sanity. "But you can rest assured that once you're gone, I'll get my hands on your dear William again and everything I'd like to do to you will be served up to him." She smirked.

"Talk, talk," I taunted. "I don't see you doing anything about it." Marsden had been circling wide from the tomb and I could make out the white gleam of his trousers among the tombstones far to the street side.

Alice launched herself at me while her companions stood and watched—the kreanou straining with desire for carnage and blood. She wasn't as fast as the kreanou, but she was fast enough, and only a very quick spin aside kept me out of her clutches. She still managed to rake my face and arm with her nails as she passed and turned. The wind of her passage stunk of rot. Simeon's spell to knit her back together might not be working quite as well as she thought.

I'd never seriously faced off against a vampire in a fight before and I'd had no idea what to expect. Mostly they intimidated and charmed and manipulated. Now this one was coming on like a street fighter, eyes gleaming red and her hands hooked into claws as she crouched. I didn't like having Simeon and the kreanou at my back, so I circled, making an arc that forced Alice to counter. She drew downhill a bit, toward Simeon and away from the Hardy tree. I stood my ground. I wasn't going to bring the fight to her. She wanted me dead; she'd have to come get me.

Behind her I saw a flash of white as Marsden jumped to ambush the sorcerer. Simeon whirled, jumping away—more spry than I'd have expected—and made a gesture with his hands that sank a bright field of green light into the turf. The ground shook and the kreanou darted toward him. But Simeon made a fist and twisted it, and the kreanou came to a quivering halt, poised like an attack dog waiting for the command.

The ground near the fence heaved and a phalanx of the dead struggled up from their graves. Whole or part, they rose and lurched toward Marsden, throwing themselves onto him.

Alice snatched at me and spun me toward the ground. I dropped my shoulder and rolled back up to my feet, reaching behind my back for the knife Marsden had given me in the sewer. I pivoted. I was a little clumsy on the moist lawn of the cemetery; my body ached from the shocks of the guards' deaths and my legs burned from the infected cuts Jakob had inflicted, so I bobbled to the right. Alice jumped and missed me by inches as I ducked to recapture my balance.

In the distance, Marsden struggled under the weight of the lyches, plunging his hands into them and tearing out the burning threads that animated them. They fell down but only one at a time, and he was badly outnumbered. The kreanou watched with avid eyes, waiting for an opportunity to slip its leash, its head turning back and forth as it watched Marsden and then Simeon, whose hands were burning with the gather of power.

I rushed at Alice and she hesitated a moment as I got close. Then she reached out and grabbed me by the shoulders, trying to wrestle me down to her shorter height. Her mouth gaped and her fangs seemed to grow longer, glinting with saliva. I put my weight into her, bowling her under me as her teeth scraped against my collarbone.

The fangs felt like knives and seemed to pierce deeper into my flesh than was possible, cutting past the bone and diving for the arteries that sprang from my heart. I pushed my left arm between us as we tumbled and gripped her jaw, shoving her head up with a wrenching thrust. The agony of her bite eased as her head snapped back and the fangs slid out of my skin. Blood coursed down the front of my shirt.

Marsden yelled and I jerked my knees up, separating Alice from me with a hard thrust of my legs. I raised my head a moment and saw Marsden vanish under a pile of dirt and bodies as the angry dead pulled him down into their mass grave.

The smoke black line that connected the kreanou to Simeon lay less than a body length from me and I lunged for it, throwing myself through the air and snatching at it as I arced into its path.

The kreanou screamed a hunting cry of bloodlust and frustration and Simeon yelled as the magic tugged on them both. Alice scrambled across the churned earth like a deadly crab as I gripped the power link with both hands.

The burn of the energy forced a scream from my throat as I tore the binding apart. The hot fragments of control whipped like fractured guy wires, and half of the kreanou's leash dissolved.

The silver-eyed monstrosity howled bloody anticipation and rushed at Simeon. It looked like a thin streak of red against the darkness as it pounced.

Simeon screamed as it hit him and he spun, trying to fight off the embodiment of rage, but it tore at him and blood flew. The grid of the Grey trembled and warped to suck in the hastening flow of magic that poured out with his life. The kreanou made bestial sounds of delight as it gorged on him, tearing him to shreds.

The death-shock doubled me over as Alice shrieked in rage and lashed at me, catching her hands in my clothes and dragging me close. She gripped me tight a moment, grinning with a sick parody of a lover's desire. "You cannot stop me this time," she whispered, trying to capture my gaze in hers, to hold my will and force me to submit to death.

I flipped the knife in my hand and jerked my arms into her with all my remaining strength, driving the blade into her side. She gurgled and twitched, losing her concentration on me. I ripped the blade down, feeling the rough black fabric of her strange bindings tear and fall away. I felt the power that held her together falter. Simeon was not there to reinforce it. Her legs buckled and I kicked her away. But her upper body stayed clutched to mine by the grip of her hands on my shoulders.

The clothes, after all, were nothing but bandages, holding her severed parts together. As she unhinged her jaw to snap her teeth again into my flesh, my gaze fixed on the choker around her neck. The ruby drops were blood that leaked from the edge of the band.

Footsteps rushed toward us—two pair: one fleet, the other desperate. As I reached for the band around her throat, I felt someone can-non into us, knocking Alice and me tumbling toward the fence that contained the Hardy tree and its sunburst of graves.

The kreanou snarled close enough to ring my ears.

I cut the ribbon and Alice screamed, her grip weakening. I thrust her away and she fell backward, scrabbling as blood leaked from the ragged, half-healed wounds that marked her body, glowing white and ringed in black.

"Kreanou, no!" she gasped.

Trembling, the creature teetered to a halt, only barely human, barely controlled, its limbs pulled around into impossible geometries and its face elongated into a lupine snout bristling with rows of gore-splashed fangs.

"It doesn't want you," Marsden called to me, running toward us, covered in dirt and grave mold.

I dropped to my knees and brought the knife down across Alice's neck, feeling the stitches pop and the magic that held her together wrench apart. And I felt nothing else: no pain, no remorse.

The last leash of magic parted and the kreanou lurched forward. I kicked Alice's body away from me as the monstrosity pounced onto it. Her head screamed and thrashed, gnashing its jaws as her breath ran out. I picked it up and staggered to the edge of the magical vortex hidden in the core of Mr. Hardy's tree.

I started to tumble into the sucking hole among the keening, churning ghosts, but I felt hands grab me at the waist and hold me to earth. I flung Alice's head away into the pit and watched it vanish in the unknown dark. One of the creatures who'd caused my death—the important death at least—was gone, and though it didn't change me back, I felt relieved by her passage.

Marsden hauled me backward, away from the tree. The sound of distant sirens floated on the haunted breeze. I glanced across the churchyard, the turf torn, muddied, and gleaming with the slowly ebbing spells of magic. Of Alice and Simeon, only bloodied shreds of cloth remained. The half-decayed corpse of a young man lay among the wreck of Alice's bandages—the remains of the kreanou, extinguished with his creator.

Marsden kicked the moldering corpse into the vortex. Then he shoved on the shapes of time, and I tumbled through to a sunny afternoon in the churchyard that stretched nearly to Euston Road. We staggered, exhausted, toward Regent's Canal and the waiting *Morning Glory*.

A little over twenty-four hours later, I was on a plane back to Seattle. I thought I should have stayed to help Michael with Will, but there was nothing I could do. Will's injuries had been worse than I'd hoped and not as bad as I'd feared, but ironically well cared for. I supposed that Simeon was responsible—that seemed like the sorcerer's style, to keep his victims as well as possible until he was ready to dispose of them—and I was grateful for that much. Michael told me that the surgeons wanted to try some reconstruction on the torn flesh and muscle of Will's hands, arms, and feet but Will had nixed it in an unexpected fit of anger, saying he just wanted to go home without anyone else cutting on him.

Will had become unpredictably moody, swinging from anger to despair to manic, unreasonable joy over the smallest things. It worried his brother and Michael thought they would return to Seattle as soon as the work, school, and immigration issues were straightened out. London no longer held any charm for them.

The condition of the churchyard at St. Pancras Old Church was written off to vandals. Clerkenwell's vampires sank into the darkness and kept their own counsel. Of the asetem, I heard nothing. I supposed the one I'd met in the club had reported to Wygan and they were re-grouping or carrying on with whatever could be salvaged of their plans. I could have asked Sekhmet, I suppose, but I hoped I'd never see the Lady of Dread again. Not in this life or any other.

I'd accomplished what I'd come for. Will was found and safe. The problems of the Red Brotherhoods of St. James and St. John no longer concerned me. The paperwork to reestablish Edward's control of—or at least the material grip on—his European holdings was on its way to Seattle and would be there within a day of my own arrival. If he was still around by the end of all of this, I imagined he'd find a way to reassert himself once the smoke had cleared. At least I'd done that much. I didn't yet know who the mole in his organization was or what was going on, but that was a problem that would wait until I got home.

And I wanted to get home very badly. There were problems there yet to be faced, threats to the world I knew. Wygan was moving to do something, of which I could only guess a small part, and none of his plans would be good for anyone I knew or loved. I didn't kid myself that destroying Alice had put any kind of drag on his plan. He'd wanted her to change me and her failure would piss him off, but he'd either try again or find a way around it—he was nothing if not tenacious, as I'd discovered.

He'd pushed my father and then me to be his tool, and so far we'd both resisted him, but he kept trying. I knew he wanted to make some kind of gateway in the Grey and that I was the thing he needed to do that. I wasn't certain how he expected to accomplish that, what power I didn't yet have that he needed, but I'd figure it out. And I'd stop him.

I no longer had to ask "Why me?" Meeting Marsden and my experiences in London had answered a lot of my questions about why I was a Greywalker and how. I'd removed one of the enemies who'd made me what I was and I felt I was on the road to reasserting control of my own life.

I still had questions, though, and I thought I'd have to find a way to my father's ghost to answer them. But I suspected he wasn't as deeply buried as Wygan thought. I was sure it was he who had opened the door to the ghosts I'd been seeing and hearing. They all called me "little girl," after all, and I was far from little anymore. And I knew things about my father—and my mother—I hadn't suspected. I loved him a little less blindly and despised her a little less deeply now. I'd have to learn more, but for now, I just longed for home.

There was a lot waiting for me in Seattle. I was heading into an unknown with consequences I couldn't imagine but envisioned the worst. And I hated the thought that I might have to do worse than I had done in London. I'd killed Jakob and destroyed Alice. They'd wanted me dead and they were monsters, but the grim weight of having killed still hung on me. It wasn't the same as having plucked a poltergeist apart or torn a trapped soul free of a rotting zombie body. Self-defense drove me to it, I knew, but killing hurt, and there was more ahead, I was sure. Would it become easier, as Marsden had suggested? Would I come not to care? I prayed not. Changes were imminent and I feared what I might have to do and what I might become. But at least home would bring me back to Quinton. Who loved me. I hoped that was going to be enough.

Somewhere over the Atlantic, my cousin Jill appeared, still drowned, still bitter. She glared at me. "It was your fault," she muttered.

Narrowing my eyes, I reached into her, tangling my fingers in the buzzing energy at her core, and then flicked her away. "You were the one who wanted to go swimming," I muttered after the vanished ghost. I didn't need her recriminations—I was sure I could heap enough on myself without her help. But that, too, would have to wait. For now, home would be enough.

Since I'm not British and had never been to England before, research for *Vanished* was a bit tricky. I had limited knowledge to start with and very limited time. One great thing about this situation was that Harper had also never been to England, so my experiences as a first-time visitor were useful in forming Harper's impressions and thoughts.

I was also very lucky to have friends and family in the UK and they all contributed something and helped vet things and fill in information for me. They also became the patterns for some of the English characters in the book, though I also blatantly lifted characters from British literature, TV, and film for the personalities of the caryatids and poor Barnaby Smith. I hope no one minds too much.

Initially I started with some rough ideas about what I wanted to use. For instance, I'd read several books that mentioned the buried rivers of London and I thought that would be a nifty addition. Living on a boat, myself, the idea of the rivers and canals of London charmed me. My friends Rik and Carol pointed me at the Canal Museum and also suggested several other marvellously creepy and crazy things, such as the Old Operating Theatre, and Sir John Soanes' tomb and the museum of his home. The tomb made it into the book, but alas, the old surgery in the attic of a church and the eccentric museum of Soanes' collections did not.

I was only able to spend twelve days in England during my research trip and much of that was spent doing things that weren't strictly research at the time, but certainly were interesting. Many seemed unlikely to yield useful material, but some did, anyhow. Such as a lunch with my publishing group that led to the suggestion of Clerkenwell as the haunt of vampires. The run across Horse Guards Parade and down to Westminster Abbey which my husband and I undertook in the rain on our one free day to play tourist. Discovering pasties at Victoria Station. Walking in reverse what turned out to be the route of the motorcycle chase. And finding the barred doors to one of the "ghost stations" on the Underground.

People became the most valuable asset, however. Not just the ones we knew already, such as friends and family in England, but also those we met, such as my agent and editor, and those we never met, including the mobs of tourists in Trafalgar Square on a sunny May Friday; crowds on the sidewalks outside the pubs at commuter hour; and the wonderful mix of people from all over the world who populated the streets everywhere we went: running cafes in Theatreland where we had tea, chatting with their friends on the Tube; and simply being part of the crowd that is uniquely London.

And of course, the caryatids, which we found quite by accident on our walk past Euston Station and then had to discover more about. At the time, there was a sign on the fence announcing the upcoming restoration, but I had to guess as to whether it would go ahead and exactly how. I assumed the best—at least for my purposes—and we were off! With a lot of help from my friends, of course.

And of course the pubs of London, which served my husband and me many lunches and dinners since the walking and staring and taking photos and notes often bored my poor spouse horribly and fortification by "pie and a pint" became the rallying cry whenever the hubby got too annoyed.

Once home in Seattle, I had to follow up on many of my notes and photos with internet research and lots of emails to friends and family, but in the end, I think I did all right for a goofy American in only twelve days. I hope you do, too.

KR

Also available in Kat Richardson's Greywalker series
Published by Piatkus:

GREYWALKER

Harper Blaine is a small-time private investigator trying to earn a living when a low-life savagely assaults her, leaving her for dead. For two minutes, to be precise.

When Harper comes to in the hospital, she begins to feel a bit … strange. She sees things that can only be described as weird shapes emerging from a foggy grey mist, snarling teeth, creatures roaring.

But Harper's not crazy. Her 'death' has made her a Greywalker – able to move between our world and the mysterious, cross-over zone where things that go bump in the night exist. And her new gift – or curse – is about to drag her into that world of vampires and ghosts, magic and witches, necromancers and sinister artifacts. Whether she likes it or not.

978-0-7499-3896-3

POLTERGEIST

In the days leading up to Halloween, Harper's been hired by a university research group that is attempting to create an artificial poltergeist. The head researcher suspects someone is deliberately faking the phenomena, but Harper's investigation reveals something else entirely – they've succeeded.

And when one of the group's members is killed in a brutal and inexplicable fashion, Harper must determine whether the killer is the ghost itself, or someone all too human.

978-0-7499-3895-6

UNDERGROUND

In the cold of winter, Pioneer Square's homeless are turning up dead and mutilated, and zombies have been seen roaming the streets of the underground – the city buried beneath modern Seattle. When Harper's friend Quinton fears he may be implicated in the deaths, he persuades her to investigate their mysterious cause.

Harper and Quinton discover a pattern to the deaths in the city's past that points to an inhuman killer stalking the modern citizens of the underground and raising the walking dead in its wake. But when Harper turns to the city's vampire denizens for help, they want nothing to do with her or with the investigation.

For this creature is no vampire. Someone has unleashed a monster of ancient legend upon the Underground, and Harper must deal with both the living and the dead to put a stop to it . . . unless it stops her first.

978-0-7499-0873-7